Running Haunted

A paranormal romance

by

Effrosyni Moschoudi

© 2020 Effrosyni Moschoudi. All rights reserved.

Effrosyni Moschoudi asserts the moral right to be identified as the author of this work.

Cover design: © 2019 Melinda De Ross. All rights reserved.

This book is licensed for the personal enjoyment of the original purchaser only. This book may not be resold or given away to other people. If you would like to share this book with another person, please purchase an additional copy for each recipient. If you are reading this book and did not purchase it, or if it was not granted to you directly by the author for your use only, then please purchase your own copy. Thank you for respecting the hard work of this author.

This is a work of fiction. Names, characters, places, and incidents either are the products of the author's imagination or are used fictitiously, and any resemblance to locales, events, business establishments, or actual persons - living or dead - is entirely coincidental.

Effrosyni Moschoudi

Nothing compares to mother's love... I am dedicating this novel to my mother, Ioanna, and to all mothers out there. This is a humble tribute to you all.

Contents

Chapter 1	7
Chapter 2	10
Chapter 3	18
Chapter 4	23
Chapter 5	36
Chapter 6	45
Chapter 7	52
Chapter 8	60
Chapter 9	67
Chapter 10	73
Chapter 11	77
Chapter 12	82
Chapter 13	92
Chapter 14	97
Chapter 15	104
Chapter 16	111
Chapter 17	121
Chapter 18	127
Chapter 19	132
Chapter 20	144
Chapter 21	150
Chapter 22	155
Chapter 23	162

Chapter 24	170
Chapter 25	175
Chapter 26	180
Chapter 27	187
Chapter 28	197
Chapter 29	203
Chapter 30	211
Chapter 31	218
Chapter 32	224
Chapter 33	233
Chapter 34	244
Chapter 35	251
Chapter 36	259
Chapter 37	267
Chapter 38	276
Chapter 39	286
Chapter 40	293
Chapter 41	303
Chapter 42	310
Chapter 43	315
Chapter 44	326
Chapter 45	333
Chapter 46	342
Chapter 47	350
Epilogue	357
More from this author	364
A note from the author	368

Acknowledgements _____ 369
About the author _____ 370

Chapter 1

Kelly gave a luxurious sigh as she took a seat at a seafront café with her best friend, Efi. The girls had a view to the fort of Bourtzi, the magnificent landmark of the historical town of Nafplio. Under the strong sunshine, it looked as if it floated gently in the serene sea like a resting, off-white bird.

Leaning back in her comfortable chair, Kelly felt the pained muscles all over her body sing with relief. Thinking back to her amazing feat, she couldn't help but give a cheer. 'I've just finished my first marathon! I can't believe it!'

Efi, who sat beside her, beamed at Kelly for a few moments, then said, 'You'd better believe it, girl! I'm so proud of you! You've come so far to get this medal, and I don't just mean the forty-two kilometres you just ran.' She winked and hooked her mouth to the side.

Kelly gave a huge sigh, a shadow crossing her face. Instinctively, to hide it from her friend, she looked the other way and said with regret, 'I know. Please don't remind me...'

'Hey, what's this? It's been over a year, Kelly... Let it go. Besides, you just proved you're not the same girl any more. You've left all that misery behind you for good.'

'You're so right, Efi. And, from now on, I just want to look ahead, you know?'

Efi smiled, but before she could say anything, a young waiter arrived to greet them with a bright smile.

'Kalimera! What will you have?' he asked, and the girls ordered coffees and toasted sandwiches.

As soon as he walked away, Efi leaned towards Kelly and said, 'Back to our conversation... Of course, you should only look ahead from now on. So, what's the next challenge? And I don't mean the next marathon run... Why don't you move out of your late grandmother's apartment? You should start a new life somewhere else... Somewhere where no memories of "Mucky-Makis" can soil it.'

Kelly scrunched up her face at the sound of the name of her ex-boyfriend, Makis. She could tell another lecture was coming.

Before she could open her mouth to protest, Efi added, 'Kelly, you know I'd miss you terribly if you moved far away from me, but I really think you should go back to England. Life in Greece clearly hasn't worked out for you.'

Kelly tossed a strand of her long brown hair behind her shoulder and twisted her lips. 'Nuh... I've told you before, Efi. I don't see it that way. I've made a wrong choice of career, I know—'

'And boyfriend...' Efi cut her off.

'Yes. Wrong choices on both counts,' said Kelly, putting up a finger. 'But that's got nothing to do with living in Greece or England. There's plenty more fish in the sea, when it comes to careers and boyfriends. Now that I've finally found strength in myself, I know I'll do better next time. I'm not leaving Greece. I love it too much. It makes me feel alive. You know that, Efi.'

Efi leaned over and patted Kelly's hand. 'Girlfriend, I'm with you all the way, whatever you decide.'

Kelly, once again caressing with her eyes the fortified island of Bourtzi in the distance, let out a soft sigh. 'To tell you the truth, I wouldn't mind leaving Athens behind.'

'To go where?'

'Well, somewhere smaller than the capital, where there's more green, beautiful scenery, a seafront... a quiet, more laid-back way of life.' She looked around her with a huge smile and added, 'A place like Nafplio. Just look at it! It's amazing. I never imagined it'd be so beautiful. I know we only arrived yesterday morning, but I think I've fallen in love with it already.'

'Yes, it's easy to fall in love with... And, really, you haven't even seen the view from the two fortresses up there yet...' Efi turned around in her seat and pointed vaguely high up in the distance. 'Only if you see Nafplio from a height will you know just how magical it is.'

'Really?' said Kelly, following Efi's gaze, but the strong sun made it hard to see clearly. Through the glare, she could barely make out the two hills that stood, side-by-side, over the town. The fortress of Palamidi seemed like a bejewelled crown of stone on top of the higher peak.

'Don't get your hopes up, though,' warned Efi when Kelly turned to face her again. 'I doubt it'll be easy to get a job here. Unless you visit again and again and ask in every hotel or shop maybe, going from door to door.'

'Well, I can surely try online first, see if I can find any job adverts, and take it from there,' said Kelly, setting her jaw.

Efi leaned forward in her seat. 'So you're serious? You want to move here?'

'Yes... This place has an amazing energy. It's calling to me, Efi. I feel it deep inside my bones.'

'Okay, but where would you live? 'I hate to break it to you, but I doubt you could afford a place on your own here. It's a touristy place. The rent must be sky-high even for tiny apartments.'

Kelly raised a single shoulder. 'You forget I have sound experience in hotel administration? If I land a job in one of the many hotels here, I could get room and board for free.'

'That could work...' said Efi, her voice trailing off when a male voice boomed at the next table, causing both girls to turn and look, startled.

'You don't understand, Dimos! My housekeeper is leaving today! TODAY! What am I going to do? How am I going to find another woman to run the house at such short notice?'

Chapter 2

Kelly and Efi listened in silence as the men continued to talk animatedly.

'Calm down, Alex. It's not the end of the world...'

'How can you say that, Dimos? Don't you see? My life keeps getting worse and worse! First my wife, and now this. And don't get me started with the problems at the hotel. Oh, God... What am I going to do about my children? Who's going to take care of them while I work?'

At that point, the man named Dimos reached out and squeezed the shoulder of the other man. The latter crouched over in his chair and hid his face in his hands for a few moments. Then, removing his hands, he raised his head and said, 'I just don't know, Dimos. I need a miracle, I guess.'

Kelly and Efi kept watching despite themselves, and what saved their dignity was that the men appeared to be too distracted to notice them.

Kelly felt her heart constrict with feeling for the man in turmoil that was apparently called Alex. He was about her age, in his early thirties, incredibly handsome, and dressed in a smart suit. The other man, Dimos, was around the same age too and just as impeccably dressed. Had it not been for their distressing private conversation, you'd think they were two professionals having a business meeting. That's how well-groomed and stylish they both looked.

Kelly's eyes couldn't leave the face of the man who continued to look upset. Her heart twinged with sympathy but, at the same time, she couldn't help but admire his flawless features. He had brown hair and kind eyes of the same colour, their expression pained right now, but she could tell from the way his jaw was set that he was a strong man in heart and mind.

His Roman nose and fleshy lips got most of her attention, as well as his impressive height. His legs were so long he seemed to have trouble tucking them adequately under the small table. As his friend spoke to him in a hushed tone, he kept bending and stretching one of his legs and looking quite uncomfortable, like a proud, wild animal that had been captured and put in a cage two sizes too small.

Alex continued to listen to his friend, who tried to reassure him, and, every now and then, brought a hand to rub at his chin or over his mouth. Finally, he checked his watch, saying he had little time left and had to go home soon.

At that point, Dimos offered to give him the number of an agency he knew of, saying they had good Russian and Bulgarian housekeepers for hire. He scribbled the number on the back of a card and handed it to him, saying there was a good chance that several of the women might speak adequate Greek, enough to be up to scratch for the job at hand.

Kelly felt concern grow inside her for this man. It can't be easy to trust a total stranger to live in your home at best, let alone when it comes to caring for your children. She turned to Efi, about to whisper how sorry she felt for the poor man, but was surprised to find she had stood up and was taking a step towards the men.

'Excuse me...' she heard Efi say, and her heart skipped a beat. *What on earth is she doing?*

The men turned to look at Efi and she said, 'I am really sorry to interrupt, and I apologise for listening in to your private conversation, but my friend and I couldn't really help it...'

Efi pointed towards their table and Kelly swallowed hard. Her heart thumped in her chest when the men turned to face her. *What is she doing? You crazy girl!*

Her mind went blank when Alex locked eyes with her, something that caused, somehow, the whole world around her to shrivel into nothing. He held her gaze, rendering her hypnotized for what seemed like an eternity. Finally, he looked away, turning to Efi again to hear what she had to say.

That's when Efi dropped the bomb. 'Well, the thing is, my friend here is job-hunting right now. And I think she'd be a perfect fit for your need.'

'What?' said Kelly, despite herself, and banged her hand on her chest with an open hand. 'Efi! What are you doing?'

Efi turned to her with a glare for a split second, then her eyes softened as she said, 'But, Kelly, you have sound experience from the hotel—'

Alex shook his head. 'I'm sorry, you misunderstood,' he told Efi. 'I'm looking for someone to work in my *home*, not in my hotel.'

'I know,' cut in Kelly, without even realizing. But once the words had come out, it was too late, too late to stop those mesmerizing eyes from searching her face again. 'We heard what you said. Hard not to, as my friend said earlier...' she added with an awkward pause and both the men nodded, lips pressed together.

All three were looking at her now, and suddenly she felt conscious of her bare legs. She hadn't put on her jogging bottoms since finishing the marathon and was still in her running shorts. Still, she noticed, much to her relief, that neither of the men had let their eyes wander down to her bare limbs.

Alex seemed to be hanging from her lips, hoping for his miracle, no doubt. But was she the answer to his wish for a miracle? Did she have the skills to be a housekeeper in a house with children—she guessed they were under age for him to feel so lost—and, presumably, no wife in sight? But if there was one thing Kelly had learned about herself in the past year, it was that she didn't cringe at challenges. And if this had happened just as she wished for a job in Nafplio, surely that was a sign from above. Or, at least, this could be one of those lucky days that very seldom come in life. Either way, she was damned if she was going to miss this chance.

Finally, Kelly said, 'We realize you need a housekeeper, sir. And I have suitable experience, I believe...' She'd said the last word without being entirely sure, but the man's eyes ignited with hope, and she smiled in return.

'Really?' he said and beckoned with a gallant gesture. 'In this case, ladies, please join our table. Let's discuss this properly.'

The girls moved their things over to the men's table, and Kelly sat beside Alex. As soon as she did, he offered his hand.

'It's a pleasure to meet you. My name is Alex. Alex Sarakis. I own a hotel here in the old town. This is my friend and associate, Dimos Orphanos. He runs a catering company on the outskirts of Nafplio.'

'Pleased to meet you,' replied Kelly, shaking his hand first, then Dimos's. Smiling brightly, she placed a hand on her chest to say, 'My name is Kelly Mellios. This is my friend, Efi Sofos. We live in Athens and came here for the marathon.' She pointed to the bib number on her running top and chuckled, then rolled her eyes. 'Well, obviously.'

This elicited peals of laughter from the others as Efi shook hands with the men. Then, Alex said, 'It's a pleasure to meet you both. And, if you have suitable work experience like you say, Kelly, then the fact we came here today and bumped into you is nothing short of a miracle.'

'Yes, I thought that too,' said Kelly, lost in his eyes, before she could stop herself.

Efi leaned forward in her chair and pointed at Kelly. 'My friend here has sound experience as a cook, as a maid *and* as a nanny! As an office administrator too.'

Impressed, Alex turned to Kelly. 'Is that so?'

Before she could say anything, Efi, who sat beside her, jabbed her in the ribs. 'Go on! Sell yourself, you silly girl. You're so qualified for this.' Then, turning to the men, she rolled her eyes. 'English girls! So modest!'

Alex's eyes sparkled in response. 'You're English?'

Kelly smiled sweetly. 'Half-English, actually. My mother is English, my father is Greek.'

'Wow. Your Greek is impeccable.'

'That's because I was born and raised in Athens. I moved to England with my parents in my early twenties, after finishing my studies in Athens in Hotel Administration. But I returned to Greece on my own a couple of years ago. I'd come to miss the country and the people here a lot. The way of life here agrees with me a lot better than that in the UK.'

'Really? But what about the crisis? Isn't it easier in England to get jobs and live a comfortable life than it is here?' burst out Dimos.

Kelly gave a dismissive wave. 'Oh... The crisis doesn't bother me. On a personal level, life can be as prosperous and positive as you wish it to be. You just have to focus and try your hardest to pursue your goals, and if you don't let fear or doubt get in the way, you can only get what you want. No matter what that is.'

'I like that... And I must say, you sound like a person who's very goal-oriented, very determined... That's exactly what I'm looking for in my employees,' said Alex, catching her attention again. 'So, about that experience Efi mentioned earlier? Please tell me more.'

'Well, when my family and I moved to England, my parents realized a lifelong dream—'

She stopped short because the waiter arrived then to gawp at the empty table where the girls sat earlier. Dimos whistled to him humorously, and the waiter turned, his good spirits restored to find the girls sitting there. He served their coffees and toasted sandwiches, then the men ordered a coffee each. When he was gone, Alex turned to Kelly with an easy smile, his eyes crinkling at the edges, 'Well, Kelly? You were saying?'

'Yes, as I said, we went to England to live there and that's when my parents bought a small hotel. They'd wanted to do that all their lives. They picked a small property on the coast in Cornwall, and it proved to be a wonderful choice. Of course, my studies came in handy... I practically took over all the administration of the business while my father manned reception and my mother ran the kitchen. I helped them both with their duties and also cleaned the rooms with the hired maid. I even did heaps of baby-sitting in the evenings.'

'But that's amazing! I don't believe it... You might as well have fallen right from the sky to save me today!' said Alex. He then told her what salary he is offering, and asked how that sounded.

'I must say, it sounds very satisfactory,' she said. She wanted to say it was very generous, more than she expected, but she didn't want to sound too keen. Smiling, she looked away from his eager face and took a sip from her coffee. Dimos's face was animated with relief for his friend, and Efi seemed equally pleased. Kelly believed she had a good chance of getting the job. She had told the truth, after all. She was fully qualified and ready for this new challenge. The very thought of living in Nafplio, of starting a new life there, made her feel exhilarated.

'So, when can you start?' asked Alex.

'She got the job?' asked Efi wide-eyed. She was holding her toasted sandwich before her mouth, about to take a bite.

'Of course! As you ladies may have guessed earlier, I am in a bit of a hurry.' Alex cringed, then added with haste, 'Not to say that I feel like I am compromising in the least here, of course!' He put up a hand and extended his palm towards Kelly. 'Even if this wasn't an emergency, I'd still hire you on the spot, I'm sure.'

'Thank you,' said Kelly, feeling overwhelmed by the effect his laughing brown eyes had on her. She wasn't sure if they were specked with gold, or if it was the sunshine streaming in under the awning that made them look that way.

'So? Can you start today?'

Kelly almost jumped in her seat. She'd just had a big bite of her turkey and cheese sandwich, and it nearly went down the wrong way. 'Today? So soon?' she said, clutching her chest after swallowing hard.

'I'd really appreciate it. It means I won't have to take time off work. My current housekeeper has a family emergency, you see... She is leaving town this evening. Her son-in-law is driving her to Athens tonight. Her daughter is very ill... in hospital.'

'I'm sorry to hear that... but... but...' Lost for words, Kelly turned to Efi to find her flashing her a meaningful look.

'It's okay, Kelly. Of course, you can start today.'

'But, Efi... How can I? All I have here are the basics I've packed for the weekend.'

'That's more than enough to go by for a week, and you know it. It's March, after all... It's not like you'll be going to the beach or anything. You have a couple of sweaters, your jeans, your coat... You'll be fine.'

'But, what about the rest of my stuff back in Athens?'

'Easy. You'll give me the keys to your apartment, and I'll pack for you. Then I'll meet you here next Sunday to bring you clothes and anything else you may need. Just make a list and I'll get it all, no worries.' Efi chuckled and leaned closer to Kelly, then added in a hushed tone, 'I'll even let you have my make-up bag and clean underwear from my suitcase, so there. Just say "yes", you silly girl. What's wrong with you?'

The words weren't whispered low enough and the men had obviously heard, judging from their soft chuckles. Kelly cringed with embarrassment. Efi could be embarrassing like that. Still, she was right. 'This is very kind of you, Efi, thank you...' she finally said. 'I can't believe you're offering to drive back here next Sunday for me.'

'It's nothing for you, girlfriend. Just say "yes" to the man. Sounds to me like you've both just saved each other's necks!'

A fresh round of laughter echoed then, and Alex looked beside himself with excitement. Kelly turned to him and matched his expression. 'Yes, Alex,' she finally said, smiling widely. 'Sure, I can start today.'

His face turning bright, he rubbed his hands together and leaned forward to say, 'Excellent! You could start right now, if you like. I can drive you ladies to your hotel so you can get your luggage…'

Kelly's eyes ignited with alarm, and she froze, holding her coffee cup mid-air.

Efi put up a hand and giggled, then said, 'Easy, Alex. I know you have an emergency, but not so fast. My girl has just finished a marathon, for goodness sake. She and I are heading back to the hotel to take a shower and catch our breaths for a while. And then, we'll go grab some lunch before she falls flat on her face from exhaustion. So how about you do your thing in the meantime, then meet us back here around five p.m.? Will that work for you?'

Offering a cute, crooked smile, Alex checked his watch, and Kelly did too. It was ten past two. Plenty of time.

'Sure, that works,' said Alex and everyone heaved a sigh of relief. The waiter brought the men's coffees, and Alex took a sip as soon as he was served, then turned to Kelly with a bright smile.

Kelly gazed back at him, mirroring his expression, and a familiar twinge at her heart told her she was smitten. She hoped that wouldn't complicate things. But most of all, she hoped the situation back at his house would be something she could handle. Panicking somewhat, she considered what she'd just done: she'd said yes without knowing anything of his home or his children and their way of life.

She rested her eyes on his charming smile and took heart. *He's a professional, for heaven's sake. A hotel owner, at that! I bet he lives in a good home. And his children will be well-behaved, surely. This is going to be a piece of cake…*

Chapter 3

In the late afternoon, having left Efi's luggage in her car, the girls walked briskly along the port to meet Alex at the café as prearranged.

From the distance, bathed in a soft, golden light, the fort of Bourtzi stood out like a sun-drenched pebble that, somehow, floated in the sea.

Kelly, who held her gym bag in her hand, hurried along deep in thought, wondering what living life out of that bag for one week was going to be like. But, most of all, she was wondering what she was getting into.

Before leaving the café, Alex had told her that he had three under-age children, all boys. Upon hearing their ages—thirteen, eight, and six—her mind had drawn a blank. She was an only child and didn't really know much about little boys or—even worse—teenage boys. It was one thing to mind them for a couple of hours on an evening at her parents' hotel, and another to be responsible for them around the clock. Still, she was willing to try…

'Don't worry, Kelly!' piped up Efi, snapping her out of her deep thoughts. 'I'm not leaving you unless I see a business card at least. We both got so excited about this amazing coincidence that we forgot to check the man out. Didn't even ask him what his hotel is called so we can look it up online. What if he's a liar? A criminal? I need proof before I let him take you away in his car!'

Kelly nodded firmly. 'Yes, it makes sense. Though I'm quite sure he's okay. I saw it in his eyes. His honesty, his decency… My instinct about people never fails me.'

In lieu of an answer, Efi rolled her eyes, obviously itching to contradict her by mentioning Kelly's awful ex-boyfriend, Makis.

Kelly gave a little laugh. She felt thankful Efi hadn't mentioned him again. 'I know what I'm saying, Efi. Alex is okay. You'll see...' she said as they neared the café.

Efi tutted. 'Well, at least, he's a gentleman, I'll give you that. He's still in his suit and already waiting for us. Look! He's right there...' She poked Kelly in the ribs with her elbow, causing her to turn and look.

'Oh, yes...' said Kelly, perking up. *Goodness me... I'd forgotten how handsome he is!*

As if Efi had guessed her thoughts, she jabbed her in her side again, this time harder. 'And please. I know he's a looker, and I bet his ass is tighter than the Gordian Knot, but try not to fall for him, okay? You're forever doing that, falling for the wrong men, and then I have to pick up the pieces.'

Kelly eyed her for a second, enough to know her friend wasn't serious. After all, Kelly had only had one boyfriend her whole life. Other than Makis, no one had ever really broken her heart before.

'Oh shut up already!' Kelly retorted with an amused smile just as they crossed the road to step onto the pavement outside the café. Alex was looking the other way at the time, towards a square. Efi reached him first and tapped him on the back.

Alex whirled around, his face lighting up as he raised a jovial hand in greeting. 'Oh! Hi, ladies. Good to see you again!'

They both greeted him happily, then Efi took over. 'Listen, Alex, I hope you don't mind, but could I have your business card, please? No offence, but this is my best friend,' she pointed to Kelly, 'and you're practically about to whisk her off to your house in a car. For all I know, you could be an axe murderer.'

Kelly flinched to hear all that, unsure as to how Alex would take it. Still, deep down, she felt grateful for her friend who cared enough to be so blunt. And she made good sense, after all.

Alex broke into a big smile and nodded fervently. 'Of course, I fully understand.' He reached into his breast pocket and produced his card, handing it to Efi. Then, his eyes turned to Kelly and he added, 'Actually, I had thought of that too. This is why I intended to ask you, Kelly, if you'd like a little tour of my hotel before we head off to my house…' he put out a hand towards her, palm up, '…in case you have any hang-ups about getting in my car with me. I fully understand we are, after all, practically strangers.'

Kelly melted inside to hear his thoughtful response. Before she could say anything, Alex turned to Efi to add, 'You're more than welcome to come with us to the hotel, Efi. You can inspect the trunk of my car too if you like. Make sure I don't carry a hatchet. Or a buzz saw.'

For a split second, both the girls froze, searching his face, wondering if, after all, he had taken offence. But then he broke into a loud guffaw and put a gentle hand on Efi's arm, then Kelly's too, to say, 'Relax, girls! I'm only joking. And now, let's go. This way!' He pointed towards the lanes. 'Hotel Nostos awaits!'

*****

Hotel Nostos turned out to be located in an enchanting cobblestone lane near a derelict Turkish bath, and a stone's throw away from St Spyridon's church – the one where, on its doorstep, Kapodistrias, the first governor of Greece, was murdered. Kelly noticed the plaque mounted on the wall as they passed by it, and Alex eagerly began to share with the girls what he knew about that fateful day.

Kelly admired his knowledge of Greek history and imagined it came in handy at his hotel, something to share with his guests at every opportunity. Kelly didn't possess the gift of the gab, so she was impressed by his diction and the confidence he exuded with every word.

But all that was insignificant compared to the experience that awaited her moments later when they entered the small, yet imposing, Hotel Nostos. Housed in an old, but beautifully renovated neoclassical building, it was labelled outside as the home of one of the heroes of the War of Independence, something that filled Kelly's heart with awe as she crossed the doorstep.

Once inside, she was immediately enveloped by the whimsical aura of a bygone time. She stood at the reception hall with the others and admired the decoration. Everywhere she looked there was polished olive wood and varnished stone.

When the receptionist greeted Alex using his surname, the latter smiled with confidence, then beckoned to the girls to follow him to the adjacent hall. It turned out to be a quaint breakfast room that served as a tea room at the time. The windowless space was lit moderately by a series of intricate antique lights mounted on the surrounding walls. A quiet couple sat in a corner sipping hot drinks from white porcelain cups and reading paperbacks. Behind them, stood a small bookshelf filled to the brim with tattered old volumes. Tea lights were lit on every table, their delicate flames flickering softly in the semi-darkness.

While Kelly took everything in, Alex kept talking, giving the girls information about the hotel, the day-to-day activities of the hired staff, and the amenities on offer. Nostos hotel had a wonderful energy about it. Being in that room felt like an immersion into a distant century, thanks to the fabulous old-style decoration, down to the red carpet and the gilded chairs.

Kelly didn't fail to notice that the two members of staff behind the counter were just as courteous as the receptionist had been. They had both greeted them with wide smiles. Everything and everyone in this hotel seemed impeccable, each element a part of a ticking clock that never skipped a beat.

As Alex pointed back to the reception with a flourish and began to walk towards it, Kelly stole another glance at his upright stance, his charming grin, and guessed he was a savvy and organized professional who didn't compromise when it came to quality in his business. Inside her, other than feeling admiration for him, a little hope nestled and began to take root. It was the hope that things in his house would be ticking away just as impeccably.

Outside, a little later, feeling satisfied with the proof of his identity, Efi said her goodbyes. She gave Kelly a hug that was tighter than normal, then gave one last wave and walked away, heading back to the port and her car.

As soon as she was gone, Alex pointed to a derelict stone gate that stood at the end of the lane, over what looked like an ancient canal. Judging from the weeds that had sprouted everywhere through the rocky ground, Kelly guessed it hadn't seen water in centuries.

'This way, Kelly. I've parked just beyond the Land Gate.'

Kelly was intrigued by the decrepit ruin, but this wasn't the time to ask for an extended sightseeing tour. She began to walk beside him, the first step towards his car now a little harder than she thought it would be, knowing her friend was walking in the opposite direction at the same time, the last remnant of her life up until today distancing itself from her by the second.

He turned to her then, his eyes kind, his smile dashing, and her mind filled with sunshine again. He put out a hand. 'I'm so sorry. Where are my manners? Let me carry your bag please, Kelly.'

As if in a dream, she saw her hand rise as she offered her luggage to him. In his hand now, as they resumed walking, the bag seemed weightless. And, just like that, she felt herself float effortlessly, rising off the ground a little then as if he'd just picked up a little more than her bag; her life too, giving it the boost it needed, the fresh start she'd been wishing for.

Chapter 4

Having left the town traffic behind, the car was now cruising speedily along a single carriageway that carried on uphill. It was edged by orange orchards and vegetable plots, the view growing more lush by the minute.

Not ten minutes later, they drove off the road to enter a quiet residential area. Alex turned right onto a wider street and parked the car.

'Here we are,' he said with a luxurious sigh and opened his door to get out, causing Kelly to follow suit. Despite the growing darkness, as the sun was almost fully set, she could clearly see the serene beauty of the place.

The street was lined with bitter orange trees and all the buildings in sight were detached, moderate-sized villas that consisted of a ground and an upper floor.

The one they had just parked in front of, was fenced with railing and a low gate. In the garden, Kelly could make out freshly cut lawn and flower patches. Bushy trees on both sides of the property stood laden with lemons and oranges. A concrete path led to the front door. Beside it, a small porch with wicker furniture stood before the lawn. The tall window shutters on the ground floor were open, unlike the ones on the upper floor. Kelly could see ample electric light shining indoors behind the thick curtains.

Alex must have guessed she liked what she saw because he smiled pleasantly and pointed to the same villa. 'Welcome to my home, Kelly.'

'It's beautiful...' she said breathlessly as she watched him remove her bag from the trunk. Without offering it to her, he returned to her side and smiled widely. 'Thank you. This way please.'

Alex opened the garden gate and gestured her to walk ahead of him along the path. He rang the doorbell, saying something about that being easier than him fumbling in the semi-darkness with his keys, and in the few seconds it took for the door to open, Kelly thought her heart would burst. Her only happy thought at the time was that she could hear no children shrieking or screaming. She knew she wouldn't handle it if his sons had bad manners or threw tantrums, the way so many young children tended to do.

A large lady in her late sixties opened the door and gave a tight smile.

Alex smiled amicably and spoke first. 'Hello, Mrs Botsari! This is Kelly, the young lady I spoke to you about this morning. Kelly, Mrs Botsari will show you around before she leaves tonight.'

The two women shook hands, then Mrs Botsari gestured them to come in. Kelly followed her inside first, her eyes fixed, for some reason, on the woman's snow-white hair that was wound tightly on top of her head in a bun. When they reached a wide single space that consisted of a kitchen, a dining area and a living room, Kelly's jaw dropped.

Everywhere she looked, there was order and cleanliness. Immediately, she felt appreciative of Mrs Botsari. The other thing she noticed was that the furniture was high quality and in pristine condition. Polished wood, seemingly cherry wood and mahogany, dominated the dining room and the living room respectively. The kitchen was decorated in bright colours, pastel yellows and blues, making it a joy to cook there, no doubt.

'I'm sure there's a lot to take in, and Mrs Botsari has to leave in an hour or so,' said Alex, clapping his hands once, and giving Kelly an encouraging smile. 'I'll get out of your way while Mrs Botsari shows you the ropes. Talk to you later!'

As soon as he said these words he was gone, dashing to the other side of the kitchen, then onto a corridor, where he went up a staircase, disappearing from view before she could utter a peep.

Mrs Botsari smiled sweetly and beckoned Kelly to follow her to the kitchen area. 'Let's start from here, shall we?'

What followed was a detailed report of everything in the kitchen. Not just where the oven was and how to turn it on, but down to the last pack of pasta stored in the pantry. Upon showing her all that, Mrs Botsari pointed to her collection of shopping lists mounted on the refrigerator, one for every supermarket she went to, apparently, so she could take advantage of all their weekly special offers.

They moved on to the living room, where she showed her the TV, the DVD player and the mini hi-fi system, then launched into a needless demo of all the buttons on the remotes. But Kelly took it all in and nodded pleasantly, all the while wondering where the children were.

But, instead of the children, what appeared all of a sudden was a pug, of all things, that had appeared seemingly out of nowhere. Kelly watched as the dog approached the tall window to her left at a leisurely pace. It was the sound of its nails hitting the marble floor that had caused Kelly to turn her head and see it before it saw her.

When it finally clocked her, its relaxed features, down to its tongue that fell limply from its mouth, morphed into something bordering on evil. Galloping like a fine horse, it neared her and Mrs Botsari barking loudly. It stopped an inch from Kelly's feet and started to yap endlessly, growling every time it stopped to catch its breath.

Kelly had frozen by then. Even though she loved dogs, she had a thing for yappy small ones, and this one was a fine specimen of the kind of dog that gave her the willies. In her mind that had gone numb, she felt lucky she was wearing jeans, imagining the little ogre would probably not think twice before sinking its teeth into her bare flesh.

'Charlie! Stop! Behave!' admonished Mrs Botsari in what felt like an eternity later. The dog growled one last time and backed away as she shook her hands in a shooing gesture.

Charlie sat down quietly at the nearest corner but his little eyes, dark and glistening, looked like two live embers thrown into the water, resisting to let go of their heat just yet.

Kelly, who had been clutching her chest all this time, took a steadying breath.

'I'm sorry, Kelly. Charlie can be like that with strangers. I am proud to say that in the last three years that I've worked here, I've managed to discipline him in a few things, but have long made peace with the fact that he will never be perfect. But don't worry. He'll get used to you before you know it.'

'I hope he will. I like my legs. I'd like to keep them,' she replied, attempting to make a joke.

'As I said, don't worry. He has more bark than he has bite. And once he's seen you with the children, interacting and sitting together, he will realize you're not a threat and warm up to you.'

'I hope so… Is he house-trained, by any chance?'

Mrs Botsari eyed her then as if she'd asked her if the dog sleeps. 'Of course. I wouldn't have it any other way. He does his business outside in the garden. It's a pain because you'll have to clean up after him, but at least he doesn't do it in the house.'

'What about walks?'

'Walks?'

'Yes, walks. You know, with a leash? Outside?'

Mrs Botsari laughed and gave a little wave. 'Oh no! He's a small dog. Plenty of room for him to run around in the garden. Just make sure to let him out every couple of hours, and certainly when he walks up to the door scratching at it or whimpering. You'd better hurry and open the door then!' She gave a hearty laugh. 'I still remember the mess he made the day I didn't get there on time.'

Kelly pressed her lips together, not sure how to respond. It was typical of Greek people to think that small dogs who had a garden to themselves didn't need to be walked. Hell, so many thought the same for dogs as large as German Shepherds. But dogs are pack animals that daily need both the exercise and the companionship involved in being walked by their owner – their pack leader. But this woman was leaving today and she was taking her place. She guessed a lot had to be changed, and not just the way the dog was left to do its business.

Clearly unaware of Kelly's bemusement, Mrs Botsari beckoned happily, leading her back to the kitchen, then onto the corridor to show her a small bathroom and a tiny storage room. Then, she stood behind a closed door that read "Keep Out" in Greek and whispered, 'This is Stratos's room. He's the eldest. Thirteen. Seeing that it's Sunday and he did all his housework earlier today, he's probably playing games on his console now or listening to music with his headphones. Either way, better not disturb him. I've raised two teenage boys of my own and I know. It's best to let them do their thing, you know?'

Kelly gave a tight-lipped smile, a little disappointed. The anticipation to meet the children was killing her. She couldn't wait to see just how good or bad she had it.

Mrs Botsari eyed her sideways and gave a crooked smile. 'I'm guessing you don't have any children yet, right? How old are you?'

'I turned thirty last month... And no, no children. I am single,' said Kelly, after clearing her throat.

'Well, let me give you a tip then, young lady. Teenagers can be a mystery, and they don't like grown-ups sniffing about their business. My advice to you is, make sure Stratos is off to school fed in the morning, and that he's given a warm meal when he's back shortly after one o'clock. He can get cranky if he's not fed enough and on time. Don't get me wrong... Stratos is a good kid... but some days, he's so aloof he doesn't even say hi. But don't take it personally. That's how he is.' She shrugged for effect.

'I see…' said Kelly, not sure how to take the news. Then, Mrs Botsari led her upstairs via a wide internal staircase. It was stunning, made of dark wood and a gilded balustrade that glinted in the overhead light.

The landing was a long corridor with five doors – three on the left side, two on the other. Mrs Botsari turned right and beckoned her to follow her to the end where a large blue glass window stood. She opened the door closest to the window and led her inside.

'This is your room. It used to be a study but, well, it's a guest bedroom now. I hope it's to your liking.'

'Oh it's lovely, thank you,' said Kelly. The first thing she noticed was that her gym bag stood on the carpeted floor before her. She guessed Alex had left it there in the meantime.

Looking around her appreciatively, she admired the view to a grassy hill beyond the window panes, then her eyes lingered on the beautiful dresser with the oval-shaped mirror on her left.

Stepping towards the bed, she smiled to herself. It was made with two plumped up pillows and a duvet cover that looked like a patchwork quilt, very colourful, reminding her of similar ones she had while growing up. That, alone, was enough for her to love the room, but everything about it was endearing, down to the vibrant salmon colour on the wall and the seascape paintings hanging all around.

She turned to Mrs Botsari, who waited by the door with a relaxed smile on her lips. 'This duvet makes me feel right at home. So cheerful…'

'Glad you like it, my dear.'

Kelly scrunched up her lips, then said, 'Mrs Botsari… You mentioned this used to be a study… I won't be depriving the children from using this room to study for school, I hope?'

Mrs Botsari gave a wry smile, her brow furrowed. 'No, don't worry, young lady. This used to be Mrs Sarakis's study. Sadly, she passed away… three years ago.'

Kelly's heart twinged with sympathy for Alex and the boys. 'I'm so sorry, I didn't know. It must have been hard for the children. And... Mr Sarakis, of course.'

'Oh, you wouldn't know how hard. It all happened very quickly and, having known the family for years, I immediately volunteered to help with minding the children in those hard first few days... Before I knew it, I was properly employed...' She gave a bitter smile and continued, 'Frankly, I needed the extra money so this has been a lifeline for me. Of course, my being here has helped the children too. This way they continued to have a female presence in the house...'

'Yes, I'm sure... And you've been living in this room all this time?'

'Oh goodness, no! I live two doors down. I'm a widow, have been for decades, actually, but I love my home and living on my own. I've been spending my days here, then popping down to my house after Mr Sarakis came home from work in the evening.'

'I see... Does he work long hours?'

'Oh yes. And his work days vary greatly. But he's been wonderful, checking with me throughout the day, forever texting or phoning to keep me updated with his schedule and to see how the boys were doing. I am sure you'll find this habit of his most convenient, as I did. And, of course, since he always dedicates his Sundays to his children, you'll have the day off to spend it as you please.'

Shortly after, Mrs Botsari beckoned her out of the room so that she could give her a tour of the first floor. Coming out onto the corridor, she opened the next door down to reveal the master bathroom. A strong smell of disinfectant mixed with pine reached Kelly's nostrils. The porcelain and glass fittings gleamed clean. A plethora of towels in various colours hung from the tiled walls.

Pacing along the corridor, they passed the staircase to stop near three more doors. Mrs Botsari pointed to the one that stood on its own on the right side. 'This is the master bedroom where Mr Sarakis sleeps, obviously. And these doors here opposite are the bedrooms of the little ones. Nikos, who's eight, and little Tommy, who's six but is quite tiny and looks much younger. He and Charlie, the pug, are inseparable, by the way. If you want the dog to like you, make sure he sees you being nice to Tommy. You know, cuddle him, talk sweetly to him, that sort of thing. You'll be all right then.'

'So, no shouting at the boy. Duly noted,' said Kelly as a joke, but Mrs Botsari didn't seem to get it. Her face grew distressed when she said, 'Oh no! Mr Sarakis doesn't allow any shouting, and any drama, in this house. Plus, you will find that the boys are all good-hearted, obedient and disciplined. I've been running a tight ship. But with love, at all times. I'm sure Mr Sarakis expects you to do the same.'

'Oh yes, of course! Sorry, I was joking just then, I assure you—'

Before she could finish her sentence, one of the bedroom doors opened and a little boy came out. 'Charlie! Where are you?' he shouted. He was dressed in slacks and a sweater and had only socks on his feet. He had come out running, his steps eliciting soft thuds against the carpet. He stopped short when he reached the women and looked up at Kelly, his jaw a little slack. His eyes were baby blue and made him look like a little angel. His straight blond hair amplified that picture of innocence. 'Hello,' he said, tilting his head. 'Are you our new housekeeper?'

Kelly crouched down to match his eye level and felt her heart melt. This was going to be easy if the other boys were as well-mannered as this one was. 'Hello. Yes, I am. You must be Tommy.'

'Yes, that's me.'

'My name is Kelly. Pleased to meet you.' She offered her hand and he curled his hand over the tips of her index and middle finger, smiling sweetly. 'How do you do?' he said, saying the last sentence in English, in an impeccable British accent.

Kelly was taken aback. 'Wow! You speak English? How old are you?' she said, speaking in Greek, like before.

'I am six,' he replied in Greek. 'I don't go to the *frontistirio* to learn English yet, like Stratos does, but he teaches me sometimes.' He stopped for a moment to catch his breath, his eyes dancing, then carried on, 'And I love movies. I learn English that way too.'

'You watch English movies? On your own?'

Mrs Botsari, who had been making cooing sounds at the boy on and off, cut in then with a grin. 'I do confess I enjoy watching movies with Tommy. I read the subtitles for him so he can follow the story. There's a large selection of DVDs in the house and many are English movies. The little one and I have watched a few of the classics together.'

Tommy opened his eyes wide and raised a hand high. 'Yes! I love Jane Eyre. She's my favourite.'

'But that's remarkable!' said Kelly, impressed that a six-year-old would have such an odd taste in films for his age. She was about to say something along those lines when she heard another child's voice echo from behind her. 'Scrooge is my favourite! Bah, humbug!'

She spun around to see another boy coming from the same room Tommy had emerged from. In a second, Alex materialized through the door behind him. Both he and the boy smiled widely as they neared them. The child's dark curly hair and intelligent brown eyes were the first thing she noticed about him. Then, she couldn't help noticing that his build was a far cry from both Alex's and little Tommy's. This boy was rather large for his age, which she guessed was eight. He didn't seem to be the thirteen-year-old she was still to see. This boy was quite chubby, down to his hands and puffy cheeks. His tummy and his thighs seemed desperate to burst through his cotton slacks. The look of him brought on a stab at her heart. She used to have similar weight issues when she was his age.

'I see you've already met the runt of the litter,' said Alex with a chortle as he approached to tousle Tommy's hair. The little boy leaned in and clung to his father's waist with a toothy grin. Standing on the other side of Alex, the older boy continued to look at Kelly full of interest. Her expectation that he'd be just as well-mannered as Tommy was confirmed when he offered his hand to her and smiled. 'Hello, pleased to meet you. I am Nikos.'

'Lovely to meet you, Nikos. I am Kelly,' she said, shaking his hand. Turning to his father, she added, 'I must say, Alex, your children have astounding manners. Believe me, over the years I've babysat a few children so wild they'd be better suited to living in a forest hanging upside down from trees.'

Alex and Mrs Botsari laughed heartily at that, and more so Alex, whose sense of pride blossomed on his face. The children smiled broadly to hear her comment, their cheeks flushed.

'Well, I guess one has to prepare them early on for their business life as adults,' said Alex brightly. 'And I'd love for my boys to be successful businessmen someday. They'll inherit my hotel when I'm gone, that's for sure, and I hope to have grown the business by then, you know? Hopefully, one day, I'll have *three* hotels downtown, so I can give them one each!' Everyone chuckled, and then Alex bent over to pick Tommy up high. He tossed him in the air, and the boy began to squeal with laughter.

'What is this racket? Tommy! Shut up already!' thundered a voice from the ground floor. Mrs Botsari flinched, her eyes darting to Alex, who pursed his lips, put Tommy down and hurried down the steps.

Kelly could hear hushed whispers from below, and it was quite clear Alex was telling off his teenage son. Towards the end, she heard him clearly urge the boy to follow him upstairs and introduce himself.

By the time they'd both come upstairs, the vibe on the landing had shifted. Mrs Botsari now stood with her head bent, seemingly fascinated by her loafers as she turned one foot on the floor this way and that, while the boys stood tight-lipped, shifting their weight from foot to foot, eyes wandering, focusing on nothing in particular.

The teenage boy stepped on the landing first, his father following closely behind. 'Hello. I am Stratos,' he said quietly, without offering his hand, his eyes kept low. He looked up to meet Kelly's gaze only after he'd spoken.

His expression was laden with tension that enveloped Kelly, causing a sense of discomfort she didn't expect. She had always been able to sense people's auras, and generally to guess their mood, sometimes without the exchange of any words. From this particular youngster, she had received a strong serving of pent-up anger in a harsh blow. It had almost knocked her off her feet.

Stratos had his hands in his jeans pockets and she found herself wondering if she should offer him a handshake, but decided against it in the end. Perhaps he didn't want to shake hands and she didn't wish to force it on him.

The boy's face was covered with angry-looking acne spots and her heart went out to him. She imagined looking like this must be even more detrimental to this teenager's obvious frail confidence. She rested her eyes on the stamp of his shabby t-shirt that was about a band of some sort. She'd never heard of that band before, but the lettering and the symbols on the image told her it was of the hard rock variety. That baffled her. If the boy was a fan of hard rock, then why was his hair short and immaculately groomed? Instead of the messy tangle of long hair that she'd expect, it was even gelled, for goodness sake. *Does he intersperse his hard rock listening with boy band music?*

All at once, he took her by surprise when he took a hand out of his pocket and offered it to her. As they joined hands in a limp handshake, he said, 'I'm sorry I shouted earlier. I didn't realize you were here, miss.'

'It's okay, Stratos. And you can call me Kelly. Pleased to meet you.'

'Yeah. Me too, Kelly,' he said distractedly, but before he looked away to seek his father's eyes, for a split second, she caught a faint smile creeping up on his lips. He didn't let it bloom into a proper smile, though. Instead, he bit his lower lip and jutted out his chin as he turned to face his father.

Alex nodded when the boy glanced at him, then Stratos dashed down the stairs, loud thumps reverberating around the walls.

'Stratos! For goodness sake,' said his father. He lowered his voice and, as he approached the centre of the staircase to look down towards the boy, added, 'Please, son. I've told you before. I don't want you guys hurrying up and down the stairs. Your little brothers look up to you, Stratos. If you keep doing it, next thing you know they'll be doing it too. And there's a danger they might fall. How would you feel if they had an accident following in your footsteps?'

'Sorry, Dad...' echoed from below, then a slam of his bedroom door followed, from what Kelly could gather.

Alex turned to Kelly sheepishly. 'Sorry about that. Teenagers! Need I say more? Huh!' He gave a nervous laugh and added with a shrug, 'But, on the upside, you've just met my whole family, warts and all. I can assure you this is as bad as it gets. You will find the children are well-behaved, and even Stratos has some good days. Please forgive his bad mood just then. He was probably playing games and begrudged the rude interruption.' He rolled his eyes. 'He always complains about noise when he retires to his room, which is a lot, sorry to say.'

'No problem. As you said, he is a teen... Of course, I understand.'

'Mrs Botsari, what time are you leaving again?' Alex asked, turning to the elderly lady, who had gathered Nikos and Tommy on either side of her, her hands on their shoulders.

'Oh... I'm nearly done here. I just need to go over some notes with Kelly... I've left them in her room. Directions to the shops, a list of pending errands, etc. Then, I'll be ready to go.'

'Sounds great,' he replied.

Mrs Botsari smiled pleasantly. 'Meet you downstairs in about fifteen minutes then? I'll say goodbye, then you can all sit and eat together. The *moussaka* is being kept warm in the oven.'

'Yes, that's fine. Thank you, Mrs Botsari.' Alex beckoned to the boys to follow and the three began to descend the stairs. After he'd gone down two steps, Alex stopped and turned around. 'Kelly, can you and I sit quietly for a chat downstairs after dinner? I won't keep you long. I realize you've had a long day, what with your marathon and all. I just want to answer any last minute questions you may have, and to make sure you feel ready to begin with your duties. I'm off to work early tomorrow morning, and you'll be on your own for hours.'

'Of course,' said Kelly, and he resumed descending the stairs, the boys way ahead of him. A short silence ensued as Kelly stood with Mrs Botsari at the top of the stairs watching them go.

Alex's last words had landed inside her heavily, trepidation gnawing at her insides. She'd be fine with the little ones, she knew. It was the teenager and the pug that were going to be a little more difficult to manage. Already, she knew it deep in her bones.

Chapter 5

As soon as Mrs Botsari left the house, Alex gathered everyone in the kitchen. He took the roasting tin out of the oven, and the children made appreciative noises to see the *moussaka*.

Kelly offered to serve, but Alex shook his head. 'No, Kelly. This must have been a long day for you. So, tonight, you don't have to serve dinner or do the dishes.'

Kelly opened her mouth to protest, but he raised a firm hand. 'No, I won't hear it! Please, take a seat! Dinner is coming!' Gesturing to the kitchen table and facing the children, he added, 'Go on, guys. Grab a seat!'

The boys sat at the table with haste. When Kelly joined them, from the three empty chairs, she picked the closest one, which was at the top of the table. As soon as she touched its back to pull it out, Charlie, who was sitting quietly at Tommy's feet at the time, burst out in loud barks and reached her in a second, snarling at her sneakers. Kelly froze, looking up from the pet, her eyes locking with Stratos's.

The boy waved dismissively. 'Oh. Sorry. We should have warned you. He doesn't like people sitting in that chair.'

Tommy reached over and pulled the dog away by the collar. Next, he cut a piece off a biscuit from an open pack that stood on the table and gave it to him. The dog snatched it mid-air and devoured it. Tommy petted him as Nikos cooed along.

'Ah... I don't think you guys should be rewarding him for bad behaviour...' said Kelly before she could stop herself. She'd had a couple of dogs over time in England and had learned from books and TV shows enough to know that immediate rewards after unwanted behaviour in terms of treats, affection or verbal praise, only resulted in that behaviour to be solidified in the dog's brain.

'Ah, don't let Charlie bother you,' said Alex when he approached with a plate of *moussaka*. 'You can sit here, Kelly.' He pointed at the vacant seat beside Stratos.

Kelly sat and gazed at the delicious-looking, large piece of *moussaka* that Alex had placed in front of her. Only then did she realize just how ravenous she was. Her mind wandered to her pizza lunch with Efi in the early afternoon. It felt like ages ago. Another lifetime even.

Alex soon returned with two more plates while Kelly made small talk with the boys. On and off, she kept an eye on Charlie, who now sat in his pet bed in a corner. He was busy chewing one of his toys and she was thankful for that. Every now and then, he'd turn his dark eyes towards her, two of his bottom teeth protruding from his lower lip. He looked cute then, but she still felt apprehensive, plus thankful he'd sat over there so she could eat in peace.

Trying to get the dog out of her mind, she continued to talk to the boys while Alex served the last two plates. When she asked Stratos about the band on his t-shirt, he smiled and seemed delighted to be asked about it. He started to say it was his favourite band, but as soon as his father arrived to leave a plate in front of him, he stopped short and never finished his sentence.

Alex sat at the other end of the table to where she'd earlier been advised not to sit on. Her eyes flew to the dog, who seemed unaffected. *Crazy dog! He minds people sitting on one end of the table but not the other. Interesting.* She wondered what that was about but didn't voice it. Instead, she tucked straight in, like everyone else did.

For a few moments, she was lost in the bliss of the warm, rich *béchamel* sauce that was heavily enriched with the woody taste of nutmeg. The tomato sauce, the mincemeat, the aubergines and potatoes, all made up a culinary work of art. Surreptitiously, she looked at everyone as they enjoyed their meals and wondered if her cooking, as good as she regarded it to be, could compete with Mrs Botsari's obvious mastery that they were all accustomed to.

But, to be honest, and that was no nit-picking, the *moussaka* was a tad too salty for her liking, plus, she didn't like the rich oil residue on the plate. She guessed Mrs Botsari had used lashings of oil in the sauce as well as when frying the vegetables. Kelly had learned an old trick from her grandmother to put the fried aubergines in a colander in the fridge overnight before cooking the *moussaka* the next day. The cool temperature squeezed the oil out of the vegetables, resulting in a healthier meal. Still, she had to admit, healthy or not, this meal was divine.

The sound of Charlie barking anew snapped her out of her deep thoughts and, instinctively, she raised both feet high off the floor in case he had run to her and was about to bite. But, it turned out the pug had run to Tommy's side. The boy was dangling a piece of potato in mid-air and now fed it to him. As soon as he had the piece, the dog fell back on his hind legs and started to beg for more. Peals of laughter ensued from the others as they watched. This time, she didn't voice her disagreement and forced herself to ignore the scene and to resume enjoying her meal.

Nikos finished his meal first, even before his father did. Kelly was amazed to see that. Earlier, while he ate, she had noticed he wasn't exactly chewing it but rather funnelling it down his gullet with the fork. And now, he had just turned to his father, his eyes pleading, asking if he could have another piece.

'No, Nikos. No way. The piece I gave you was as big as the one I'm having! We've discussed this before. I don't want you to eat too much,' Alex replied, serving him a stern look.

Kelly felt awkward to witness the scene because it was obvious Alex had been annoyed by the request. Still, she admired his discipline. He had managed to stop his vexation from growing any further. As for the child, he clearly needed a healthy diet and close supervision. *If not an exercise program.* Already, she was mentally going through the contents of the fridge from when Mrs Botsari had shown her earlier. Some of them were a no-no. *No worries. I'll get it all sorted after a single supermarket run!*

'Sorry, Dad,' replied Nikos, head bent. Then, he put his fork down and sat back in his chair, turning around and whistling to the dog to come closer. The pug did so, and the boy petted him, but his eyes looked sad, making Kelly feel sorry for him. All the while, she threw furtive glances towards Alex, who was chewing away while looking at the back of Nikos's head, a deep frown on his face. *Oh, no! What fresh hell have I just landed myself in? First the teenager, now the overweight child... This father thinks he has it all in order but clearly he has issues with both this boy and his eldest...*

After dinner, the children went to their rooms, Charlie following them upstairs, tail wagging. Apparently, there was another pet bed in Tommy's room, even though the dog often abandoned it to sleep on the boy's bed over the duvet.

Kelly stood from the kitchen table and began to pick up the dishes, but Alex, who had just started to do the same, insisted that she lounge before the TV while he did the washing up. He beckoned her to follow him to the living room where he turned on the TV and handed her the remote, urging her to sit on the sofa while he did the dishes.

Seeing that he was adamant, she obliged and, a few minutes later, he was back in the living room. He went straight to the drinks cabinet and poured two glasses of brandy.

'Here you go,' he said, handing her a glass as he came to stand before her. He emitted a soft sigh when she took it, and ran a quick hand over his hair. 'I don't know about you, but I need a nightcap...' He gave a lazy, sweet smile that made her heart leap. 'I expect this must all be a little daunting for you, Kelly. For me too, to be honest. Not that I don't have full faith that you'll be fine here; of course I do.'

'Thank you, Alex,' she said and he clinked his glass with hers.

'To new beginnings,' he said with a grin.

'To new beginnings,' she replied, feeling rather light-headed looking up at this tall, dashing man before her. The exhaustion of the day had begun to take its toll on her and she could barely keep her eyes open.

Alex took a long sip from his drink and she did the same, then he sat in an armchair, leaned back and crossed his legs. He seemed relaxed, almost regal in his manner, as he rested his glass on the armrest, his hand curled around it loosely.

She nodded, tight-lipped, and a little mesmerised by his charm, but before she could say anything, he piped up, 'We've had Mrs Botsari here for such a long time... The children have grown accustomed to having her around. When I tuck the little one in a little later, I expect there'll be tears over her departure today.'

She took a sip of her brandy and said, 'Oh I am sure, Mr Sarakis. It must be hard, but—'

He raised a hand. 'Please. Alex.'

'All right... *Alex*... Rest assured I will try my best, so the children continue to have all they need.'

'I'm sure you will, Kelly.' He drank from his glass, then leaned forward. 'So, I trust Mrs Botsari has left you her keys to the house, and to the city car that you'll have at your disposal? It's parked right outside on the street.'

'Yes, she did. And I am very grateful for the car, by the way. It'll certainly come in handy. For the grocery shopping, if anything.'

'Yes, and on your days off too. Feel free to use it to go to town, if you need to shop for yourself, to go sightseeing, or whatever. It's yours to do with as you please while you work here.'

'This is most kind, thank you... By the way, Mrs Botsari mentioned that the children walk to school. Is it safe? Are you sure you don't prefer that I drive them there and back?'

'Oh no, definitely. Both the elementary and the junior school are a few blocks away, down the residential road we're on. It's safe in our area, I can assure you; plenty of people about all day long. Besides, my eldest is protective of his little brothers and escorts them to school in the morning, then heads to his own school. When the school day ends, Nikos and Tommy return home with a bunch of their friends who live around here so they never walk alone.'

'What about any extra-curricular activities?'

'There are none really.' He raised his chin slightly, then set it. 'I am not one of those parents who deprive their small children of their idle and playing time by adding a bunch of activities for their evenings and weekends. I am a firm believer that a small child needs both these things by the buckets.' He hooked a finger to point at himself, raised his brows humorously and added, 'I enjoyed plenty of playtime as a child and look how I've turned out!' They both chuckled loudly at that, then he added, his face serious now, 'No, I won't exhaust my children that way. Once they're teenagers they can pick the hobbies and the sports they want to do themselves.'

'What about the eldest? Stratos? Tommy mentioned he learns English in a *frontistirio?*'

'Yes, evening classes only. Three times a week. Monday, Wednesday and Friday. Again, the *frontistirio* is close by and he walks there and back on his own. You don't need to worry.'

'I see. Good.' A short lull followed while they both enjoyed another sip of brandy, then she added, 'Stratos seems like a good lad. You must be very proud of him.' She didn't know why she said it. But perhaps it was because she was so intrigued about the boy. Something was quite off between him and his father. She just knew it.

Alex smiled, but she wasn't fooled. She'd seen it. That passing shadow on his face. He looked up from the glass on his lap and tilted his head. 'He sure is. But I... I am not convinced that he likes me, you know?' A nervous chuckle and then, 'And he often forgets his good manners... I'm not sure he doesn't do it on purpose to taunt me.'

'Sorry to hear that...' she replied, then cautiously, 'You know, Alex... Teenagers are in need of gentle guidance. If I may say so, pushing them often has the opposite result.'

'Yes, I suspect this is true. It's just that sometimes I lose my patience, you know?'

Kelly nodded mutely and took another sip. Glancing at the wall clock, she saw it was coming up to nine o' clock and was shocked the time had passed so quickly. At the very thought of her long day, she gave a yawn, her hand flying up with urgency to cover her wide open mouth.

Alex saw her and his face fell. 'Oh Kelly. You must be so exhausted. And I am keeping you here, forgive me.' He glanced at the clock. 'Oh my! Better down this quickly and go say goodnight to the little ones! Then I'm off to bed with my book.'

'You read in bed?'

'Oh yes. Can't fall asleep without reading a few pages.'

Kelly was impressed. She hadn't met another Greek who read, and as for her awful ex-boyfriend Makis, the only thing he ever read for pleasure was either Disney comics or the football newspapers. Intrigued, she asked, 'What do you read? Fiction? Non-fiction?'

'Mostly thrillers, but I also read the odd biography for inspiration, you know? You?'

'Fiction and self-help.'

'Self-help?'

'Yes.'

'What about?'

'Oh... various things. Fitness, esoteric philosophy, mind hacks and relaxation methods, anything that can make me a better person and reshape my character.'

Alex pinned his beautiful brown eyes on hers for a few seconds as he nodded slowly. 'Wow,' he finally said. 'I just hired my own Oprah. I feel like I've hit the jackpot,' he added with humour but seemed to be serious about it at the same time. He drained his glass and stood up.

She followed suit and he took her empty glass from her hand. 'I am serious, by the way. Not only did you fall right out of the sky to save me today, but it seems to me I just hired a knowledgeable person in many diverse things. I heard what you commented earlier about the dog, about not rewarding bad behaviour. I hadn't thought of it that way. You got me thinking, Kelly. And I think I'll give you full rein… See what other problems you may find in my house to report.'

He smiled wickedly, nodding firmly. 'Make a list! And know I am all ears. One thing I've learned as a businessman all these years is to listen to my employees. In my hotel, they're all talented, each one a gem of knowledge in their own right. All together we form a mastermind that makes us a better business a little every day. I strongly feel that my home was enriched the same way today. Thanks to you, Kelly…'

They locked eyes for a few moments, both of them smiling amicably, then his eyes ignited when he added, 'But keeping you up is no way to thank you. So, if you have no other questions, Kelly, you're officially dismissed to hit the sack. You must be exhausted after your marathon, you poor thing.'

She smiled sweetly, mind reeling to hear his praise, something she really appreciated. She thanked him and said good night. Reaching the bottom of the stairs, she heard his footsteps echoing behind her so she spun around.

'One last thing, Kelly… I don't know if Mrs Botsari told you. She ran out of time and never did the weekly shopping yesterday. I'd appreciate it if you could use the car tomorrow to do it while the children are in school. The shopping list is stuck on the fridge door, and the supermarket is down our road a little further after the elementary school. You can't miss it.' He gave a crooked grin. 'Big ugly thing standing on a corner.'

'Yes, Alex. I know. Mrs Botsari already covered all that.'

He did a thumbs up. 'Oh great! Thank you. I will leave you the money here on the kitchen island tomorrow morning. That is, if I don't see you before I go. I have a quick coffee around seven, then leave shortly after.' He shook a finger and added, 'You don't have to be up so early on my account, by the way. I can make my own breakfast. All I ask is that the children are fed and ready to leave for school at half past eight.'

'Yes, of course. Mrs Botsari informed me about your morning schedules. I'll certainly make sure the children are never late for school.'

'Wonderful.' He raised a hand. 'Well, good night, Kelly. And welcome to my home.' With a dashing smile, he turned about face, the glasses still in his hands, and headed for the sink.

Her mind was in a whirl, not just for the way his eyes had just stirred her heart again, but also for the daunting new life that awaited her the next morning.

Kelly carried her tired legs up the stairs with effort. After the marathon and the walking she'd done around town in the day, they felt like two chunks of old wood that didn't belong to the rest of her body. As she continued to ascend, while resisting the need to moan with discomfort, she wondered how this new marathon was going to end, and if all the self-help books she'd read in the past year were likely to help her.

Chapter 6

Kelly woke up with a start when the alarm on her phone went off. She'd slept like a log all through the night. The area was perfectly quiet, a far cry from her place in central Athens where traffic rushed along the surrounding avenues day and night.

Checking her phone, she gave a chuckle. She had two text messages from Efi. The first, sent at half past seven the previous evening, read: "Got home safe. Thinking of you smooching with your new boss." The emoticon at the end had its tongue sticking out. Efi's second text was sent at ten in the evening. "Have you tucked him into bed yet? Dying to know. And I can't fail to notice your silence to my previous message!"

Kelly chortled and keyed in a quick answer: "Oh do shut up. All okay here. Talk later, as I have to get the kids' breakfast ready!" As soon as the text was sent, she left her phone on the bed and rushed to get dressed. She put her sweater and jeans on and made a mental note to buy a pair of slacks and another sweater that morning.

She was itching to go out and explore the place. A quick glance towards her window told her the weather was going to be mild again today. She had a view to a line of quiet residential buildings on the back road and a green edged by a hill in the distance. No shops in sight. *Alex mentioned there are some in the area. I'll have a nice look-see once the children are off to school. Can't wait!*

She left her room and, following Mrs Botsari's detailed advice, knocked on the doors of Nikos's and Tommy's rooms, calling them out to get up and join her downstairs for breakfast. Alex's bedroom door was wide open so she knew for sure he had gone to work.

She'd been so tired last night, and he did say he wouldn't mind if she missed him, but she planned to wake up earlier each morning to catch him before he went. She wanted to do that in order to seem eager, and to communicate anything needed for the house or the kids at the last minute... Yet, she knew, deep down, there was another reason, too. She wanted to catch another glimpse of him before he went. Just to be able to start her day with his gorgeous smile...

She was deep in thought, standing before the boys' closed doors when echoes of their rushed voices reached her ears. 'Be down shortly, Miss Kelly! Almost ready!' echoed Nikos's voice behind his closed door.

'Me too!' it sufficed little Tommy to chime in from his own room. His response was followed by a volley of loud barking.

Of course. The pug. God help me... Kelly thought, wondering how her first day in the house alone with the unruly pet was going to pan out. But she had a plan. A training plan, as a matter of fact, for the little devil. *But I need to go shopping first.*

Downstairs, on the kitchen island, she found three fifty-euro notes. Beside it, a scrap of paper read in neat handwriting:

"Kelly, I am leaving you one hundred euro for the weekly shopping as discussed. The extra fifty is for you. Please use it to buy anything you may need for yourself until your friend brings you your things on Sunday. It just occurred to me that you may need some toiletries or something. This is a gift – not an advance on your pay, by the way. Use it as you wish or keep the money. Thank you again for accepting this position at such short notice. I'm off to work now, but I'll give you a call later. Thanks, Alex."

Kelly clutched her chest with one hand, deeply moved by this gesture. And even though there was nothing to hide, when she heard footsteps on the stairs, she shoved Alex's message and the banknotes deep in her jeans pocket, like a happy secret she preferred to keep for herself.

Before the two little boys had arrived downstairs, Stratos emerged from the small bathroom at the end of the corridor.

'Oh! Hi Kelly,' he said, surprisingly bright and breezy. He was dressed in jeans and a sweater. 'I'll be there soon,' he added before disappearing into his bedroom.

'Sure!' she said just as the younger boys came in. They emitted equally jovial greetings and sat at the table looking expectant.

Kelly checked her watch. 'Oh no! Sorry guys, running a little late.'

'Don't worry, Miss Kelly,' said Nikos. 'Mrs Botsari used to come in late some mornings too.'

'Yes, when she had a bad back, for sure,' said Tommy, then bent down to caress Charlie on the head. It was true what Mrs Botsari had said. Tommy and the pug were inseparable. The pet had followed the boy closely down the stairs as if tethered to him.

Kelly gave a little sigh and turned to open the fridge. Her eyes fell on the tub of margarine, and that caused the corners of her lips to curl downwards. The sight had seemed just as offensive the previous day when Mrs Botsari showed her the fridge contents and told her what the boys had for breakfast. Everything had sounded great except for the margarine. Feeding it to the kids went against everything she stood for. She also noticed there was no butter to speak of in the fridge.

She took a carton of milk into her hands and turned to the children just as Stratos breezed in to sit at the table.

She bit her lower lip. 'Ah... I was thinking... what if we tried something else for breakfast, Tommy?' She knew he was the only one who didn't like cereal. Mrs Botsari had said he only ate margarine on sliced bread or toast.

'Like what?' asked the little boy.

'Well, what if instead of margarine, I put hazelnut paste on your bread today? Or maybe honey?'

The boy shrugged, clearly about to acquiesce, when Nikos piped up, 'Why? Are we out of margarine? Can't be. There's a big tub in the fridge.'

Kelly twisted her lips, then said, 'I know, it's just that I don't think it's healthy. I'm sorry. I can't sit here and watch you guys eat it. It's really bad stuff.' Kelly registered the puzzled looks the boys exchanged with each other but couldn't spare the time to explain herself further, at least not now. Kelly rummaged through cupboards and drawers getting out plates, cups and cutlery. Then, she rushed to get a *briki* for her Greek coffee. Already, a small pan with milk in it was warming up on the stove so Stratos and Nikos could use it for their cereal.

Stratos pointed to the pan. 'There's no need to do that, Miss Kelly. Mrs Botsari microwaved the milk instead. Cereal and all.'

'Nuh. No way. Microwaves are the devil. Not feeding you nuked stuff.'

'What?' they all said at the same time, a vision of frowns, raised brows and tilted heads. For a few seconds, she froze, wondering what the hell she was doing. The last thing she needed was for them to dislike her for trying to change their habits, or even worse, complain to their dad, which would undoubtedly result in her getting fired for being plain weird.

But then, she looked at their eager faces in succession and took in a steadying breath, deciding the risk was worth it. She, herself, had once paid the ugly price of bad eating habits. She couldn't just let these innocent children eat unhealthy stuff. Nikos had a big weight issue. Stratos had an evident skin problem. A wholesome, healthy diet would benefit them both.

She heaved a long sigh, then said, 'Look, kids. Let me go shopping this morning, and we'll have a talk lunchtime when I can show you what I got, okay? No time now. You're all rushing and so am I.'

For the next quarter of an hour, the children enjoyed their breakfast, and Kelly was amazed by how well-behaved they all were. Even the pet sat quietly at Tommy's feet. Luckily, the child didn't try to feed it any bread. Which reminded her...

Kelly took another sip of her coffee, then stood to get some dog food in dry pellets. She put some in Charlie's bowl that lay by his bed in the corner, and he went straight to it, then started to munch.

'Good boy!' she said and, albeit reluctantly, caressed the top of his head with her fingertips. Charlie raised his head and met her eyes for a few seconds dispassionately, then resumed eating.

At least he hadn't seemed to mind her touch, so she took heart, hoping she'd be okay alone with him in the house, after all. Smiling to herself, she returned to the table just as Stratos stood up and wiped his mouth with a napkin. He turned to Tommy, who had finished eating and was caressing the dog.

'Tommy, go get your school bag, okay?' Then, leaning in, he opened his eyes wide with a wicked grin. 'If you're not back in five minutes, Nikos and I will go without you!'

Tommy dashed out of the kitchen, the pet rushing behind him. Kelly panicked then, as she recalled what Alex thought about them running on the stairs. But Stratos spoke first. 'No running on the stairs, Tommy!'

Tommy froze right at the bottom of the steps, then began to go up the stairs in slow motion, a cheeky smile on his face, just to make a point.

'That's better,' said Stratos with a chortle, then turning to Kelly he added, 'Thank you for our breakfast, Miss Kelly. It was great. And no problem about the margarine. Actually, I hate the stuff. It tastes awful. Mum used to give us butter for breakfast... It was Mrs Botsari that first bought margarine for us. Can you get us some butter, please? That would be nice.'

Kelly smiled openly, relieved. 'Yes, that was exactly what I intended to get for you boys.'

Nikos, who had long since finished his cereal and was now enjoying a second slice of bread with hazelnut paste, screwed up his face. 'Dad says that I'm not supposed to eat fatty foods. He won't let me eat butter.'

'Actually, Nikos, the body needs fat to burn fat.'

Nikos raised his brows, his ruddy cheeks puffed up as he chewed, the sides of his mouth smeared with hazelnut paste. 'Really?'

Kelly nodded firmly. 'Really. Now finish up, Nikos. It's almost eight-thirty.' Taking heart to have found an ally in Stratos about her diet changes for the kids, she shooed the boys playfully out of the kitchen. 'Now go get your bags or you'll be late for school. We'll talk at lunch about butter and anything else you may want to know.'

Two minutes later, right on time, the boys were all laden with their school bags. Kelly escorted them to the front door, the pug running up and down the hall. When the boys went out into the porch, Charlie tried to follow, but to no avail. Mrs Botsari had warned Kelly about this so Kelly had made sure to get hold of the dog's collar before the boys had even opened the door.

Kelly waved to the boys and shoved the door shut, ignoring the pug's frantic wiggling as it tried to break free. As soon as the door was shut, he began to growl, causing her to jump out of her skin. She removed her hand from his collar as if scalded, and even took a step back.

Charlie began to whimper, scratching at the door, leaving Kelly at a loss. 'What is it, Charlie? Are you sad because Tommy left, or do you need to wee?' she said in desperation as if the pet could answer.

Seeing that Charlie continued to whimper, she thought it best not to take any chances and opened the door. Charlie ran all the way to the closed gate, then looked at her across the distance, the sorrow alight in his dark eyes, seeing that the boys were no longer in sight.

'Right. You wanted to be let out, so sit out there for now. Do your business while you're at it, I got work to do!' she said with a mischievous smile and shut the door.

Chapter 7

Kelly parked the car outside the house feeling elated. She was still overjoyed to have been given access to the small city car. That would make all the difference in doing the shopping and going out to explore on her days off.

It was easy to find the supermarket, just like Alex had said. On the same street, there were a couple of retail shops where she was able to buy a sweater, slacks and some underwear too.

Returning home, she parked the car on the same spot as before and, laden with four large shopping bags, opened the gate and began to walk down the path to the door.

Charlie emerged from the trees on the right side of the garden and ran towards her silently. He stopped short at her feet, his body rigid as he took in her scent.

'Yes, it's me, you little ogre!' she said, amused, about to resume walking, when she heard a jovial voice greet her from her left. She turned to find a woman in her late twenties waving her hand, a wide smile on her face.

'Hello! You must be the new housekeeper,' she said.

'Yes, I am,' said Kelly politely. She put down the bags and approached the woman. 'I am Kelly,' she said, offering her hand.

'Lovely to meet you, Kelly,' said the woman as she shook hands with her. 'I am Stella. Mrs Botsari told me she was leaving, and that Alex was looking to find someone new at short notice. She seemed quite upset and said she had to go to Athens urgently but didn't say why.' She lowered her voice a few notches and leaned in. 'Do you know why she was upset, by any chance? I do worry about her. I hope she's okay.'

Kelly cleared her throat and looked away, partly with dismay, and partly to check on Charlie in case he was tampering with the bags. She found him chewing a weathered piece of wood on the lawn so she turned back to Stella reluctantly. She couldn't suffer busybodies. Stella's vibes were unmistakable. 'I'm sorry. Mrs Botsari didn't say.'

'What about Alex? Surely he must know.' She waved her hand dismissively. 'Oh, never mind. I'll ask him when I see him.' She half-closed her eyes and pulled a face of concern, but it didn't fool Kelly much. 'Just to put my mind at rest, you know? So many people fall ill these days. I'd hate to find out she had a medical emergency.'

Well, if you'd hate to find out, then maybe you should not ask, thought Kelly, itching to say it, but her good manners allowed her only to press her lips together, give a single nod, and look away. A moment later, with a fleeting glance towards Stella, she said, 'Well, I'd better go. Lots of work to do in the house.' She had already begun to walk away from the fence when she heard Stella call her name. She spun around, pushing herself to assume an expression of mild interest. 'Yes?'

Stella put up a finger. 'Please, Kelly. Can you wait a moment? I've made some muffins for the kids. Back in a sec!'

Before Kelly could say anything, Stella had already dashed to her front door to enter her house. It looked almost identical to Alex's, except for the colours on the railing and the shutters, and the lanterns that were made in a modern style. Alex's had an antique look. She also noticed that Stella's garden was unkempt. Just a couple of trees, and only one small patch of flowers near the gate. On both sides of the path, the land was covered with weeds.

Kelly stood by the fence, waiting, and a few seconds later, Stella reappeared with a plate of large muffins. They were covered with a generous dusting of icing sugar.

'Here you go! I make the kids a fresh batch every Sunday evening and bring them over Monday morning. But since I saw you, you can give it to them.' She gave a chuckle. 'It's my way to treat the kids with a little something. It must be hard for them, you know? Losing their mother like that. Tsk Tsk!'

Bemused, Kelly took the plate and mumbled a "thank you" while forcing a thin smile. It wasn't so much what Stella had said, rather than the way she had said it. It had sounded like another attempt to acquire feedback, some private information on Alex's family. It felt so intrusive it made her skin crawl. 'Thank you. I'm sure the children will enjoy them…' she said without looking at her, then turned away to check on the dog again.

'I made the muffins with banana and nutmeg this time. I alternate the flavours. Last week it was coffee and walnut.'

Kelly turned in time to see the woman give a little wave. 'I love making them, but my elderly parents, who live with me, don't eat them. So I get to enjoy a spot of baking and do something for the kids too.'

Kelly took a step back from the fence, about to mumble an excuse and leave her, if only a moment sooner, but Stella leaned over then, both elbows resting on the fence, poised for a good chinwag. Not having the time for that, Kelly said, 'Okay… Got to go. I have cooking to do—'

Stella didn't seem ready to let up. 'I live on my own here on the ground floor,' she pointed vaguely behind her, 'My parents live in their own flat upstairs. Feel free to come over for a chat anytime. I make good filter coffee.'

'Yes… right, thanks…' said Kelly, taking another step back.

Stella tilted her head, eyes flashing with interest. 'How old are you? I'm guessing you're late twenties like me? And single, no doubt, yes?'

Numb, and unbelieving of this woman's tactlessness, Kelly only nodded.

'Huh! I knew it! We single girls should stick together!'

Panicking now, for she'd rather stick needles on the back of her fingernails than give this woman one iota of encouragement, Kelly put up a hand, balancing the plate on the palm of the other, and said firmly, 'Right! Got to go, Stella, and thanks again for the muffins!' This time she didn't wait for a reaction. She turned around and made straight for the door.

The pug followed her inside, and she hurried to the kitchen island to leave the plate there, then dashed back out to pick up the bags. Luckily, Stella had vanished by then. *Crikey! What is this woman like?*

*****

Kelly opened the bags and placed all the shopping on the kitchen island. In the last bag, she found the dog lead she had bought with her own money. Chuckling, she showed it to Charlie, who sat in his bed on the floor. 'This is for you! You and me. Walking. It starts tomorrow, buddy!'

Charlie raised his head, then tilted it to the side, looking very cute.

Amused, she shook a finger. 'No, you're not working that charm on me. You've gone too long without exercise. And discipline. But Kelly's here now. Trust me, you'll enjoy it.'

Charlie emitted a single bark as if in conversation, causing her to go to him and pet him on the head. Already, he seemed accustomed to her presence, and that made her feel relieved. She didn't know much about pugs and was glad that, at least, this little soul seemed to have no aggression in him, after all.

Her eyes lit up. 'Oh! I forgot. Look what I got you, Charlie!'

The dog picked up on her excitement and followed her back to the island as she rummaged through the last shopping bag. 'Look! I got you chocolate treats! But you'll have to work for them, matey. Come. Let me show you.' She stood before him and spoke firmly, the way she knew how, for this wasn't the first dog she'd trained.

After just three attempts, the pug finally worked out that he'd get a treat immediately after sitting on his hind legs. 'Good boy!' she said, patting him on the head, and causing his mellow dark eyes to look back at her almost adoringly. 'So the way to your heart is through your stomach, huh? I knew it! A typical guy!' she said, chortling.

'Sit!' she said once more, to make sure he'd got it and, sure enough, the pug obeyed the command once more to get the last treat of his first training session.

When she set about putting the shopping away, the pug came to lie on the floor between the kitchen island and the pantry. It was sweet he'd followed her there, but she was concerned she might wind up stumbling over him while milling about. 'Go to your bed! *Pigene sto krevati sou!*' she said, pointing to the corner.

To her surprise, Charlie obeyed at once. He sat in his bed looking at her, a solemn look in his eyes. 'Good boy! *Kalo pethi!*' she said, impressed. 'Training you will be a piece of cake. You're so clever,' she cooed, then resumed putting the food stuff away, except for the ingredients she needed for lunch – a chicken curry.

She checked her watch. It was a little after eleven. Without further ado, she began to prepare the meal.

*****

While the curry simmered on the stove, Kelly checked her phone to find another inquisitive text from an impatient Efi. Even though she was rushing, she made a quick call to her and hung up a little later, once she'd filled her in on her first impressions about everyone and everything.

Efi had asked her to email her a list of everything she needed her to bring on Sunday, which Kelly made a mental note to do in the afternoon when she expected to have some free time. Then, the house phone rang, and she hurried to the edge of the kitchen counter where a wireless device sat in its cradle. It was Alex, just checking in, to ask if all was okay.

Kelly assured him the kids had left on time for school and that she'd done the shopping. When she mentioned meeting Stella, the muffin-bearing neighbour, she heard him emit a soft sigh. Was he stressed at work? Or was it a hint of annoyance she had just detected?

'Yes... She does that every Monday...' he said after a short pause. With that said, he said goodbye and they ended the call. Without wasting time, Kelly then headed upstairs to tidy up the bedrooms.

*****

Kelly tidied up Nikos's and Tommy's bedrooms first, making beds, putting toys away, and folding any clothes lying about. She checked the furniture surfaces and emitted a silent thanks to Mrs Botsari. Despite her urgency and distress, the old woman had ensured to hoover and dust the house before leaving.

When she entered Alex's bedroom, she froze on the spot. A feeling of warmth, mixed with deep sadness, hit her hard. It had almost knocked her off her feet. But, it wasn't just that that had caused her to look around her wide-eyed, jaw gaping open. The room had an odd scent about it. *Candy floss... Where's it coming from?*

Ignoring the unmade double bed and the clothes that were messily draped over the back of the armchair, she headed for the wardrobe where the odd smell seemed to be coming from. She opened the double doors in the centre, to find it full of shirts, trousers, jackets and coats, all hanging neatly. Underneath, Alex's shoes had been placed just as tidily. *No candy floss smell in here...*

She opened every other compartment, one by one, starting from the left, exposing drawers and shelves into the morning sunlight that streamed heavily through the tall balcony doors. In the last compartment on the very right, she found yet another set of shelves with drawers underneath, but this time, far from turning away from it at once, her eyes searched the space thirstily. All the while, her nostrils filled with the eerie smell of candy floss in this crammed little space where it didn't belong.

Kelly's hand began to tremble slightly as she reached into the middle shelf, for she already knew this scent wasn't real, but a result of her special gift inherited from her late grandmother. Feeling her heart begin to race, she took into her hands a colourful scarf that lay on the shelf on top of a pile of women's sweaters. Taking it into her hands, she leaned in and smelled it deeply. *Oh, my!*

She almost buried her face in the neat pile of sweaters and tried again. The same spooky smell, now even stronger, caused her to straighten abruptly as if pushed back, her heart giving a thump. She steadied herself by holding on to a doorknob and turned around feeling light-headed.

'The scent fills the whole room... and only this room...' she mumbled. Deciding it had something to do with Alex's late wife since these clothes had clearly belonged to her, she told herself right there and then that she wouldn't let it bother her.

Obviously, her new boss was holding on to his late wife's memory, seeing that he had kept some of her clothes. It brought deep sadness to her heart, but she knew it was all part of the grieving process.

Deep in thought, she went to the window to open the panes and let fresh air in. Then, she made Alex's bed and tidied up. By the time she'd made her own room a little later, she'd convinced herself not to think about that eerie smell any more. This didn't concern her. But, in the deep recesses of her mind, she couldn't help but feel sad. It'd been three years, after all. By not letting go of his wife, Alex was holding her spirit back from total deliverance. Because that's what the smell suggested. He was keeping her spirit here, somehow, still.

Shaking her head to clear her mind from this disconcerting thought, she went to Stratos's room downstairs. As she made his bed, she found a plectrum on the duvet, much to her surprise. She promptly recognised it as the tiny plastic thing people use when learning to strum the strings of a guitar. Bewildered, for she wasn't aware that Stratos played this instrument, nor could she see one lying around, she put the plectrum on his bedside table, and thought about it no more.

Chapter 8

'I can't believe he's doing it!' uttered Tommy with a squeal of delight. 'Can I try too?'

'Sure! Just one treat, though, as he's already had three,' said Kelly, handing Tommy a chocolate treat from the pack in her hands. Shortly after the boys had come home from school, she thought she'd quieten down the dog that had got too excited, by asking him to sit. The children had been speechless so she explained she'd started to train him. While she demonstrated, the boys kept clapping and whooping with delight every time the pug obeyed the command.

'Wow!' said Tommy when Charlie sat and took the treat from his hand. He cuddled the dog and left a kiss on his snout.

'What other tricks can you teach him, Kelly?' asked Nikos.

'A few. Stay, roll, twirl, speak, lie, play dead... and fetch, of course.'

'Can you teach him now?' asked Tommy, who was sitting on the floor tiles beside the dog, his arms laced around him.

'Not now, Tommy. And please get off the floor.' She clapped her hands, then shooed them all playfully. 'Go wash your hands and let's eat, guys! The meal is ready!'

Nikos and Tommy dashed out, Charlie following suit, but Stratos hovered by the table with her. 'What is the meal? It smells divine.'

In the strong sunlight that streamed in through the kitchen window, the acne spots on his flushed face looked thick and unsightly, like chickpeas swimming in a bowl of tomato soup. She flinched inside as she remembered her own experience with spots as a teen. She recalled how stress used to make matters worse. At least this boy looked laid back. When his father wasn't around, at least.

'It's chicken curry,' she finally said. 'A mild one. I hope you guys like it.'

His eyes lit up. 'Wow! I haven't had a curry in years...' Before she could reply, he was gone in a rush, leaving her somewhat perplexed. He had sounded happy about her choice of meal, but the shadow that had crossed his face as he ended his sentence and quickly turned away told her otherwise. *Teenagers. Who could ever suss them out?*

The table was already set, and by the time she'd served all the plates, the boys had returned to take their seats.

Kelly, who was still standing, eyed the dog with a lopsided smile. He was sitting by Tommy's feet and she decided to tease him for fun. As soon as she pulled back the chair that had set him off the previous day, he hurried to her feet with a growl.

'O-kay!' she said, putting up both hands and smiling openly, causing the boys to laugh out loud. 'Just joking, matey! I'll sit here, see?' She chose another seat.

'Oh, I think it'll take a little more than teaching him how to do tricks for him to let you sit there,' said Stratos before taking the first bite. He rolled his eyes when he began to chew. 'Oh my! Kelly, this is delicious.'

'Thank you,' she said as she turned to the other boys to find them eating hungrily. Then, she saw Tommy take a tiny piece of chicken in his hand. The dog sat at his feet looking up at him pleadingly. She put up a hand, catching the boy as he was about to feed the pet. 'No, Tommy! I am training him, remember? We agreed earlier, didn't we? No more feeding him while we eat. Discipline and manners will make him a better and a happier doggie, trust me.'

Tommy put the chicken piece back in his plate and nodded. 'Yes, Miss Kelly.'

'Miss Kelly... How did you know we love curry?' asked Nikos.

She shook her head and straightened in her chair. 'I didn't. I just thought you might enjoy it...' She gave a bright smile and gazed into everyone's faces in succession to add, 'And you guys can call me Kelly.' She hoped that would help the boys feel at ease with her even more.

'Okay, Kelly...' said Nikos. With a wry smile, he added, 'Granny used to make curry for us all the time. But she's dead now, so... We hadn't had one in ages.'

'And Mrs Botsari, of course, didn't know how to make chicken curry.' Stratos looked up from his plate, pinning his eyes on Kelly to add, 'Mum would make it sometimes, but she's also...' With a shrug from his shoulders, his voice trailed off.

The sorrow in his eyes had been palpable, his gaze electrifying. The vibe had hit her like a racing car coming at full throttle. Swallowing hard, Kelly turned to Nikos. 'Sorry to hear your granny passed away. Do you have any other grandparents?'

'Yes. But not here. They live in Salonica. They're our Dad's parents,' cut in Stratos.

'Stratos says our mummy left to join her parents in heaven,' piped up Tommy.

'And I'm sure they're all happy up there together...' She forced a thin smile and added, 'I bet they smile as they watch over you boys every day.' She willed her voice not to waver as her eyes flitted from face to face, her heart twinging. The boys' eyes were filled with a terrible sadness that permeated through her, making it hard to breathe properly.

Other than feeling uncomfortable to receive these vibes, she also felt amazed by how quickly the boys had opened up to her. *But I'm just a stranger... Why are they so eager to discuss their deceased loved ones with me?*

'Do you have grandparents, Kelly?' piped up Tommy, removing her from her thoughts.

Kelly took a steadying breath, then said, 'Like you guys, I only have one granny and one grandad now. They're my mother's parents and they live in England. They're English, you see.'

When she said that, she noticed they all exchanged excited glances but didn't say anything. She wondered what that was all about, but quickly gathered her thoughts and continued, 'As for my father's parents, they are Greek, and they've passed away. My granny died last year. In Athens.'

'Sorry to hear that,' said Stratos. A short pause ensued, then he added, 'Is your mother alive, Kelly?'

Kelly saw the deep sorrow return in his eyes and felt a lump lodge itself deep in her throat. She felt almost guilty to admit her mother was alive and kicking. 'Yes, Stratos... She lives in England too, with my father and my grandparents.'

'Our mummy died three years ago,' said Nikos quietly, then put out a hand and placed it tenderly on Tommy's shoulder. 'Tommy was only small then. He doesn't remember her.'

The lump in her throat grew bigger. 'Well, your little brother has you and Stratos, though. You guys can tell him what you know about her.'

'Only when we're alone...' mumbled Tommy, playing with a piece of chicken in his plate using his fork.

'What was that, Tommy?' she asked.

He didn't answer, so Nikos cut in, 'Dad doesn't like it when we talk about Mum.'

Kelly raised her brows, despite herself. 'He doesn't?'

Stratos shook his head profusely, lips twisted. 'No. We don't mention her when he's around.'

Lost for words, Kelly simply nodded. An awkward silence ensued for a while, then she forced a smile and piped up, 'So, what did Mrs Botsari cook for you guys? Give me an idea of what you like.'

'Can you bake cakes?' said Tommy.

Kelly chortled. 'Yes, of course, I can, and I will. But I'm asking about food, not dessert.'

Nikos scrunched up his face. 'Mrs Botsari made a lot of *ladera*...'

'Vegetable stews?'

'Yes. And no matter which vegetable, she used *a lot* of oil!' Nikos widened his eyes for effect.

Stratos chuckled. 'Actually, we could almost see the veg swim in the oil around the plate. A little more and we'd have had to get them *vatrahopedila* so they can float in the oil without sinking.'

Kelly gave a belly laugh. Her mind had conjured up an image of okra swimming around a plate wearing flippers and the effect was hilarious. *Who would have known the demure, quiet teen I met yesterday can be so chatty and funny?*

'Please don't make any *ladera*, Kelly!' said Tommy in an adorable, pleading way, snapping her out of her thoughts.

Kelly smiled at him and felt her heart melt. 'Well, I could make them from time to time, but I'd be more frugal with the oil.'

Nikos gave a cheeky smile. 'That'll work.'

'Speaking of oil,' said Kelly, 'I bought butter today. So if you guys agree, we can throw away the tub of margarine. I'll run it by your dad first tonight, of course.'

'I thought butter is bad for you. Isn't it supposed to clog arteries or something?' asked Stratos.

Kelly put up a finger. 'Ah! Only if you eat a lot, I guess. Moderation is key, as is the case with anything we eat or drink.' She leaned forward. 'Did you guys know that people have died from drinking too much water?'

'What?' said Tommy with a squeal, then exploded in peals of laughter.

'It's true. As I said, *Pan metron ariston*, as our wise Greek ancestors used to say. Moderation in all things. And don't forget that butter is a natural food while margarine is artificial.'

'Artificial?' asked Nikos with a tilt of his head.

'That's right. Plus, its oils are heated in high temperatures during preparation so they're actually oxidized. So, far from protecting the heart as the adverts say, the truth is it can actually hurt it.'

'How do you know all these things?' asked Stratos, who, like the others, was eating greedily. His plate was nearly empty.

'I have researched heavily online, that's all. I wasn't always slim like this, you know. I had a major lifestyle change once I realized how my diet affected me in all sorts of bad ways. And, trust me, margarine is plastic food. For one thing, it doesn't spoil, no matter how long you leave it out of the fridge. I think that says a lot.'

'It doesn't?' asked Nikos, his brows raised.

'Nope! Not one bit. It doesn't smell, it doesn't change its colour, shape, or texture. Plus, no flies or other bugs will ever go near it. Unlike butter, of course.' She gave a wicked smile and added, 'Actually, margarine is more suitable for motor engines than it is for the human body.'

'Really?' asked Nikos and Tommy in unison. Stratos seemed just as interested but, at the time, seemed more intent on devouring the last morsels on his plate.

After they ate, they each had one of Stella's muffins. The boys seemed to enjoy them but when Stratos asked who had baked them, Kelly confirmed what he seemed to already know. The moment Stella's name left her lips, the boys pulled faces of dismay and threw each other knowing looks. As curious as she was, she didn't comment on that.

When Nikos and Tommy left the kitchen a little later, Stratos stayed behind. Kelly went to the stove to transfer the rest of the curry from the pot into a container. With the corner of her eye, she caught Stratos placing the dishes in the sink.

'That's kind of you, Stratos, thank you.'

'Do you need help with the dishes?'

'Oh no. I'm fine, thanks. You can go to your room now and rest, or study, whatever it is you do at this hour.' With a bright smile, she waved dismissively.

'Thanks again for the meal, Kelly. It was like a blast from the past.'

Kelly moved to the sink and reached for the liquid soap and the sponge. Stratos came to stand beside her, looking forlornly at the sink.

Before she could ask him if there was anything he needed, he cleared his throat, then said, 'Um... Kelly, I found a plectrum on my bedside table. Did you put it there?'

'Yes. I found it on your duvet while making your bed.' She gave a frown. 'It's yours, isn't it?'

He looked away and shoved his hands into his pockets. 'Yes... yes, it's mine. It must have fallen out of my jeans pocket when I dressed this morning...' He gave a soft sigh and met her eyes again. 'Please? Can you not tell my dad about it?'

Kelly nodded firmly. 'Of course...' Her voice trailed off as her bewilderment rose inside.

'Thanks, Kelly. You're the best!' he said and hurried down the corridor to his room.

Chapter 9

Alex came in around eight in the evening looking quite tired, but he was chatty as usual. After dinner, the boys went to bed. While Kelly did the dishes and tidied up, Alex sat in the living room watching TV. When she finished, she asked to talk to him and he eagerly picked up the remote to turn down the volume.

She sat with him and told him about the changes in the boys' diet that she wanted to try. Starting from their breakfast, she expanded to their school lunches as well. Mrs Botsari never packed anything for them for school, so they all bought a snack daily with their pocket money, whatever they wanted. Kelly had asked the boys earlier in the day and they admitted that they often had cheese pies, crisps or chocolate, the healthiest choice being a cinnamon bun with raisins.

Alex agreed with her that Nikos, especially, needed a healthier lunch at school than the fatty *tiropita* he'd admitted to buying daily from the school canteen.

Seeing that Alex was open to all her suggestions, she felt at ease with him and wondered if she should tell him that the boys had spoken about their mother at lunchtime and, furthermore, that they seemed to think they couldn't do it openly with him. Finally, she decided against it, thinking she'd be breaking the children's confidence if that were true. Besides, she couldn't do it without sounding nosy, or critical, or both.

Moments later, she said goodnight and retired to her room. Tired as she was, she fell asleep as soon as her head hit the pillow.

*****

Running Haunted

Kelly heard a creaking sound that woke her up with a start in the middle of the night. She sat up on the bed in the semi-dark room, eyes pinned on the door that was left ajar from her earlier visit to the bathroom.

The corridor was dimly lit with a night light, allowing her to make out clearly a small shape just in front of the door, low on the ground.

What's that?

Then, she heard the familiar tapping sound of Charlie's nails hitting the wooden floor as he neared her bed silently. 'You little ogre, you scared me half to death...' she whispered, clutching her chest with her hand. *Panic over...*

Before she could finish her thought, the bed shook briefly. The dog had just landed on her duvet with a soft thud.

'What are you doing here, Charlie?' she whispered, half-annoyed he had woken her, and half-amused. In the semi-darkness, she could just make out his dark eyes that were pinned on hers. They reflected the faint moonlight coming in through the window with an eerie effect. Somehow, those wistful eyes were the only part of his face she could make out at the time. A few more silent moments passed as they continued to gaze at each other, and they felt surreal in an odd way.

Kelly rubbed her eyes and yawned, about to scold Charlie for his audacity and lead him out, when the pug jumped back down and left the room in a hurry.

Bewildered by this odd nightly visit, she turned to the clock on her bedside table. *Half past three.* Rubbing her eyes again, she realized her earlier panic had chased her sleepiness away. Now, she was wide awake and felt parched too.

She was wearing only a t-shirt so she put on a sweater and cotton slacks and headed downstairs to get a glass of almond milk.

Halfway down the stairs, she thought it odd that strange sounds were coming from the kitchen. *Just what is that crazy dog doing tonight?* But, when she reached the bottom step, she realized that a beam of light was shining on the kitchen tiles. *Torch light! Intruders? Oh, my God!*

Her heart pounding in her chest, she was about to go upstairs to distance herself as much as possible first, then think what she was going to do, when she heard a familiar sound that didn't make sense. Someone had just opened the cutlery drawer. *Huh? A hungry robber? With a huge flat TV and a stereo standing on the other end of the huge open space, I don't think a thief would check out the cutlery instead, somehow...*

Willing herself to calm down, and quite sure this was no intruder, after all, she inched back down the stairs and entered the kitchen on tiptoe.

Her jaw dropped to find Nikos eating a piece of cold *moussaka* from the fridge. He had placed it on a napkin and was leaning against the counter chewing, his back to it, his head hung low. A handheld torch sat on the counter, shining towards the kitchen island. Beside it stood the container with the *moussaka* leftovers, a knife lying on top.

Nikos obviously heard her approach because he looked up abruptly. Freezing in place, he gulped his last bite so hard his shoulders twitched. 'Ke... Kelly... I...'

'Oh, Nikos...' she said with regret, walking up to him.

Nikos bent his head, looking at the leftovers on the napkin forlornly, and she guessed his appetite was gone.

'You're eating it stone cold? Are you that hungry, Nikos?' she asked, her hand on his shoulder.

Avoiding her eyes he said, 'I am sorry... Please don't tell my dad... He'll kill me if he hears.'

'Don't worry. I won't tell him. But, really, Nikos, how can you be hungry after your hearty meal? Hungry enough to eat cold *moussaka* from the fridge at this hour?'

He looked up to meet her eyes, his own misted over. He sniffled, then said, 'I know. I have no excuse...'

She squeezed his shoulder gently. 'You want to know what I think?'

He nodded, tight-lipped, his eyes pinned on the floor tiles.

'I don't think you're hungry, Nikos. You're eating for the sake of eating... I've been there. And I'm guessing this is not the first time you're doing this.'

He gave her a fleeting glance. 'No, it isn't.'

'Thank you for your honesty. Now, give me that... You and I know you don't really need it.' She took the half-eaten piece of *moussaka* from his hand and tossed it in the bin, then lifted his chin with one finger. 'Now, tell me, Nikos. Do you want to change?'

'Change? Like, get thin?'

'No... Not just get thin. The change required here is not just about dieting. It involves changing your thinking too. But first of all, you need to be honest with yourself, the way you were with me just now, and admit why you are doing this to yourself. Why you are coming in here with a torch in the middle of the night doing something you know is wrong.'

He shrugged and looked down again. She removed her finger from his chin and caressed his head, causing him to issue her with a sheepish gaze.

'Come on, tell me, what's really bothering you?'

He heaved a long sigh. 'Some boys bully me at school.'

'Do they?'

'Please don't tell my dad. He doesn't know...'

'I won't if you don't want me to... but bullying is not something you should suffer alone, Nikos. It is something you should always talk about.'

'I know... It's just that I'm ashamed to tell Dad... and scared to tell my teachers... in case those kids...' He bent his head, his voice trailing off.

She raised his chin again, seeking his eyes. 'Tell me. What do those kids do to you?'

He twisted his lips, then said, 'They... they call me fat and ugly... that I'm worthless... and... other things... And every time I want to eat a *tiropita*, I have to hide in the loo to do it. I can't eat it in the yard or in class at recess because they will come over and call me names... laugh at me... until I lose my appetite and throw the food in the bin.'

Kelly's stomach kept doing backflips as she listened. The vibes the child gave off as he relayed his daily turmoil struck a familiar chord inside her. She took a steadying breath and said softly, 'I am sorry to hear that, Nikos... But, you know, you have the power to change this around.'

His eyes lit up. 'I do? But, how?'

'For starters, you won't eat a *tiropita* again, starting from tomorrow. Cheese pies are fat, as you know. You're only giving those bullies kindling to throw on the fire. Besides, cheese pies won't help you to become the thin boy you'd obviously prefer to be. Or am I wrong?'

'Of course, I want to be thin. I just don't know how.'

'I'll help you, Nikos.'

'So what can I buy in school? There isn't much choice really...'

'Nah-uh. No buying. I went shopping, remember? I'm packing you all lunches as of tomorrow. When those boys see you eat a cheese and ham sandwich instead of a *tiropita*, they won't bother you that way... You'll still get some attention when they notice the difference at first, but not in the long run, trust me. And you won't be hungry at all. I'll give you some nuts and an apple to have as a snack too. And I'll make some energy bars tomorrow with all sorts of good stuff for you guys to take to school every day.'

'And, you think that those boys will leave me alone if I change my diet?'

'Give it time, and yes, they will... I've been there, kiddo, and someone helped me change once. And now, I can do it for you too, if you want me to. But, I'll tell you now, Nikos. You have to really want to change. You have to put in the effort. And persevere.'

'Yes! I want to change! Thank you, Kelly!' he said as he squeezed her arm, eyes dancing.

'Shhh!' she responded. He'd been so excited he'd raised his voice. The last thing they needed was to have Alex come down holding a baseball bat, to find, instead of intruders, his housekeeper and his son raiding the fridge and chatting.

'So, you used to be fat too, Kelly?'

'Oh, yes… Twice. Once as a school girl, and once more, as a young girl… up until a year ago, actually.'

'Wow, I don't believe it.' He eyed her up and down, his face bright in the faint torch light.

'Believe it. So, if I could do it, so can you.' She pointed at him with a single finger and winked.

'I don't think I'd be any good with running, though…'

'Don't worry. Diet is way more important than exercise. Having said that, mild exercise speeds up the process, plus keeps you healthy. You and I could walk Charlie together to the green around the back every afternoon… We could start tomorrow! Do you want to try?'

'Yeah! I'd love that.'

'Great. I was going to get some almond milk. You want some?' she asked, moving past him to get a glass from a cabinet.

He declined, so she said, 'Well, off to bed you go then, matey, and take that torch with you. We don't want your dad to find it here tomorrow morning.' She switched on an overhead spotlight, then Nikos turned off his torch and began to walk away.

'And you? You're staying up?' he stopped to ask a moment later.

'Goodness, no. I'll have my milk, put away the *moussaka*, then head back to bed in a flash.' She checked her watch and gave a titter. 'Got to rise in just over an hour actually, for my early morning run.'

Chapter 10

Kelly got out of the house in her running gear, excited to start practicing in a new place that waited to be explored. She jogged to the corner, then headed down the side street, running until she found herself at the edge of the green she'd seen through her bedroom window.

The grass was covered with frost. Purple and yellow wild flowers dotted the field here and there. Enchanted by the beauty of the setting and the quiet, she took a dirt path that ran across the green, then stepped onto a paved path that took her all the way up to the top of the hill at its other end.

Tired, but deliciously exhilarated by the time she'd got there, she stopped at the edge of a precipice to catch her breath and enjoy the sunrise. It was still in progress, the sky a vivid painting that changed by the second, filling the magnificent vista of the bay with pastel and golden hues.

The rooftops of Nafplio were alight with a pink glow in the face of the morning sun, and Bourtzi seemed to have caught fire, resembling a flaming twig dropped in the middle of the sea. As for the castle of Palamidi, it looked sleepy, having just emerged from under a cloud of mist that still circled the top of the mountain like a crown made of candy floss.

Candy floss... The thought inevitably brought back eerie memories from the house. *Alex's family is still grieving... and that poor spirit is trapped here. Alex keeps his late wife's clothes in the wardrobe... and doesn't talk to his kids about her...* For a while longer, she stood admiring the celestial masterpiece in the sky, feeling awestruck. It kept evolving with masterful strokes as she began to wonder if she could help this family at all. *Perhaps I could use my gift... to help Alex and the children move on. Maybe the spirit would find it easy to depart then. That would help everybody...*

She was glad that her special ability involved nothing drastic or scary like being able to see spirits, for example. But, back in England, by sitting quietly in a haunted place and concentrating on making contact, she had managed many times to see images or hear words in her head that gave her answers about the spirits that dwelled there. She'd used her gift numerous times to help others receive messages from their departed loved ones. But these people had come to her, being aware of her special power. This family hadn't asked her for assistance of this kind. *Still... knowing that I could help, how can I sit and watch them all suffer? This spirit is bound here because Alex and the kids are still grieving...*

She checked her watch and began to jog down the hill, her mind still mulling things over. As her feet picked up speed, her thoughts began to die down until they dispersed completely. The familiar feeling of bliss that came from emptying her mind hit her like the most glorious high. Smiling to herself as the morning sunlight warmed her face, she ran across the green sure-footed, heading home.

✴✴✴✴✴

Kelly checked her watch again as she entered through the garden gate. It was half past seven. Alex's car wasn't parked outside, and that caused her heart to sink a little. She'd hoped to catch him before leaving, just to exchange a few words over coffee, and maybe see that luminous, killer smile of his as he said goodbye.

She entered the house and went straight to the stairs, her mind still deep in thought. Alex had blown her away with that same smile two days ago when she first laid eyes on him. She had fallen in love before... so, she was fully aware what it was she felt about Alex. But that didn't bother her, nor did she try to control it, as much as having a crush on her boss could complicate things. *Yes, he seems to be highly problematic, but so what? Problems come and go, but a man's personality stays. And what a terrific personality he has!* She loved his finesse, his polite manners, his sense of pride about his family and his business.

When she reached the landing, echoes of drawers and wardrobe doors opening and closing echoed from the boys' bedrooms, jolting her out of her reverie. As if on cue, Nikos opened his door and headed for the bathroom, his shirt draped messily over his jeans.

'Hi, Kelly...' he said sleepily, his hair tousled. As he paced with socked feet along the carpeted floor, he kept rubbing his eyes, patting his hair and generally doing anything but meeting her eyes.

He's embarrassed... Of course, he is. I caught him binging in the middle of the night. She raised her hand and caught his eye just as he was about to enter the bathroom. 'Hey, Nikos! You and me. We're walking Charlie this afternoon, yes?'

She flashed him a huge grin and he served her one back, his eyes igniting. 'Yes! Look forward to it!' With a thumbs up, he closed the bathroom door behind him.

Kelly rushed into her bedroom. Now wasn't the time to shower or change. She'd do all that after the boys had left for school. She took a small face towel from the chair and wiped the excess sweat off her face and neck. Then, she changed into her long running bottoms. She opened her door halfway, about to leave the room, when she noticed a scarf on the foot of her bed. *What's that doing here?* Her mind went numb when she recalled Charlie's short visit in the middle of the night. *He jumped on the bed... Did he leave this here?*

A split second later, she heard a door creak open down the hall. She guessed the noise had come from Tommy's room because the pug materialized at her door a few moments later. In his mouth, he carried a string of pearls.

'Oh no! No, you don't—' she burst out as soon as the pug rushed past her to leave the necklace on the floor before her bed. He turned around, raising his head slowly, and looked deeply into her eyes. It was such an intelligent look, as if he were human and about to speak.

'Charlie? What are you doing? Why are you bringing me this stuff?' She had spoken to him as if expecting an answer and wondered if she had lost it a little. Still, the pug kept magnetizing her with his eyes. Then, out of the blue, a whiff of candy floss hit her nostrils, causing her heart to give a thump. Her brow furrowing, she looked around her, even though she didn't know what she was looking for.

As soon as she darted her eyes back to the dog, she heard words inside her mind, loud and clear, which she knew were not her own. 'Wear them! Please!' the eerie voice told her.

Kelly froze in place, her mind in a whirl. She barely registered the soft thudding of the pug's paws hitting the wooden floor as he rushed out of the room. *Whoo! Did I just hear a spirit speak inside my head?*

Feeling strange still, as if this were a dream, Kelly bent over slowly and picked up the pearl necklace from the floor first, then the scarf from her bed too. She already knew what to expect but buried her face in them anyway. They both smelled like candy floss.

Heaving a huge sigh, she left both items carefully, reverently, on her bedside table, willing herself to keep calm. *Why am I surprised? I have the gift, after all... Surely, that's why the spirit has made contact with me... I have to think about this carefully, though, before I decide what to do. But not now.*

Without further ado, she dashed outside, then headed downstairs to prepare breakfast.

Chapter 11

Feeling numb from her earlier other-worldly encounter, Kelly set out to prepare breakfast for the boys and herself. The first thing she did was prepare the coffee percolator, and after a few gulps of the strong brew, she felt herself grounded back to reality again.

Nikos and Tommy soon came into the kitchen, followed by Stratos. The latter joined his brothers at the table just as Kelly put their cereal bowls in front of them all.

'Almond milk in your cereal as of today, guys. It's very nutritious and tastes wonderful. Try it!'

'Yum!' said Nikos, and Stratos soon expressed equal appreciation.

Kelly winked at Nikos. 'This will help you especially, Nikos! It has less calories in it. Athletes drink this stuff, including me, of course.'

Nikos's face lit up to hear that and he resumed eating with gusto. Sitting beside him, Tommy was licking his lips with relish. He seemed to love the butter and honey on his toasted bread.

Kelly giggled as she joined them at the table to enjoy a plate of cereal too.

Stratos gave a tut, then a huge sigh, drawing everyone's attention. He was looking at his fingertips. His index finger had a smear of blood on it. A large spot was bleeding on his chin. 'Not again!' he said with exasperation. 'It bled again last night.'

Kelly took a napkin and leaned over to wipe the blood from his face and finger, then asked, 'Why is it bleeding? Did you squeeze it?'

Stratos shook his head forlornly. 'I did... Hard not to...' He gave a sigh of vexation, then burst out, 'Oh! Acne is so annoying!'

'Do you take anything to treat it?'

'Nah... I have a liquid soap Mrs Botsari got me from the supermarket. But it's not doing much...'

'There are other treatments... Wait a minute...' she said as she stood to open the fridge.

'Oh no! No more doctors! The one Mrs Botsari took me to last year gave me meds that burned my face. I had to go to school looking more red in the face than a monkey's butt. Not doing that again!'

Kelly chuckled, despite herself, when she returned to his side. 'Not to worry. I'm the last person that would suggest taking you to a doc to prescribe nasty chemicals.'

Stratos frowned at the sight of the half lemon she held in her hand. 'So, what would you suggest then?'

'A natural approach,' she said, showing him the lemon. 'Open your hand.'

When he did as she asked, she squeezed a little lemon juice onto the palm of his hand. 'Use one finger to dab a little juice on the spot. It will sting a little, but it will dry it out perfectly. Trust me.'

He followed her instruction and she told him to repeat the application before bedtime, promising the spot would be dried out by the next morning.

Happy to see his jovial expression return as he resumed eating, she picked up her spoon to do the same. They all ate quietly for a few moments, then she gave a sigh. 'You know, Stratos... I had a terrible problem too at your age... and my grandmother suggested a few natural tricks that worked for me at the time. If you want, I can tell you more.'

He nodded eagerly, so she continued, 'There are many ways to treat acne the natural way. Personally, I swear by a mixture of apple cider vinegar and water as a lotion, but you can also use cinnamon and honey in a mask. Tea tree oil, green tea, aloe vera and witch hazel are great remedies too.'

'Wow! I had no idea you can use natural stuff to treat acne.'

'Of course, you can. But diet is also very important.' She pointed to his cereal bowl that was nearly empty. 'Glad you're enjoying almond milk. For you, that's a life saver, right there. You should avoid dairy. You told me that you have cheese pastries in school, but if you want to clear your skin of acne, you really should avoid them.'

Stratos put up his hands and smiled openly. 'Sure! I'll try anything!'

Kelly turned to Nikos. 'Same goes for you, buddy. No more *tiropita* as of today.'

Nikos nodded his assent, his eyes sparkling when he gazed back at her, giving her the impression he was feeling one hundred per cent committed.

'What about me?' asked Tommy with a frown, and a cute tilt of his head that made her melt.

'How could I leave you out, Tommy?' she said, cooing at him. 'I'll be making sure you *all* have plenty of fruits and nuts, and lots of other healthy choices for your school lunches as of today.'

'Oh, we love nuts!' said Stratos, causing her to jump upright with enthusiasm and glide to the fridge. Moments later, she returned to the table with a flutter in her chest. She'd taken great care in choosing healthy snacks for them for school and hoped they'd like them. She put three lunch boxes on the table and pointed at them with a theatrical flourish.

'Here you go! You'll find an orange juice, a sandwich, an apple and a cereal bar in each lunch box. I've also included a few assorted nuts and a piece of dark chocolate wrapped in aluminium foil.'

The boys made excited noises, grabbing a lunch box each to open it and take a look.

With a happy smile, she continued, 'I'll alternate the contents, of course, so you don't get bored. The sandwiches today are ham, tomato and lettuce. The cereal bars are bought but I'll make some from scratch later today. So, as of tomorrow, you'll be eating one hundred percent wholesome, home-prepared food in school. Nikos, you can buy milk from the canteen, if you wish, but only skimmed, and no chocolate.'

'Yes, of course,' said Nikos. 'And I'm excited about the walk this afternoon. I can't wait.'

'What walk? Where?' asked Stratos.

'Oh, I was just thinking that Charlie needs some daily exercise. It'll also help improve his discipline as he can be such a naughty little devil!' She pointed to the dog and they all agreed with her, giggling.

The dog, who had been leaning against Tommy's legs all this time, sat up, eyeing them all curiously, causing new peals of laughter to reverberate around the walls.

'And Nikos is coming along because he said he'd like to exercise, too.'

Both Stratos and Tommy said they wanted to join them, and, for a while, Kelly got flustered. She had to get their father's permission first and hadn't expected that all the boys would want to come along. It might prove difficult to get the dog to exercise calmly if all the boys were present. But surely they'd be fine if she held the lead and asked the boys to not distract the dog.

In the end, she told them that as long as their father agreed, they could all come. Stratos could join them on the days when he didn't have English classes. The fresh air and the exercise would help with his acne too.

'Kelly, you're a treasure,' piped up Stratos to hear that. Thank you for taking such good care of us all!' He leaned over and laced his arms around her neck, squeezing her in a bear hug.

Kelly was overwhelmed. She hadn't expected that and, as she hugged him back and giggled, spared a moment for the demure, annoyed teen she'd met just two days earlier.

Her thought evaporated and she snapped back to the present moment when Nikos and Tommy stood to hug and thank her too, causing Charlie to jump about and bark excitedly. Finally, the dog settled by her feet, his tongue sticking out as he gazed up at her.

'Of course! We love you too!' she said, chortling, as she bent over to pat the dog's head.

Tommy knelt before the dog for a close hug. 'Yes, we all do, Charlie! We love you soooo much!' He kissed his head and the pug responded by leaving a slobbery kiss on Tommy's face.

'Eeeww!' said Kelly, then shook a playful finger at Tommy. 'Hey! You'd better go wash your face, matey! I don't want your teacher calling me to complain I sent you to school smelling like a dog's bum!'

Howls of laughter ensued, then Nikos pretended to sniff his little brother and burst out, 'Uh-oh! Tommy smells like dog's balls!'

'No, *you* smell like dog's balls!'

'No, *you* do!'

Kelly watched amused and, for a moment, didn't know what to do. Stop them or keep laughing? In the end, she clapped her hands together and said, 'Right! Off you go, boys, and get your school bags! It's almost half past eight!'

All three froze mid-laugh and turned to check the clock on the wall. Then, like soldiers following an order from their drill sergeant, they left the room in a hurry.

Only the pug remained on the floor before Kelly, eyeing her with rapt concentration. His eyes sparkled under the overhead light, and she got the strange impression he was trying to convey something to her. But, as to what that was, she didn't have the faintest idea.

Chapter 12

As soon as the boys left, Kelly marched upstairs to load the washing machine. The weather was perfect today for hanging the laundry outside. Sunny with a moderate wind.

Having switched on the washing machine, she hoovered everywhere, then began to make the beds. When she entered Alex's room she felt apprehensive, even though, other than the dog, she was alone in the house.

Ignoring the ghostly smell of candy floss, she began to plump up the pillows, then folded Alex's pyjamas. Thoughts of him dressing—or rather, undressing—in there flooded her mind, and she wondered what he looked like in his pyjamas, or better yet, without any clothes on at all.

Shaking her head profusely, she chased the tantalizing thoughts away. They felt inappropriate, seeing that his wife was obviously very much present in the house, not to mention in this man's heart and mind.

She had resumed her bed-making effort, with full gusto this time, when, somehow, the eerie scent began to grow more and more intense, demanding her attention. She straightened and whirled around, instinctively turning her eyes towards the door on the very right of the wardrobe.

What she saw then made the hairs on the nape of her neck stand on end. The door was wide open, even though she was sure it had been firmly closed when she walked in earlier, just like all the other doors of the wardrobe.

Intrigued, she moved cautiously to it, her vivid imagination conjuring up images of a ghostly hand creeping out of it at any second.

Surprised by her own courage, she stood by the door and reached out to close it. She did so, but the door wouldn't close completely. She heard a soft clunk, a metallic sound she couldn't place, and reopened the door. As she did so, a tin box at the very top of the clothes pile on the lowest shelf tipped sideways and fell onto the floor.

'Oh no!' she said, as the lid came off and a plethora of photographs scattered around her feet. She knelt on the carpet and began to pick them up, putting them back into the box. Intrigued as she was, though, she had a look at a few of them, eager to see snapshots from Alex's married life and what his late wife looked like.

There were wedding photos and others of the couple—alone or with other people—in what looked like central Nafplio or on the shore. In plenty of them, they were photographed with the children in various places and in that very house as well. Alex's late wife was a tall woman with long blonde hair and an intelligent look in her eyes. Classy and elegant, she looked perfect by Alex's side.

A feeling of warmth settled in Kelly's heart to see Alex's wife with her children in many photographs, holding them in her arms as babies or on her lap as small children. The tug at Kelly's heartstrings intensified to see Alex's beaming smile in these family photos. Even these days, Alex was always upbeat. He smiled and joked, but, in these pictures, his face had a glow she'd never seen before.

After a while, looking at the photos made Kelly feel like an intruder. Shamed, she picked the last photos off the carpet without looking and placed them in the box. Standing up, she put the lid on and moved to return the box to the shelf when the same eerie voice she'd heard earlier in her bedroom echoed in her head again.

'You're wrong... It's okay to look. I want you to... And I need you here...'

Kelly was so stunned she literally jumped backwards. Clutching her chest with her free hand, she stood before the open door and froze, pricking her ears. Nothing else came so she moved to place the box on the shelf again.

Before she could do it, the voice echoed anew, this time amplified. 'I know you don't want me to appear before you, so I won't... I don't want to scare you. But at least now you know what I look like.'

Kelly felt her blood chill in her veins. 'What... What do you want from me?' she mumbled with difficulty.

'I told you... Wear what Charlie brought you. Please.'

'But how could I? Alex—'

'Trust me!'

'No! Leave me alone!' Her heart thumping in her chest, Kelly placed the box on the shelf and closed the door quickly as if trying to contain the spirit inside. Then, with her peripheral vision, she noticed a presence at the threshold. Turning to see, she gave a sigh of relief.

'Charlie?' she muttered breathlessly.

The dog was gazing back at her, tilting his head and whimpering softly.

'That's right...' she heard the woman whisper in her head, her voice crystal clear. 'It's through Charlie that I could give you the necklace and the scarf. He helps me around the house. Only when he's near you I can get you to hear me, though. And only if something that once belonged to me is present too. That's why I need you to wear something of mine. So that I can guide you at all times...'

Still gazing at the dog, Kelly felt helpless. All she could do was tremble softly for a few moments. She swallowed hard and asked, 'What's your name?'

'Lauren.'

'That's not a Greek name, is it?'

'No, of course not. I was English in life. Like you...' came the eerie echo reverberating around in her mind.

Right then, Kelly made sense of the boys' excited reaction the previous day when she said she was English. 'Now, I understand...' she mumbled. 'They need you still... the boys. I am so sorry...'

'Don't be. It was my time to go. And my boys will be all right. Their father is the best they could ever have. I'm only sorry that he isn't helping them to move on after my passing.

It won't happen while my things are still stored away in this wardrobe. And while the photos are put away here too, out of sight... The boys have not seen half of them...'

'Wait a minute! You want me to tell Alex and the kids that their mother is still here and wants them to see these old photos?'

'No... Not the kids. But Alex, surely. He needs to show our children these photos. They convey so many precious memories they all need to share together. I want my children to be able to talk about me with their father. So they can all let me go. They haven't yet... and they never will while they have to keep silent about me and my passing. Do you understand, Kelly?'

'Yes, yes, I think I do... But I can't just... If I tell him that I can hear you... he'll think I'm crazy.'

'No, he won't. Not if you let me guide you every step of the way...'

'I don't know... I can't...' muttered Kelly. Brushing her brow with an urgent hand, she dashed out of the bedroom, leaving the dog and the spirit's demands behind, at least, for now.

*****

Kelly carried a full laundry basket down the steps, her mind in a whirl. Behind her, Charlie descended closely by her feet. So close, as a matter of fact, that she feared she might trample over him. She paused on every other step, peering over the side of the basket to check where she was going.

Rushing past the kitchen, she arrived at the hallway and put the basket on the floor. She took the key from the lock, about to go outside to hang the clothes on the line. Charlie, who had followed her, came around to stand between her and the door, barking his head off.

'What is it now, Charlie?' she said as she opened the door. 'Shoo! Go play with your toys! Go! *Pigene!*' she shouted, exasperated, wishing he'd leave her alone at last. After her earlier interaction with the spirit, she needed time alone to think. The last thing she needed was this dog—a haunted one, from the looks of it—while she tried to collect her thoughts and calm down.

She held the basket against her torso with one arm to open the front door, then held it in both hands again and used her foot to open the door further. The whole thing was rather awkward, especially as in one hand she was also holding the house keys. All the while, the dog kept barking and jumping about at her feet.

'No! You're staying in here. Shoo!' she shouted and went out the door, but the dog followed. Huffing loudly, she got in again in an attempt to trick him, which caused Charlie to follow her back in. Quick as a flash, she stepped out and clear of the door, about to close it and trap the dog inside, when the keys slipped off her hand.

Letting out an exasperated sigh, and feeling like she were living a real-life episode of Mr Bean, she bent over to put down the basket so she could pick up the keys. But, what happened then, left her at a loss.

The dog, possibly thinking this was some kind of game, rushed over, took the keys in his mouth and bolted down the hallway. Then, a strong gust of wind came from indoors, oddly enough. It made an eerie noise as it rushed past her ears, blowing her hair. She blinked, shocked, and the front door closed with a slam, leaving her locked out.

'Noooo!' she exclaimed, realizing she'd have to stay outside until the boys returned from school. Thankfully, Stratos had a key to the house. *But I have so much to do from now till lunchtime... and to cook too! Oh, God, why? Why me?*

Distraught, she dissolved into tears. Putting the basket down, she moved to one of the chairs on the porch and fell heavily on it as if she weighed a ton. She buried her face in her hands and continued to cry for a while, one sob after another rising from her throat to find vent through lips that quivered with emotion. All her stress and apprehension about starting a new job in a stranger's house mixed with her horror to be suddenly chit-chatting with her boss's dead wife had left her in a state of total cluelessness mixed with upset.

'Psst!' she heard then and, at first, she panicked. *Spirits don't say 'pst', do they?*

'Hey! Young lady!'

A man's voice. No doubt about that. Kelly looked up to find an elderly man looking at her from behind the fence to her left. She'd noticed from the first day the beautiful villa that stood there. The garden had stunning flower patches she'd admired many times through the front windows of Alex's house.

Kelly was delighted to finally meet one of the villa's owners, even though the timing was terrible. The old man had an open smile across his face. He eyed her with benevolence across the distance, dressed in a chequered blue shirt and a fisherman's vest in the same colour. His short hair had a parting on the side and was white like cotton.

Embarrassed, she turned her face away from him for a moment to wipe her wet cheeks with an urgent hand, then looked at him sheepishly. 'Hello there.'

'Are you crying? What's the matter, young lady? Can I help at all?' he asked with a frown.

'No, I... Oh, it's nothing.' As her manners dictated, she approached him with a smile, offering her hand, even though she was well aware that from a close distance he'd be able to see her tear-sodden eyes. Luckily, the sunlight was in his eyes.

Surprised, she saw that their colour was a striking blue, so rare for a man of his age, and she was hushed by their beauty for a moment.

'*Hero poli*! Pleased to meet you,' he said, shaking her hand.
'Pleased to meet you, too. I'm Kelly.'

'You're English?' he asked, and she was surprised to hear it. How had he guessed? She spoke Greek like a native, and her name didn't necessarily point to a British nationality.

'Yes, I—' she began to say, still perplexed.

He chortled and hooked a finger to point at his chest. 'I'm Alan! Bet you didn't expect a Brit living next door?' he said switching to English readily.

Kelly gawped at him for a few moments. Finally, she said, 'Hey, what's this? Where am I? I thought this was Greece!' She looked around her, amused.

He laughed again, then said, 'Oh, you'd be surprised how many Brits live all around Greece! Your country is too beautiful to resist.'

'I know, I'm sure... It's just that...' She threw a wistful glance at the house she lived in, then faced Alan again to say, 'Well, I am English... and the boys' mother was too... It's so strange. It's like a British colony on this street.' She goggled her eyes for effect.

He laughed, then his bright eyes lost their lustre when he said, 'Ah... Lauren... A lovely woman, she was. So tragic, her death...'

'You knew her?'

'Yes, of course. Both my wife and I did. We've been living here for many years and had relations with Alex and his family.' He raised his eyes to the sky and gave a wistful smile. 'Oh! Lauren was a wonderful cook! The dinners we used to have in her house!' A small pause, then his features darkened. 'But, sadly, she's gone now and the family, well... I'm sure you know how it is...'

Kelly pressed her lips together and nodded in lieu of an answer. *Oh... Far more than you think, actually.*

'So, you must be the new housekeeper!' he added, evidently trying to lift the mood.

'Yes. Mrs Botsari had to leave... for family reasons, as you probably know...' Kelly had guessed that Alex had no trouble sharing about his personal life with this lovely man—obviously, a cherished old friend—who was a far cry from that awful busybody, Stella.

'Yes, we were saddened to hear Mrs Botsari's distressing news...' He took a deep breath, then added, 'Don't get me wrong, Kelly. She is a lovely lady, and she helped the family a lot while she was here, but the boys need someone younger to be around, you know?' He leaned forward, resting his forearms on the fence, and his eyes ignited in the glorious sunshine as he added, 'Someone like you.'

He probably guessed from her expression how he'd surprised her with that, because he then waved dismissively, moved back from the fence a little, looked away and said, 'You know what I mean... A woman closer to their mother's age... God knows these boys need a mother.'

The words rang true in Kelly's heart. She had sensed that much already in the way the boys looked at her. Thoughts of their shared laughter and the hugs they had given her at breakfast flooded her mind, causing her to smile.

He chuckled then, breaking her reverie. 'I'm so glad you came, Kelly. You seem like the right girl for the job.'

'Well, thank you for saying that, even though I'm proving to be a right idiot at the moment.'

'What do you mean?'

She turned around and pointed at the closed front door. The laundry basket still sat before it where she'd left it.

'I got myself locked out.'

'Yeah? How?'

'It was the dog... Charlie... or a sudden gust of wind... Or both. I don't even know. I'm not well in my head today.' She was laughing now, impossibly enough. For a while, they both did, looking at each other across the fence.

Alan had just dissolved into a guffaw, brought on by the roll of her eyes while she relayed how the dog had acted at the door earlier.

'Oh, Charlie... He's always full of beans. And mad as a hatter!'

'Yes, he is. And if he had opposable thumbs, he'd be perfect. But sadly, he can't open doors, and I'll be stuck here until the boys come home from school.' She gave an exasperated sigh.

'Oh, I beg to differ! See that geranium plant over there? The bright pink one?' He pointed to a big pot beside the front door.

When she nodded, he carried on, 'Well, there's a decorative ceramic little house sitting on the dirt hidden under the foliage. It's an old tea-light holder. Lauren always hid a spare key inside it. Go and check! I dare say it's still there.'

Excited, Kelly rushed to the pot. It took a bit of bending over and fumbling through the foliage, but she finally found the little ceramic house as Alan had said. It was hand-painted and depicted a whimsical Tudor English cottage with dark beams. For a few moments, she simply admired it, wondering why it had wound up there out of sight instead of being cherished inside the house. Then, she noticed a large chunk of it was missing at the bottom, the part that served as the tray where the tea light would sit. She lifted the cottage to reveal its content, an old golden key that was a little rusty at the top.

'Got it, thank you so much!' she shouted across the distance, turning around and holding up the key in her hand.

'Glad to be of assistance! And chin up, Kelly! You'll be fine, you'll see!' called out Alan and turned away before she could comment.

She watched him as he went up his front steps and disappeared through his front door. A divine, spicy smell of roast chicken emanated from his half-open kitchen window.

She guessed his wife was busy cooking in there. *Oh! I have cooking to do too! Better get a move on!*

Without wasting another moment, Kelly put the rusty key in her pocket, left the tea-light holder in the pot and set out to put the laundry on the line.

The sun warmed her skin, the refreshing soft wind helping to clear her mind. *What's the worst that could happen if I told Alex his house is haunted? And that his wife is asking that he shares the old family photos with the kids? Yes... I could get fired. But so what? It's a small price to pay if it means Alex and the boys will find healing... and if it sets Lauren's spirit free at last. Not sure why she wants me to wear the scarf and the pearl necklace the dog brought me, though... I'll have to think about that. Yeah... I guess I could talk to Alex... But I can't just blurt it out. I must wait for the right time to do it. When it feels right...*

Chapter 13

In the afternoon, Stratos left for his English lesson and Kelly spent the next hour in Nikos's room. She had a good chat with him about school and his interests, and he proudly showed her his collection of action hero figurines and toy cars. Later, she asked if he needed any help with his lessons. To her surprise, he told her he'd done all his studying already.

'I like to get all my studying done first thing after lunch. Get it over and done with,' he said with a cute smile. 'This way, I can enjoy playing games in the evening or watching TV without worrying about all that.'

Kelly was amazed to hear that. 'You have a good head on your shoulders. Good for you, Nikos.'

He shrugged. 'Thanks, Kelly.'

'Sorry I ran out of time today and didn't take you guys walking with Charlie. I haven't forgotten, Nikos. We'll do it tomorrow afternoon, okay?'

Nikos nodded fervently, and she turned away with a thumbs up, leaving him to play with his games console. Next, she knocked on Tommy's bedroom door that was slightly open. No reply came, so she opened it fully to check on him.

At first, she froze with surprise at what she saw, then gave a chortle as she walked in. The dog was sitting before Tommy on the carpet, a plethora of fashion necklaces around his neck. A colourful scarf was tied in a round loop and placed on the top of his head like a crown of silk.

As soon as he saw her, Charlie gave a single bark but didn't move. Tommy, on the other hand, froze in place, his mouth agape. Not even the sound of Kelly's laughter seemed to snap him into motion. His hand that held a string of colourful beads was poised in mid-air before the dog's face.

Kelly paused mid-step when she sensed the boy's embarrassment. It had hit her intensely, mixed with a good measure of worry. *Whatever this is, he would have preferred I hadn't seen it. What is he doing? Oh... This jewellery can only belong to...*

Kelly stepped closer. The eerie scent of candy floss hit her nostrils as she'd expected. She took a steadying breath and said, 'Wow! Can't believe Charlie is still standing with all these necklaces around his neck!' She laughed to lighten the mood, but the boy didn't seem to relax. If anything, he looked as if he'd stopped breathing.

'Sorry... I'll take them off him...' he said finally, his little hands busy removing the scarf and the jewellery from the dog. He dropped it all on the carpet carelessly in a tangled mess, his eyes pinned on hers now, misty all of a sudden, his lower lip slightly trembling. 'Please... don't tell Dad.'

She put up her hands, eyes wide as she shook her head. 'It's okay, Tommy. Don't worry... I won't tell.' She sat on the carpet beside him and caressed his head, her heart sinking. *All the children have secrets from their father... That's not good at all...*

'Do you want to talk about it, Tommy?' she asked when he seemed to relax a little, his head bent. The dog approached and lay down between them, belly up for a rub.

Tommy obliged him readily. And even though the dog seemed to be lost in the pleasure of the experience, the boy looked tormented as his fingers tickled and caressed his pet.

'Tommy?' she repeated in a little whisper.

He turned to face her, his jaw set. 'You promise you won't tell Dad?'

'Of course, I promise. Don't worry about it. But tell me, Tommy, why do you put the jewellery on the dog?'

Tommy shrugged in lieu of an answer, his eyes pinned on the dog's ecstatic face.

'These necklaces belonged to your mummy?'

He nodded.

'Where did you find them?'

'In Daddy's room... They were in this box... Found it in the wardrobe with Mummy's clothes...' He pointed to the top of his bed where a wooden jewellery box lay empty, its lid wide open. It had beautiful carvings of vines and flowers on it.

'And your daddy doesn't know you've taken the box?'

He shook his head. 'Please don't tell him. He doesn't like to talk about Mummy. I just wanted to have something from her. To remember her by... I didn't take any of the ones with the stones. Just these simple ones.'

Kelly bit her lip for a few moments, then said, 'So you put the jewellery on Charlie and you talk about Mummy with him?'

Tommy faced her, his jaw slack, eyes igniting with starbursts under the overhead light. 'How did you know... that I talk to Charlie about Mummy?'

'I guessed... I didn't know... And, if you want, you can talk to me about her too. I'd be happy to listen.'

*****

In the evening, Alex came through the door looking visibly drawn. His features were pinched from his busy day. He'd relayed a little about it earlier in the day over the phone. Still, when he found her milling about in the kitchen, he flashed a tired smile and she smiled openly back.

He headed straight upstairs for a shower while she prepared dinner. Stratos had not long returned from his English class at the *frontistirio*.

Half an hour later, they were all sitting around the table eating their meal. At some point, Charlie jumped on the empty seat he didn't like anyone to sit on. From the seat, he watched them all as they ate, a forlorn look in his eyes. Every now and then, he emitted a soft sigh.

'Why does he do that?' asked Kelly.

'Don't mind him, Kelly. He's a crazy old thing. We gave up trying to make sense of him long ago!' said Alex. Dressed in an old jumper, cotton slacks and slippers he was a huge contrast to the impeccably dressed man that had walked through the door earlier.

Kelly stole a glance at him, admiring his nonchalant charm. His hair was still wet from his shower. Dark, long strands fell over his forehead, brushing against his thick lashes every time he leaned forward to take another bite of his meal. It was *biftekia* and roast potatoes that she'd served with salad.

'This is delicious, Kelly!' he said then, as if on cue, snapping her out of her trance.

She threw him a happy smile, then her eyes flitted towards Nikos and Tommy. The former had gone for a piece of Mrs Botsari's *moussaka* instead and had almost emptied his plate already. Kelly thought back to the strict admonishing he had received from his father when he asked for a second piece. As she eyed Nikos surreptitiously, deep sympathy caused her insides to tighten. She still recalled quite well what it felt like to be permanently besotted with food.

Then, Stratos, who had opted to have the leftover chicken curry from the previous day, pointed to his plate and said, 'Dad... Yesterday, when Kelly made this meal, my brothers and I told her that Granny used to make curry too...'

'Yes, she did,' he replied, eyes glued on his plate, and took another bite.

Stratos cleared his throat, then added, 'And... Mum made it sometimes... Didn't she, Dad?'

Alex continued to have his head bent. Stratos was looking at him, waiting for his response, and seemed decisive, almost like he was daring him to answer. Or not.

A few moments of awkward silence passed, then Alex finally looked up, and nowhere in particular. He cut a piece of bread from his slice, dipped it in the tomato and cucumber salad that sat among them all and ate it.

'Dad? Did you hear? I said—'

'I heard what you said, Stratos!' Alex ran a hand across his forehead. 'Please don't start again! I'm too tired to deal with you right now.'

In an abrupt move, the young teen stood up in response, his chair legs screeching across the tiled floor. 'I'm sorry, Kelly...' he said to her with a fleeting glance that conveyed his upset, then stormed out of the kitchen.

Alex, who remained seated, gave a bitter smile, then tutted. 'Teenagers...' He met her eyes only for a split second, then resumed eating in total silence. Nikos and Tommy exchanged sympathetic glances and eyed Kelly sheepishly for the rest of the meal.

As for Kelly, the tension that had built up had caused her throat to constrict. Losing her appetite, she set her fork down and mumbled something about being full. She grabbed her glass and took a few sips of water, every gulp painful as it travelled down her throat.

Chapter 14

A soft knock on the door caused Alex to look up from his computer, and he found himself eager for a distraction. For the past hour, he'd been checking expenses and planning future purchases. His mind was going numb.

The young receptionist materialized at the half-open door, her features pinched with apprehension. 'I am sorry to interrupt, Mr Sarakis. Your friend, Mr Dimos Orphanos, is here to see you.'

As she finished her last sentence, Dimos came into view behind her, his typical jovial smile already working wonders on him.

With an eager smile, Alex waved his friend in. '*Ela, Dimos.* Come in. Thank you, Tatiana.'

The receptionist closed the door behind her with a faint click just as Dimos took a seat across the desk from Alex.

'What? They let you escape, you lunatic?' Alex asked him, flashing a lopsided smile. His heart was lifting with humour already.

'Yep! For just an hour, mind you. Thought I'd drop by and pick you up for a coffee at the seafront. Come on! It's gloriously sunny outside!'

'Nah... I have to go through my budget this morning. Can't leave.'

Dimos shook his head, giving Alex a look of mock-pity. 'I swear, my friend... You'll turn into a mole before you know it.'

Alex gave a dismissive wave. 'It's not just the work. My head's not right today.'

Dimos's expression darkened with concern as he leaned forward. 'Why? What's wrong?'

'I had the dream again...'

'The same one?'

'Exactly the same.' Alex raised his arms with desperation, only to drop them on the desk with a bang a moment later. 'It's driving me nuts! Every time I see this dream, I wake up with a heavy heart. And I don't even know why... Or what it means.'

'Why don't you go see a therapist or something?'

'What? And tell him I see my wife and me chained in our bed together? With heavy chains tightly wound around us that clank loudly with every move? He'll only think I'm a nut job and have me committed, seeing that my wife is dead!'

Dimos gave a snort. 'Are you sure it's not a remnant of your fond memories from... you know...' He gave a mischievous smile. 'Your private moments together in the past?'

'It's not funny, Dimos. And may I remind you that this is my deceased wife you're talking about.'

Dimos put up his hands. 'Sorry, Alex. Just trying to lighten the mood. I meant no offence.'

Alex ran an urgent hand through his hair and gave a huge sigh. 'I know... I know...'

Dimos stood and came around the desk to place a hand on Alex's shoulder. 'Yes, you'd better know! Back in school, I had your back, and I still do. I'm here for you, buddy.'

Alex looked up at him, feeling grateful for his old friend. Indeed, he'd always been there.

Dimos returned to his seat. 'Look, Alex... This recurrent dream has to mean something. I wasn't joking before. I really think you should see a therapist. It's obvious that you're not over Lauren's passing yet. That's why you keep dreaming of her.'

Alex shook his head. 'I've told you before... I miss Lauren and I'll always love her. But I don't mourn any more. Not in the way you think anyway. It's been three years, after all...'

Dimos eyed him with disbelief. 'But you've kept all her stuff. It's not right.'

'Yes, just a few items...'

'But why?'

'I can't just give everything away, Dimos!'

'Why not?'

'You want me to throw away her jewellery? The wedding ring she wore? I have three sons, Dimos! One day, I hope to be able to give that jewellery to their brides, you know?' His eyes misted over, a knot beginning to expand at the base of his throat, making it hard to breathe.

Dimos gave a soft sigh. 'I know, Alex... I understand.' A small pause, then he added, 'But what about her clothes? Come on, you have to admit it, it's not okay to keep those.'

'And by "okay", you mean it's not normal...'

'You said it, buddy...'

Alex stood tiredly and paced to the window. A bougainvillea laden with bright pink blossoms cascaded over the railing on the property across the paved lane. Pinning his eyes on it, his mind travelled away, to a time when he and Lauren sat in their garden shaded by a bougainvillea just like that, watching their children play on the lawn.

He heaved a long sigh and turned around to face his friend. 'I don't know, Dimos. Maybe I am still mourning... in a tiny way, perhaps. And I guess I should give the clothes away... See if it'll help.' Even as he said it, though, he knew he didn't have the strength to do it. But he tried to smile, to hide his feeling of defeat.

Dimos watched Alex until he flopped down in his chair, then gave a faint smile and said, 'Yes, you should. And you know what else you should do, Alex? Find yourself another woman.' He tilted his head. 'Isn't there anyone at all that you like?' He raised his arms and waved them about as he added, 'Come on, Alex! You're surrounded by gorgeous women!' Lowering his voice, he added, 'Your receptionist is a looker... Start there!'

Alex scrunched up his face and waved dismissively. 'Choose a woman among the hotel staff? You must be mad...'

'Then what about that gorgeous marathon runner you hired?' He chortled. 'She's already living in your house, mate! You have a good head start there!' he said with a devilish grin.

Alex looked at him, stunned for a few moments. Finally, he said, 'I can't believe you said that!' but couldn't help laughing out loud. He knew his friend wasn't serious and was only trying to brighten his mood. But, the moment his friend said it, something clicked inside his head. Sure, Kelly was a beautiful woman... but to see her that way? Did he fancy her? Of course, he did. But for him, trying anything with a woman he employed was against his principles. For him, it would be like taking advantage. And to consider flirting with her in his home... where his children lived... where he and his wife used to live together... This felt wrong right from the start.

'Hey, what's wrong? Why so quiet all of a sudden?' he heard his friend say, and his shoulders jumped. Startled, and realizing he'd been staring into space for a while, he darted his eyes to Dimos to find his expression was mirthful.

Dimos gave a guffaw. 'Please tell me you're considering my suggestion! It would make my day! I've been trying to get you to go out with a woman for longer than I can remember. I hope Kelly is the one. She's a stunner, with a body to die for!'

Alex shook his head. 'Don't be daft. I can't try anything with an employee. It's against my principles.'

'Oh! Principles-Sminciples! It's what keeps you warm at night that matters!'

Instead of answering, Alex pressed a button on his desk phone. The woman at the breakfast room answered the call quickly. 'Can you bring two Greek coffees please, Sandra? One for me, and one more...' He paused to look up at Dimos as he added, '...with two sugars. *Glyko.*'

Dimos confirmed with a nod.

'Thank you, Sandra. That'll be all.' Alex hung up the phone and Dimos began to tut, his eyes twinkling.

'What is it now?'

'If you talk to Kelly at home the way you just spoke to Sandra, nothing will ever happen with her or anyone else.'

'Why? How did I talk to her?'

'Like a boss. If not a grandad.'

Alex threw him a thunderous look but Dimos hadn't finished. He put up a finger and shook it. 'And unless you aspire to be a monk, you should get it into your thick skull that you're doing things wrong with women. At least, get it right with Kelly, for goodness sakes!'

Alex leaned back in his chair and gave a huff. 'What would you have me do with her?'

Dimos leaned forward. 'Tell me the truth. Do you fancy her? Because I know she fancies you. That morning at the seafront she looked at you like you were the last cupcake on the tray and she was on the verge of diabetic shock.'

Alex threw him a look of mock-disapproval. Still, inside his heart, he felt a twinge of excitement. 'Yeah, right.'

'I'm telling you, Alex! If you like this girl, you should ask her out!'

'But, how—'

Dimos put up a hand. 'Nuh-uh! It's simple, my friend! Do you fancy her?'

Alex shrugged.

'That's not an answer.'

'Yes, yes, I suppose I do.'

'Good! Then ask her out!'

Alex shook his head fiercely. 'I can't... She lives in my home.' He gave a shudder. 'It's creepy!'

You know what's creepy? Keeping your dead wife's clothes. That's what's creepy!'

'I can't just ask Kelly out! What will she think? I just employed her...'

Dimos sat back in his chair, eyes focusing far, two fingers of one hand tapping his closed mouth. Alex could tell he was busy thinking and didn't want to interrupt. Wonderful things had turned out from his best friend's thinking process over the years, and he had full confidence in it.

After a few moments, Dimos put up a finger, his face brightening up like the city of Patra on Carnival Day. 'Got it!' He began to laugh, much to Alex's annoyance. Half an hour ago, it hadn't even occurred to him that he saw Kelly that way. Now, he couldn't wait to find a way to ask her out. Dimos never ceased to amaze him. 'Tell me, already!' he burst out when his intrigue reached boiling point.

Dimos gave a belly laugh. 'A-ha! So you *are* interested in her!' He took a glimpse of Alex's stern face and continued, 'As you know, I am celebrating my company's ten-year anniversary with a formal reception in a couple of weeks. You're already invited. You might as well seize the opportunity to bring Kelly along.'

Alex's heart gave a thump at the very thought. 'Invite her to dinner at your event?'

'Yes. Dinner and dancing. It's perfect. And it won't be a date as such. Just tell her you need someone to escort you to this thing you have to go to. That's not awkward, is it? You can just tell her you're asking her so she can have some fun... Get out of the house and enjoy a bit of dancing. And this way, you'll have the opportunity to let your hair down and get to know her better.'

Alex had grown excited to hear all that, but then a new thought destroyed everything. 'Wait a minute. I can't. You forget the kids. Who's going to mind them?'

Dimos waved dismissively. 'No problem. Use that weird neighbour of yours, Stella.' He cocked his eye and gave an impish smile. 'You know she'll come running to oblige you if you ask. She's crazy about you.'

Alex shook his head. 'No way. You know I'm keeping her at bay since "the incident"...' He did air quotes and added, 'And she still bakes muffins for the kids. I accept them to avoid offending her, but that's my limit. I've learned the hard way not to encourage her any further.'

Dimos flicked his wrist. 'Beggars can't be choosers, mate. Ask her. It's only one evening. You can avoid her all you want after that.'

Chapter 15

Kelly and the boys left the house with Charlie so he could have his first walk. Once his paws touched the pavement outside, he got so excited he kept twirling, getting the lead entwined around his legs and causing the others to have to keep stopping to unravel it. Kelly, who held the lead, picked up the slack so he had to walk closely beside her.

That seemed to help. By the time they'd reached the green, they were strolling at a steady pace, Charlie walking along happily.

When they reached the other end of the green, Nikos suggested they go to the top of the hill and everyone eagerly obliged. As they began to walk up the slope along the path, Kelly watched him surreptitiously, feeling proud of him for sticking to his commitment. As a child his age, she'd also worn the uncomfortable proverbial shoes of the kid who got bullied at school.

A loving aunt had come to the rescue then, advising Kelly's mother to use a healthy diet for her daughter and to get her to exercise regularly. That advice had changed Kelly's life. And now, she felt herself glide just a little off the ground as she walked beside Nikos, grateful that she could finally pass on the same advice to help someone else.

❋❋❋❋❋

Just under an hour later, they all returned to their street, their faces flushed, and went through the garden gate chatting excitedly. The moment they closed it, Tommy bent over and took Charlie off the lead, and the dog went straight for a puddle at the edge of the lawn to drink water.

The boys began to laugh and Kelly asked Stratos to get the dog, then rushed through the front door announcing she's going to get him some water. Stratos picked him up to place him before the front door just as Kelly returned.

They all stood for a few moments, chuckling, and watching Charlie drink from his bowl. Then, Kelly prompted the boys to go inside and have some water as well. She stayed behind, waiting for the dog to finish so she could get him inside too.

'Were you thirsty, Charlie? You enjoyed that walk, didn't you, you little devil?' she said with a little laugh.

Charlie raised his head and looked up at her with a goofy expression, his tongue sticking out. He looked as if he was smiling at her. That caused her to chortle. Just as he resumed drinking, a voice echoed from the left.

'Hey, Kelly!'

It was Stella. She was leaning against the fence, her eyes that sparkled with that familiar glint of intrusive curiosity trained on her.

'Oh, hi.' Kelly did her best to smile as if she meant it.

'You guys went for a walk? Couldn't help seeing you pass by earlier.'

'Yes. This little fellow had his first walk today.' Kelly pointed to the dog and smiled genuinely this time.

'Oh, good…'

'Wait a moment! Let me give you your plate back,' said Kelly and, without waiting for an answer, she dashed indoors. She'd left the plate on a side table so she would remember to return it. Somehow, she didn't like having it in the house. It felt like an intrusion.

'Here you are! Thank you for the muffins…' she said when she handed it to her a little later.

'I hope you guys liked them,' said Stella when she took it.

'Yes, thank you.'

Stella's face brightened. 'Well, there's more to come. Every Monday, as you know!'

'Actually, I meant to say… The boys are trying to cut down on sugar now… so it would be best, perhaps, if you didn't go through the trouble of making any more for us.' She saw Stella's stupefied expression and cleared her throat before adding, 'I don't mean to be rude or anything, Stella... But the truth is... Nikos is on a strict diet now. He has decided to lose some weight, and I'm trying to be supportive. You understand... And as for Stratos, he's eager to eat more healthily so he can keep his acne problem under control. In any case, sugar's not a good thing to eat much of, as I'm sure you know... I'm just looking out for the boys, that's all.'

'Oh... I was just trying to be nice...' Stella blurted out, looking unsettled.

'Yes, well, as I said, we're very grateful—'

'It's okay... I understand.'

Stella looked anything but understanding, though. For a few moments, Kelly didn't know what to say. Stella had stepped back from the fence as if about to run into her house in tears. Her face had darkened with a mixture of upset and annoyance.

Best to sweeten the pill. 'Look. Maybe if you bake muffins for the kids every two weeks from now on? And maybe bring only six or so? I don't have any myself, and neither does Alex, so two for each of the boys would be more than enough...'

Stella's face mushroomed with surprise. But not the happy kind. 'Oh. I didn't realize Alex doesn't eat my muffins. I was... Well, I was just trying to be nice, as I said. The last thing I wanted was to cause any trouble.'

'Well, of course, you didn't cause any trouble! I was just trying to—'

Stella's face contorted with scorn and, all of a sudden, she pointed a sharp finger at Kelly. 'Oh! I know very well what you were trying to do! Well, look at you! So clever! So slim, so athletic!' She banged her open hand on her chest, eyes wide open, as she added mockingly, 'Aww! Now you're here and suddenly everyone's on a diet! You think you're better than me, huh? Coming here out of nowhere, telling me my muffins are no good? I've been living next door to this family forever, you know! Now you're living in there, and all of a sudden Alex doesn't eat my muffins any more? And his kids don't want them either?'

Still holding the plate with one hand, she put the other on her hip and sneered. 'Well, I got news for you, missy! You won't last in there, you hear? And when you get fired, I'll still be here! With my damn muffins and all!'

Kelly gawped at her, stunned by Stella's insults and ridiculous forewarnings. Finally, she found her voice to say, 'What the hell are you talking about? I don't know what looney pills you're on, girl, but they're clearly expired! So why don't you go get a fresh batch from your shrink before you wind up roaming the streets screaming "Redrum" all over the place!'

Stella's jaw hardened, her eyes sparkling with rage. Without saying another word, she whirled around and strode to her porch.

'No need to go right now... You can go later!' Kelly teased, but Stella didn't stop for a moment. She grabbed her door knob as if it were a lifesaver and she were sinking amidst an ocean, then disappeared behind the door, slamming it shut.

As Kelly walked back to her own front door, she wondered what had driven her to respond in such a deriding manner. Her happy mood of moments ago had been destroyed at the flip of a coin, it seemed. What had just happened? Stella had gone off on a tangent and was clearly deranged... But that wasn't all. Stella had *offended* her. Simple as that. And Kelly didn't handle offence well. She'd made a conscious decision long ago never to be mistreated, disrespected or bullied. Ever again.

*****

When Kelly walked into the kitchen, the boys were running around the table playing with the dog, making one hell of a racket.

The breakfast cereal packet was open on the table, a scatter of cereal before the opening. Three empty water glasses stood together a little further away.

'Boys, please! Quieten down!' said Kelly.

'We're just playing!' replied Tommy, stretching out his hand to show her some cereal on his palm. 'I gave some to Charlie and he went crazy!'

'Give that to me!' said Kelly, and when the boy obeyed, eyeing her with surprise, she felt sorry for her abrupt manner. 'I'm sorry, Tommy, but it's not okay to feed the dog willy-nilly. He should only snack with his own treats and at set times. Remember we are trying to discipline him?'

'Yes, I'm sorry...' he said bending his head.

She tousled his hair. 'It's okay, Tommy. I'll tell you what. You can give him three chocolate treats now. And you can choose what tricks he'll do, okay?'

Tommy squealed with excitement when she took the treats from the pack and handed them to him. 'So far, he knows how to sit, to stay, and to twirl only, remember.'

'I'll do one each!' With the others looking, Tommy moved to stand before Charlie, who stood proud and rigid like a sentinel, surely knowing what was coming.

'Sit!' said Tommy, and the pug obeyed to earn his treat readily.

'Sit!' repeated Tommy, and as soon as he did, the boy added, 'Stay!' but then the dog twirled instead. Everyone laughed. 'No, Charlie...' said Tommy. 'Stay!' He put up his hand, just like Kelly had shown him the previous evening, and the dog got it right this time. Tommy moved away a few steps, and then, as soon as he said 'come' and beckoned him over, Charlie approached to get his second treat.

When Tommy said 'twirl' next, the dog sat instead. 'Oh no!' said Tommy comically, and they all burst into guffaws.

Charlie looked at everyone's faces in succession, tongue sticking out, clearly wondering where the next treat was coming from.

'Oh, put him out of his misery and give it to him anyway,' said Kelly. 'Pugs are not the easiest dogs to train. Considering that, he's doing great!'

'No, I want him to do it right... Come on, Charlie!' insisted Tommy. 'Twirl!' This time, he did a cartwheel in mid-air with his finger, the way Kelly had done the previous day to show him, and the dog got it right this time. As Charlie chewed his last treat, everyone clapped their hands, then they all patted his head.

Tommy took one of Charlie's toys from his bed in the corner and ran to the living room, shaking it in his hand over his head. 'Come! Come, Charlie! Come and get it!'

The moment Tommy said that, the dog ran towards him like a hound hearing the foxhunt horn echo across the plain. Everyone followed him to the living room and began to chortle.

Tommy handed Charlie the toy and the dog sat on the carpet, growling at them all. It was hilarious to watch and Kelly laughed her head off along with the boys.

Tommy knelt before Charlie and tried to pry the toy from his jaws, but that only made the dog move his head from side to side, and to growl even more fiercely than before.

'He sounds like a lion!' said Stratos.

'No! Like a bear! Aaaaarrr!' said Nikos with a belly laugh.

All the while, Kelly was laughing so hard she couldn't speak.

Somehow, Tommy managed to snatch the toy from Charlie's mouth and began to run around the coffee table. Rushing behind him, Charlie began to bark excitedly. In the end, Tommy let him take the toy, and Charlie sat on the carpet again, shaking his head fiercely, the toy in his mouth. He acted as if he'd just snatched a living thing and was trying to end its life.

Everyone fell on their knees roaring with laughter around him and patted him on the head.

Then, Tommy put his arms around Charlie, cuddling him, which seemed to have a calming effect on him. He finally fell silent and grew still, the toy now lying on the carpet before him as he enjoyed everyone's attentions.

'Oh my goodness! I can't remember the last time we laughed so hard!' said Stratos.

'That's right; I think the last time was when Mum was still alive...' said Nikos.

'Aww...' Kelly mumbled, her insides twinging with upset just like every time the boys mentioned their mother.

Nikos looked up at her and added, 'Dad used to laugh too... But now, when he laughs, it's not the same.'

'Why is it not the same?' asked Kelly, noticing Stratos had agreed with Nikos's statement by nodding firmly, his lips pressed together.

Nikos scratched his chin and said, 'Well, his eyes don't laugh any more. They look tired now. Even when he laughs.'

Chapter 16

A long silence ensued after Nikos's remark about their father's lack of genuine laughter. Still sitting on the carpet with them all, Kelly watched as Stratos and Nikos exchanged mute glances, then bent their heads in contemplation, their expressions grim. Only Tommy seemed unaffected. He had picked up a toy truck—one of his three large car toys that permanently sat by the TV stand—and was playing with it silently.

Then, Kelly heard the jingling of Charlie's dog tag on his collar that signalled he was approaching. She hadn't realized, deep in her thoughts until then, that he had left the room earlier.

They all turned to see that he was carrying a photograph in his mouth. Several sounds of astonishment broke out from everyone.

'What's that?' said Tommy when Charlie went straight up to him to let the photograph drop on the boy's lap. Everyone gazed at the dog with equal wonder.

Tommy took the photograph in his hands as the other three leaned over to take a better look. Kelly recognised Alex and Lauren in it. 'Where did you get it, Charlie?' said Tommy, and everyone looked at the dog as if he could answer.

Kelly imagined the photograph must have been kept with the others in Alex's wardrobe. The dog amazed her... How did he get it? Or did Lauren remove things from the wardrobe, somehow, to give them to the dog to deliver? *That's how he must have brought me the scarf and the pearls as well...*

'Is it Mum and Dad?' Tommy asked his brothers, snapping her out of her thoughts.

Stratos asked to take the picture and take a closer look, and Tommy let him, a galaxy of stars exploding in his eyes as he waited for his big brother to confirm.

Kelly felt a twinge in her heart. The little boy didn't remember his mother at all and, because of his father's obscure reasons, hadn't had the chance to see any photos of his mother either. Until now.

'Yes...' confirmed Stratos in what sounded like a reverent whisper moments later, causing Tommy to lean closer to look at the photo again. Nikos did the same, and Kelly fought against the lump in her throat for a few moments, trying to say something. Yet, all she could do was watch as the boys huddled together, looking at the likeness of their mother, the mother they all missed beyond words.

'Oh... Mummy was so pretty...' said Tommy.

'Yes... Yes she was,' said Stratos. 'Remember, Nikos? How she used to wake us up in the morning?'

Nikos giggled, then said, 'Yes! She'd come and wake us up with kisses every morning, and we'd complain...'

'Then, she'd laugh...' said Stratos, his eyes dreamy when he looked up to meet Kelly's eyes for a few moments, before turning his attention to the photograph again.

Kelly cleared her throat, then finally managed to say, 'She must have loved you, boys, very much.'

'She did...' said Stratos quietly. He paused for a moment, then added, 'And she'd do this thing if we didn't get out of bed quickly enough. Do you remember, Nikos?'

Nikos chortled, his ruddy cheeks turning a dark red. 'Yes! She'd start to sing! Really loudly! *Ta paidia tou Pirea*!'

The two boys began to laugh, then to sing the chorus of the famous song by Hatzidakis that was sung by Melina Merkouri in the movie 'Never on Sunday'. Every Greek knew that song, including Kelly, who began to sing along gaily. Only Tommy stared at them giggling, and when they stopped, he piped up: 'Did she sing it to me too?'

'Ah, Tommy... You were only three at the time... The apple of her eye. I don't think she ever used this ploy to get you out of bed,' said Stratos with a chortle, then added, 'But I am sure she kept the best songs for you, to sing them to you as you lay in your bed,' said Stratos, melting Kelly's heart.

'Did your mother sing a lot around the house then?' asked Kelly.

'Oh yes, all day long! I guess that's why I—' Stratos stopped abruptly, then looked down at his lap to mumble, 'Mum was the best.'

'Can I see it?' asked Kelly pointing to the photograph.

Stratos handed it to her and she admired the carefree young couple in the photo. Their faces were glowing, eyes sparkling as they held each other in an open field. 'They look so young...'

Stratos gave a firm nod. 'Yes... They were both seventeen in that photo. They were in the same class in school.'

'Wow! And where are they pictured, do you know?'

'This was taken here in Nafplio on their first date... Mum told Nikos and me about it many times. See that?' He pointed at something his mother held in her hand. 'It's candy floss. Mum had already had most of it when the photo was taken, but you can see a bit of it left on the stick if you look hard enough...'

'Candy floss?' asked Tommy, leaning even closer to see, his expression full of surprise for some reason.

Kelly eyed him with intrigue but didn't ask him about it. In her mind, she was already deep in thought. *Candy floss... so that's why... it must have been such a special day for her... Aaaww...*

'Yes, Tommy,' said Nikos. 'That's what Dad bought her that day. Mum told Stratos and me about it only a million times...'

Nikos gave a sigh. 'Yes... I remember...' he said pointing to the picture, looking at Kelly and Tommy. 'They were walking back to mum's house after visiting a church festival when they asked a passer-by to take the photograph.'

'Mum and Dad used to go to school together here in Nafplio...' Stratos interrupted, looking now just as excited as

Nikos did at the chance to talk about his mother. 'It had taken Dad ages to pluck up the courage, apparently, and ask her out on that first date!' He giggled.

Nikos rolled his eyes and said, 'Mum told us many times that when Dad bought her the candy floss, her heart melted the same way the candy floss melted in her mouth.'

'And every time Mum said that, Dad would kiss her, then Nikos and I would make barfing noises asking them to stop while we looked away,' said Stratos.

Nikos gave a wicked smile. 'But deep down we liked it that they were kissing, didn't we, Stratos?'

'Yeah, Nikos... It was great when Mum was around... We were all happier then. Dad especially...'

'If only we'd been able to say goodbye to her at least! She died so suddenly. We never got the chance...' Nikos heaved a huge sigh, his brow etched deeply. The fragility in his voice caused the others to look at him with sympathy.

The short silence that followed brought on a sadness that hung awkwardly over them all like a cloud, then settled among them, sticking like glue, causing them to huddle together closely as they resumed looking at the photo.

Finally, Stratos's voice, a little frail, broke the silence. 'Can I take the photo please, Kelly?'

Kelly handed it to him and Stratos thanked her, then turned to his brothers, his expression solemn. 'I'll hold on to this, guys, if you don't mind, since I'm the oldest. I'll take good care of it in my room, and you guys can come and see it anytime you like.'

The boys accepted happily, then they all turned to Kelly. 'So, what was that yelling we heard earlier coming from the yard?' asked Stratos with a devilish grin. 'Tell me I don't have to see another of this awful woman's muffins again and my day will be made.'

'Oh come on! You like her muffins, I saw you eat them!' said Nikos as he nudged his brother with his elbow.

'I do, of course, but I like the idea of Stella leaving us alone even better.'

'I take it you don't like her then?' Kelly asked him with a snorting laugh.

Stratos made a cartwheel mid-air beside his ear with his index finger and said, 'That woman is not all there, you know?' All traces of humour vanished from his face when he shrugged and added, 'She gives me the heebie-jeebies... I don't know why. It's just a feeling.'

*****

An hour later, having had a bit of a rest, Kelly thought she'd check on the boys. Being thirsty, she had a glass of water in the kitchen first, then went straight to Stratos's room. She stood before the door, unsure if she should knock. It was firmly shut, plus, she could hear quiet singing.

Despite her best intentions not to, she stuck her ear to the door. It wasn't so much curiosity as it was admiration. *He sings like an angel from heaven!* It was a new English pop song she'd heard on the radio. A ballad. *He sings it like a pro... I wonder if he practices... and not necessarily in this house.* Her mind flew to the plectrum she'd found on his bed the other day. *He's a dark horse, that one... but maybe, if I win his trust I'll learn more, so that I can help him. He has such a remarkable gift! Does his father know he sings like that?*

She guessed he didn't, knowing what Alex was like, and it made her feel sad. Pressing her lips together, she unglued her ear from the door and headed upstairs.

She found Nikos playing on his games console. His door was wide open and when he spotted her at the threshold he raised a hand and smiled. She asked if he was done with his homework, and when he confirmed, she left to check on Tommy.

In the pocket of her cotton slacks, she carried the scarf and the string of pearls the dog had brought her. Maybe Tommy could shed some light on the mystery.

The door was open, Tommy sitting on the carpet. Before him, Charlie was patiently receiving his attentions. The same scarf he wore last time as a crown was now tied around his neck in a bow. Lauren's fashion necklaces were scattered on the floor. Tommy was holding a long one with blue beads in his hands, admiring it, probably about to put it on the dog.

'Tommy...' she said with a soft knock on the door. The boy smiled and beckoned her in.

'Come and see Charlie! Isn't he cute with the bow?'

Laughing, Kelly knelt beside Tommy just as the dog tilted his head and eyed them both silently in quick succession.

Tommy put the necklace on him, while both he and Kelly chortled.

Charlie stood like a statue while Tommy looped the necklace around his neck a couple of times. When he leaned back to admire the fruit of his effort, the dog gave an excited bark, then reached over and left slobbery kisses on Tommy's face and neck.

Peals of laughter ensued while they both cooed over him and petted him. Afterwards, Charlie lay on the ground with a soft sigh.

Kelly took the scarf and the necklace out of her pocket and showed them to Tommy. 'Tell me something... Have you seen these before?'

To her surprise, Tommy sniffed them, then said, 'No, I haven't. But they're Mummy's. I can tell. Where did you find them?'

'Charlie brought them to me,' she said matter-of-factly.

'Oh, right.'

Why isn't he surprised? 'Tommy? Does Charlie bring stuff to you too? Stuff that belonged to your mummy?'

'All the time.' He pointed to the blue beads that the dog wore. 'He brought that to me earlier today.'

Weird. 'Can I ask you something? Why did you sniff these just now?' She pointed with her eyes at the articles in her hands.

He shrugged. 'I wanted to see if they're Mummy's, that's all.'

She leaned a little closer. 'What do you mean by that?'

'Mummy's things smell. Like candy floss.'

Kelly was astonished to hear that. She thought she was the only one who could detect that scent. 'Really?'

'Yes...' He rolled his eyes. 'Look... I know I'm the only one who can smell it... Just take my word for it.'

If only you knew! 'Okay...' she said instead, then reached out with a tender hand and caressed the dog. Charlie came over to lie before her knees, resting his head on her lap. That made her melt. *To think he was growling at me on my first day. And already, he...* But then she remembered her earlier notion and it made sense. The dog was haunted by Lauren, somehow. She bent down and kissed the dog's head, but what she really wanted to do was to smell him surreptitiously. The result confirmed her previous thought. *Wow!*

As if on cue, the boy chuckled and said, 'Even Charlie smells like Mummy. Like candy floss. Again, I'm the only one who can smell it...'

Before she could say anything, Lauren's voice boomed inside her head. 'That's because I'm always with you, my darling...' Realizing that Lauren was addressing the boy, even though only she could hear, her heart twinged with upset.

Kelly's eyes fell on the dog, who met hers, his gaze intelligent, almost human. *Lauren haunts the dog so she can spend time with Tommy? That would explain why Tommy is able to detect this eerie smell, unlike Alex and the other boys. But why just him? It doesn't make sense. What else does Tommy know?*

She turned to the boy and tried to seem nonchalant as she asked, 'So, Tommy... This candy floss thing... is it the only odd thing you can smell that the others can't in here?'

'Yes, that's right.'

'And what about Charlie? Does he act weird in any way?'

Tommy gave a snorting laugh. 'All the time. Have you not seen what he's like all day?'

'No, I'm serious, Tommy. Anything that perhaps you know and the others don't?'

Tommy looked away, biting his lower lip as he seemed to think for a while, then said, 'Well, Charlie spends a lot of time in my room, and he brings me all sorts of stuff when we're alone.'

'Your mummy's stuff?'

'No... not just my mummy's stuff. He also brings me English movies to watch from our DVD collection in the living room... Old movies, all very nice... I used to ask Mrs Botsari to watch them with me, but sometimes I'd sit and watch them on my own. But even then I felt... I felt like I wasn't...'

Kelly gave a deep frown. 'Yes? Go on... You can tell me...'

The boy looked down at his lap. 'Nothing. Never mind...'

Kelly was intrigued, but didn't want to press things further, so she asked, 'So, what else does Charlie bring you?'

The boy gave a soft sigh and said, 'He brings me pens too. Then he goes to my desk there,' he pointed to the small desk in the corner where the boy did his homework, '...and doesn't stop barking until I sit to write.'

'Write what?'

'A letter... to my grandad.'

Kelly remembered that the boys had grandparents in Salonica. Alex's parents. The notion that the dog urged Tommy to write to his grandfather seemed absurd. 'What makes you think Charlie wants you to write letters? I don't understand.'

The boy looked down at his hands that were laced together on his lap. He gave a sigh, then said, 'Sometimes, I get upset playing with mummy's things... And when I do, Charlie brings me a pen and goes to the desk, as I said, and he insists that I sit to write...'

'So you write to your grandad when that happens?'

'Yes. Every time I feel sad...'

'Do you write to him about your mummy?'

In lieu of an answer, the boy just nodded.

'Does it help, Tommy?'

'Yes, it does. And I think...' He stopped short and looked at his lap again.

Her throat constricting with feeling, she put out a hand to caress the boy's head. 'It's all right, Tommy. You can tell me. I promise I won't tell anyone.'

The boy seemed to take heart. His eyes ignited with excitement when he met hers to confess, 'I think that Mummy talks to me. She uses Charlie to do it... I can feel her sometimes... When Charlie's in the room, late at night. Many times, I have felt a warm caress on my hair or on my forehead... But that doesn't scare me. It always feels like...'

'Like what, Tommy?' she said with effort. A growing knot had lodged in her throat, her voice barely audible.

His eyes exploded like supernovas under the overhead light when he replied, 'Like... love.'

'Oh Tommy...' it sufficed her to say as she took his hand in hers and squeezed it. But instead of speaking again, still holding his hand gently, she set her jaw and looked away, determined not to break into tears.

His voice sounded frail when he spoke after a short pause. 'Please don't tell anyone, Kelly. They'll think I'm crazy.'

She nodded firmly and looked him squarely in the eyes. 'You're not crazy, Tommy... I believe you.'

'You do?'

'Yes. And you don't need to worry. I won't tell.'

'Thank you, Kelly!' Tommy opened up his arms and looped them around her neck.

Overwhelmed, Kelly held him close as Charlie watched silently from the floor. The bow around his neck had long since come undone from the fierce rubbing of his face against her knees as he coaxed her to keep stroking his fur.

When they pulled back, Tommy heaved a long sigh. 'I'm glad I could talk about it... I didn't dare tell my brothers... or Dad. I guess, if I could talk about Mummy more often, I wouldn't feel so sad...'

'You can talk to me about Mummy anytime you like. Thank you for trusting me, Tommy... Your secret is safe with me.'

With a tousle of his hair, Kelly stood and went to the door. Standing at the doorjamb, she turned around and eyed him lovingly for a moment, then left the room, striding down the corridor, her head bent. *I have to find the nerve to talk to Alex. And soon! It's incredible that he has no idea his wife is haunting the house... And his kids... Those poor children! By not mentioning Lauren to them he's making things worse! The boys need to come to terms with her loss so they can let her go. Because no one seems to have done it yet. And that is why she's stuck in here still...*

Chapter 17

Kelly was standing before the stove adding chopped herbs to the tomato sauce she was preparing for dinner. When she heard the front door open, she was startled. The kids were in their rooms, and it was too early for Alex's return.

Alex emerged from the hallway, his features pinched. 'Hi, Kelly. Where is Stratos?' His manner was terse and she knew instantly that something was wrong.

'He... He's in his room. Do you...' she replied feebly, her voice trailing off when she realized he wasn't going to wait for her to finish her sentence.

Alex lunged forward, speeding towards Stratos's room. Despite herself, she followed him, then froze by the bottom of the stairs when he began knocking profusely on the boy's door.

'Stratos!' Without waiting for a response, he swung the door open and barged inside.

Kelly put a hand over her mouth, the vibes of Alex's obvious agitation hitting her like darts at the heart. Slowly, she took two steps forward. From where she stood, she couldn't see them but could hear their exchange clearly. Stratos had just issued a startled greeting and Alex had said something about a phone call.

As Kelly listened, Nikos and Tommy came down the stairs on their tiptoes and stood one on each side of her. 'What is it? Why is Dad home so early? Why is he shouting?' whispered Tommy, his eyes sparkling, threatening with tears.

Kelly held him close against her legs and soothed him, coaxing him to hush for now and listen, just as Nikos did. Listening didn't take much effort seeing that Alex continued to shout in Stratos's room.

'What do you mean, you don't know what I'm talking about? They called me from your English school today! They said you've been skipping classes! So, don't deny it! What's going on, Stratos?' echoed from the room.

Kelly gave an inaudible gasp during the lull that followed. Suddenly, Stratos erupted, 'Yes, Dad! It's true. I admit it! Happy now?'

'Happy? Do I look happy, Stratos? And where exactly do you go when you skip class?'

A rumble followed, during which the screeching of a chair echoed, then Stratos appeared at the door. He stopped short for a moment to find the three of them standing there. His expression was wild, his hair tousled. Then, as if someone had pushed him from behind, he sprang forward and began to stride towards the kitchen.

Nostrils flaring, Alex came out too and caught up with him by the dinner table. He grabbed his son's elbow and tugged him closer, then swung him around. 'Stratos! Where are you going? We're talking here!'

When the boy looked up to face his father, something in Alex's eyes melted. He let go of the boy's arm, tilted his head to the side and, with an outstretched hand, palm facing up, he said to Stratos, 'Come on, Son. I just want to know what's going on. That's all. If you don't want to do English any more, just say it. I won't make you.'

Stratos ran an urgent hand through his hair and looked away. 'Huh! As if you'd ever let me stop my English classes!'

'Why? Is that what you want?' Alex's manner remained quiet, eyes pleading for understanding, but Stratos was still looking away, chest heaving.

Kelly and the boys had come to stand at the entrance of the kitchen like three apparitions. Neither father nor son seemed to notice them standing there. That suited Kelly just fine. This, she already knew, was a wonderful development. Anything but this ongoing pretence that everything was fine and working in this family was going to be an improvement.

She looked down at her feet to find Charlie had joined them. Not a thing belonging to Lauren was in sight, though, which explained why she couldn't hear her in her head. She caught herself wishing she'd worn or carried something of hers in her pocket at least. She'd have loved to hear any insights on what was unfurling before her eyes.

Stratos's tired voice brought her back to the present. 'You know I love English, Dad... Because of Mum.'

'Then, why? Why do you play truant? Where do you go anyway? Are you in trouble, Son?'

Stratos's wry laugh reached Kelly's ear like a sting to her insides. The boy's pain was palpable. Before she could absorb it fully, Stratos spoke, this time bursting with anger.

'Trouble? I'm not in trouble! Is that all you care for?' he shouted, distancing himself from his father.

This time, Alex didn't try to approach him. With his feet glued to the spot, he started to gesticulate frantically. 'Then, what is it? Talk to me, Son! And what do you mean when you say that's all I care for? You boys are *all* I care for!' He turned towards Nikos and Tommy, who clung to Kelly, pointing at them with trembling hands. His eyes met Kelly's for just a split second, enough for her to feel his upset. He was at a loss. That, she knew for sure.

Alex faced Stratos again and heaved a long sigh. 'Why don't you talk to me? What is the problem here?'

'The problem, Dad, is that you don't care, okay? Regardless of what you say, you don't!'

'How can you say that? Why do you think I work all day? So you and your brothers can have a comfortable life. So you want for nothing!'

'I want my *mother*, Dad!'

'Stratos, what is this now? Your mother has passed away!' He banged his fist on his chest and added, 'What do you want from me? I can't bring her back from the dead...'

'I'm not asking you that!'

'Then what are you asking for?'

'I want her *memory*, Dad! Her memory that you refuse to share with me. With *us*!'

Alex watched mutely as his eldest son first pointed to himself, then to his brothers. Alex's eyes were burning, and he seemed like he was about to lose his grip. Whether he was going to break down in tears or start shouting again, Kelly knew she had to intervene, lest this would get even worse.

'Sorry to interrupt,' she said as she approached, the two boys following her as if tethered to her waist by an invisible thread.

'Yes, Kelly?' said Alex, his voice weak. His furtive glance told her he felt mortified.

She gave a faint, yet sweet smile, and said, 'Why don't I make you a nice cup of herbal tea, Alex? I know you love to have one late in the evening, but how about having it now today, before dinner?'

When he nodded tiredly, she continued, pointing to the living room, 'Go sit on the sofa, and I'll bring it soon... I'll put the kettle on, then Stratos and I will go back to his room, have a quiet chat, and you guys can talk this through calmly after dinner. How's that?'

Alex nodded again, about to speak, but Stratos beat him to it. Taking a step towards his father, he produced his parents' old photo from his jeans pocket and showed it to him, shouting, 'Look at this! See? A picture of you and Mum! My brothers and I looked at it together earlier and remembered the old days!' His expression turned derisive, nostrils flaring when he added, 'And you know what, Dad? Nobody got upset! We even cracked a smile! Something we never do when you're around any more. So what are you afraid of? Huh?'

Alex's face morphed into that of a man on the verge of madness. Brushing his hair urgently, he shook a rigid finger at his son, then at Kelly, much to her surprise. 'What is this? Where did you get that? Kelly? Did you open my wardrobe and look through my things?'

'Excuse me?' said Kelly, bringing her hands to her waist. 'How dare you assume that I've done that?'

'Well, forgive me, but my boys would never look through my things!'

'So, you suppose *I* did, huh?'

'Well, who else could?'

'Your dog, that's who!'

'My dog? That's preposterous!'

Stratos was now staring in disbelief while Kelly did the rowing with his dad. The boy's face was ablaze with a mixture of shock and amusement.

'Yes! That's what I'm saying, Alex! Your dog keeps bringing us stuff that belonged to your wife!' Kelly caught Tommy's eyes, whose face went alight with panic. *Oh, no! I can't expose him! And I'd better not say Lauren has been getting the dog to bring me stuff either...* She blinked profusely as she shook her head. 'Sorry. I meant the dog brought the photo. Just the photo...'

Alex's brows knitted. 'What do you mean he brought it?'

Tommy took a step forward and mimed the dog walking towards them, his hands paddling like paws in mid-air, lips pressed together as if holding something in his mouth. Then, he smiled. 'Like that, Dad! He held it in his mouth and brought it to us! We all saw him do it!'

Alex looked from Tommy to Kelly, then sought the eyes of the other two for confirmation. The dog had retired to his bed in the corner and was now chewing one of his toys, none the wiser.

'You're telling me the dog took this photo from my wardrobe?'

'I don't know where he got it from, but—'

Stratos didn't wait for Kelly to finish her sentence. He threw his hands in the air and shouted, 'Is that our issue here, Dad? How the damn dog got the photo from wherever you'd hidden it?'

'Now, watch your language, Son! Remember your little brothers look up to you!'

'That's not our issue either, Dad! And you forget they look up to you too!'

'What's that supposed to mean?'

'It means they expect you to talk about their mother, Dad! As if she actually used to live here! And I ask you, why aren't any photos of her on the walls? Why are you hiding them in your wardrobe? We had to wait for something totally weird to happen, like a dog bringing us a photo of her, so we can see her likeness again!'

'Stratos, just because I don't have her photos on the walls it doesn't mean I didn't love her. It doesn't mean I don't care that she's gone. Of course, I do!'

'You do? Then prove it!' He shoved the photo into his father's hand. 'Blow this up for me. I want to put it up in my room and see my mother's face every day!'

'What good would that do? I'm trying to help you boys move on... and what you're doing, Stratos, is... you're upsetting your brothers and me! For no good reason! And you still haven't told me why you're skipping classes! I'm starting to think this whole charade is nothing but an attempt on your part to change the subject!'

'What? I'm not changing the subject. There's only one subject and that is Mum! The fact that I love her... that I miss her... that I honour her memory and *you don't...*' His voice, frail as it was, broke towards the end of his sentence. He stormed out of the kitchen and, moments later, closed his bedroom door with a slam.

Alex shook his head, his eyes pinned on the carpet.

The boys, frozen, stared at their father, then looked up to Kelly, clearly waiting for her to do something.

Chapter 18

Kelly didn't waste a moment. Calmly, she asked Nikos and Tommy to return to their rooms so she and their father could talk alone. Once they were gone, Kelly led Alex to the sofa. She sat closely beside him as he heaved a long sigh and buried his face in his hands.

For a few moments, he stayed like that, his hands stuck on his face like a faulty mask that had no holes cut into it for eyes. His breathing eased with every passing moment, and Kelly wondered if that was indeed the case. Perhaps the mask he wore had finally ripped a little, allowing him to see a little better.

Alex removed his hands and eyed her with apprehension. 'I'm so sorry, Kelly. You shouldn't have had to witness all that. You've only been here two days... But I assure you this isn't the norm. Come to think of it, I've never had to quarrel with my son like that. I have no idea what came over him, to be honest.'

Despite herself, Kelly felt her features harden as she blurted out, 'You don't? But Stratos just told you, Alex. Plain and clear. He misses his mother. That's all... And I...' Her voice trailed off when she wondered if she had the right to pass judgement. She hardly knew the guy.

As if guessing her thoughts, he gave her an encouraging smile. 'Don't hesitate, Kelly. Please. Your honest opinion. I am lost here.'

'Well, I think the boys are right to want to share memories of their mother with you, Alex. To be frank, I do wonder as well why there are no photos of Lauren around... I noticed yesterday too... the tension around the table when Stratos mentioned her. He was clearly challenging you to talk about her. He's practically begging you, Alex... Don't you see?'

Alex shook his head, his gaze dropping to the floor. 'I don't know... I am reluctant to bring her memory back into their lives. What if it hurts them? Isn't it better to move on?'

'What do you mean it will hurt them? It's clear to me they are hurting *now*! What's more, I don't know about the little ones, but Stratos surely thinks you don't care about their mother, or for them.'

His face went alight with dismay. 'What? That's not true...'

'Well, they don't know that, do they? And you know what the other problem here is?'

His eyes locked on hers, begging her to continue. He seemed like a man at the end of his rope, ready to try anything that could help. This gave her the courage to be fully honest. 'Well, because your children feel you don't care that their mother died, I know it sounds harsh... but I believe they've distanced themselves from you. Emotionally, I mean... They don't share stuff with you any more. They keep secrets from you, Alex. That's not a good sign.'

'Secrets? What secrets? You mean like Stratos skipping classes?'

'Yes, that's one of them, obviously. But it's not just Stratos.' She drew a long breath and added, 'Yesterday, all three of your children, on three different occasions, uttered these words to me: "Don't tell, Dad." And I am someone who's just entered their lives, Alex! They trust me more than they trust you... What does that tell you?'

Alex ran a hand through his hair, his face contorted with upset. He rubbed his lips with the back of his hand and sprang upright, now pacing up and down before the sofa where Kelly still sat.

Her lips pressed together, she watched him, giving him the time he needed to process all that she'd said.

Finally, he turned to her, the light returning to his eyes as he replied to her question, 'I guess it tells me that they need their mother. Or... a woman of her age, like you, to talk to, perhaps.'

'Yes, you could say that, I guess. But they need a father too, Alex. They need *you*! They look to you to keep their mother's memory alive. You're the one who holds the key to the past, a plethora of memories of her, in so much detail. And they are dying to know all the things you know about her. But for three years, you've been telling them, albeit without words, that it is forbidden to mention her... Don't you see? They disagree, yet they've accepted it to keep you happy. But it's making them miserable. And they can't endure it any more.'

Alex's face melted with sorrow to hear the last words. He collapsed on the sofa, dropping like a big clump of lead. 'Oh, God! What have I done?' He turned to her, taking her hand, shaking it. 'Thank you so much, Kelly!' His eyes glinted as he continued to shake her hand. 'You know... Dimos, my best friend whom you've met, has also been telling me this from time to time, but it's only now that I can truly see it...'

Kelly nodded, not sure what to say. When he let go of her hand, he took another steadying breath, then said, 'You know, when Lauren died, Nikos had a meltdown... He was only five then, and didn't want to go to kindergarten... didn't want to eat or play... Every morning I had to coax him to leave his room, his bed... had to take him to a therapist for months. It was hard fixing him again, you know? Luckily, Stratos wasn't affected like that. And Tommy, of course, was too little to know his mother was gone at the time. But what happened to Nikos scared me senseless...'

He sought her eyes, looking for understanding, and she nodded firmly. 'I am so sorry, Alex... Now, I begin to understand. Poor Nikos... It must have been so hard for him. For you all.'

'It was... But I kept telling myself that I owed it to Lauren to take care of our children first and foremost. I guess it was then that I decided that by removing any reminders of her from the house I'd be protecting the kids, helping them to get over our loss.'

'That was clearly the wrong thing to do... Mourning is a live thing inside us, Alex. It needs to be processed. I've lost my beloved grandmother. I know... The sorrow creeps up on you when you least expect it.'

'Oh, don't I know it...'

'I'm sure you do, Alex. But to heal you need to face the pain squarely in the eyes. The pain will punish you if you try to sweep it under the carpet. Do you understand?'

'Yes, yes I do...'

'Forgive me for asking, but... Have you processed that pain yet yourself?'

'It's been a long time now, so I guess I have.' A shadow crossed his face. 'I think of her a lot still, though...'

'That's understandable...'

'And I dream of her sometimes.'

'Often?'

'Quite.'

'Then, I think you still need to process her loss, if that's the case... Alex, the subconscious mind creeps up on us in our sleep to remind us of the unfinished business in our hearts...'

'This is so wise, Kelly...' He tilted his head. 'How do you know all these things? Seems to me I've employed a housekeeper and got myself a dietician and a philosopher, too. If not a therapist. I hit the jackpot with you, Kelly...'

'I've just read a lot, that's all... Relationships and the workings of the mind always fascinated me.'

'Well, lucky me!'

She marvelled at his change of demeanour, and the sweetness of his smile magnetized her for a while. *He is so handsome! Pity he's not over his wife yet...*

'So, what do you think I should do?'

'Well, start from the photo that Stratos showed you. Blow it up like he asked.'

His expression darkened as he went quiet. 'My poor boy... What have I done to him?' he lamented, shaking his head ruefully. 'To all three of them. I'm such an idiot...What if they hate me? What do I do? Oh, God! What a mess!' He crouched over, his elbows on his thighs as he planted his hands on either side of his head.

Kelly placed a tender hand on his back and rubbed it gently. 'It's okay... it's not that bad. They don't hate you. Your children *love* you. They need you, Alex.'

He looked up and took her hand. This time, he didn't shake it like before but held it like a man looking for salvation. 'Kelly, can you help me? I don't know what to do.'

'It's simple... Just listen to your children...' She gave an encouraging smile. 'Start with Stratos.'

Alex furrowed his brow, bottom lip twitching, then he said, 'So what does he do when he skips classes? Do you know?'

Remembering the plectrum, Kelly gave a knowing smile. 'He hasn't told me, but I have the impression he's involved in another kind of learning. And it's all good. You don't need to worry.'

'What kind of learning?'

She chuckled and pointed towards the corridor with her head. 'Just go. Ask him! He's your son. You guys ought to find a way to talk openly to each other from now on.'

'I'm afraid that if I go to his room now, he'll start shouting again... I don't want to fight with my boy any more.'

'Do you want me to go first? See if he's ready to talk?'

'Oh Kelly... you're such a treasure.'

Chapter 19

Kelly knocked gently on Stratos's room and, when he responded with a numb "enter", she walked in with a thin smile. 'Can I talk to you, Stratos?'

He was lying on his bed, a tablet in his hand. He placed it on his bedside table and said with a nod, 'Yes, of course, Kelly.'

He swung his legs around to sit on the side of the bed, hands on his knees, and she sat beside him in the same manner.

'Do you want to talk about the plectrum?' she asked him with an amused smile. It did the trick, causing him to smile too, albeit bitterly.

'You guessed?'

'So, you skip classes to play the guitar?'

'Yes... My best friend's dad is a musician. He doesn't know I skip classes, of course. My friend told him I wanted to learn how to play, and we lied that I had no money to go to a music school...'

'Because you didn't want to tell your father?'

'That's right.'

'But why not?'

The boy gave a laboured sigh. 'He doesn't want me to play the guitar or sing.'

'What? But I heard you sing. Your voice is amazing.'

He bent his head, taking the compliment with humility and a wry smile. When he looked up, he seemed angry. 'He doesn't care about Mum. Or what she wanted for me.'

'What did she want, Stratos? Help me understand.'

He gave a soft sigh, raising his eyes to focus them far, the light streaming from the ceiling causing them to sparkle. 'Mum loved to hear me sing... And she knew I loved the guitar. I wanted to learn when I was little, and she said I could start when I was a little older. But then she died, and...'

Kelly put a gentle hand on his back and he leaned towards her, like a felled tree. Her heart constricting with feeling, she squeezed him in her arms lovingly.

She couldn't see his face now, as it was buried in the crook of her neck, but from the wet feeling on her skin, she could tell he was shedding quiet tears.

Her insides clenched, and a devastating feeling, like a freight train barrelling through her, caused her own tears to begin rolling down her face. His upset was coming on too strong for her to bear. Her special gift had its shortcomings. Feeling other people's pain was one of the worst. She began to sob, and it caused him to pull back.

'You're crying too?' he asked with a frown.

'Don't mind me, Stratos... Tell me, why do you think your father doesn't care for you?'

'Because since Mum died, every time I wanted to talk about her, in his way, he stopped me from doing it. Then, overnight, all her photos from the table tops and the walls disappeared. Her clothes that lay around, her jewellery on the dresser... even her books and her magazines in the study. It was like he wanted to wipe out the memory of her existence completely.'

'Stratos, do you remember how your mother's passing affected Nikos?'

'Yes... He was sick for a long time.'

'Well, your father wanted to protect you, boys... That's why he did all that. So Nikos can get well, and you and Tommy don't suffer in any way like that either.'

'But... we didn't. Not that way. And then Nikos got well...'

'I'm not saying your dad did the right thing, Stratos. I'm only letting you know why he did it. Of course, he loves your mum. Of course, he misses her, like you guys do. And he told me he sees her in his dreams still. Did you know that?'

Stratos's face brightened, eyes glazing over. 'No...' it sufficed him to say feebly.

'See? You were wrong about him.'

'So... if I talk to him, do you think he'll let me carry on with my guitar classes? Because I'm good, Kelly! My teacher tells me so! I don't want to stop!'

'Well? Do you want me to get your father to come in here so you can ask him yourself?'

The boy gave a long sigh. 'Okay.'

She saw the trepidation in his eyes and put a reassuring hand on his shoulder, squeezing it gently. 'Just remember your father loves you. And that to him, you and your brothers are the most precious things in the world. Okay?'

Stratos nodded, finally understanding.

Without further ado, she went and got Alex, who had been sitting on the sofa crouched over in silence. He looked like a schoolboy waiting outside of the principal's office, already scolded once by the teacher, now waiting for the final reprimand. The thought made her heart melt as she called him over.

Alex brushed past her at the doorway acknowledging her with a firm nod and walked into Stratos's room. Father and son sat quietly at the edge of the bed, the cautious glances they threw each other sufficing to tell her they were open to mutual understanding. The vibe was crystal clear. Satisfied, Kelly moved to close the door when both called her name, asking her to stay, so she stood at the open door, lips pressed together as her heart began to swell.

Alex had just put an arm around his boy's shoulders, drawing him close. 'I love you, Son. For whatever I've done to hurt you, I apologise. I didn't mean it. Please forgive me.'

Father and son held each other in a tight embrace, both bursting into tears. Kelly wiped a tear from her own eyes and continued to watch in silence as Stratos confessed about the guitar lessons. Apparently, he'd been skipping only one class a week, careful not to neglect his English lessons. He'd been making sure to get the notes of the lessons he missed from a classmate and had recently run out of excuses to tell the teacher for his absences. He said he'd been expecting his dad would find out sooner or later. He'd been dreading it but didn't have the guts to tell him what he'd been doing.

'It's only because when I asked you to do guitar lessons last year, you said no.'

'I'm sorry, Son. I didn't realize it was so important to you. I guess I wanted you to concentrate on your English classes.'

'I thought you said no because Mum wanted me to learn how to play. I thought it was just another way for you to keep her memory away from me.'

Alex's voice wavered when he replied, 'No, Son... That's not the case. I'm so sorry...' He turned to face Kelly, and she admired him for not minding her seeing his tear-sodden eyes.

'So many misunderstandings, you two...' she said with an encouraging smile. 'But that'll change from now on, right?' She gave a thumbs up.

Father and son chuckled and laughed, tightening their embrace.

*****

After dinner, Alex went upstairs without saying anything and returned a little later holding a tin box in his hands. His face was ablaze with enthusiasm when he entered the living room where Kelly and the boys had sat to watch TV. She'd just done the dishes and the boys had insisted they all sit and watch a movie together.

However, when they saw Alex's expression, the movie was instantly forgotten. Kelly recognised the box from the wardrobe and gave an inaudible gasp. Nikos and Tommy became animated with intrigue, but before they could ask what was in the box, Stratos beat them to it.

He jumped upright and switched off the TV, then started to jump about. 'Oh, Dad! Thank you! I remember this box!'

Turning to his brothers, he added, 'Our old family photos are in there, guys!'

Chortling, Alex sat on the sofa with the boys and Kelly beamed at them from the armchair beside it, the pug lying on the carpet by her feet.

Before Alex had the chance to speak, Tommy, much to everyone's intrigue, sprung upright. Asking everyone to wait, he went upstairs to return moments later, Lauren's scarf in his hand, the one he'd been putting on the dog secretly in his room. As if on cue, Charlie ran towards him and Tommy put it around his neck as the others watched, dumbfounded.

'I hope you don't mind, Dad. I dress Charlie with Mum's things sometimes. Whatever he brings me from the wardrobe in your room.'

The dog moved closer to Alex, who gasped when he obviously ascertained that the scarf once belonged to Lauren. Lost for words, he gazed into the pug's face for a while, then said, 'Charlie? Is that what you've been doing? Taking things from my room and giving them to the kids?'

His face erupted with humour as he patted the dog on the head. 'But... you don't even have opposable thumbs! How do you open the wardrobe door? Ah! I've always known you're a special little doggie! No wonder Mummy loved you so much!' Everyone laughed at that, clearly too caught up in their elation to really wonder, as Charlie barked excitedly.

Finally, they all quietened and began to look through the photos as Alex started to relay stories of their family past.

Charlie soon returned to Kelly's feet to lie there, and she struggled to listen to Alex and Lauren's commentaries that went on at the same time; his, out loud, and hers, inside her mind. Before her eyes, and in her heart, the story of a romantic young couple and, later in life, that of their growing family, unfurled, causing her heart to shudder with emotion.

As Alex generously shared his memories of Lauren, Kelly saw the same light that shone in his eyes dance in those of his children, who listened, oohing and aahing along.

✻✻✻✻✻

The children had just gone to bed after a frenzy of excited squeals, hugs and kisses with their father at the bottom of the stairs. He and Kelly were still smiling widely when he offered her a nightcap back in the living room.
'It's getting late, but, somehow, I feel rejuvenated. Wide awake!' he said when he handed her a glass of brandy. His eyes exploded like stars in the soft light that streamed from the side table.
Kelly chinked her glass with his and they drank a few sips in silence for a while. Then, he piped up, 'Oh Kelly! I cannot begin to express my gratitude to you...'
She flicked her wrist. 'Oh please. I did nothing but remind you all what you have in common. And that's your love for each other. And Lauren, of course.' She met his eyes as she said the name, and wondered just how often he still had dreams about her. And what kind. *If only he weren't so charming... So damn, heart-stoppingly handsome.*
He smiled sweetly then, bringing her back to the present. 'I beg to differ. What you managed here tonight was nothing short of a miracle.' He pointed at her and shook his head with disbelief. 'No. *You are* the miracle, Kelly! You've been here just two days and, already, you've transformed my relationship with my sons. With Stratos, especially. We hadn't really seen eye to eye in ages... I've been fooling myself thinking that it was all because of his age and hoping he'd eventually grow out of it. And, all along, it was *me* that was the problem.' He shook his head, took another sip, and added, 'Stupid me.'

'Don't chastise yourself, Alex. Life doesn't come with a manual. We all plod along, learning as we go. What's important is to seek assistance when the going gets tough. And that's simply because every single one of us is too involved in our own *pathos*, in our own perspective of things, to understand our problems and our feelings clearly. It takes the fresh, objective viewpoint of an outsider to do that and let us know what we're doing wrong. That's all I've done. It doesn't make you stupid, or me a miracle worker...'

To her surprise, he leaned closer then, a wicked gleam in his eye. 'If that's the case, then is there a problem you have that I can help you with? To repay you?' He chortled and pointed at himself with both hands. 'Try me, Kelly! See if I can help you too!'

Kelly eyed him with disbelief, hushed to silence for a few seconds. She recalled he'd had an extra glass of wine or two after dinner while showing the old photos to them all. *So the man had a bad evening and needed some extra alcohol. No harm in that... Except... Is he flirting with me?*

He had a breathtakingly sexy look in his eyes at the time. The lopsided smile that wrinkled the side of his mouth and his lower cheek would put the biggest Hollywood heartthrobs to shame. Mesmerised, she gazed back at him some more.

'Well? Out with it!' he coaxed.

She shook her head, unwilling to open up about any of the problems she'd had in the last year. The loss of her grandmother, the loss of her job, and the whole sad chapter that involved her ex-boyfriend, Makis. 'What's the point in talking about old problems? They're all in my past, thank goodness. I have no problems now, I'm happy to say.'

He gave a grin. 'Oh, that's good to hear. Except, it seems to me you have one big problem still.'

'What's that?'

'Well, isn't it obvious? You live in here, with a widower who doesn't have a clue about how to raise his kids on his own!' He burst into peals of laughter, clearly owed to the wine and the brandy. To make matters worse perhaps, he'd just moved to the coffee table to pour himself another glass. 'Another one, Kelly?'

'Oh no, thank you.' She wanted to say that perhaps he shouldn't drink any more either, but the dog was faster. He arrived swiftly from the corridor, Lauren's scarf still around his neck.

'Oh, I could kick him!' she heard Lauren's voice in her head as the dog approached. 'Tell that fool not to drink any more! Go on! Last time he drank this much, that awful woman next door took advantage! And now I can't get rid of her!'

'What?' screeched Kelly, despite herself, almost jumping from her seat on the sofa.

Her sudden reaction caused Alex to jerk backwards in his seat, almost emptying the contents of his glass onto his clothes. 'What is it, Kelly?'

'Oh! Nothing, nothing...' she said as a wicked laugh from Lauren rang in her ears. *Great to know that death and humour are not mutually exclusive*, Kelly thought.

She met Alex's eyes and chuckled. 'I thought I felt an earthquake...' she lied, raising a shoulder. 'A slight tremor. Hardly felt it, actually. I may be wrong.'

'Oh, I didn't feel a thing. But maybe I drank a lot,' he said with a chuckle.

'Well, it's been a long day...' She stood. 'I'm off to bed. You should go too. Get some rest... Best not to drink any more.'

He stood with a huge grin to give her a mock-military salute, then put the full glass down on the table. 'Yes, ma'am! Of course, you're right.' His smile disappeared as he neared her to add, 'But you can't blame me for letting my hair down a little, after that awful start to our evening. Thank you again, Kelly. For what you did today.'

Kelly nodded. 'It's okay. It was my pleasure to help.' Standing so close to him felt wonderful. His mild intoxication made his chiselled features come to life, with his cheeks flushed and his eyes incredibly bright. Having got enough Dutch courage that evening, she wondered if now was perhaps the right time to hint that Lauren's spirit hadn't departed yet.

But then, he spoke, and her plan was abandoned instantly. Especially as he reached out and squeezed her forearm gently, causing her heart to give a thump. 'Listen, Kelly. Earlier, while I was showing the photos, I thought it'd be nice, perhaps, to take the kids to Bourtzi this coming Sunday... What do you think?'

She wiped her brow, faking nonchalance, even though the touch of his hand on her arm had caused her mind to go numb. 'Bourtzi?' she mumbled, trying to will the frenetic beat of her heart to subside. His face was so close to hers... It felt both uncomfortable and amazing at the same time.

Clearly none the wiser, he said, 'Yes... Lauren and I took Stratos and Nikos there once, before Tommy was born. It was many years ago and I doubt either of them will remember it much. I thought I'd start from Bourtzi to take my kids gradually to all the places in town Lauren and I enjoyed going to. I think it'll be good for them. What do you think?'

'Yes, yes, of course. It's a great idea,' she said numbly, seeing that he still hadn't removed his gentle hand from her forearm. The warmth it radiated on her skin felt blissful. His eyes, not fully open, hypnotized her with a deep gaze, and she guessed he had more to say.

He cleared his throat, as if on cue, and said, 'I was thinking... Since Efi is coming to bring you your things this Sunday, why don't you girls come along to Bourtzi with us? The boat ride should be fun, and I'll give you a little tour of the fort itself with the little I know.'

'Oh, that's a lovely offer! Thank you, Alex. I'll ask Efi, and I'm quite sure she'll say yes.'

'Great... and maybe a coffee after?' Alarm flashed in his eyes, and he removed his hand as if scalded when he added, 'With the kids, I mean! And Efi.'

'Yes, that would be lovely, too.' As soon as she said this, she heard Lauren's voice in her head say, 'Oh that's wonderful!'

Instinctively, Kelly looked down at the pug that now half-lay at her feet. The dog raised his head to return a mute gaze, and Lauren continued, 'Please make sure to wear my scarf on Sunday, Kelly... Bring Charlie along and keep him close to you. This way I can talk to you when you're out. I have my ways to help you all. Please allow me to do this...'

Taken aback, Kelly grew rigid while she listened, then gave a single nod as she issued a mental acceptance to Lauren's suggestions.

She turned to Alex to find him gazing absently at Charlie, a faint smile on his lips. And now, he looked up, his smile brightening, rendering her star-struck.

He shook his head. 'You know, Kelly, I still can't believe I've just shown the old photos of Lauren and me to the kids. It's a major breakthrough for me. And they seemed so delighted...'

Kelly nodded, about to speak, when he slapped his forehead with an open hand to pipe up, 'Oh! I almost forgot! Remember my friend Dimos who runs a catering company?'

'Yes...'

'Well, he's doing this event, a reception... Basically, it's a posh lunch with live music. He's celebrating a milestone in his successful business and, naturally, being his best friend, I am invited but completely lost as to whom to take along. So, I was thinking, would you mind terribly accompanying me?'

He gave a nervous chuckle and added, 'Knowing you, you're probably a proficient dancer too.'

She chortled. 'I wouldn't say that, but I do all right...'

'Good! Perhaps you can teach me how to move on the dance floor without stepping on any toes.' He laughed and put out a hand, tilting his head to the side. His look was somewhat pleading, but more in an amused way, rather than serious. 'Come on. Take me out of my misery and say yes? I really don't have anyone else to ask.'

Before she could speak, he put up a finger, eyes widening. 'Wait! That sounds bad. I didn't mean it that way. Sorry, Kelly. It's been a long time since I asked a woman out.' Another bout of panic animated him, causing both his hands to start shaking before her face. 'Not that this is a date, of course! Not by a long shot!' He pressed his lips together and eyed her with caution, clearly assessing the damage following his outburst.

Kelly burst out laughing. The whole routine had entertained her from early on. The initial surprise had given its place to amusement, and now she was over the moon to have been asked. 'Thank you, Alex. I'll gladly come!'

'Oh, wonderful!' he said, then gave a long exhalation.

'When is it?'

'Not for another couple of weeks. At the end of the month.'

'Great.' She mirrored his elated expression for a few moments, then a thought caused her to frown with dismay. 'Oh no...'

'What is it?'

'What about the kids?'

He gave a dismissive wave. 'Oh, that's okay. I'll ask Stella from next door... She's minded the kids before.'

'Oh... About her. I may have put her nose out of joint.'

'What do you mean?'

'Well, I sort of mentioned to her today that the boys are on a diet now, Stratos and Nikos especially, as you know, and I may have asked her—albeit very politely—to, well, not bother bringing us any more muffins...' She finished her sentence with a slight cringe as she awaited his response. Now she wondered if she'd overstepped the mark.

What right did she have to tell Stella that? This wasn't her house or her kids. She was just an employee here. And Alex, even though he didn't want Stella around, he surely didn't seem reluctant to invite her into his home to mind his kids. And, according to Lauren a few moments earlier, Stella and he had... She couldn't even picture it in her head. If these two had been an item in the past, or if they'd just shared a night of passion here together, wasn't it awkward for him? Stella still wanted him while he clearly didn't. *What is he doing asking her to baby sit in his house then?*

She ventured a look his way, and, to her relief, he didn't seem angry. He looked expectant, if anything, so she added, 'I'm sorry. I shouldn't have done it. I can see it clearly now.'

Giving a wicked smile, he said, 'Oh don't worry. It's only Stella.' He gave a soft sigh. 'Believe me, there are leeches in the river with less staying power than she has when it comes to what she wants.'

'What do you mean?'

'I don't know what her problem is, exactly, but she seems to think that she and I... you know... may become an item sometime in the future. But that's never going to happen.'

Huh? thought Kelly, her mind drawing a blank. She looked down, then around her, but the pug was nowhere to be seen. *Thanks a lot, Lauren. First, you drop the bomb, then you leave me in the lurch.* Her mind whirling, she shook her head, then said, 'Anyway... it's late. I'm going to bed. Good night, Alex.'

'Good night, Kelly. And don't worry about Stella... I'll ask her. She'll be fine.'

Chapter 20

In the days that followed, Kelly and the children bonded further, especially during their walks in the afternoons with the dog. She ran every morning too, which helped not just to keep her body in shape but also to clear her mind from the eerie happenings in the house.

Every morning, as she entered Alex's room to make the bed, Charlie would follow her inside and Lauren would start coaxing her to wear her scarf but Kelly wouldn't do it. As much as she wanted to help the spirit find peace, the thought of having that eerie voice in her head at all times around the house—if she were to don the scarf—felt too unsettling.

On Saturday morning, Kelly set about doing her chores deep in thought. Alex was at work, as usual, and the boys had gone to an open-air basketball court near the green to play together.

As she put clothes on the washing line in the garden, she willed herself to stop worrying about Lauren and to focus on the happy times she had in the house. Soon, images of Alex and the boys' smiling faces filled her mind. Since that harrowing evening earlier in the week, all their interactions had been fun-filled and effortless. Even Stratos smiled genuinely now every evening and had heart-to-heart talks with his father as they discussed Lauren.

Kelly smiled to herself. Even the dog had started to act differently – he'd now listen to her at all times. He was out in the yard with her at the time, happily chewing a tennis ball a little further away. His soft growling reached her ears as she began to daydream. She couldn't wait for her morning out with Alex and the kids the next day. Knowing she'd see Efi again and get more of her own clothes back made her want to sing.

But then, her mind wandered to Stella, and the smile on her face faded away. Kelly couldn't fathom why Alex wanted her to mind the kids on the night they'd go to the party. And she was shocked still, having heard from Lauren that Stella had 'taken advantage'. Surely that meant Stella had had her way with Alex, somehow... Whatever Lauren had meant, it couldn't have been something good. And it certainly wasn't a good sign that Alex was encouraging her further. *Maybe... he doesn't find her as much of a leech as he'd have me think...*

Her reverie ended abruptly when Charlie broke out in a deafening fit of barking. She looked down and scolded him, telling him to stop, but he wouldn't do it. Perplexed, she followed his gaze to see Alan sitting in the middle of his garden on a plastic chair, his legs crossed as he read from a letter-sized sheet of paper, an amused smile on his face. She noticed the paper was creased as if it'd been folded many times. It was also heavily stained with what seemed like mud.

Asking the dog to stop barking, once again to no avail, she approached the fence to say hi. Charlie began to follow, his bark increasing in volume with every step. Alan kept reading, totally unaffected by the racket.

Halfway to the fence, she changed her mind and took the dog by the collar, taking him to the front door. Using the keys she'd left in the lock, she opened it, let go of the collar and told Charlie to go inside. She half-expected him to disobey and head back out towards the fence to bark some more but, to her surprise, he looked up, gave her a wistful look that seemed almost human and went inside silently, tail hanging low.

Not wanting to miss Alan while he was outside, she set her thoughts of the strange pet aside for now and headed back to the fence without delay. She had enjoyed chatting to Alan the last time and hoped for a chance to meet his wife too. Perhaps, if Alex agreed, they could invite them over for coffee one day. She thought that perhaps the children might benefit from talking to their parents' old friends, now that Alex didn't mind them discussing their mother any more.

Putting both hands on the fence, she called out: 'Hey, Alan! *Kalimera*! How are you?'

At the time, Alan was chuckling as he read from the paper. Hearing her voice, he snapped his head up, his eyes igniting with surprise. 'Oh! Hi, Kelly! I'm fine, and you?'

'Great, thanks...' she said, somewhat numbly, as she watched him stand up, fold the paper carefully and put it in his pocket. She put out a hand, despite herself. 'Oh! That was stained, did you not notice? You may not want to put that in your pocket.'

He chortled as he sauntered towards her. 'Oh, it doesn't matter. My hands are forever in the dirt. So are my clothes. That was a letter from my grandson, by the way. Oh, I enjoy hearing from him so much!'

'He wrote to you? That's nice.'

'Yes. He writes all the time, bless him,' he said, his eyes bright.

'And how is your wife?' She couldn't help pointing to the open window with her head as tantalizing aromas of tomato sauce reached her nostrils. 'She must be a wonderful cook. Lucky you!'

'Oh yes, she loves to spoil me!' he said, taking hold of his tummy with a loud guffaw.

Kelly wondered if she should hint that she'd like to meet her but then thought better of it. It would sound rude, perhaps. Besides, she hadn't asked Alex yet if it'd be a good idea to call them over.

'Hey, Kelly...' said Alan, leaning closer over the fence.

'Yes?'

'How are things in there? A little better now, I hope?'

There was something sinister in his eyes then; it was unmistakable. *What does he mean?* She followed his eyes to gaze back at Alex's house for a while, then faced Alan again to say, 'Good. Really good, actually. The boys seem happy with me. Alex too. So that makes me happy too.'

'And what about...?' He leaned even closer, a suggestive look in his eyes.

'About... what?'

'You know... Look... I know, okay?'

'Sorry, Alan... What are you referring to? I'm not with you.'

He gave a soft sigh. 'I'm referring to... Lauren, of course. I can see her sometimes.'

Kelly's eyes opened wide, the air escaping from her lungs in one loud exhalation. 'What? Where?'

'In your garden... She often goes to sit on these chairs by the table...' he said wistfully, pointing to Alex's garden furniture on the porch.

'Are you psychic?'

'I can see the unseen, yes. And, it takes one to know one, Kelly. I can tell you have the gift. So, forgive my asking... It's not curiosity, I can assure you, but only my concern for Lauren and her surviving family members that urged me to ask.'

Kelly stared at him aghast and tried to process in her mind what she'd heard. Could Alan help her at all? For one, he'd just helped her see she wasn't crazy. Even though she knew she had some kind of gift, she'd never heard spirits speak inside her head before and had started to doubt her own sanity. Finally, she found her voice to say feebly, 'It's okay, I don't mind you asking. Actually, I am relieved to hear I'm not the only one.'

'So, do you see her too? His eyes darted to the house. 'In there?'

'No... But I hear her voice clearly in my head. We get to talk back and forth, actually.'

'Wow. That must be something.'

'Yes... and it's quite unsettling at times, but I have to admit that my conversations with Lauren are helping me understand the dynamics in the family... to try to help them find healing.'

'Ah! Healing! You're a true medium then. You understand what your purpose is, and why the spirit is grounded here, unable to depart to a better place.'

'Yes, I think I do... And it seems that something's starting to happen now, to help Lauren's family process her passing.'

'I'm glad to hear it.' He shook his head forlornly. 'Alex is a great guy but it seems he's been doing things the wrong way. By trying to protect the boys he's only been prolonging their suffering.'

'So, you know.'

He chortled. 'Let's just say I don't just see Lauren. She and I often enjoy a little chat, too.'

Kelly gave a gasp. 'Really? Out here?'

'Anywhere.'

'She comes to you? Even in your house?'

'Lauren and I had a strong bond in life. So yes. That makes it possible. Which is why she is able to communicate with her pug so effortlessly too. She and Charlie were inseparable.' He shook his head and chortled. 'That poor canine soul! He's so haunted it's unreal!'

'You think it's funny? What if the dog isn't happy? I feel sorry for the poor darling!'

Alan's face turned serious in the blink of an eye. 'Oh no, don't be! For a dog, it's the ultimate connection with its owner. That pug is in heaven having his master so close, believe me.'

She shook her head, lips pressed together, then said, 'I hope you're right.'

'I know I am! Lauren's connection with Charlie is so strong that she can use it to channel her voice to you... That's how you can hear her... Am I right?'

'Yes! How did you know?'

'I talk to Lauren too, remember?'

'Yes. But something that belonged to her must be present too so I can hear her...'

'Yes. That's why you need to start wearing her things like she asked you.'

'She told you about that too?'

'Yes... But why don't you do it? Are you afraid? Alex won't mind if you wear Lauren's scarf. Put it in your hair... Do it tomorrow, when you go to Bourtzi.'

'You seem to know everything!'

He laughed. 'Kelly, things will get easier for Lauren, Alex and the kids if you listen to her instructions. She'd been waiting for three years in that house hoping for a girl like you to turn up and help her, to help them all! You're the one, Kelly! You have to find the courage to do as she asks. Believe me when I say it will lead you to happiness as well.'

'Happiness? In what way?'

'I mean exactly in the way you imagine your happiness...' He tilted his head and gave a playful smile. 'And don't worry about Stella. Lauren has a bone or two to pick with her. She's not a problem for you.'

Overwhelmed by the revelations and cryptic advice, Kelly's mind began to race. And even though she stood in the garden under a clear blue sky, her eyes half-closed in the sunshine, fresh air getting into her lungs, she began to feel claustrophobic. Clutching her throat with one hand, she shook her head. 'Um... Sorry, Alan. I've left a pot simmering on the stove. I need to go check it,' she lied.

Alan moved away from the fence and raised a hand. 'Okay... See you, Kelly. Have fun tomorrow! Please wear the scarf... And, here's a tip: When Alex makes sounds about going for a coffee, ask him to take you all to the café in the old train station. It's in the railway park in town...'

Nodding silently, Kelly retraced her steps and rushed into the house as if she were being chased. The rest of the laundry would have to wait to be put on the line a little later. Preferably when Alan was no longer in sight.

Chapter 21

It was a mad rush at the house the next morning when everyone gathered in the kitchen to get some breakfast before heading to town.

Kelly was worried Alex would notice Lauren's scarf that she was wearing. She had used it to tie two thick strands from either side of her head together high on the back. The two ends of the scarf fell freely over her long hair, the flowery pattern showing, making her uncomfortable. This was amplified by the fact that, with Charlie scampering around by her feet, she could hear Lauren's encouraging words loud and clear.

The spirit sounded excited that Kelly had agreed to wear her scarf today. She said it would help them all immensely, promising Kelly she'd be able to see the difference before the day was done. Kelly had no idea what that meant but was too busy frying eggs and buttering bread to give it much thought.

With the spirit's words booming inside her head, it was hard to communicate back and forth with the family. At best, it felt as hard as trying to talk to someone while wearing headphones, music blasting in your ears.

'Kelly?' she heard Alex say and turned to find him standing beside her on the counter. He was holding a green tea teabag in one hand and an Earl Grey one in the other. 'You said you wanted tea, right? Which one do you prefer?'

'Green, please. Thank you,' she said, grateful that Lauren had finally fallen quiet. Smiling, she turned to face him squarely so he couldn't see the scarf on the back of her head. It was futile, she knew, as they were going to spend the whole day together. What was she hoping for? Swallowing hard when he looked away, she resumed transferring fried eggs from the pan to the boys' plates.

'Are you sure it's okay to take Charlie with us, Kelly?' he asked, causing her, once again, to whip her head around.

'Yes, I think he'll benefit from the exercise. And this way he won't be alone all morning in here. You don't mind, do you?'

'No, of course not. If you don't mind walking him, I don't.'

'Yes, I'm more than happy to hold the lead. You guys won't have to worry about him.' She shook a fist in the air and widened her eyes to convey enthusiasm. 'It's all part of his training! And this is the next step. To see if he'll remain calm and obedient among many people in a foreign environment,' she lied, but, of course, the only reason she was bringing him along was so she could oblige Lauren.

She hoped the day would unfold without any problems and began breathing freely again the moment Alex turned away, telling herself that, of course, everything would be all right. If anything, she was going to see Efi again today and felt enthused about that. She couldn't believe it had only been a week since she'd last seen her. It felt like weeks on end. But that wasn't necessarily indicative of her having a hard time in the house. On the contrary, despite the eeriness and all, this place had felt like home right from the start. Furthermore, this family had also recently begun to feel like more than just the people she'd been hired to take care of for money...

*****

When they arrived at Nostos hotel to pick up Efi, they found her sitting in the lobby. A big suitcase was standing on the floor by her feet, which Kelly identified as her own.

'Heeeeey!' shouted Efi as she sprung upright and flung her arms around Kelly in a tight embrace. Everyone greeted her and Kelly introduced the boys. Then, Alex made sounds about heading for the seafront. He took Kelly's luggage to carry it outside and everyone followed.

Alex put the luggage in the trunk of his car, which was parked nearby. Then, they all began to saunter along the lane, Alex with the boys ahead, while the girls followed a little further behind.

Kelly was holding Charlie's lead as he trotted happily by her feet.

'What a nice, doggie!' said Efi, cooing over Charlie. 'He's so good!'

'Oh!' said Kelly, chortling. 'He is *now*. He was a right monster on my first day. He growled at me and everything!' For a while, she relayed a little about the dog's antics and they laughed, while Kelly mentally thanked her lucky stars that, at least for now, Lauren kept quiet inside her head.

'And the boys? They seem like well-mannered children.'

'Oh yes, they really are, Efi. Quite marvellous...' Kelly's voice trailed off as she wondered if she should mention how their mother's passing had affected them. Despite texting and phoning back and forth with Efi the whole week, Kelly hadn't really imparted any information about what was going on in the house.

'And... how are things with... you know?' Efi's hushed tone caused Kelly to return to the present and face her again just as Efi lifted her chin to point to Alex, an impish smile on her face.

Alex, who was walking a good distance up ahead, too far to hear, was chatting to his kids at the time. He was holding Tommy by the hand, a sight that caused Kelly's heart to melt. She loved the tenderness he showed to his children, and the sweet manner he had with his youngest especially, like the way he held him against his chest in the evenings as they all watched TV, when the little one's eyelids began to grow heavy.

These days, the children spent more time with their father in the evenings and it seemed precious to them all. It meant they went to bed a little later than they used to, but it was the norm in Greece for children to go to bed around nine o'clock or even later. Alex and the boys were benefiting from this new arrangement as the extra time they spent in the living room after dinner often led to cheerful chats and laughter. And cuddles. Lots of cuddles between him and the boys.

'Kelly?'

She turned to find Efi eyeing her with curiosity.

Kelly shook her head. 'Sorry, I'm a bit tired, Efi. My mind's a little slow this morning,' she lied.

'You're daydreaming, more like...' Efi whispered, nudging her on the arm. 'I saw how you looked at him just now! Tell-me-everything!' she commanded with a snort.

Kelly rolled her eyes. It was futile to hide from her. 'Okay. But not now... Later...' she promised under her breath, then smiled. 'Now let's go catch up with the others! Alex says the caiques depart for Bourtzi every hour or so.' She checked her watch. 'Oh! The next one's leaving in five minutes. Hurry up!'

'Is that why they're rushing?' asked Efi, looking amused as she picked up her pace to match Kelly's.

They sped up, Charlie scampering along, his tongue lolling out of his mouth, making him look like he was offering a goofy smile as he met Kelly and Efi's gazes successively.

The girls reached Alex and the boys, laughing with the cuteness of the dog, and causing the others to turn and look at them over their shoulders. Now everyone was chortling at the sight of the pug's animated face. Realizing he was the centre of attention he began to bark with excitement.

'Come on, everyone!' said Alex, beckoning frantically. They'd just reached the seafront, and a caique with a canopy was in view. Out at sea, but close enough to be visible in stark detail, Bourtzi looked like a giant off-white seabird floating blissfully on the water.

A couple was boarding the caique at the time and it seemed half-full already. 'Thank goodness! No one else is waiting to board!' said Alex, checking his watch. 'Come on, everybody! Bourtzi, here we come!' he exclaimed, causing Tommy to explode into enthused squeals as they all hurried along.

Chapter 22

The caique departed shortly after everyone had boarded, leaving behind the bustling cafés along the promenade.

Kelly sat beside Efi, Charlie lying on the floor by her feet. She grew silent as the caique picked up speed, and the cool sea breeze intensified, causing her senses to come alive as it hit her face. On the opposite bench, sat Alex and the boys, their faces bright as they looked back at her and Efi.

Tommy grew excited, bordering on delirious, as they neared Bourtzi. Nikos's eyes caressed the fortified little isle as Alex began to talk about their mother, and the day they'd been there last. As for Stratos, he had grown quiet, just listening to Alex relay their old family memories, his eyes, wistful, focusing far.

Kelly watched Stratos, her chest tightening with sympathy. She could feel with every fibre of her being his nostalgia for the days when his mother was still around.

All at once, she heard a faint whisper. At first, she thought it was Efi, so she turned to her and said, 'Huh? What was that?'

Efi gave a frown. 'What? I didn't say anything,' she said with a shrug and returned her attention to her phone screen to resume her communication with her boyfriend in Athens.

Kelly shook her head and looked towards Bourtzi again. Another whisper came, and it was a little louder this time, but she still couldn't make out the words. She wondered, mystified, if it was Lauren. As if willing herself to prick up her ears more efficiently, she raised a hand on one ear, cupping it to block the breeze as her gaze lowered to meet the dog's. Charlie returned a mute gaze, his face serene.

Yes, it's me... she heard clearly inside her head. Lauren continued talking but Kelly kept losing her after every few words. *...weak away from home... not enough energy*

Running Haunted

channelled from you yet... turn on the radio... ask Alex to name his favourite station.... Do it! Now!

Nothing else came after that urgent request, and Kelly, willing to help, took her phone out of her bag and tapped on the radio app. Attaching the headphones, she turned to Alex. 'Do you know of any good stations? Thought I'd put on some music for us all.'

Alex's face brightened. 'Good idea, Kelly. There's a local station that plays beautiful folk music on Sunday mornings.'

He gave her the frequency and Kelly tuned in as quickly as she could. For some reason, Lauren had seemed to be in a hurry, which she didn't understand, but was happy to oblige, now because of her mystification more than anything else.

As soon as she tuned to the station, nostalgic chords of a well-known folk song by Hatzidakis filled the salty air. Everyone began to move their heads along to the rhythm and Alex whistled the tune as well. The song ended soon and another one came on – a famous bouzouki melody. Somehow, this one caused Alex, Stratos and Nikos to become rigid at once. It took Kelly a few moments to work out the reason. When she did, she gave an audible gasp, then said, 'Oh... *Ta paidia tou Pirea* by Melina Merkouri. What a wonderful song! Perfect for a Sunday morning...'

'Of course, it is. It's from her movie Never on Sunday, after all,' said Alex, chuckling, obviously in an attempt to hide his inner thoughts, but the shadow that had darkened his features was too evident to miss.

'It's the song we were telling you about the other day, Tommy,' said Stratos to his little brother.

'Yes! That's the song Mum would sing to us to get us to wake up if we were being lazy in the morning,' commented Nikos with a smile. His cheeks were flushed pink, eyes dreamy when he turned them towards Bourtzi again. They were nearly there. Every detail on the aged fortress walls and in every nook and corner was becoming more alive by the second.

'Strange that song should come on the radio now, don't you think, Dad?' asked Nikos.

Alex seemed too overwhelmed to speak. It was no surprise Stratos beat him to it.

'I think Mum knows we are thinking of her today. It's a sign from her. It has to be! What do you think, Dad?'

Alex squeezed Stratos's arm, then put out a tender hand to caress the heads of his younger boys in succession. Finally, with a little effort, he said, 'Yes. I am quite sure of it,' he said in a frail voice, looking away.

As the song continued to play, Kelly watched them all and silently gave kudos to Lauren for what she had done. *She certainly is amazing... I'd better listen to all her requests if that's the kind of impact they're likely to have on Alex and the boys... But, the only thing that bothers me... He doesn't seem to be over her yet. Not one bit...*

Kelly felt disillusioned in her own pursuit for romantic happiness, yet she was determined to help Lauren and her family find healing, no matter what. With a shake of her head, she chased away the sad thought that Alex would never be interested in her that way.

When the song ended, she exited her radio app and looked up, managing a bright smile, just as the captain moored the caique on the tiny dock at Bourtzi.

*****

As soon as they disembarked, Tommy began to run towards the castle gate. 'Don't go too far, Tommy! Stay where we can see you!' shouted out Alex, then repeated the same instruction to Nikos, who nodded his head in agreement as he hurried to follow his little brother, eager to explore.

The others sauntered behind them. Only about a dozen or so other tourists had got off the caique so it was fairly quiet.

The tourists had spread out in all possible directions like sheep let out of the pen to graze freely on a green pasture.

Stratos turned to Kelly, his face eager. 'Shall I take the lead now, Kelly?' He pointed to Charlie.

Kelly paused, happy for the offer, but had to keep the dog near her in case Lauren wanted to communicate again. 'Sure!' she said as she handed him the lead. 'But please don't wander off. I need to monitor him, make sure he behaves at all times.'

Stratos was happy to oblige and they all resumed walking towards the castle gate. With every step they made, the fortified castle seemed all the more magnificent, its ancient stone walls gleaming under the strong sunshine.

'Wow... It's so beautiful... How old is it, Alex? Do you know?' asked Efi.

The question seemed to prompt Alex to shift into full work mode. Kelly admired him silently as he assumed his professional stance, chest puffed out, an arm sweeping theatrically to point to the ancient edifice as he began to say, 'Oh! It's quite old, yes. Bourtzi was built by the Venetians in 1471. Originally, thick chains connected this fortress to the mainland to stop enemy ships—pirate ones included—from reaching the city. At some point, the executioner of Palamidi Castle...' he pointed to the magnificent fort on top of the taller peak over Nafplio, '... lived here in Bourtzi. This was his home, as strange as it sounds!'

'But why here?' asked Efi, a deep frown on her face.

Alex shrugged, then chuckled. 'I guess no one in the city wanted an executioner as their neighbour.'

'Makes sense!' said Stratos, bursting into a snorting laugh.

'Bourtzi was a prison too at some point, wasn't it?' asked Kelly, who'd heard that somewhere once.

'Indeed. Theodoros Kolokotronis, the hero of the Greek War of Independence, was jailed here as well as on Palamidi.' He pointed at the castle across the distance again and added, 'His tiny prison carved in the rock up there is a bleak tourist attraction today.'

A few silent moments ensued where, undoubtedly, they all spared sorry thoughts for the great man, who had been treated so unfairly by the very people he'd fought to save. Then, as if in a conscious attempt to lift the mood, Alex's eyes lit up and he burst out, 'In the 1960s and 1970s, would you believe, there used to be a small hotel with a restaurant right here in Bourtzi!'

This caused everyone to gawp at him as they went up the steps of the castle together. Guessing their disbelief, Alex assured them he wasn't joking.

The castle seemed too small and lacking the individual spaces to house a hotel, let alone a functioning restaurant too. Stunned to silence, Kelly began to look around at the forlorn surroundings with new eyes.

Tommy and Nikos ran towards them then, their faces flushed. They'd been dashing here and there around the courtyard all this time.

'Dad! Nikos and I went up those steps on the far wall! The view is great from up there! Come! I'll show you!' said Tommy tugging Alex's hand. Excusing himself, Alex told the girls he'd be back soon and hurried away.

Stratos followed behind them with Charlie scuttling along at the end of the lead.

*****

Kelly and Efi stood for a while to admire the magnificent view of Nafplio, and that of Argos Castle on the other side of Bourtzi, then went through the gate on their own, leaving the others behind. Kelly wasn't keen to lose visual contact with the dog, but Efi was insistent.

They entered a medium-sized room that was empty of furniture. Its stony walls were just as bare. A small canon stood by a window and an ancient-looking canon ball sat beside it inside a cradle made of iron and stone. Having taken a few moments to admire them, Kelly moved towards the window. It was arched, with beautiful ironwork.

She admired the sea view that it offered and, all the while, enjoyed the eerie silence, thankful that Efi wasn't unleashing the volley of questions she'd expected.

Kelly gave a luxurious sigh as she continued to gaze out to the vast sea. It shimmered silver in the morning light in a mesmerising way, flowing peacefully. Small waves crashed softly against the castle wall underneath, eliciting plopping sounds and faint sighs that delighted Kelly's ears.

Then Efi's voice echoed, breaking the spell. Kelly turned to see that she'd just put her phone away. 'So, tell me everything! I've waited for so long! Start with the juicy details. Alex and the kids could come in any minute!' Efi nudged Kelly on the arm, eyes twinkling.

Kelly's heart sank. *So much for avoiding the third degree. But what is there to tell her? Nothing really. I can't tell her about Lauren. Efi has neither the knowledge nor the experience necessary to believe me or to even understand...* She took a deep breath of the salty air, then shook her head. 'Really, not much to say. And there are no juicy details. Don't be ridiculous.'

'But I've seen how he looks at you! You must be joking!'

Kelly knitted her brows. 'What? How does he look at me?'

'Hello? Like he wants to gobble you up?'

'Now I know you're being absurd, Efi. The man's a widower. He's not over his wife's passing yet and has no romantic interests in me, that's for certain.'

Efi put her hands on her waist and huffed. 'That's not what his eyes say, girlfriend.'

'Why? What could you possibly decipher from that?'

'You forget my amateur dramatics classes? Body language is one of the skills actors are required to master and I've learned a lot! I know what I'm talking about. Throughout the—albeit short—boat ride just now, Alex didn't take his eyes off you. And, there's the other thing.'

'What other thing?' Kelly had grown excited to hear all that. Her voice had sounded breathless in her own ears.

'The toes of his shoes.'

Kelly screwed up her face. 'Huh?'

'He kept shifting his position, but no matter how he sat, the toes of his shoes never stopped pointing to you.'

'Oh come on! When did you see all that? You barely took your eyes from your phone!'

'I'm telling you, I kept watching him. In between texting, of course.'

'And the shoes thing means he's into me? Are you sure?'

Efi rolled her eyes. 'Hello? Totally!' She waved dismissively. 'And surely you've noticed how his voice turns velvety when he talks to you. He even mirrors your expressions. Haven't you noticed that, at least?'

Kelly shook her head and grimaced, unwilling to take all that seriously for fear more disillusionment awaited her in future. All she knew was that his face had crumbled with upset earlier when his wife was mentioned. 'Whatever…' she said with a vague wave of her hand before turning around.

Right on cue, excited chatter echoed from the threshold as a bunch of tourists entered to look around the space. Alex and the boys arrived closely behind, wide smiles spread across their faces.

Chapter 23

Everyone came out to a paved stone terrace, high up over the sea. Their faces grew bright with admiration when they stood at the battlement and gazed out to sea through the wide rectangle gaps.

Efi, presumably taking the initiative to give Kelly and Alex a few private moments, coaxed the boys into taking a wide staircase to explore a small yard below.

Eager to keep the dog around in case Lauren needed to communicate, Kelly called after Nikos, who held the lead at the time, asking him to hand it over before following the others down the steps.

The other visitors had all done the same already, and now, she was standing alone with Alex, who gazed out to sea silently, while the dog returned to her a mute gaze.

Alex broke the silence first, a dreamy look in his eyes when he turned to her to say, 'I'm so glad you and Efi could join us today, Kelly. I have to say, my boys seem different when you're around... I really feel they are benefiting from your presence in their lives. Me too, of course... We all are. You're such a treasure to us all.'

For some strange reason she couldn't comprehend, a huge lump lodged in her throat then and all she could do was smile faintly, nodding her understanding. She was still trying to find something to say when the dog barked. They both looked down at him, to find him looking all goofy and adorable, his tongue lolling out of his mouth. Kelly bent over to pat his head and Alex chortled when he followed suit.

'Yes, you little rascal! You're a real treasure to us, too... You make us laugh, don't you?' said Alex. Straightening to meet her eyes, he added, 'I feel so blessed, Kelly! Suddenly, I see it. I can't explain it, but something shifted in me since that night when I had this awful quarrel with Stratos... You helped me so much to see the truth that had been staring me right in the face all along. I've been such an idiot. And I can't thank you enough for helping me to see the truth.'

'Oh, it was nothing,' she said with a pleasant smile.

'No… it was *everything*…' He reached out and touched her upper arm gently. Through the fabric of her long sleeve, she felt the warmth of his hand and her heart fluttered, sending shivers to travel down her spine. *Did the breeze just pick up?*

Lost in a whirl of thoughts for the next few moments, as his gentle gaze kept her captive, she wondered if her hopes for romance with him could ever be realized. Lauren felt so real… so very much alive. That made her interest in Alex feel wrong; it was like she had her sights on someone else's man, if that made any sense at all.

Suddenly, as if in a dream, she saw his brow etch deeply, then his mouth gaped open in surprise. The scarf that she had tied in a knot on the back of her head had come undone following a strong gust of wind. She knew in an instant, when the strands she'd tied with it fell on her temples and shoulders, confirming the panicking thought that the scarf was airborne. In a split second, she saw one of its ends fly, like a battle banner, just over her eyes.

Her heart giving a thump, she raised a quick hand to catch it before it got swept away, and over the edge, by the wind. At the same time, he raised his hand too, capturing hers that had got hold of the scarf, his fist closing in around her own as comforting as a warm blanket.

'Oops, sorry!' he said, chuckling nervously, but didn't let go. Her gaze locked with his as she lowered her hand slowly, lips twitching.

And now, she'd frozen in place, realizing he still hadn't let go. Delicious warm sensations shot arrows of bliss up her chest. They caused her heart to bloom as if it were about to explode like a firework on a clear night sky.

When she looked down at their joined hands, he let go as if scalded.

'Oh. I didn't mean to do that, sorry. Glad you got the scarf in time...' He chuckled, then turned away to look out to sea. 'Wow. The wind picked up quickly. Let's hope it remains sunny, though,' he added, still looking away.

She cleared her throat, then said, 'Oh, I wouldn't worry about that. I checked the weather report first thing this morning. It'll be warm and sunny all day.'

Now, she was playing with the scarf nervously in one hand, unsure if she should wear it again in case the wind reclaimed it. *Maybe I should just put it in my pocket... Surely it will still allow Lauren to speak to me if she wants to.* Suddenly, she heard Alex's voice ring heavy with intrigue.

'Wait... I know that scarf...' A shadow darkened his features. 'Is it... Lauren's?' he mumbled a moment later, eyes intense.

She scrunched up her face and felt herself cower a little. 'I'm sorry. Charlie brought it to my room the other night. I wasn't thinking, and back then I didn't know he had a knack for sharing Lauren's things with us from your wardrobe. It was silly of me to wear it. I can see it has upset you... I do apologise. Here...' Even though she needed the scarf, it felt right to offer it to him, but instead of taking it, he put up both hands to wave them fiercely.

'No, no! Keep it! I insist.' Looking down at the dog, who sat on his hind legs now, an intelligent look in his eyes, he added, 'Seems to me the dog has more sense than I do these days. I'll go with his instinct. If he thinks you should be wearing Lauren's scarf, then so you should.' He flashed a bright grin. 'Besides, it was just sitting in the wardrobe, and it does look good on you.'

In the short silence that ensued, the look in his eyes deepened as he held her gaze captive. This caused Kelly's mind to be hurled into a torrent of pressing questions anew. *Is he flirting with me? But he's still grieving, isn't he? Is he just being nice then? But what about that deep gaze, the way he held my hand earlier? Oh, so many mixed signals!*

'Okay then... I'll just put the scarf in my pocket for now. You never know with the wind,' she said finally, looking away. He chuckled to that, and then, Lauren's voice echoed in her head, albeit faintly. *Good... Finally, he listens. Now, let go of the lead please, Kelly! Do it now!*

Running on automatic, Kelly opened her hand. At once, Charlie lunged forward and began to sprint towards the top of the stairs. Two elderly women were ascending at the time.

The moment they reached the terrace, they both cooed over the dog, bending over to shower him with affection.

Mystified as to why Lauren had asked her to do that, Kelly remained glued to her spot as she watched the strangers take turns in patting the dog and scratch his chin. The little scoundrel seemed to be enjoying it all and now fell on his back, exposing his belly to their affectionate attentions.

Alex gave a guffaw and rushed over to the women, causing Kelly to approach too, albeit numbly.

As soon as he got there to get hold of the lead and say hi, the ladies began to pose questions about Charlie. When Kelly joined them, the ladies were offering the information that they were Americans living in Italy and touring the Peloponnese on their bicycles. Without being asked, they began to recite the names of the places they'd visited already.

'Wow, lucky you... And I must say, you chose well to travel in this manner,' said Alex, standing tall, having no trouble in shifting to his professional mode in an instant. 'I expect it allows you to sample original Greek life, since you travel off the tourist trail, taking time to absorb the world around you fully, at your own pace.'

'Hey, that was the whole idea!' said the one that seemed to be the chattier of the two. The women looked almost identical. Tall and skinny, dressed in similar-style sandals, capris and t-shirts, they both wore baseball hats and dark sunglasses, their hair long and flimsy grey. One had a ponytail, the other a plait.

The former was the chattier one, and she continued to talk, relaying their experiences.

A few moments later, Efi and the others materialized at the top of the stairs behind them, causing Alex to beckon them over, his eyes ablaze with excitement. 'Come! Let me introduce you to these lovely American ladies from Italy!'

As Efi and the boys approached, he chuckled and added, 'Wait! How can I? I don't even know your names yet. I am Alex, by the way.' He extended his hand to shake, causing them both to break into wide grins.

'I am Kelly,' said the chatty one with the ponytail. 'And this is my friend, Lauren.'

'Kelly? Lauren?' said Alex glassy-eyed, his hand still extended mid-air, even though the ladies had retracted their hands moments ago, having both shaken hands with him. Suddenly, he seemed to realize and pulled back his hand, hiding it in his jacket pocket. 'Wait... that's incredible...'

'Why? I don't understand,' said the woman with the plait.

Kelly had frozen, mystified again. *Lauren did this! Of course. But wait... Why does the plait seem familiar?*

Alex cleared his throat, snapping her back to reality. 'Sorry... It's just a weird coincidence, that's all. This lady here is my housekeeper. Her name is Kelly. And we were just discussing my deceased wife... whose name was Lauren.'

'Wow, that is amazing!' said the ponytailed woman, her face bright.

'Perhaps it's a sign. Sounds like your wife is watching you from heaven,' said the woman with the plait.

'Yes...' he said after a short hesitation, 'My children and I had this very impression earlier on.' He brushed his hair back from his forehead, sounding a little breathless when he added, 'It's a little creepy, actually.'

'Oh, there's nothing creepy about our loved ones. They're just trying to communicate, that's all,' said the woman with the ponytail.

'I guess so,' said Alex, then turned to Efi and the boys to make introductions. The boys seemed exuberant and began to make sounds about this being a sign too. Alex was looking at the ladies with an open smile, and to the long plaited hair of the lady called Lauren especially.

A little later, the Americans said their goodbyes and moved to the battlement, while the others turned around to get out of the castle the way they'd come. Alex fell into step beside Kelly, who walked alone at the back with the dog. She thought he was about to speak, but he got hold of her arm instead. It caused her to stop and look at him as the others kept sauntering along.

'Kelly? Do you also think that Lauren is sending us signs today?'

'Yes, I think so.'

'But what does it mean? What does it all mean?'

'I think she's trying to tell you that you've made the right decision to open the subject about her with the children...' She saw his eyes sparkle with contentment at that notion and continued, 'If you ask me, I think that the more you stay that course, the more she's likely to confirm you're doing the right thing by bringing to you little coincidences such as these.'

He shook his head and resumed walking, causing her to follow. 'Being a Greek, I am spiritual enough, Kelly... Don't get me wrong... I do believe in God... I believe the spirits of our departed loved ones watch over us but, to tell you the truth, I don't know how to deal with this. Spooky things don't happen in my world. But, if it helps me and the children, I'm game, you know?'

'I'm glad to hear it, Alex. Just keep an open mind. That's my advice to you.'

The others had sped up in the meantime and were out of sight already. The two of them were making their way out through a series of adjoining chambers when he suddenly turned to her and whispered, 'You know... Lauren only wore her hair in a plait once as I remember. On one of our earliest dates. You may remember her wearing her hair like that in one of the photos you saw with us the other day. We were in an Italian restaurant, would you believe?'

'Really?' she said wide-eyed, realizing why the plait rang a bell. Of course, she remembered the photo. The both of them were pictured with full plates of spaghetti before them, a glass with breadsticks in it sitting beside a salad platter between them.

'Perhaps I'm reading too much into it... but to meet a lady who lives in Italy, wears a plait and is called Lauren... just as we were talking about her... This is just too much to put down to coincidence, don't you think?'

'I guess...'

'And what about Charlie, huh? What he just did, running to these ladies... What happened there, Kelly? You were holding the lead, no?'

'Yes. But it just slipped away. I must have been holding it loosely...' she lied, dropping her gaze to the dog.

'But... Charlie is acting strange, isn't he? Bringing you Lauren's scarf, bringing the boys that old photo of her and me... Could... Could it be that the dog can communicate with her? I know it sounds strange but... they'd always been very close.'

Kelly was tongue-tied. What was she to say?

'Kelly?'

'Sorry, I heard you, but I don't know. Maybe you're right.'

He sniggered. 'I wouldn't put it past Lauren, you know... She always had a wicked sense of humour. She's probably in heaven right now looking down, orchestrating these pranks on us and having a right laugh,' he said with a wry smile.

Before she could comment, Kelly was silenced by the sound of laughter, clear as crystal, echoing inside her head. 'Oh, Alex! Finally I'm getting through to you. You're not as daft as I remember, thank goodness...'

Alex's eyes remained glued to Kelly's face, but she was too distracted listening to Lauren to reply to him. All she managed was a non-committal shrug as she pressed her lips together.

Right then, Lauren's voice turned serious inside her mind as she said, 'Thank you, Kelly. You're doing wonderfully! And I'll be out of your hair soon, I promise. Just keep doing as I tell you… Please. You're all I have.'

Chapter 24

When they disembarked from the caique back at the port, Alex made sounds about coffee and refreshments. Being the gentleman that he was, he pointed vaguely at the cafés lining the promenade and addressed Kelly and Efi to say, 'We boys will leave it to you ladies to decide. Take your pick.'

Efi chuckled, but before she could say anything, Kelly, remembering what Alan had advised her to do, piped up, 'Perhaps if we don't sit here at the seafront?'

Alex turned to her swiftly, eyes dancing. 'Sure. Would you prefer Syntagma Square?'

Kelly smiled sweetly, then shook her head. 'Actually, I was thinking of the café in the old train station building.' She tilted her head and shaded her eyes against the sunshine so she could see him more clearly against the glare. 'At the railway park?'

Alex widened his eyes, lips parting with what looked like a silent gasp.

Before he could speak, Stratos cut in excitedly, 'Oh! Great idea! I remember that café, Dad. You and mum used to take us there on Sundays, remember?'

'Yes, of course, I do.'

'You remember, Nikos?' asked Stratos.

His face bright, Nikos nodded frantically, then looked up at his father. 'Can we go there please, Dad? I'd like to see it again.'

Alex patted the boy's shoulder, a wry smile playing on his lips. Then, his expression brightening, he turned to Kelly. 'Great idea. Let's go, guys!'

He pointed the way and they took a bustling lane that led them to Syntagma square, the heart of the historical quarter. Every corner seemed to swarm with visitors from all over the world, it seemed, judging from the various languages that reached Kelly's ears as they made their way leisurely.

The children were chattering to each other, bantering and joking, their exuberance alight on their faces. Efi started a conversation with Alex, asking about the tourism in the town, its ebbs and flows throughout the year, and he offered his plans for the future to expand his business.

At first, Kelly contributed to the conversation but, as they left the bustling lanes behind to emerge into Trion Navarchon Square, she fell silent, wondering where Lauren's plan was taking her. The spirit had grown quiet for now, and she felt thankful for that as she ambled across the square with the others, Charlie making his way alongside her at the end of the lead.

The strange coincidences about Lauren this morning had seemed to overwhelm the family, filling their hearts with a sense of wonder.

But what is the spirit trying to do exactly? I guess she wants them to discuss her openly more and more... like the boys wanted. Like Alex needed, perhaps, without even realizing it, so he could heal too...

Still, there was something else that nagged at Kelly from the darkest recesses of her brain. It suggested Lauren had another motive which she couldn't fathom, somehow. *I'll carry on doing as she asks, all the same. I'll do all I can to help that poor spirit move on to a higher plane and find peace at last...*

*****

The railway park was lush and just as busy as the rest of the historical town centre, owing to a craft fair that seemed to be in full swing when they got there. The numerous stalls that stood side by side displayed all sorts of jewellery and gift items as well as organic soaps and scented candles that released their heavenly fragrance into the tender breeze.

The stalls were placed on either side of a path lined with leafy trees and bushes. When they came across what seemed like an antique steam engine, the boys ran forth to explore it all around.

Alex chuckled as he watched them go and pointed at the café a little further away, telling them this was the original building of the town's old train station. Soon, they had all gathered to stand before the steam engine to admire it. Alex said it was on permanent display there and that it dated from the 1880s. In Venetian times, this area was out of the city walls and was covered with water. During the second Turkish occupation in the 1720s, the Turks had brought in soil to turn it into land.

Nowadays, the old train station building, having been compartmentalized, served the people of Nafplio as a music school, a children's museum and a café too. The latter operated at the centre of the building.

Behind the large glass panes on either side of the beautiful entrance, the seating area of the café spread out to the back end of the building. Lush sofas and armchairs made the many patrons appear super-relaxed as they lounged and enjoyed their coffees, in typical Greek-style, while chattering with friends and family.

An eager waiter showed Kelly, Alex and Efi to a large, empty table near the façade. The boys were still lingering by the steam engine, reluctant to walk away just yet. A toddler, held by the sure hands of his father, was sitting on the top, his face bright as he clapped his hands together. When Tommy turned to his father across the distance, a pleading look in his eyes, Alex put up a shaking finger, his face stern.

'No, Tommy. Don't even think about it. You're a big boy now. You can't sit up there any more.'

Tommy bent his head, defeated, and Alex turned to the girls and chuckled. 'Boys, huh! The turmoil never ends. And I got three!' Everyone laughed, then Alex called the boys over. 'Come and tell us what you want to order, guys!'

As his children rushed over, Kelly felt amazed by the transformation. Not that the boys had been insolent at any point, but it was evident now that they were more eager than ever to listen to their father.

The boys went first to order refreshments and cakes, then the waiter turned to Kelly and Efi. 'Ladies? What will you have?'

As Efi gave her order, Lauren's voice sounded loud and clear in Kelly's mind. 'Would you mind if I ordered for you, Kelly?'

Kelly didn't know what to do. *Should I nod?* she wondered. Just then, Lauren laughed, a sound crystal clear like running water on a mountain waterfall. 'I can hear you, Kelly. All you need to do is think. Thank you. Please order an almond-flavour coffee... And a *kataifi*. I always enjoyed these here.'

Amazed that she could hear her so clearly now, much better than she had at the beginning of the day, Kelly looked up, feeling rather disoriented. That's when she realized, panicking, that everyone, including the waiter, had turned into frozen statues as they waited for her to speak.

Kelly cleared her throat. 'Sorry. I was miles away just now...' she said feebly, fanning her face like an idiot.

'That's okay,' said Alex with a cute grin. 'So what will you have?'

Her eyes glued to his, she said, 'I think I'll have an almond-flavoured coffee.' With a lot of effort, as she found it hard to break away from Alex's astounded gaze, she looked up to the waiter to add, 'And a *kataifi* please.' She forced a nonchalant smile, but only she knew how hard this was. She was aware she'd just dropped a bomb. Alex and the two older boys, who obviously remembered Lauren's usual order in this café, were gawping at her.

She smiled again, a little more confidently now, and ventured another look towards Alex.

His eyes were huge, studying her intently. 'I can't believe it...' he said in a faint whisper, his lips trembling slightly.

'Neither can I...' mumbled Stratos, his eyes glazed over as he shook his head softly from side to side.

'What?' she said, feigning nonchalance.

Alex looked at Stratos, then Nikos, and they all pressed their lips together. 'Nothing,' said Alex, then shared a giggle with the boys. Tommy nudged Nikos on the elbow, obviously demanding to be told what was so funny. Nikos leaned over to whisper in his little brother's ear, causing Tommy's eyes to come alive with exploding stars, his lips parting with awe as he turned to Kelly.

'That's it...' Kelly heard Lauren say in her head then. 'The connection's made. I'm so pleased!'

Connection? What connection? thought Kelly, but even though Lauren had said she could hear her, she never gave her an answer. All Kelly heard now was the sound of Lauren's giggles that slowly began to fade until they disappeared from her mind altogether.

Chapter 25

When they left the park behind, Alex made sounds about returning home with the kids. He then asked the girls if they wanted to come along, or if they preferred to spend some time alone in town. In the latter case, he offered to return to Nafplio to pick them up in the car later so Efi could visit the house.

Before Kelly could ask Efi what she wanted to do, Efi checked her watch and yelped. 'Goodness me! It's one o' clock already! Time just flew by!'

'Yes, that's what usually happens when you're having so much fun...' said Alex, his eyes flitting to Kelly towards the end of the sentence.

'I've had a wonderful time with you guys...' Efi began to say, placing a hand on her heart.

'Surely you're not leaving Nafplio yet!' cut in Kelly. When they all turned to face her, startled, she realized her voice had sounded a little louder than she'd intended. She'd hardly spent five minutes alone with her friend all morning. She'd missed her a lot, even though it'd been only a week since they parted.

'I'm afraid I have to...' said Efi. 'It'll take me almost two hours to get to the city in my old banger, and I need to prepare for my presentation tomorrow.' She rolled her eyes and added, 'The big bosses are arriving early in the morning from the headquarters, and we're all expected to present our sales stats for the trimester. I told you on the phone last Friday, didn't I?'

Kelly pressed her lips together and nodded. 'Yes, you did...'

'Don't worry, Kelly. You and I can chat lots on the phone tonight.' She gave her a wicked smile, then pointed the way forward with a little wave. 'So let's go, guys. I parked my car near the hotel. Take us there on the shortest route please,

Alex. These lanes all look the same to me!' Efi gave a loud guffaw and everyone burst into laughter, causing Kelly's mood to lift again.

Kelly scolded herself inwardly for sounding so dramatic earlier. After all, she had found herself a bunch of new friends since last Sunday... *Or rather, a new family...*

She half-expected a comment from Lauren to her peculiar thought, but the eerie silence in her mind continued, surprising her. Lauren had been silent since placing her order at the café about an hour earlier. Furthermore, Kelly's previous notion to think of Alex and his kids as her new family had seemed foreign, somehow. As if it'd been put upon her by Lauren herself...

With an inaudible gasp, she brought a hand to her mouth, her eyes dropping to the cement tiles as she continued to walk with the others along the pavement. *Is this what she is after? Of course... She wants me to take her place!* Oddly, instead of panicking or bothering her, the realization caused her heart to thump, then bloom with excitement.

She stole a glance towards Alex, who was busy chatting with Efi at the time. In the strong sunlight, his face looked bright, eyes dancing. He had rolled up his shirt sleeves to the elbows, veins and sinews bulging under his translucent olive skin. His well-shaped, long legs made quick progress as he paced energetically in his black, stylish boot-cut jeans, the tight fit on his hips and around his thighs causing her to reel with desire. Of course, she noticed him... every day she did. But, until that moment, he'd felt out of bounds.

That was because of Lauren, who felt so very much alive to her. *But now, knowing she wants me to take her place in her home... Goodness me, in her bed too! Is that what she referred to when she spoke of a connection earlier? My connection with her family?*

Her head began to spin with tantalizing images of her and Alex together, wearing very little or nothing at all in his bed, their bodies entwined, the smell of his skin and his aftershave rich in her nostrils. Now, thanks to Lauren's obvious intention, dreaming of him was becoming a different matter altogether.

She chastised herself silently for allowing her mind to wander like that as if she were some stupid schoolgirl. But then, she thought, why not? *Having Lauren's blessing makes Alex fair game. And he seems to like me… like, a lot…* She turned to steal another glance at him and, as if on cue, he turned his head and captured her gaze, his lips curling up into a sweet smile.

Boosted by a newfound sense of confidence, Kelly offered him a wide smile, her heart blossoming.

*****

Efi kissed Kelly goodbye and shook hands with Alex, then waved playfully to the kids before getting in her car. With one last wave and a blown kiss from the driver's seat, she was gone.

As if sensing Kelly's sense of sadness at Efi's departure, Alex placed a tender hand on her shoulder. 'You okay, Kelly?'

She offered a faint smile and nodded. 'Of course, I'm okay.' She gestured them all forward and began to walk ahead towards Alex's car. It wasn't that she was hurrying to return home, but rather an attempt to escape Alex's penetrating gaze. It was evident he could sense her sadness and hadn't been convinced by her answer.

She heard Alex prompt the kids to follow him, then his heavy footfalls echoed in her ears as he hurried to fall into step beside her. When he did, he got hold of her hand, much to her surprise, and that caused her to stop short.

'Hey… it's okay to feel sad, Kelly. Nothing wrong with that…' He looked deeply into her eyes.

Kelly, frozen by surprise, and by the warm, delicious sensation of her hand encased in his, realized in panic now that they had both stopped walking. What's more, the kids had gathered around them, but she didn't dare break her gaze with Alex and look at them. She could see them with her peripheral vision and also knew that the dog, who Nikos was holding by the lead at the time, had come to sit by her feet. That, she knew from the heavy panting that echoed from the pavement.

When Alex squeezed her hand in his gently, she snapped out of her trance. To her horror, with the kids still watching, she saw his hand let go of hers, then move up, ever so slowly, to brush her cheek with light fingers. She raised her own hand too, just as he removed his, to find her face was wet with tears. *How long have I been crying? Oh, God! They've all seen me cry! What they must think!*

As if guessing her thoughts, Alex shook his head. 'I am so sorry, Kelly. I shouldn't have asked you to join us. I can be such an idiot sometimes. Now I realize you'd have preferred to spend time alone with your friend and catch up. By inviting you, I put you on the spot and, of course, you had to say yes.'

'No! It's not like that at all!' she protested, lowering her hand, and then, somehow, he took it in his again. This time, despite herself, she ventured a look towards the boys. Surprisingly, they didn't seem to mind their father holding her hand. If anything, they were watching with rapt attention, and Tommy was even smiling to his ears.

Before she could recover from her astonishment, Alex's voice, heavy with regret, caused her to face him again. 'Of course, it is like that, and please don't say otherwise, Kelly. I was so selfish, so insensitive. I know we had a great time together, and I am thankful for that, but I think you'd have been happier today had you spent some quality time alone with your friend.'

She shook her head profusely and opened her mouth to tell him that he was wrong to think that, but before she could speak he put up a firm hand.

'No! I must insist. Please, Kelly, have a think about it and tell me in your own time how I can make it up to you. Perhaps you'd like to invite Efi to return to Nafplio another weekend? I'd happily give you the whole Sunday off to spend with her, possibly half of the Saturday too. I'll work things out with the boys, somehow, if you let me know in advance. And I'll gladly book Efi in my hotel for the weekend. Free of charge, of course...'

Finally, Kelly found her voice. 'What? No way! But thank you. And it's not like that. Not at all. Yes, I wish I'd spent more time with Efi today, but I am not devastated or anything...'

'But you were crying just now, Kelly...'

'I know... It wasn't about Efi, though...'

'It wasn't? Then why were you crying?'

Kelly grew speechless. What was she to say? She had no idea herself where those tears had come from. *What's going on? Is it Lauren? Is she haunting me now the way she does with Charlie? Causing me to do things despite myself? Or is there an underlying sadness about Efi's departure I hadn't realized?*

Seeing that all four of them continued to stare at her, she grew so embarrassed that she had to lie. 'It's... erm... personal. But it's nothing serious. No need to worry. I'm fine.' She resumed walking, and everyone followed behind her. In the few moments it took them to reach her, she almost felt their eyes on her back, their mystification palpable, penetrating her flesh like bullets.

Chapter 26

When they got out of the car outside the house, Tommy rushed in through the garden gate first, the others following, laughing out loud.

Tommy was practically running, holding the dog before him with outstretched arms. Charlie had been whimpering for the last five minutes in the car, and they'd all guessed he was desperate to relieve himself.

As soon as his paws touched the lawn, the pug rushed like a shot to the far corner of the garden where he usually did his business.

Kelly moved towards the front door and was in the process of retrieving the key from her bag when she heard Alex's voice behind her. He was greeting someone and she turned around to see who that was.

To her dismay, she found him approaching Stella's fence. Following his gaze, her heart sank to find the odious woman standing by the railing of her porch, a deckchair laid out behind her. She had just removed a pair of stylish sunglasses from her face and was now holding them in her hand half-hidden behind her back. *Mad as a hatter! What's she hiding the glasses for?*

Kelly guessed Stella had been lounging in the deckchair and shot up eagerly as soon as she saw Alex. Her eyes that shone with enthusiasm told her as much. Kelly grimaced at the thought. *She's so eager, but it's all for nothing. She'll never put her grubby mitts on Alex!* She heard that thought inside her head and, again, it felt foreign. *Lauren?*

A low guttural sound echoed inside her mind. The sound turned into a laugh she easily identified as Lauren's.

'Yes... it is I. But don't worry, Kelly... I got your back. Go to her. Play nice. She shouldn't suspect...' Kelly didn't understand what Lauren meant, but since she'd decided to follow her instructions to the letter, she went along.

Kelly looked over her shoulder before moving forward. The dog had returned to the boys and they were now spread out on the lawn playing with a Frisbee, Charlie running to whichever of the boys held it at the time, only, of course, to start running anew, to the next one who caught it and so on.

She gave an open smile at the carefree sight, then looked ahead, sashaying towards the fence in her tight-fitting jeans, now fully aware she had an edge over that awful woman.

Not only did she live with the man Stella wanted, but she also had the ghost of his dead wife pining for her to take her place. *Beat that, weirdo!* she heard herself think as she reached Alex to stand beside him. *Yes, that's definitely my own thought,* she mused with a wicked smile. Stella had stepped down to her garden by then to stand before them on the other side of the fence.

Stella's features grew pinched with discomfort. She brought up a hand to fan her face, saying something about it being hot that day, but Kelly knew better. Delighted, she decided to crank it up a notch. She placed a hand on Alex's arm, offering him a sweet smile, then turned to glue her eyes on Stella. 'Hi, Stella. How are things?' she asked casually, acting like the man's wife.

When Stella's face contorted with evident annoyance, it took all of Kelly's restraint to keep a straight face.

'Good...' she mumbled, then ran an urgent hand through her hair.

'I was just saying to Stella... that we've been enjoying her delicious muffins...' cut in Alex, giving Kelly a meaningful glance before turning to face his neighbour again with a generous smile. 'But sadly, Stella, it's been a long winter and the boys have been putting on weight. We're all on a bit of a diet these days. That's why Kelly mentioned to you that there's no need to give us any more muffins.' He offered a charming smile and added, 'Honestly! It takes a lot of discipline to turn down culinary triumphs such as yours, Stella, but it's got to be done.' He winked at her for good measure, something that caused Stella's eyes to twinkle, first with surprise, then with something that bordered on adoration.

Huh! I'll show her! heard Kelly inside her mind. This wasn't Lauren's voice but, again, she was unsure if that was her own thought. Still, she was well aware her dismay was mushrooming inside. Having to hear Alex butter Stella up in this manner had made her nauseous.

'Ask her about her glasses, Kelly! Ask her if they are Dolce e Gabbana!' echoed Lauren's voice in her mind again.

'What?' whispered Kelly to herself, then brought a fist up to cover her mouth. She coughed, then whispered again as the other two continued to chat idly. 'What did you ask me?'

'Dolce e Gabbana! Ask her if those sunglasses she's holding in her hand are of that brand! Hurry! Before she goes! And stop whispering, Kelly... Just think the words. I can hear you, remember?'

Kelly nodded, even though there was no need for that either, then thought how peculiar Lauren's request was.

'Doesn't matter. Trust me and ask anyway! Please!'

Kelly cleared her throat to catch their attention. Then, she made an effort to sound nonchalant as she tilted her head, pointed to Stella vaguely and said, 'Say, Stella... I love your glasses. Couldn't help noticing them earlier when I saw you taking them off... Are they... Dolce e Gabbana, by any chance?'

To her surprise, Stella's whole demeanour changed in an instant. She banged an open hand on her chest with a gasp, then squinted her eyes to say, 'What? Why would you ask me that?'

'I... erm...' Kelly, who noticed Stella still kept the glasses out of sight behind her back, looked to Alex for help but of course he was of no use to her. He seemed to look at her just as inquisitively as Stella did, albeit without the kind of upset her eyes conveyed.

'It's just that.... I saw something similar in a fashion magazine the other day. Just wondering, that's all,' she said with a dismissive wave, then turned to look behind her and clear her head, her eyes seeking refuge to the delightful scene of the kids playing on the lawn. *That went well... Cheers, Lauren. Any other great ideas?* From the deep recesses of her mind, Lauren's laugh echoed maniacal this time. 'Good work, Kelly. She got the message. You're a star!'

Message? What message? Kelly thought, but no explanation came. Alex said her name then, and she turned to face him. He was smiling widely at her and then, to her pleasant surprise, he reached out and put his arm around her shoulders before turning to Stella to say, 'Anyway, Kelly and I have a favour to ask...'

Kelly's mind began to whirl, the earth under her feet threatening to disappear. *He put his arm around my shoulders!*

Stella's eyes had narrowed into slits as she looked back at her with disdain.

Alex, seemingly unaware of the two women's silent communication, went on, 'We're off to a night of dancing in a couple of weeks from now and we were wondering...' He turned to Kelly to flash a smile at her again, then looked at Stella to add, 'Well, can we count on you to mind the kids that evening, please? I'd be more than happy to compensate you for your time, of course.'

'Compensate me? Like, how?' Stella asked in a shrieking voice.

'Pay you, of course.'

'I never asked for your money.' Stella put a hand on her hip, her brow furrowing deeply, lips twisting.

Alex put up his free hand, then waved it frantically. 'I meant no offence, Stella. Just saying I need some help and that I can reimburse you for your time, that's all.'

Stella pursed her lips, threw Kelly a vitriolic look, and then turned to Alex again, her face sour. 'Sorry, I can't help you.'

'But, why? I don't understand…'

'Um… it's… I'm just busy. So very busy.'

'Busy? Oh… uh… well…' said Alex, using his free hand to rub the nape of his neck.

Kelly, judging from the fiery looks Stella continued to offer, knew very well the reason for Stella's refusal. She stepped away from Alex's embrace, then leaned over the fence. 'Look, Stella… I realize you and I may have started off on the wrong foot but, I can assure you, that was no intention of mine. As Alex said earlier, it's just that the boys are on a diet now… I say this in case I caused any offence the other day when I asked you not to bring us any more muffins. I certainly didn't mean any offence…'

As she waited for Stella to respond, her mind began to race with her own inner thoughts. *I recall you offended me that day, you mad cow! But I need you… so I can go to the dance… but I can always fix you later!*

She heard Lauren laugh inside her head then. *For a dead woman, she certainly has a lot of fun*, thought Kelly.

Stella's indignant voice brought her back to the present. 'This is not about that. Forget the damn muffins already!' Stella had her hand on her hip still, and now, her eyes were glinting with evident scorn.

'So, what is it?' asked Alex. 'Not that we mean to insist, of course… If you're busy, that's fine, but if the reason for your refusal to mind the boys has to do with us, then please tell us… If I've done something wrong, do let me know, give me a chance to defend myself, or to explain, or to apologise, or whatever…'

Stella took a few moments to eye them both with uncertainty, her arms now folded firmly before her. In the end, she tutted once, then said, 'I don't see the point. It seems to me you don't need me any more, Alex. So why are you asking me for help?'

'I don't understand, Stella. I just said Kelly and I will be going out that evening... and there'll be no one to mind my children. Hence asking you for help—'

Stella huffed then, cutting him short, her voice taking on a deriding tone. 'Oh, I see. I am like a Jack in the box to you. All forgotten until you open the lid. I'm tiny little Stella in the box. Open it and get me out when you need me. Close the lid and forget about me when you don't!'

'What?' said Alex, his eyes wide.

Kelly stared at her, unbelieving. 'Yes, Stella. What the hell? That doesn't even make sense.'

'Oh, I made a lot of sense before you came to live here, Kelly. Trust me. Suddenly, you're here, and I am crazy?'

Kelly couldn't believe her ears. Before she could utter a word in her defence, Stella moved closer to the fence and put up a shaking finger at Kelly. 'And I still don't get the reference to Dolce e Gabbana! What was that all about, huh? Because if you have something to say, you should just say it!'

'Excuse me?'

'Yeah! Excuse you! If you have something to say, then out with it. Don't just insinuate! How *dare* you insinuate?'

Kelly shook her head and waved her hands profusely before her. 'Stella, uh... Sorry, you're making no sense!'

At that point, Stella began to shout so Alex got in front of Kelly, trying to calm his neighbour down. Moments later, he was patting Stella's hand on the fence, and she was like a lamb before the shepherd, adoration alight in her eyes. She took a hankie out of her pocket and began to dab on her nose, sniffling.

Kelly studied her and wondered if she wasn't just a disillusioned loner who simply had Alex in her sights without him ever having given her one iota of romantic encouragement. If anything, she now seemed nothing else but a raving madwoman, a proper lunatic on her way to an asylum on a single ticket.

As if on cue, Stella raised her eyes from her hankie and threw Kelly an intense look of hatred, before turning to Alex, her expression changing in an instant from hateful to pained.

'Okay, Alex. I will do it. Because it's important to you. But don't ask me to have anything to do with *her*!' Her eyes hardened at the last word, and she didn't remove them from Alex to look at Kelly when she said it. 'If you want me to help when you go out with her in two weeks, fine. I'll mind the kids. But don't expect me to talk to her again.'

Chapter 27

Back at the house, Alex prompted the boys to change into sweats and wash their hands for lunch, while Kelly went straight to the fridge to take out a roasting tin of *gemista*. She had baked it the previous evening and turned on the oven to reheat it. With haste, she set about getting vegetables together to make a salad.

Alex had just washed his hands in the sink and now approached her at the kitchen island, then put a hand on her shoulder. Kelly loved the gesture that suggested what she was well aware of by now; that something had shifted between them, making them eager to touch each other casually whereas that was unthinkable before.

She turned to meet his eyes and found his gaze was deep, his lips curled up in a relaxed smile.

'You're wonderful, Kelly... You just never stop, do you?' he said, his eyes alighting. 'But you don't have to do everything. And certainly not today. I can make the salad.' He pointed to the table. 'Have a seat, relax... It's your day off, remember?'

Kelly tilted her head playfully and offered him a pleasant smile. 'It may be my day off but I'm only preparing lunch for us all. It'll take a moment. And, besides, it's my pleasure...'

He insisted, trying to pry a large beef tomato from her hands. Giggling, she relented and let him have it. As he began to cut it into thick chunks over a large salad bowl, she opened a cupboard to get the plates and set the table.

'What was that with Stella just now, huh?' he said with a chortle.

'No idea... That girl is certified...' She paused for a moment, then said, 'Alex? Are you sure it's safe to have her mind the children on her own?'

Alex waved her dismissively. 'Don't worry. It won't be the first time. She does a good job. And she's harmless...' He pressed his lips together and eyed her with humour. 'I guess... she doesn't like you, that's all.'

'Well, yes... I think she made that clear.'

'Quite.' He chortled, then added after a short pause, 'I guess she's jealous. Of you.' He threw her a meaningful glance.

'Yeah. Go figure,' Kelly replied as she set the table, avoiding his eyes. She wondered if he was trying to suss her out. That was the oldest trick in the book, but she wasn't going to fall for it and show him any of her secret cards. *If you fancy me, Mister, you'll have to try a little harder than that...*

As if on cue, he piped up then, 'Well, I guess that if I were to find someone else after Lauren's passing... If I...' He paused to clear his throat and, when she turned to look at him, having placed the last napkin and fork on the table, she was astonished to see that his look was electrifying. Like a stunned wild animal before the headlights, she straightened, lost in his eyes.

That's when he carried on, 'I guess... If I were to find someone else, it would have to be someone like you, Kelly. Someone who would care for my children and for my home, the way you do.'

As if released from the glare of the proverbial headlights when he dropped his gaze to the table before them, she came back to life and, with a steadying breath, commented, 'And for you.'

'What about me?' he asked, his brows knitted.

'You forgot to mention you. If that woman were to care for your children and your home, I guess she'd better care for you too. And I... I wish it for you, Alex. You deserve a happy life in this beautiful house, with your beautiful children.'

She saw his face melt with something that bordered on adoration, and she felt her heart skip a beat. Before either of them could say anything else, footsteps echoed from the stairs as Nikos and Tommy descended, squealing and conversing loudly.

Soon, they emerged from the corridor, Stratos coming in last a moment later. Charlie began to skip excitedly around their feet like he always did when they gathered to take their seats at the table. They chatted excitedly while the food was getting reheated in the oven, and Tommy decided to use the waiting time to show his father the latest tricks he had taught Charlie with Kelly's help.

Soon, everyone was laughing and cheering as Tommy, having taken a small amount of chocolate treats in his hand, stood before the pug and began to direct him, rewarding him as soon as he sat, spoke, twirled, stayed or played dead.

Before they knew it, Kelly had served stuffed tomatoes and peppers with roast potatoes on everyone's plate. Shortly after they'd begun to eat, Alex looked at the dog, amazement evident in his eyes, and piped up, 'I don't believe it! The dog doesn't beg at our feet any more! Well, I'll be damned.'

'Did you just notice, Dad? He hasn't done it in days,' said Stratos before taking a big bite.

'I guess I've been too tired from work to notice in the evenings, my boy,' he replied. 'Kelly, you're amazing. You even fixed the dog!' said Alex and everyone laughed.

Kelly beamed at the compliment and looked around the table as everyone continued to eat their food with relish. *Indeed. Look at them all. Stratos's spots are no longer angry. The fish supplement I got him worked wonders... Actually, his skin looks today the clearest it's ever looked since I came here a week ago. And he looks calmer, happier now... And Nikos.... he doesn't seem so bloated any more. His cheeks definitely seem less puffy. The daily walks are helping... I'd love for him to lose the weight, to stop getting bullied. As for Tommy... bless him, it's done him a lot of good to see his mother's pictures, to be able to talk about her openly...*

Her thoughts, instead of making her happy though, made her sad instead. Sad, because she could feel in those moments Lauren's shadow watching over them at the table. It made her sad that she couldn't tell them about her. Right then, she wondered if they'd welcome the news – that Lauren was there, watching over them, worrying about them, so much so that she'd been delaying moving on to paradise to make sure they were going to be okay first.

Her torrent of uncomfortable thoughts was disrupted by a soft thud. She turned to find the pug had jumped onto 'the forbidden chair' as the boys often called it. The pug had just landed on the upholstery cushion on the seat and was now lying on it, returning a wistful look back at her.

'There he goes again, jumping onto his favourite seat,' Kelly said, chuckling, then turned to the others, hooking her finger to point. 'I guess that's why he doesn't let anyone else sit on there.'

The children all shrugged and kept chewing, their mouths full. As for Alex, he pressed his lips together and tilted his head for a few moments as he observed his pet, then said, 'Who knows? It used to be Lauren's seat, you know... Back then they often shared it.' He leaned forward in his seat and smiled faintly, eyes igniting with a strange warmth, never leaving the dog. Then, he broke into a grin and added, 'Hey buddy! Is that why you sit there? You miss your *mama*?'

The knot that had grown in Kelly's throat in the last few moments didn't let her say anything other than a faint, 'Awww...'

His eyes still glued to the dog, who returned a solemn stare, Alex continued, 'You loved to sit there on her lap as a puppy, didn't you, Charlie?'

Kelly thought he missed his wife very much and her heart sank a little at the thought. But then, he met her gaze, and in them, he found a tenderness she knew instantly he was directing straight to her.

'Well, Kelly... I'd just like to say a big thank you—'
'What for?' she asked, raising her brows.

'I feel we owe a lot to you. For one, you helped me see sense the other day... Since the boys and I began to talk about Lauren openly, the whole energy in this house has shifted... Do you know what I mean?'

Kelly simply nodded, too overwhelmed to speak.

Eyes still locked on hers, he carried on, 'And these strange incidents today... I feel they are signs Lauren is sending to us... Maybe to let us know she's still here, watching over us, you know?' he said, raising a hand in a twirling motion. 'And I can't help feeling we have received all these messages from her because of you...' He turned to look at his children in succession, pensive. 'What do you think, boys?'

'Yes. I totally agree, Dad. We owe it all to Kelly,' piped up Stratos. 'She's, like, our lucky charm... She helped us connect with Mum, somehow. This morning, it was she who played on her phone the song Mum loved to sing to us.'

'And it was Kelly who ordered Mum's favourite coffee and dessert at the train station café!' said Nikos.

'Yes! And it was Kelly who trained Charlie to be good and do lots and lots of tricks!' said Tommy, who obviously had lost the thread, causing everyone to split their sides laughing.

Alex tousled the boy's hair when everyone's amusement had dissipated. 'That's not linked to Mummy, buddy, but thanks for playing.'

The room filled with uproarious laughter and even Charlie sat on his hind legs and began to howl and bark in an adorable way, causing them to laugh even more. Then, they moved on to other subjects and chatted endlessly until they had devoured every morsel left on their plates.

After lunch, the boys went to the living room to watch TV, Charlie following them there eagerly to lounge on the sofa, his head resting on Tommy's lap.

Alex stayed behind to help Kelly and offered to do the dishes. He had to convince her to let him help, and in the end, they agreed to do it together – he would do the washing up and she would dry it all up with a towel.

'Kelly?' he said after a few moments as he placed the salad bowl on the dish rack.

Kelly was taking a glass from the rack at the time and their hands touched for a split, electrifying second.

'Yes?' she said as she began to dry the glass with the towel, standing too close to him for comfort as it was. And now, the after-effect of that momentary contact of his skin against hers had made it hard to breathe. She wanted him to touch her again, so badly. *What have I got myself into?*

His gentle voice brought her back to the present deliciously. 'I was thinking... What I said earlier about Lauren and those spooky incidents... Do you think I'm crazy to believe her spirit is still around? That she's watching us in here, perhaps?'

Oh goodness... What do I say?

'Kelly?'

She turned to find him frozen as he waited for her reply, his eyes trained on her, his hand holding the soapy sponge mid-air, a handful of dirty forks in his other hand.

She cleared her throat. 'Alex, if you think so, then it must be true. I dare say you had strong enough a bond with Lauren all those years to be able to sense these things by instinct.'

'Thank you, Kelly. I had begun to fear that perhaps you thought I was two bats short of a belfry.'

'No, of course not,' she said, shaking her head frantically.

He resumed washing the cutlery and, after a while, added, 'I think that is why Charlie brings stuff of hers to us from time to time... because she is here. She's trying to communicate with us, and she's using the dog to do it...'

'What?' It had escaped her lips of its own accord, and now she wished she could take it back. She was simply amazed by his astuteness.

He chuckled in an awkward manner, obviously misreading her reaction. 'Feel free to call me a lunatic. Not sure I am not one, myself, to be honest.'

'No, as I said, I don't think you're crazy, Alex... And I agree, a lot of weird things have been happening here.' *Finally, I can say something I really mean!*

He sighed with evident relief. 'Thank goodness I am not the only one to think that then! And I think it's great that Charlie brought Lauren's scarf to you. Goodness knows how he took it from the wardrobe, but I got to say... I am glad he did. I think it means that Lauren likes you...' He pointed to the scarf, his eyes soft. It was holding Kelly's hair in a ponytail at the time, its edges tickling the nape of her neck every time she turned her head.

Kelly felt too overwhelmed to speak. Avoiding his eyes now, she continued to dry the cutlery, the corners of her lips curved up in a tight smile.

He gave a soft sigh and added, 'Speaking of Charlie bringing stuff from the wardrobe... It's not just the photo of Lauren and me that he brought the kids... Did you know that he also keeps bringing Tommy stuff from the wardrobe?'

'Oh? Really?' she said, looking down at the open drawer where she was arranging the cutlery.

'Yes!' he continued, none the wiser, 'All are Lauren's things; the odd item of fashion jewellery and some scarves... The boy told me earlier today.' A small pause ensued, then he exclaimed, 'Oh! Of course!'

Kelly looked up, then whipped her head around to find his face alight with surprise. 'What?'

'I just realised, Kelly. I believe Lauren is using the dog to try to give me a specific message...'

'A message? And what do you think that would be?'

'I think she's trying to tell me that it's wrong of me to hold on to her things... My friend Dimos has been trying to tell me too, but... I guess I've been finding it hard to consider giving Lauren's things away. But now, I believe it's time to give away her clothes, at least. They're just sitting in the wardrobe collecting dust. All her accessories too. And it's not like they're fit for the bin... Her father was in the fashion business and kept Lauren's wardrobes well-stocked. After her passing, I couldn't just give it all away. That's why my wardrobe is still full of clothes, bags and scarves by the finest designers of Milan, Paris and New York.'

Kelly nodded knowingly. The scarf she was wearing had an impressive designer label on it that confirmed what he'd said. And then, something inside her began to nag for her attention, but she couldn't place it as she listened to Alex recite some of the brands of Lauren's clothes and accessories. When he mentioned Dolce e Gabbana, Kelly made the connection. *Why did Lauren ask me to mention this specific brand name to Stella?*

'Kelly?' she heard him ask and, with a start, resumed drying the glass she was holding. She felt stupid to realize he'd caught her looking frozen, deep in thought, and avoided turning to look at him.

'Earth calling Kelly?' he said with a loud chuckle.

'Sorry, I was miles away just then,' she said, finally meeting his eyes. 'You were saying?'

'I was saying that I think it's time I gave Lauren's stuff away. Not the jewellery, of course. That, I hope to give to my boys' future wives to wear one day... But I'd love to donate the clothes and the accessories to a local charity. Do you know of any? For the life of me, I can't think of one. The designer clothes may get a good price in a charity shop or during a charity bazaar, don't you think?'

'Yes, yes of course. I can ask around, or surf online. I am sure there are local charities that would love to have them.'

'Thank you, Kelly. You are a treasure.'

Kelly's heart melted as she gazed back into his handsome face, those eyes that danced with excitement, and that warm smile of his that made her heart race.

She heard the sound of the pug's paws hit the tiles and looked down. Charlie scampered towards her and sat by her feet, his eyes gazing up at her expectantly, tail wagging.

Just then, Lauren's voice reverberated inside her mind loudly to say, 'My plan is working out wonderfully, Kelly! And don't you worry... I've got just the right charity for you!'

*****

As soon as Kelly entered her room, having bid everyone goodnight, she marched to the small dresser, threw herself a disgruntled look in the mirror and began to untie the knot on the scarf as if her life depended on it.

A mirthful laugh echoed in her mind then, causing her fingers to move back from the knot and to hover in mid-air. Her eyes widened and she stared back at her own reflection in the mirror blankly.

'Oh Kelly... is it such a big burden to you?' she heard Lauren utter in her head with a hint of regret.

Kelly turned around as, for some reason, seeing her own reflection in the mirror while hearing Lauren's voice had freaked her out. 'No, it's not that, Lauren. It's just that, well... I need some privacy,' she mumbled.

A short pause ensued, and then realisation hit her, causing her brows to knit together like long lost friends. 'Wait a minute!' she whispered to herself. 'How can I hear you when the dog's not here?'

Lauren giggled. 'Charlie's sitting on the carpet right outside your door, Kelly.'

Kelly opened her door and confirmed that Charlie was sitting right behind it. He looked up and offered a tired yawn, then lay down on the carpet.

'I'm tired, Lauren. I need to sleep... Please go away. It's been a long, and very weird day,' she whispered, her expression pleading, as she gazed into the dog's eyes.

Charlie yawned again, then lowered his head on his paws and closed his eyes, dozing off.

Kelly held her breath as the dog began to snore softly. She stepped back, about to close the door, when Lauren's voice echoed again. 'Please wear the scarf, Kelly... Tomorrow, and the day after that... I need your energy to keep talking to you. The scarf will channel it to me. You'll know why in time...'

Exhausted from a long day of having to manage this weirdness, Kelly said nothing. She simply closed the door shut, changed into her pyjamas and climbed straight into bed.

The darkness and the sweet warmth of the duvet provided the perfect refuge, the perfect oblivion from it all, if only for a while. The image of Alex, looking as gorgeous and happy as he'd looked all day, caused the corners of her lips to curl up into a dreamy smile as she surrendered herself to sleep.

Chapter 28

In the morning, Kelly's mind was still churning from her strange day of hosting Lauren in her head the day before. She wore the scarf again, still willing to do the spirit's bidding and help them all but, somehow, she felt nervous too. The previous day, it had become clear to her that what Lauren was after was to fix Kelly up with Alex. Still, she had her doubts…

Once everyone had left the house, she pushed aside any worrying thoughts and set about doing her chores. When she entered Alex's bedroom to tidy up, Charlie materialized behind her at once. He'd come in running, his chest heaving, tongue lolling out of his mouth in that cute way of his. For the last couple of days, he'd got into the habit of following her from room to room as she went around the house.

'There you are, you little ogre, you!' she said with a giggle. 'Are you lonely? Are you following me around for company?' Laughing still, she let Alex's pillow drop onto the bed and went down on her haunches to caress the dog's head. Charlie responded with yelps of affection and a slobbery kiss on her face.

She stood back up, smiling at him, but then he suddenly stiffened, his head turning to stare intently at the dresser in the corner. Before she could say anything, he ran to it and started barking.

Intrigued, Kelly followed him there and gasped at the sight of the mirror over the dresser.

Instead of reflecting her shape and the wardrobe behind her, it reflected what could only be described as a thick white mist. It flowed and swirled like a fluffy cotton cloud caught in a fierce wind. In seconds, it turned pink, and now it looked like… *Candy floss?* Kelly gasped and clutched at her chest as she took two steps back. *Oh, God… What now?*

'Don't be afraid…. It's only me…' she heard then and, impossibly, this time a face materialized, clear as day, in the mirror.

'Lauren?' Kelly said, inching forward. She'd recognized her readily from the photographs.

'Yes!' Lauren smiled amidst the pink confectionery background.

'But… how? How is that even possible?'

'Why are you surprised? How is it possible you can hear me in your head? Why is seeing me any different?'

Kelly felt a sharp pain on her lips and only then did she realize she'd been pinching her lower lip with two fingers all this time, clearly giving vent to her agony despite herself. The pain felt welcoming, anchoring her to reality, whatever reality she could grasp in this madness. She was awake. She was sure of that. She'd had a tall mug of strong coffee earlier, for goodness sake.

Lauren frowned. 'Oh, Kelly… Please don't look so scared. I am not that ugly, surely?'

'Oh no… Of course not. Sorry. It's just that… that…'

'That you're not used to seeing spirits, I get it.' She nodded firmly. 'Listen. I don't have much time. I wanted to thank you for wearing the scarf. Just from you sporting it for one day yesterday, I was able to communicate with my family a lot. When you cried and Alex held your hand, I felt his touch through you for the first time… Thank you, Kelly, for that. It was so precious.'

Kelly felt a little weird to hear that. 'My pleasure…' she managed feebly, without being sure she meant it.

Lauren went on, thanking her, her face beaming amidst the eerie, cotton-candy background. Her face was animated with excitement. 'I've now accumulated enough energy so I can anchor myself to the living world a little better. This is how I can finally get you to see me too…' Kelly heard Lauren say in her head, the words hitting her hard like a basketball on the nose.

'Energy? What energy? Are you siphoning it from *me*?' shrieked Kelly despite herself, one sharp finger shooting up to thump herself in the chest with such gusto that it hurt. Now it made sense! The previous night she had felt sleepy earlier than normal. When they all sat to watch a movie on TV, her eyes had begun to droop of their own accord during the first advert break. Everyone was puzzled when she announced she was going to bed because she couldn't see straight from exhaustion. They all said this wasn't like her and she was just as surprised but hadn't really thought much about it. Not until now.

'You're draining my energy, aren't you? That's not nice, Lauren!' she added, stepping forward determinedly until she was right in front of the mirror.

'Please, Kelly! Please don't be angry with me! I need you!' pleaded Lauren when Kelly's hands flew up, ready to remove the scarf from her own hair. Lauren had spoken just in time, causing her to reconsider, but not to calm down in the least.

Kelly put up a rigid finger and thumped the mirror with it, right on Lauren's chin. 'Don't you dare trick me, Lauren! I'll be gone before you know it, I swear! I won't let you hurt me in the process of doing whatever it is you're planning to do. I know enough about spirits to know it's not advisable to let them stick around for long. And I won't let you haunt me like you do Charlie. I have my own mind! And, right now, my own mind is to head back to my room, pack my bag and get the hell out of here!'

As Kelly's last irate words faded away, Lauren's face disappeared from the mirror, the pink goo turning into a grey cloud. Lauren began to sob, the heart-wrenching sound filling Kelly's mind, the whole room, it seemed.

'Oh... Please don't cry, Lauren... I...' Kelly felt guilty now, and utterly confused. 'Just tell me, okay? Tell me what you want me to do for you. It's just that, well, I *hate* surprises!' She flung out her arms and huffed. 'There, I said it. I have read widely on ghosts, and I have a vivid imagination as it is... I am willing to help you, Lauren, but I won't do just anything!'

Lauren stopped crying at the sound of that, her face reappearing in the mirror, her expression puzzled. Her voice echoed frail when she asked, 'What exactly are you afraid of, Kelly? What horrible things could you possibly be imagining I could ask you to do?'

Kelly drew a long breath to steady herself, letting it out with a long sigh before saying, 'Look, Lauren... To be honest, and with all due respect and all that, I'm not too happy to hear you can feel through me.... I mean... you're not going to ask me to do anything else with your husband so you can feel it, will you? Because let me tell you something. There's no way I'm going to stick around for that sort of thing!'

Lauren's face melted with surprise, then she burst out laughing, causing Kelly to gawp for a few moments, not sure how to interpret her reaction.

When Lauren sobered, she said with a loud chuckle in Kelly's mind, 'Oh no... Of course not. I'd never do that. What kind of woman did you think I am?'

Kelly let out a sigh of relief. 'Okay, then. Glad we cleared that up.'

'Me too, Kelly. So, we're good?'

'Yes, we are.'

'Good. And let me tell you. All I want is for my family to be happy. And they are happy around you. So, I thought, what would be a better thing than to make a family out of you guys? You and Alex look great together, Kelly... And I know you are attracted to him...'

In lieu of an answer, Kelly eyed her sideways for a few moments, then an appreciative smile spread slowly across her face.

Lauren gave a giggle. 'See? I got your back, girlfriend!' she said with a roll of her eyes. 'So, as I said, I want you guys to be together and I want it to be perfect... Will you let me make it happen, Kelly? And I promise it won't get weird. At all. She tittered, then added, Well, maybe a teensy bit.'

Kelly let out a guffaw. 'Weirder than this? No way.' She put out her hands, then giggled as she pointed to the mirror.

Lauren erupted into hysterics, causing Kelly to join her. By the time they'd sobered up, Kelly was amazed. She had no idea talking to a ghost face in a mirror could be so much fun.

As if guessing her thoughts, Lauren smiled fondly, then said, 'I am so glad you've come to my home, Kelly. And let me tell you... You are attuned to Alex's soul and he is to yours. Being on a higher plane it's so clear to me. Since you wear my scarf now, I grow attuned to you with every passing moment... Please keep wearing it, Kelly. It helps me stay close so I can help you all. And I won't drain your energy so much again. I guess I got carried away yesterday, too desperate to communicate. I'll pace myself from now on. I promise. Okay?'

Smiling, Kelly nodded firmly. 'Agreed. And I promise I won't question what you ask of me again.'

'Oh, you're a sweetheart... And don't worry. I'll soon be out of your hair... We're almost there. Alex has gone a long way, thanks to you, in just a week of you being here. Now he is ready to give away my things... That was music to my ears. He'll do well to give away to charity all my clothes and accessories, but not my jewellery...'

Kelly opened her mouth to tell her that, of course, Alex didn't intend to give the jewellery away, when Lauren went on, this time with feeling, 'And I have to get the necklaces, the bracelets and the rings that are missing from the wardrobe, Kelly. I have to get them all together for safe-keeping for my daughters-in-law... My precious future daughters!'

Kelly's brows shot up. It was obvious Lauren didn't mean the imitation jewellery Tommy had in his room. 'What do you mean they're missing? Where are they? Tell me and I'll get them for you...'

Lauren's beautiful face glowed with a cunning smile. 'Oh don't worry about that, Kelly. That's my own task to do. And I'm so close to getting them back. You'll see…'

Chapter 29

In the following three days, Kelly began to feel all the more confident in the house. Since seeing Lauren's face in the mirror, she'd been feeling more trusting of her, somehow, as if gazing into her eyes had served to confirm her candour irreversibly. She still wondered about those missing pieces of jewellery Lauren had spoken about. To be sure, she'd looked inside the wardrobe and the drawer cabinet in her own bedroom and found nothing. She hadn't gone looking in the other compartments of Alex's wardrobe at all but expected she'd have the chance once they went through Lauren's things together so they could pack them to give away to charity.

Nikos walked into the kitchen for breakfast that morning wearing a cunning expression of ill-concealed enthusiasm.

Kelly was placing boiled eggs, pieces of toast, cottage cheese and cut up tomato on the boys' plates at the time. When she saw his face, she wondered why he was looking at her like that, but before she could voice her question, he picked the sides of his jeans at the waist with both hands and huffed with humour.

'Look, Kelly! I'm practically swimming in these! My other pairs are the same. I need new ones!'

Kelly rushed to him, clapping her hands with elation. 'Oh my! Already? That's amazing! It's only been a few days since you started the diet!'

He gave a bright grin. 'Yes! But we also walk daily, don't we? Monday to Saturday. Running up the hill too!'

'Yes, it's true… The exercise has certainly helped to speed things up. Still, I'm amazed you burned the fat so quickly!' She saw his beaming face and mirrored his expression.

'Well? Will you come shopping with me please, Kelly? I'll go to school like this today but not again… I don't want to give those bullies a new reason to bother me.'

She pressed her lips together, then said, 'They still do, Nikos?'

'Of course, they do... Although, to be fair, it's not as bad as it used to be. Rather than call me fat, they now concentrate on trashing my efforts to lose weight. Every time I take out my sandwich to eat, or the healthy bar, they come dangling their cheese pastries and their hazelnut-filled croissants from the canteen in front of my face.'

'I hope you see that you're winning, though, right?' she said, squeezing his shoulder gently.

'I'm winning?'

'Hello?' She pointed to his frame that seemed to have shrunk overnight inside his clothes. His top looked as roomy as his jeans, and his shoulders, once rounded and prominent, seemed to have disappeared under the sagging garment.

He shrugged and said with a half-smile, 'Yeah, I guess I am.'

'Seems to me that they're trying desperately to find something to tease you about, Nikos. And it's getting harder now, don't you see? When you finally emerge through the diet and the exercise as a slim young man, in the long run, they'll find absolutely nothing to say against you any more.'

She straightened and took a long breath, then cocked her eye at him to add, 'Remember what I told you, yes? Those bullies are doing you a favour! They are the reason why you have sought a healthier body and a healthier lifestyle. Never forget that. You should silently thank them every time they come to you with a nasty comment...' She gave a cunning grin. 'And pity them too, of course! Not just because they're pathetic, but because if they carry on eating croissants and cheese pastries every day, they'll look like blobs by the time they hit thirty.'

Nikos gave a little laugh and they locked together in a tight embrace. Kelly kissed his head, and a tear she didn't expect escaped from her eye, but she wiped it quickly away.

Just then, Stratos and Tommy came in to take their seats, and she went over to them to greet them and tousle their hair.

When she returned to the counter to resume preparing the boys' plates, Charlie ran up to her and barked once. She looked down to meet his eyes and Lauren's voice echoed in her mind. 'Thank you, Kelly. I couldn't have handled this with Nikos any better than you have...'

*****

The same afternoon, instead of walking to the park, Kelly and the children visited the local shops on foot, taking Charlie with them so he didn't miss his exercise for the day.

Stratos needed a more effective face balm to use after shaving, just as badly as Nikos needed jeans in a smaller size. They entered a clothes store first and, leaving Tommy near the entrance to hold Charlie by the lead, Kelly and the other two boys walked in a little further to the counter. A helpful young girl came out from behind it and showed Nikos a half-dozen different styles of jeans. Having tried four pairs, Nikos chose to buy two, excited to see himself looking so trim in jeans for a change.

When they came out of the store, Nikos's expression was exuberant as he held the bag with his new purchases.

Kelly led them all to the pharmacy that was a couple of doors away. This time, Nikos and Tommy chose to wait outside together with Charlie, and Kelly and Stratos walked in to buy his shaving balm.

As soon as they'd got what they were after and paid, they heard frantic barking outside and knew with certainty that it was Charlie. But it was a fierce bark, which was unlike him.

Intrigued, they said goodbye to the man behind the counter and sped outside to find an ugly scene.

Two tall teenage boys were standing ominously before Nikos and Tommy, too close for comfort. Charlie was barking his head off at their feet. The taller of the boys, who had piercing blue eyes and blond hair, was pointing a finger at Nikos and laughing. The other one stood a little further back. He had curly brown hair and a pimply face that seemed a lot worse than Stratos's had ever been. It was obvious those were two of the bullies Nikos encountered in school.

Glaring at the bullies, Kelly sped forward to stand protectively in front of Nikos and Tommy. 'What's up, lads?' she asked, standing straight, chin raised.

Just then, Stratos materialized beside her, panting hard and exercising evident restraint. He seemed ready to grab the boys by the throat.

Keeping his cool, the blond boy said nothing. He only took one step back, a deriding lopsided smile breaking on his face. Unlike him, the other boy sprang back as if he'd been scalded by hot oil.

The blond boy put up his hands and said, 'Take a chill pill, girl... All's good here...' He had a putrid smile on his lips that made Kelly feel sorry for him. He was a handsome young lad, yet the ugliness inside him oozed on the outside, destroying his inherent beauty.

'Don't give me that! What the hell were you saying to my kids just now?' she insisted, but, before anyone else could utter another word, her blood chilled in her veins.

Stratos charged forward, shouting, 'You filth! Leave my brother alone!' He reached out with both hands and grabbed the two bullies from their shirts, shaking them. 'So it's you! You're the two bastards that have been bothering my brother!' he said as he shook them.

'Stratos! Please, don't! You're better than that! Please!' she pleaded, pulling him back by the shoulder with her free hand. She was holding his purchase and her purse with the other.

Somehow, Stratos relented and let go. As soon as he did that, the bullies stepped back to stand numbly a safe distance away, on the road. It was quiet in the street, with hardly any traffic. The only passers-by during the incident had been a young couple. They'd thrown them curious looks but hadn't seemed concerned enough to stop. Just as Kelly thought that, she heard a voice coming from behind her.

'You okay, Madam? Do you need any help?' It was the pharmacist, standing at the doorway. He looked at the bullies, his eyes narrowed, then back to Kelly, his expression turning mild anew.

Kelly shook her head. 'Thank you, but no. We're okay. These kids go to school with mine. It's just a misunderstanding...' She gave a faint smile. 'Boys will be boys, that's all.'

Hearing that, the man bid them good day again and walked back into his shop.

Kelly turned to the bullies. 'You ought to be ashamed of yourselves. Two big lads like you, pestering two smaller children. Is that the kind of men you want to grow into? If you boys feel like picking on someone for your own fun, at least, pick someone your own size!'

As she spoke, she could hear Stratos grinding his teeth, his hands balled into fists at his sides, so she put out a hand to hold his arm tenderly. The sound eased, then was drowned out by the boys' fierce reaction.

They both laughed out loud, or rather, the blond boy started it, followed by the other one, who sounded like a hyena.

Now, they were sniggering, their eyes fixed on Nikos. Kelly, boiling with fury, took a step forward. 'You know, I'm racking my brains, but, between you two, I really can't tell which one is Dumb and which one is Dumber.'

'What?' said the blond boy, and again his good looks were marred by the noxious expression he wore. Shaking a finger at Kelly, he added, 'You watch yourself!'

Undeterred, Kelly took a couple of steps towards him, causing the pimply one to back away further. He began to look around him nervously, and pull his more assertive friend from the arm, coaxing him to flee with him.

But the blond boy wasn't finished yet. Shaking his arm away from his friend's desperate grasp, he took one step forward to say, 'Did you hear what I said? Did you understand? Or are you really *dumb*?'

Stratos had followed Kelly by then, to remain by her side. She felt him tense up and grabbed his arm again. 'Don't...' she whispered, then her eyes flitted to Nikos and Tommy, who seemed frozen, standing near the shop window, their eyes huge with distress. The dog's eyes were pinned on the blond boy, feverish like live coal. Lauren's voice echoed then to say, 'Yes. That's him. He's the one who's been bullying my baby the most. Give him a piece of my mind, of *our* mind, Kelly...'

Kelly turned to the blond boy, a hand on her waist. 'I'll tell you what I understand... I understand that when you call people names it shows your lack of decency... And here's the thing: What you do and what you say to Nikos has no bearing on him as a person. The more names you call him, the greater your own shortcomings show.'

The blond boy drew a deep breath and began to snigger, nodding repeatedly.

That didn't deter her so she went on, 'So you want to feel like you're somebody, huh? You want to feel good about yourself?' With every passing second, her body tensed up all the more, her mouth accelerating, as if speaking of its own accord. 'I'm telling you, that's no way to do it. If you want these things, you've got to do something *meaningful*. Something useful. Something that actually makes *others* feel good too. Not just you. And it's got to be something *positive*.'

Her eyes flitted to the pimply one, who stood with slouched shoulders, hands in his pockets, then threw a confident gaze to the blond boy again. 'You're not little boys any more! You ought to behave like men, not like infants. Do you understand me?'

The blond boy tilted his head slowly to the side as he put his hands on his waist. 'You talk too much... you know that? It's not good, not good at all.'

'Yeah. And you'd better listen. If you know what's good for you!' she demanded, the words coming out of her mouth as if on automatic pilot.

She saw his eyes glint with something vile then and steeled herself preparing for the worst, fearing he would erupt at any moment, possibly assault her or the boys, but then, he suddenly threw his hands in the air and chortled, putting on an expression of perfect innocence. *'Ise trelli, koritsi mou?* Are you crazy, my girl? What are you talking about? We're just teasing the boy. It's harmless fun.'

'No. it's not harmless fun if you're on the receiving end. And Nikos is better than you! Any day of the week!'

'Better?' As soon as he said it, he erupted in a belly laugh so fierce that even his friend, who had grown pale with distress, managed to imitate him with a similar, albeit weaker, bout of laughter.

'I knew he was bluffing! Inside, he's just a wimp. Kelly! Look at the poster on the wall!' Lauren's voice echoed inside her mind then and Kelly, as if hypnotized, turned around. On the shop window, right beside the entrance, there was a poster that advertised a school run for charity. The date was printed in large lettering. It was to be held the following Sunday, in ten days' time, at the open-air track of the local stadium. *Plenty of time. Thanks, Lauren.*

With a triumphant smile, she turned to face the bullies again, tilting her chin. 'I wonder if you're as tough as you look!'

A minute later, the boys had accepted the challenge amongst mocking comments. Kelly had reciprocated in kind, telling them that Nikos was going to run faster than they ever could, that he could do it straight out of bed while yawning. Before they left, she made them promise to leave him alone once he'd left them behind to eat his dust, as she put it. That particular comment of hers had caused them to dissolve into hysterics and Nikos to cringe with apprehension.

Now, they were gone, and Kelly, still pumped up from the confrontation, pointed forward with a rigid hand and began to stride towards home.

The boys began to follow, falling into step beside her, and, moments later, Nikos began to shake his head ruefully, his voice agitated when he erupted, 'What have you done, Kelly? You've destroyed me! Forever! How am I ever going to show my face in school again? Why did you do that, huh?'

She threw him an encouraging smile. 'Oh come on, Nikos! It's only one kilometre! It's easy! We'll train together... If you can run uphill, you can run one kilometer fast enough on flat ground to beat Dumb and Dumber! Trust me!'

'Yes, Nikos! You can!' piped up Stratos, throwing a fist in the air with excitement. 'I see those idiots at the park all the time, just sitting and drinking *frappé* coffee. I've never seen them jogging or running or anywhere near a ball. Plus, they smoke. Heavily. They'll eat your dust. You'll see!'

'Yes!' said Tommy. 'I know you can do it, Nikos!'

Charlie barked excitedly then, causing Tommy to add, 'See? Even Charlie agrees with us!'

Chapter 30

When the air horn blasted out across the open-air track of the local stadium, the shrill sound wafting in the morning spring breeze, Kelly felt her heart would explode. Adrenaline coursed through her, reminding her of the short runs she had done back in Athens during several running events. She began to jump up and down on the spot, clapping her hands and whooping with the rest of the family. They were all sitting on the benches amidst an equally excited crowd.

Having arrived at the stadium early, they had found seats right in front of the finishing line. Their arrival with ample time to spare had also helped to ease Nikos's tremendous anxiety. Kelly had stayed by him while he warmed up, coaxing and praising him all the while to build up his confidence.

The two bullies had arrived typically in the last minute bringing together many of their like-minded friends to deride as they passed by Kelly and Nikos while he did his warm up.

But Kelly and Nikos had ignored their snide comments and Kelly had reminded the tough bully that if he was indeed a man, he was to keep his word if Nikos beat him. The boy had said he would, although it was never going to happen because Nikos stood no chance.

And now, watching Nikos's progress around the track, Kelly was feeling hopeful. About five minutes earlier, she had set her stop watch as soon as the air horn echoed in her ears. The runners were all boys from both the local junior high and the high school – both Stratos's and Nikos's schoolmates.

The most athletic among them were already within the last one hundred metres of the race. Nikos had covered only one full lap so far but that didn't matter as he only really had two opponents. Those two were far behind Nikos, no doubt only now realizing they'd bitten off more than they could chew.

Kelly took her eyes from Nikos, who seemed to be advancing at a comfortable pace, to drop her gaze at her feet. She had worn the scarf again but had suggested they leave Charlie back at home, expecting that the din of the crowd wouldn't allow her to listen to Lauren's voice in her head. She still thought that, but found herself, much to her surprise, wishing she could hear Lauren's comments during Nikos's effort.

Suddenly, she heard the agitated voices of Alex and the boys and raised her head with a start, realizing she had been lost in her thoughts for a while. They had sounded alarmed, speaking together at the same time, and she hadn't registered what they said. She'd only made out Nikos's name as they called it out repeatedly. Alarmed too now, in case Nikos had fallen or got hurt, she scanned the track with her eyes and froze, her heart giving a thump so hard that it almost hurt her.

The bright green top that Nikos was wearing helped to clock him easily. He was standing immobile on the other side of the track, now about three hundred metres from finishing the race. From that distance, she could see he had one hand on his waist, the other over his heart.

Before she could move a muscle, Alex seized her arm, shaking her. 'What do we do, Kelly? Can we go to him and check if he's all right?'

Kelly gave a firm nod and sprang upright. 'I'll go. Stay here.'

Without waiting for a reply, she sprinted to the booth where the school committee sat. Nikos's gym teacher, Mr Savidis, sat at the end. Nikos had introduced her to him earlier. He'd seemed impressed to hear she was a marathon runner. He still ran the odd marathon too, even though he was well into his sixties.

'Mr Savidis, Nikos stopped running! Right there!' she said when she arrived before him and pointed to the boy.

Mr Savidis tilted his head to the side and furrowed his brow. 'What's that boy doing?'

Kelly's gut began to churn when she saw the bullies finally catch up with Nikos, pointing sharp fingers at him as they passed him by. The blond boy tilted his head back and seemed to be laughing as he and his friend advanced forward, albeit slowly.

Her heart racing, Kelly grabbed Mr Savidis's arm. 'Please, sir! Will you allow me to go to Nikos and talk to him? Would that be okay?'

The gym teacher gazed into her eyes, his own glinting in the morning sunlight brilliantly, for what seemed like forever. Then, he flashed a toothy grin and pointed to the track. 'Be my guest! And you'd better put your marathon feet on, girl! I'd hate to see that boy finish last. He's been trying so damn hard!'

Kelly never waited for him to finish his words before bolting, as rude as that was, but she couldn't afford to be polite. As soon as he'd granted her permission she was off like a bullet shooting out of a pistol. Mr Savidis's remaining speech reached behind her, all the more faint and distant as she ran, thanking her strong legs and her habit to wear sneakers every day.

When she reached Nikos a few seconds later, she grabbed him by the shoulders. 'Nikos! What are you doing?'

Nikos shook his head. 'I don't know. This was a stupid idea.' He was hyperventilating.

Kelly pressed her lips together. He hadn't stopped because he was tired. He had stopped because he had panicked. She urged him to take two deep breaths, which he did, then she coaxed him to resume running but, still, he shook his head.

'What if I don't finish? What if they start running faster when I get to them? If I don't win, I am lost!'

She squeezed his arms so tightly she saw him wince with pain. 'But what if you win, Nikos? And you can! Believe me, you can!'

She pointed to the bullies up ahead; they looked unsteady on their legs, advancing like octogenarians who'd never run in their lives. 'Look at them! They don't have this! But you do, Nikos! And it's their arrogance you must beat today! If they had knowledge in their own abilities they wouldn't have accepted the challenge! Punish them for thinking they're better than you!'

Nikos gazed at the boys up ahead, who were walking, not running now, intent still, it seemed, to get to the finish line.

Kelly shook Nikos again, which caused him to turn to her. She raised her voice and leaned forward, her face closer to his. 'They're just two stupid hares and you're the tortoise they've been underestimating! You know the Aesop tale, don't you? So finish it!'

That seemed to do it. 'Thanks, Kelly!' he said, his eyes lighting up, and he was off like a shot, leaving her behind standing tall, clapping her hands together. She ran back the way she'd come but slowed down when she reached the committee booth. She raised a hand to thank Mr Savidis and he gave her a thumbs up. As she hurried past, she heard him shout, 'Bravo, Kelly! There's no stopping that boy now!'

In the few seconds it took her to go up the steps and join the others again, she didn't check on Nikos's progress at all. When she took her seat amidst the others again, she found them looking ecstatic, Alex thanking her profusely for helping out Nikos.

Following his gaze, she realized why he and the boys were so beside themselves with enthusiasm. Nikos was now advancing like a powerful steam engine. He seemed unstoppable out there. He had just reached the bullies and sped past them in perfect form and without even turning their way, as if they didn't exist, let alone to shout something deriding to them, something boastful, the way they had surely done earlier. But Nikos was different. He was a natural athlete and she was truly proud of him.

Now, Nikos was on the last stretch, less than one hundred metres from the finishing line. Many stronger young runners had already finished the race and were standing near the booth shaking hands with friends and family who had approached to congratulate them. They were getting hugs and receiving pats on their backs, their medals hanging around their necks.

Kelly's eyes sought Nikos again, the excited voices of Alex and the boys as they cheered him on booming in her ears. She kept silent, too excited to make a sound, her hands balled into fists as she willed Nikos forward, to keep going strong.

The bullies were no longer running, and no longer walking either. Now, they were standing near the side of the track, a good distance before the finish line, the blond boy bending over at the waist, his hands on his knees. His underdog was staring at him, his chest heaving, mouth wide open as he panted.

Kelly felt sweet satisfaction blooming in her chest. Standing up like a coiled spring, she whooped and clapped her hands so much it hurt, shouting Nikos's name and words of encouragement as he continued to run, incredibly sure-footed, past the benches, steady on his way to the finish line.

When he finally crossed it, she screamed with joy, then found herself, without knowing how, jumping up and down inside Alex's arms. Stratos and Tommy hugged them both in turn, and then everyone began to thank her for helping Nikos make this happen.

Now, she was overwhelmed by it all. She didn't have time to think how warm and delicious it had felt to be enclosed in Alex's arms, how full of love and joy his eyes had been, how wonderful it was to see Stratos and Tommy so happy too.

She was too busy reveling in the absolute relief and the elation on Nikos's face when he finally stopped running and a woman from the committee approached to award him his medal. As soon as she'd placed it on his chest and turned away, Nikos doubled over, hands on his knees, for a few moments, then he stood tall again and sought them with his eyes across the distance. Kelly and the others waved at him frantically, then they all rushed down to shower him with hugs and kisses.

They were still all doing that when Kelly heard heavy panting coming from a short distance away. She turned and found the blond boy on his knees, the pimply one flat on his back starfish-style, his mouth gaping open as he sought to fill his lungs with air. Mr Savidis and another man rushed to them with two bottles of water, coaxing them to drink.

Kelly, Alex and the boys fell quiet as they watched the pitiful sight. Moments later, having drunk some water from the bottles and showered themselves over the head with the rest of it, the bullies were standing on their legs again or rather teetering on them as if they were made of jello.

The thought made Kelly giggle to herself as her eyes shifted to Nikos, who had just received a bottle of water from Mr Savidis and began to drink thirstily. He finished the bottle in one go, then Alex patted him on the back to say, 'My little champion! I am so proud of you!'

Then, Mr Savidis held out his hand to Nikos. The boy shook it and the man said, 'I'll second that... I'm so proud of you, Nikos! Not just for the recent change in you, but also because...' he turned to look at the bullies, who stood close by, but not close enough to hear, and added leaning closer to Nikos, '... Someone had to show these drongo heads what it takes to be a real man! Good on you, my boy!'

At that point, only a handful of kids remained struggling on the track towards the finish line, and they were all coming in at a walking pace. Mr Savidis threw a look their way, then turned to Kelly and chuckled. 'If you ask me, those belong in the girls' race that takes place this afternoon!' Without waiting for a reply, he turned to the bullies, who were coming closer now, a sheepish look in their eyes. Mr Savidis walked up to them and patted the blond boy on the back, who seemed too weak to even acknowledge it.

'Did you hear that, you two?' he said, bending over to talk near the blond boy's face. 'Next year, I'll list you both to run in the afternoon with the rest of the girls!'

Without waiting for the boys to respond, he turned to Kelly, Alex, and the boys and winked, then laughed at his own joke as he walked away.

To Kelly's surprise, the bullies, looking even more sheepish now, walked over to them, then stood unsure on their feet, their knees seemingly ready to buckle. They avoided their eyes for a few awkward moments, then the blond boy looked up and offered his hand to Nikos. 'Congrats...' it sufficed him to say.

'Thanks...' muttered Nikos, his eyes wide. The blond boy spun around and the other one did the same, but not before acknowledging Nikos with a single firm nod, eyes full of evident shame.

Kelly knew they had just acknowledged Nikos as an equal, if not someone superior. The shift she'd been hoping for had just been made. No words were necessary. She knew then that Nikos was going to have no more trouble at school.

Nikos, obviously knowing it too, fell into her arms as soon as the boys had left, his voice cracking in her ears as he held her tightly. 'Thank you, Kelly. Thank you so much!'

Chapter 31

A little later, Alex and Stratos went to the car, which was parked near the stadium, and brought back four bags full of clothes and accessories that once belonged to Lauren.

Alex and Stratos put the bags down by Kelly's feet, then returned to the car to get the rest of the bags. Kelly stood on a concrete path near the stadium gate with Nikos and Tommy. A big stall with an awning had been put up a few paces away. It was manned by volunteers of a local charity, which accepted donations of both food and clothes for the poor. This was where Alex had decided to donate Lauren's belongings. They had brought a total of seven bags, which contained all of Lauren's belongings that Alex had kept over the years.

The previous day, when Alex and Kelly opened his wardrobe together to pack Lauren's things, Kelly had seen for herself that they were expensive designer clothes and accessories, hardly worn and used. Alex had invited her to go through them and take whatever she wanted for herself, but Kelly had declined, even though she'd have loved to own any of these beautiful things. But having Lauren in her head made it impossible to take something of hers. It felt as if she were still alive and likely to use them herself.

Besides, Lauren had already given her two things she once owned. The scarf, which Kelly had grown accustomed to wearing every day in her hair, and the pearl necklace, which she'd never worn and still had no idea why Lauren wanted her to have it. She kept it in her room, all the same, trusting Lauren knew what she was doing.

When Alex and Stratos brought the remaining bags over, everyone except Tommy took a bag or two and began to walk to the charity stall. The young runners with their families were leaving the stadium in large numbers at the time, seeing that the event had finished.

At the stall, Alex did the talking, while the others stood back a little. When the two women manning it had a quick look inside the plastic bags their jaws dropped. Alex explained the contents belonged to his deceased wife and their faces melted as they began to nod sympathetically.

He soon got chatting with them and one of the ladies said she remembered him from their school days. Kelly overheard that just as he whirled around to point their way, mentioning his three children, before facing the women again to resume their conversation.

People were coming and going, leaving bags at the stall or browsing at the items offered for sale, so Kelly and the boys moved a little further away. Now, they were unable to hear much of what Alex discussed with the women.

The people passing by before Kelly's eyes prevented her from seeing Alex on and off, and she caught herself feeling uneasy. She chuckled to herself when she realized jealousy was pricking her insides. *Look at you! He's not even yours and you're getting possessive!* The thought made her feel ridiculous, but she still couldn't help the sting burning in the core of her gut.

Trying to ignore it, she turned to Nikos to tousle his hair and began to praise him anew. His face was beaming and that made her smile with pride. Stratos then began to talk to Nikos about something trivial. Tommy kept silent beside her, waiting, like she did, for his father to rejoin them. Her stomach began to grumble and when she voiced her extreme hunger, the others said they were also feeling peckish.

Stratos gave a chuckle and suggested to Nikos that he ask their father to take them all out for *souvlakis* to celebrate his 'victory over those knuckleheads', as he put it, and then, he stopped midsentence.

Kelly, who had been looking over at Alex as he chatted to the women, snapped out of her trance and whipped her head around to check on Stratos. She found him gazing intently at three girls roughly his age, who were passing by. They were all pretty, making up a vision of sparkling eyes, long silky hair and translucent skin.

She nudged Stratos in the ribs to tease him for staring. 'Pretty girls. You know them?' she whispered, leaning towards him.

'Huh?' he said, without taking his eyes off their receding frames.

'I said, pretty g—' Her voice cut off when he let out the most forlorn sigh ever. 'What's the matter, Stratos?'

Stratos sighed again, albeit softly this time. The girls had disappeared behind the receding crowd by then, which allowed him to break his obvious reverie and turn to her. 'Oh... nothing.'

'Nothing? Are you kidding? Had these girls been Sirens singing their heads off and you'd been tied up on Odysseus's boat you wouldn't have looked more fascinated.'

'Ha-ha. Very funny,' he said in a faint whisper, looking away.

Stratos's earlier good spirits had vanished. He now had both hands in his pockets, shoulders hunched, as he looked at his shoes.

She was about to persist some more, asking if he knew those girls, when Nikos shrugged and informed her, 'The one in the middle was Eleni. He's in love with her.'

'Nikos! Don't!' said Stratos, slapping his brother's arm. Then, he bent his head, his neck shrinking to nothing as if he was trying to hide his face inside his shirt.

'It's okay, Stratos. I won't tell your dad if this is what you're worried about.'

'It's not that,' he said, avoiding her eyes. 'It's futile, that's all. She'll never give me the time of day.'

'How do you know that?'

He huffed. 'Didn't you see her just now? She's stunning. Why would she look at me?'

'Why wouldn't she look at you?'

'Hello? Kelly?' He hooked his index fingers and pointed to his face sharply. 'Why would she even throw a glance at this horrid, pimply face of mine?'

'Oh, Stratos... It's not as bad as you think. Your pimples have cleared a lot since you started this new healthy diet. The herbal cosmetics help too. You know that.'

'Still. I'll never be Robert Pattinson.'

She chuckled, despite herself. 'Robert Pattinson?'

He waved. 'Yeah. She adores him. Ever since she watched Twilight.'

He'd said the last word with an eye roll and his lips curled in disgust. Kelly found that hilarious but willed herself not to show her amusement. 'So? You don't have to look like him for her to like you.'

'I don't know about that...'

Kelly tutted, unsure of how she could lift his spirits, when he brightened a little and said, 'I may not look cool, the way he does, but I can surely do something he does really well.'

'What's that?'

He puffed up his chest. 'I can sing and I can play the guitar.'

'What? You mean, Pattinson does these things?'

'Yeah, you didn't know? He's a brilliant musician. I'll give him that.'

'Oh! There you go! Why don't you sing one of his songs to her? If you know any of them, that is.'

'Sing to her? Are you kidding? I could never pluck up the courage to even talk to her, but I often hang out in the school yard near her and her girlfriends... She talks about Pattinson all the time and plays his songs on Youtube. Her favourite is 'Never Think'. And he's good in it. But I'm better,' he said with a grin, puffing out his chest.

It was wonderful to see him look so confident for a change, and Kelly found herself clapping her hands together. 'You should play it for me! For all of us. Huh, boys? What do you think?'

Nikos and Tommy agreed, but Stratos huffed their suggestion away. 'You forget I don't own a guitar?'

In a heartbeat, Tommy said, 'Ask Dad to buy you one for your birthday! There's still time. I bet he hasn't got you a present yet. He always gets our presents at the last minute, you know him!'

'Your birthday? When is it, Stratos?' asked Kelly, taken aback.

'It's next Saturday,' he replied to her numbly, then turning to Tommy, 'I won't bother. You know how he feels about me singing. He'll never buy me a guitar!'

'But he's fine with you having lessons at your friend's house!' said Kelly. 'Surely you know he cares for you. Just ask him. What do you have to lose?'

'I'll get upset when he says no, Kelly. So I won't.'

'*If*, Stratos. *If*! Not, when. You don't know that.'

'Look, Kelly. I have enough to worry about. And Eleni is what I worry about the most, okay? And if I ever decide to sing that song to her to try to impress her, the guitar won't be a problem. My friend will be glad to lend me his.'

'If you have your own guitar you won't look so lame,' offered Nikos but Stratos twisted his lips.

'I won't look lame if I sing this song to her. She'll love it.'

'Then why don't you do it?' asked Kelly gently.

'I told you why. The very thought terrifies me. Besides, I can't just bring a guitar to school and sing to her in front of everybody. It has to be somewhere else. Not alone necessarily, as that would be impossible, but not in front of so many people either.'

'Why don't you invite her home? To study together in your room, or just to hang out and play music?'

'What? No way, Kelly! I'd die if she said no!'

'Okay... so how about inviting her home to a party?'

'A party?'

'Yes!' interrupted Tommy shaking his fists in the air. 'A birthday party for you! Do it, Stratos. Do it!'

Stratos waved it off and shook his head fiercely. 'You're all crazy. Stay here and wait for Dad. I'm going to wait by the car.'

Before Kelly could protest, he was gone, walking away with his hands in his pockets. Her heart went out to him and she knew then she wasn't going to let this go.

Chapter 32

Kelly was having a hard time washing Charlie in the bathtub. For some strange reason, he was livelier today. Normally, he'd sit still for ten straight seconds but today he kept twirling and shaking, and lifting his paws to put them over her arms as she washed him.

Huffing, she regretted picking this time to give him a bath. It was almost ten a.m. and she was alone in the house, so there was no one to help her keep him still while she shampooed him.

'If only Lauren could lend a hand!' she heard herself say with a wicked smile, something which caused Charlie to freeze and look up at her, tilting his head.

'I swear,' she said, brushing the top of his head softly with a frothy sponge, 'It's like you have a permanent connection line open with her.' She chuckled and added, 'Can you hear her now? I hope she's telling you to be good. She'd better!'

Laughing, and since he'd finally grown still, she continued to wash him, glad for the reprieve, and rushed to finish. Earlier, she'd had a shower, the way she did every morning, after everyone had gone, to feel fresh after her run. She'd been rushing to do the hoovering so never blow-dried her hair or put on the scarf so she could hear Lauren.

Her phone pinged from the top of the washing machine just as she wrapped the pug in a towel and began to dry him.

She recognized the notification sound with enthusiasm. It was from an app she used to communicate back and forth with Efi. When she made sure Charlie was dry enough, she opened the bathroom door and he rushed outside. He knew she'd give him chocolate treats straight after his wash and was surely rushing to the cabinet, ready for the treats.

Chuckling, and with his impatient barking in her ears, Kelly picked up her phone. As she headed to the kitchen she checked her message.

Hi, Kelly! Traffic was murder this morning. Got to the office with a headache. Hope your morning is better than mine so far!

Kelly frowned with sympathy and responded.

Sorry to hear, sweetie. Get some paracetamol.

Kelly took the chocolate treats from the cabinet as Charlie ran up and down the kitchen, his barking frantic. Another ping came.

I did. Duh! But my boss is working hard to counteract the effect. He's on my case again today. Sometimes, I think I ought to chuck it all in and come work in Nafplio too. Is Alex hiring in the hotel?

Kelly laughed out loud. She knew Efi was joking and teasing her about Alex. Again.

I hardly think he offers jobs for statisticians!

She leaned against the counter, waiting for a response, and ignoring the pug, who kept running around the island like a tireless wind-up toy.

Oh. I was thinking more like a maid's job. You know? I'd gladly wear a short skirt and have Alex chase me around the rooms of his hotel.

Kelly loved her friend's wicked humor. It was like she was right there and she could almost see her. She laughed with abandon, but then, Charlie barked again from the far end of the room. She'd forgotten all about him.

'Sorry, buddy!' she said, and he rushed to sit before her feet. She opened the bag of chocolate treats and made Charlie stay, then swirl and roll too, which meant he'd soon got the three treats he was expecting.

Patting him on the head, she placed the treats back into the cabinet and picked up her phone to carry on with the playful banter she enjoyed so much with Efi every day. If she didn't have that, she'd feel lost. She had no other friends to talk to these days. No living ones, anyway.

She typed her answer, giggling.

Ha ha. I think not!

She added an emoticon that stuck out its tongue cheekily.

What took you so long to reply this time? Were you worried I meant it?

Efi used the same emoticon.

No, silly! The dog distracted me, that's all!

You know I am joking, right? If anything, I am hoping it's you he's chasing around the rooms over there...Tell me if he does, girlfriend! I want to know!

Kelly smiled to read that, then sighed, despite herself. She was well aware she was head over heels in love with Alex. Since the school run three days earlier, she'd been reliving non-stop in her mind those moments when he held her in his arms, overcome by his enthusiasm, once his boy had reached the finish line.

And she'd been seeing a subtle change in him since that day, too. Now, she often caught him gazing at her across the table at breakfast and at dinner, like he was looking far, through her, or rather, into her soul. He certainly wasn't looking at her the normal way one looks at someone else.

That gave her hope that perhaps he felt the same way that she did. But while Lauren haunted the house, she wouldn't dare let anything happen between her and Alex. This is why she felt now, more than ever before, the need to help Lauren find peace so she could move on. Only after that happened, she'd feel justified to claim Alex as her own.

Her phone pinged again, and her eyes darted back to the screen. Only then did she realize she'd been in a daze for a while. Efi, impatient as usual, had written again seeing she hadn't answered.

Well? Does he chase you? You naughty thing!!!!!

Kelly gave a giggle, but before she could reply, the pug came rushing to her out of nowhere. With one of his toys in his mouth, he began to run up and down before her, looking at her sideways in that cute way that made her hysterical with laughter whenever they played chase together which, these days, was a lot.

'Not now, Charlie! A little later!'

She returned her attention to her phone and typed a short answer.

Ha-ha. If only!

As soon as she replied to Efi, she turned to Charlie, who had finally stopped running. When he met her eyes he let the toy drop from his mouth. To her surprise, he then charged towards her, bit at her slacks and began to tug.

'Hey! Stop it, Charlie!'

Another ping came.

I know you wish! Haha. Tell me, is his bum still as chewable as I recall?

Running Haunted

Kelly would have normally laughed with that, except the dog was becoming a bit of a handful. Now, he had begun to bark too, running up and down, then back to tugging at her slacks, back to barking and running, then returning for more tugging. This carried on for thirty seconds while Kelly stood gawping. 'What's wrong with you today?'

Charlie would always get really excited when his fur was damp after a bath. A little running around was to be expected, but this?

Frowning deeply, she was about to scold him, but then a text message notification echoed from her phone, snapping her attention back to it. Her heart gave a backflip. It was from Alex.

Hi, Kelly! Something I wanted to ask you. Can you call me when you have a moment, please?

Kelly smiled to her ears. He was always so tactful and sweet. Any other boss would call his employee whenever he pleased. But after he'd called her a couple of times to catch her in the middle of cooking something involved or rushing around the house upstairs hoovering and tidying, he'd heard her panting when she answered the phone and never called again. It was one of his sweet, thoughtful quirks that really made her heart melt: to text and ask her to call him at a time convenient to her if he wanted to discuss something.

Another ping from her app echoed.

Quiet again? Hey, Kelly! Just how chewable is that butt?

Kelly sniggered, her finger hovering over the digital keypad to answer when the dog did something unthinkable. Sinking his teeth in deeper, he gave her a super quick, yet rather painful little bite just above her ankle. It wasn't the kind of playful nip he'd give when excited. That took her aback.

'Ow! Charlie! Why did you do that? What's wrong with you today?' she protested, her phone dropping carelessly on the kitchen counter.

She began to shoo him and, funnily enough, he moved away without needing much encouragement. Keeping silent, he allowed her to lead him back to the bathroom where she decided to leave him for five minutes to calm down. It would also allow her to reply to Efi and to Alex with some peace and quiet.

Standing before the closed bathroom door, she lifted the fabric of her slacks to find the bite had left only a faint red mark. 'You crazy thing...' she muttered, and then, walking away, added, 'No more chocolate treats for you today, mister, that's for sure!'

She was still flustered and huffing when she returned to the counter to pick up the phone. Trying to regain her earlier light-hearted mood when reading Efi's last message, she smiled to herself and began to type, giggling as she did so.

Yes! His bum is definitely chewable.

As soon as she'd replied that, she sought Alex's message to reply that she'd call him in five minutes or so, only to realize that she was already in the text message screen, not in the app where Efi's messages were.

OH-MY-GOD!

She'd only just typed that back to Alex, instead of Efi! All at once, a cold sweat that started in her brow began to slither down her body like a deadly snake. When it reached her knees it made them buckle and, raising a hand on her head, she used the other to prop herself against the counter. With trembling hands, and with her heart pumping hard, she reached the first chair in sight with difficulty and flopped herself on it like a sack of stones, her phone still in her hand.

Oh, God, what do I do?

She brushed her brow with an urgent hand and pinned her eyes on the opposite wall. On there, her worst nightmares began to play like projections of her very own Cinema of Horrors. The movie playing was 'How to Get Fired and Ridiculed on the Same Day' and she was the leading star.

'Oh no! He's going to fire me, I know it! He's going to come straight home and fire me!' she shouted, her voice reverberating around the walls, echoing her desperation back to her, feeding it anew.

With hands that shook as if a Richter-scale-ten earthquake were in full swing around her, she looked down at her dark phone screen. She tapped on it and it came back to life. Willing herself to calm down so she could think, she looked at Alex's message above the fateful one she'd typed by error. With surprise, she saw he'd written another one in between. She guessed she must have been too busy scolding the dog for its antics to hear the ping when it came.

You must be busy... No worries. I'm off to a meeting shortly with a new supplier. I'll be at least an hour. Give me a call after eleven thirty or so when you can. Thanks.

Kelly felt relief wash over her like a jet of tepid water. *Alex, sweet, Alex! Such a great communicator!* So he probably wasn't on his phone when she wrote that. He was off to a meeting. Well, he had to be! Because that meant he never read her stupid message. The alternative was unthinkable. *And he'll be in that meeting room at least an hour! Dare I?*

She looked at her watch. 'Yes!' she told herself, pumping her fist mid-air, her heart beating fast. 'I'll get to the hotel in the car, find an excuse to get into his office while he's in the meeting, and I'll delete the message. Easy! Plenty of time to get there and back, and to rustle up a quick pasta meal before the kids get home!'

Kelly was feeling hopeful and tremendously lucky at the same time. She knew for a fact that Alex never took his phone to his meetings. He'd told her once how he thought phones made people unsociable. He detested seeing others staring into their phone screens, and that's why he allowed his employees to use their phones while on duty only for short phone calls – strictly no social media or Internet use.

'Oh, Alex! I thought you were a nut job the day you told me all that. But now I am so glad you are who you are!' she said out loud, caught up in her elation. Taking her phone with her, she hurried to the bathroom door, opening it to let the dog out. 'Detention over. Mummy's got work to do!'

Charlie walked out calmly, back to his good old self. Even though she was in a hurry to change clothes, grab her bag and go, she remained glued to her spot for a while, exchanging a mute gaze with the dog.

She gave a frown. 'Are you trying to say something to me?' She remembered then she wasn't wearing the scarf today. 'Damn!'

Beckoning Charlie frantically, she hurried up the steps and he followed, barking loudly.

In her room, with the pug by her feet, she put on the scarf in front of the mirror. As soon as she tied it to hold her ponytail in place, Lauren's laughter filled her head, crystal clear.

Kelly put her hands on her waist and turned away from the mirror in case Lauren projected her face onto it. She had no time to talk to extent. She just wanted to get out the door and delete that damn text message one moment sooner.

'Don't laugh, Lauren. It's not funny. And if it weren't for your silly dog, this would never have happened!'

'Oh come on, Kelly! It's funny, *awfully* funny!' More laughter ensued, high-pitched now, and just as annoying.

'Well, I think not. And I want you to tell me. Did you do this?'

'Did I cause you to write to Alex that you think his bum is chewable, you mean?' This time the pitch of her howl reached new heights. Not even a primadonna the likes of Maria Callas, or the maniacal laugh of Cruella de Vil, could ever possibly reach these notes.

'You know what I mean, Lauren! Did you get the dog to bite my leg to distract me?'

A moment's silence filled the room confirming her suspicion. 'A-ha! And now you're laughing? How could you do that to me, Lauren? I thought you wanted to help me, not to get me fired!'

'Don't be silly! You won't get fired—'

'Well, not if I can help it, I'll tell you that!' Without waiting any longer, she slipped out of her slacks and opened her wardrobe to get a pair of jeans.

'Listen, Kelly. You have to trust me. I know what I'm doing!'

'No, you don't! You've caused an absolute mess for me. How the hell am I going to be allowed into Alex's office when he's not in it? I have no idea!'

Lauren chuckled and said, 'That's easy, Kelly. Now listen to me… This is what you need to do.'

Chapter 33

Kelly entered through the hotel doors and marched straight up to the reception desk without breaking her stride.

The receptionist on duty, a rather snooty brunette who wore her hair in a tight bun today—like every other time she'd seen her—looked up from a register opened on the desk before her. Seeing Kelly, she puffed up her chest and raised her chin.

'Good morning,' she said with a ghost of a smile.

Kelly noticed that, once more, she hadn't used her name to greet her even though Alex had introduced them and they'd spoken since then a couple of times. She couldn't decide whether the receptionist failed to recall her name or chose not to address her with it. What she did know for sure was that the young woman was even snootier with her than she was with the customers, and wasn't sure why.

'Good morning, Tatiana.' Kelly raised up to her chest the plastic bag she was carrying so Tatiana could see it. 'I've brought something for Mr Sarakis.' She pointed at his closed office door to her right. 'Shall I?'

Tatiana put up an urgent hand, shaking her head, her red lips puckered tightly as if she'd been sucking on an ice smoothie through a straw and her mouth had stayed that way. 'I'm afraid he's not in. Perhaps you could come back in an hour?' she finally said, showing off her pearly whites with a glacial smile.

Kelly was ready to meet her resistance. Having been schooled adequately back home by Lauren, she didn't miss a beat. She smiled widely at her, then said, 'It's okay, Tatiana. I know he's in a meeting with a new supplier. He told me on the phone.' She pointed to the closed office door with her head and added, 'I'll just leave the stuff he asked me to bring and I'll come straight back out.'

Tatiana grew visibly baffled for a few moments, her lower lip twitching.

Kelly could read the inner struggle in her expression. Tatiana regarded herself too professional to let anyone into her boss's office while he was away. But, if the housekeeper was bringing something he asked for, how could she stop her from doing it?

All at once, Tatiana's eyes lit up. 'Why don't you leave, whatever this is, here with me? I'll make sure he gets the bag as soon as he's back in.'

'Oh no, that won't do. You see, he's also asked me to refresh his supply of socks, underpants and ties in his cabinet in there...' She pointed towards the office door again, this time with a playful finger, her features arranged to exude nonchalance to the max, just as Lauren had advised her.

'He said he has left a few unwashed articles in there for a while that I need to pick up immediately...' Kelly continued to lie, 'He told me he goes to the gym straight from the office and back here three times a week. And, you know, he hasn't brought any dirty laundry to the house for a while.' She let out a high-pitched laugh and gave a little wave. 'I expect his sweaty socks must be a little high in his gym bag as we speak.' She leaned forward as she stood before the counter and whispered, 'So I'd better get in and rescue them from their sad fate.' She winked, conscious she was grinning like an idiot, but it had to be done. 'What do ya say?'

Tatiana leaned back in her chair abruptly and Kelly registered in the woman's eyes a flicker of bemusement, if not suppressed abhorrence. Knowing she'd managed to elicit that from Tatiana's impassionate demeanor was a success in itself. Lauren's advice for Kelly to act that way had worked. Kelly had managed to put off the snobbish woman enough to want to get rid of her as soon as possible.

With a frantic wave that almost served as a shooing gesture, Tatiana said, 'Okay, okay. By all means. Go in there and do what you have to do.' She enunciated the last few words with disdain, her lips curled outwards, not touching her gums and teeth.

Kelly smiled as sweetly as she could muster in response to Tatiana's sour expression and hurried to the door. As soon as she put her hand on the handle, she heard Tatiana's voice and whirled around.

Tatiana's features were tight as she peered at her from over her glasses. 'And make sure to leave things tidy in there. As Alex... erm... as Mr Sarakis likes it.'

'Yes, of course,' said Kelly with a forced smile before turning to the door again. 'How did he ever hire her? Bossy cow...' she whispered, despite herself, as she pressed the handle down.

'What was that?'

Kelly looked over her shoulder with a chuckle. 'I said, "wow"! The woodwork on this door is stunning!'

Her lips puckered, Tatiana tilted her chin like a displeased schoolmistress. 'Hm. It's mahogany.'

'Well, that makes sense then.' Without giving her a second look, Kelly stepped into the office and closed the door behind her. Taking a steadying breath, she rushed to Alex's desk as if the place was on fire and every moment counted.

Just as she'd expected, Alex's phone was on his desk. She placed the bag on the chair and picked the phone up.

'Thank you, Alex, for your little quirks! For leaving it behind...' she said as she tapped on the screen. It lit up, expecting a code to be keyed in but that wasn't a problem. They all knew it back home. Nikos and Tommy used their father's phone sometimes in the evenings to play with a couple of games and fun apps they had asked him to download on there for them.

On one occasion, the kids had offered the phone to her to play a certain game. They had kept scores that night turning it into a competition. Stratos had won, but she'd won something too that night: access to Alex's phone code.

Running Haunted

Keying it in now, she saw her stupid message on the screen, and once again she hoped it had arrived after Alex had left his office. Of course, it had. The alternative was unthinkable.

She deleted it at once, along with the whole thread of their conversation, as there was no way she could delete just the specific last message. It meant he would find it strange the thread was gone, but she was happy to take her chances with that. It was a thousand times more preferable than to have him see what she'd written. He'd know for sure she was referring to *his* bum because she'd told him she was single. She was seeing no one in town, so, of course, he'd suspect she could only be referring to him.

Shaking her head, she tried to rid herself of the very idea. Now, the damned thing was gone. And she was safe. Thank goodness for that. Even if he found it baffling that the thread was gone, it would never point back to her. He'd just have to accept he must have deleted it by error.

She placed the phone back down on the desk, then picked up the bag and smiled when she opened it a little to look at the contents. She'd actually brought a couple of ties, some underpants and socks in case Tatiana asked to see the contents of the bag.

Now, Kelly's job was done and she knew that if she had any sense she should get the hell out as soon as possible. Except, she couldn't. Instead, she glued her eyes to the cabinet by the window, where Lauren said Alex kept his undergarments, and felt her curiosity prick at her insides. Soon, her gut began to clench with a growing sense of panic. *I bet Alex has charmed all the girls back at the gym... Oh, God! What if he has a girlfriend? That cabinet might hold some evidence... Photos of them together, maybe? Tickets for them to enjoy upcoming events? Or stuff belonging to her, perhaps? Like, sexy lingerie? Goodness me! He couldn't bring any of that stuff into the house. But he could hide it all... in this cabinet...*

Shaking her head profusely as she stood near the door, Kelly scolded herself for letting her imagination run wild. It wasn't like her to nose about. But... she wanted him so badly! And she'd been hurt before. What harm could it do to grab the chance and find out if he had a girl? It would save her from keeping her hopes up in vain, wouldn't it?

Oh, come on, Kelly. Just a little peek. No one will ever know.

Giving the door a furtive glance, she hurried to the cabinet to open it. The first thing she noticed was his gym bag that lay on the bottom shelf.

Oh, Alex... Good for you. So that's how you keep fit despite your long hours in the office. And that butt is certainly tight! She rolled her eyes and chuckled. *Definitely chewable.*

Turning her attention to the top shelf, she found no dirty clothes were in sight. *He must be bringing the dirty clothes back and forth between the office and the house himself. Of course, the receptionist doesn't know that. Good one, Lauren!*

Soon, she began to whisper to herself as she stared in disbelief. 'Wow... So neat...' On the top shelf, three patterned ties lay folded in rounded shapes inside a small cardboard box. Beside it, a larger one contained neatly folded pairs of underpants and socks in various basic colours. *So cool... But wait! He folds the Marie Kondo way? The plot thickens. Just how big a catch is this guy?*

Kelly threw another glance towards the door. Tatiana had to have a thing for him. Ergo the zeal to keep Kelly away and not calling her by her name. But who could blame her? If Kelly worked a stone's throw away from his office all day, she'd be enamored—if not besotted—with him, too.

Straightening, she closed the cabinet doors and picked up the plastic bag again.

She was halfway to the door when it suddenly swung open and Alex walked in. 'Kelly!' he said, his face breaking into a grin as soon as he saw her.

'Oh! Hi!' Kelly gave an awkward smile, then put a hand on her waist. Her other hand that held the bag landed on her

Running Haunted

chest with a thud as she looked away. 'Ooh! You scared me there!'

'Sorry, Kelly. You've been shopping?' he said, pointing to her plastic bag with one hand, then turned back for one moment, just enough to swing the door shut.

'Hm?' she said, shaking her head like an idiot.

'The bag?'

'Oh! That!' She fanned her face with her free hand, then lowered the one that held the bag, wishing the damn thing would disappear from the face of the Earth. 'Yes, um... a spot of shopping. Underwear. No, um, sorry. A top. A new top.'

'Oh. *Me ya.*'

'Thanks... Strange, isn't it?'

'What is?'

'You know... "*Me ya*"? What a strange wish we Greeks have! "Enjoy it with health?" I mean, who ever thought of that?'

He chuckled loudly. 'Socrates? Or perhaps Plato?' he joked. 'Who knows? I have no idea.'

'Me neither.' She shrugged, then began to shift her weight from foot to foot, not knowing where to look. Why was he studying her so intently? It made her feel extremely self-conscious. Or maybe it was her own impression, seeing that she felt bad to have been caught lingering in there on her own. Her eyes sought the window, the glorious sunny day outside. *That's where I should have been. Out there. Not in here. Serves me right being nosy, wanting to check the contents of his cabinet. Stupid, stupid, stupid!*

'Kelly? All okay?'

She turned her eyes towards him, to find him gazing at her with twinkling eyes. A mixture of amusement and intrigue oozed from that look, his smile wide, effortless.

She took a steadying breath. 'Yes, sure. Fine. Just grand.'

'Wonderful!' His eyes lit up as he shook his head to add, 'My goodness, Kelly! I'm so pleased to find you here! It's like you've read my mind or something!'

Her brows shot up. 'Really? Why do you say that?'

'Well, you know this morning when I wrote you a message and said I had something to ask?'

'M-hm...'

'Well, I meant to ask you to come over here so we could talk face to face!'

She exhaled loudly, then said, 'Well, I'd like to say I am clever enough to read minds but I can't!' She chuckled, then brushed her hair back from her brow. 'You know, I just read your message and thought, "Well, I am going to town anyway this morning, so why don't I pay him a surprise visit to talk face to face, instead?" See? Hence me. Here. Surprising you!'

She pointed at him with a loose finger, trying to appear nonchalant, and gave a giggle that sounded too girlie in her own ears.

Luckily, he didn't seem to notice. He burst into laughter that made his eyes dance so wonderfully she couldn't help but stare.

'And a wonderful surprise it is, too! Thanks for coming, Kelly!'

'Well, I'd better go now, you must be busy!'

He put a gentle hand on her arm as she moved to go, and let out a soft chuckle. 'Wait! I do need to talk to you about something, remember?'

'Oh, yes, right. Of course.'

'Well, I just got out of the meeting, earlier than expected, and I have two hours to spare. Why don't you stay and grab a bite to eat with me today? We can have an early lunch so you can get home before the kids return from school.'

'Lunch? With you?'

'Yes.'

'So, that's what you wanted to tell me? To have lunch?'

'No, of course, that's not it.'

'Oh.'

'All I'm saying is to have lunch and talk about a certain issue I need to discuss.' He tapped her upper arm playfully, then removed it, regretfully too soon. 'Sorry, if I confused you.'

Kelly eyed him, deep in thought. He was being secretive. It wasn't like him. As if guessing her thoughts, he put a hand on his heart, tilted his head and said, 'It's nothing serious or complicated, don't worry. Stratos's birthday is coming up, and I'd like your help to pick something for his birthday. That's all.'

'Oh! Okay,' she said, dropping her shoulders and taking an easy breath.

He smiled brightly and went on, 'You see, when Mrs Botsari was around, she always offered to do the shopping herself for the children's gifts around the year. I wonder if you'd be happy to take over and pick something for Stratos. His birthday is this coming Saturday. I trust a woman's choice better than I trust my own. And I'd be happy to accompany you. We could go get Stratos's present today if you like. Saves you from another trip to town. And we could eat something on the hoof if we run out of time.'

'Of course. I'd love to help.'

He prompted her to take a seat and he went to sit behind his desk. He leaned forward with a happy smile, his hands resting on his desk entwined. 'I'm happy beyond words to have you working in my house, Kelly. But I'm sure I've told you this before, haven't I?'

With a demure smile, she glanced at her lap for a few moments. There was something electrifying in his eyes today, something she hadn't seen before. It made her dizzy, and crazy with exuberance at the same time. As if she could touch the ceiling if she only raised her hands over her head.

Finally, she looked up to say, 'And I feel the same about working for you, Alex. You guys, I mean. You and the kids.'

He chuckled again. 'So? What shall we get Stratos?'

'What are you thinking to get him?'

He shook his head. 'Don't look at me. I got nothing. I never do.'

'Well, what did Mrs Botsari get him last year?'
'A sweater. A blue one, I think.'
'Hm.'
'Not good, huh?'
'For a thirteen-year-old? Nuh-uh.'
'Okay...' He put two fingers of one hand on his lips and began to pinch them absentmindedly. Raising his head, he leaned back in his chair and sighed luxuriously. Then, he looked at her again, eyes lit up, both hands clutching the armrests. 'I've got it! How about a pair of jeans? He likes those faded, heavily torn types!'
'Can we get away from clothes at all?'
'Oh...' A moment later he added, 'I know. Music!'
'Now we're getting somewhere.'
'Yes, but I don't know what he wants.'
'I do.'
'You do?'
'Yes, Alex. But it may extend your budget a bit. My idea doesn't involve buying him a CD.'
'A CD collection perhaps? Or two?' He waved both hands dismissively. 'No problem. Sky's the limit for my boy.'
'Of course. Except, I am not referring to CDs. Besides, I don't think young kids buy CDs any more. Not in the era of iTunes and iPods.'
He leaned forward, a cunning smile on his lips. 'Ooh! Something more fitted to his young, techie tastes then. No problem. Money's not an object. And I can tell you have a good idea... I know he has an iPod and a phone, so it must be something else.' He widened his eyes. 'Go on! I'm all ears!'
'A guitar. Stratos wants a guitar.'
'Oh!'
Kelly saw it then, the epiphany. She gave him a few moments to process it.
'Of course... What an idiot I am! He did tell me, after all, how he enjoys the lessons with his friend's father... See?' To her surprise, he slapped his forehead and continued, 'Stratos

was right. I don't listen. I've been too cooped up in my own inability to deal with Lauren's loss to care for my children's needs properly as a father. All this time, I've been paying no attention to Stratos's love for music. Lauren has always encouraged him to sing... And since she passed, I've been hearing him sing behind his closed bedroom door on his own... But I never encouraged him, nor did I discuss it with him. I didn't even discuss his mother with him, for goodness sake!'

'Oh Alex, don't do this to yourself any more. Stratos is fine now, with you I mean, since you guys had that talk.'

'He is?'

'Yes, of course, he is. And he'll be even happier if you get him a guitar. This way, he'll be able to practice in his room and will no longer have to go to his friend's house. I also think you ought to register him at a local music school so he takes proper classes.'

'His friend's father is a great tutor, he told me... Don't you think he'll mind if I tell him he'll have to change his tutor?'

'No he won't, trust me. I know he likes the guy, but don't you see? If you register him in a music school yourself, it will make him see without a shadow of a doubt that you approve of his interest in music. Combined with your present of the guitar, it will be the ultimate proof of your encouragement, your acceptance of his natural music talents that Lauren saw in him so early on.'

'Oh Kelly... How right you are!' He placed a hand on his heart and let out a sigh, holding her gaze, making her all gooey inside, her heart galloping like a horse that's gone wild.

After a few moments of silence, with eyes that seemed to melt with the soft light of a thousand candles, he added, 'You know, Kelly... I often think it was fate that you came to Nafplio to run that marathon... It seems to me like I've been running one myself all this time, except I didn't know the way, or how long I had to go to reach the finish line. All I knew was that I was alone, lost, and tired. But with you here now, "running the course" with me, so to speak, things are so much better.'

Chapter 34

Kelly and Alex walked together along the pavement in a central road lined with shops and leafy trees. As they commented back and forth about their beautiful surroundings and the warm weather, she couldn't help but marvel at his long limbs that moved fluidly beside her own. He was smiling widely, head tilted back, eyes half-closed, and she noticed the fringe over his forehead had grown since she'd last noticed it. It was almost touching his eyebrows now.

His face, clean-shaven as always, allowed her to admire the hard lines of his cheekbones, nose and chin. Those, in conjunction with his Adam's apple and the sinews that bulged on his neck as he turned his head this way and that, caused her to hyperventilate. She looked away, focusing on the traffic rushing past, just to clear her mind.

Alex, none the wiser, was now talking about Stratos, and how he felt intent on treating him for his big day in the best way possible. The lapels of his jacket were dancing as he walked. Kelly loved that charming spring in his step, and he seemed to walk like that more often than not these days.

Alex stopped short in front of a shop and pointed to the window, causing her to snap out of her thoughts. It took her only a split second to see why. The window offered a colourful display of stylish musical instruments, guitars of all shapes and kinds included.

'This is the store, Kelly.'

'Oh! They have a wonderful collection!'

'Wait until you see inside. I've been in here a couple of times to buy plastic flutes and Soprano melodicas for the kids when they were smaller.'

'All the boys play music?'

'You know... a little... what they learned in school.'

'Oh. That's nice.' She followed him into the shop when he beckoned and wondered again why Stratos hadn't told his father all this time that he wanted to play the guitar. If all the kids were allowed to play music in the house, then why? And then, she finally understood. Stratos had clearly associated his affinity for the guitar and for singing with his mother, who had encouraged his talents. *Because he wasn't allowed to discuss his mother at home, he must have thought singing and playing the guitar wouldn't be allowed in the house either... Poor thing... How he must have suffered for so long!*

'Kelly?' she heard him say and, with a nervous shake of her head, approached as the clerk led them to the window from the inside of the store. There, Alex pointed at a stunning black electric guitar with red flame details on it, asking to look at it more closely.

✶✶✶✶✶

Leaving the store, Alex suggested to Kelly they go straight to the hotel so he could leave in his office the huge guitar box he was carrying. He proposed they go somewhere on the seafront for a quick lunch afterwards, and she happily agreed.

Walking back along the same busy street, Alex seemed over the moon for having picked what he thought was the best gift for Stratos. Having held in his hands half a dozen guitars of different colours and shapes, he'd decided on that first one he'd asked to see – the black one with the red flame details. He told her in the shop how it looked similar to the one showing on the poster Stratos had on the wall over his bed. It was a poster of his favourite rock band. Alex said he hadn't even noticed it until recently. When he asked Kelly about it in the shop, she informed him the band was Aerosmith and agreed the guitar he wanted to buy was perfect for Stratos.

Crossing a traffic light, they entered the lanes of the historic quarter of Nafplio. They sped past a couple of tavernas, then turned left on the next corner under a cascading bright pink bougainvillea. The path was strewn with pink blooms, the aftermath of the north wind that had been blowing fiercely through town the previous day.

They turned right at the end of the path, onto the lane where the hotel was. They sped past a couple of souvenir shops, and then, just as they neared a small café, Kelly suddenly stopped mid-sentence and froze in place.

As if in an action film sequence, everything before her eyes froze too, then began to whirl around her. She blinked a few times, trying to shake the unbearable feeling of vertigo away. Everything kept spinning, except for one thing: the man who had just come out of the café, a Styrofoam cup of coffee in hand. The world stopped whirling at last and came sharply into focus before her unbelieving eyes.

The voice she heard then caused her shoulders to twitch. 'Makis?' the voice said, and only then did she realize it was her own.

The man stopped before her with a frown, just as she recalled that Alex was standing beside her. In the shock and horror of the last few seconds, she had forgotten all about him.

'Yes?' said Makis, the awful ex-boyfriend that she had tried for so long to forget.

'Makis? It's me, Kelly,' she said with a nervous chuckle, yet secretly wishing for a chasm to open wide under her and swallow her whole.

His brow grew deeply etched, and then, with a loud chuckle, he put out his free hand and said, 'Kelly! Oh, my God! Look at you!'

He leaned forward, putting his hand around her, and she had no choice but to do the right thing and kiss him back on both cheeks. Numb, she threw a look at Alex, who was smiling faintly, obviously waiting to be introduced.

She didn't want to do it, to introduce her unfortunate past to her wonderful present. The past involved being fat and miserable. Her today involved being thin and fit, happy, and madly in love. Not that there was anything wrong with being fat, per se. But with Makis in her life at the time, being as awful as he was, her extra weight had become a curse.

Ugly, infuriating memories flooded her mind. As her boyfriend, Makis had laughed at her, bullied her, criticized her, and in the end cheated on her with a girl who was so supermodel-thin she bordered on anorexic. But surely, she didn't have to be upset about all that now. It was over between them and they'd parted like friends.

After all, he was the reason why she'd resorted to running, dieting, and healthy living after their separation. And she'd become a shiny new person. She owed him that.

She pressed her lips together, then tried to smile at Makis, but still, no words came out of her mouth. He was still looking at her up and down, clearly aghast. Her stunning new looks must have knocked him back like a category-five hurricane.

'Oh, my God! What happened to you, Kelly? I can't believe it. You look gorgeous!' he finally said, his expression bright.

A warm feeling of satisfaction mushroomed in the pit of her stomach, cascading in all directions from there to fill her inner being. It caused the corners of her lips to curl wickedly, her hand to rise with a flourish when she turned to introduce Alex, choosing to ignore his comments. 'This is Alex. Alex, meet an old friend of mine, Makis.'

Makis gave a tight smile and shook hands with Alex, who responded in his formal manner, the way she'd seen him greet his guests and his associates in his hotel.

Makis turned to her, a wry smile on his lips. 'I hope you bear no grudges, Kelly. I was in a bad place when we were... well, "friends", like you said.' He did air quotes with his free hand when he said the word as his eyes darted to Alex.

'So, Alex? You guys are… "friends"?' he asked then, doing the air-quotes thing again and causing her agreeable smile to disappear. *I knew it… He's still the same tactless moron he always was! Surely he must have guessed I'd rather have Alex not knowing that he and I were an item in the past. But he insinuated anyway. What a tool he is!* Before she could say anything, Alex beat her to it.

'Kelly works for me, actually.' He'd straightened his spine, raising his head too, and she wondered why. His smile had frozen, eyes narrowed.

Makis, self-absorbed as usual, didn't seem to notice. Ignoring Alex, he turned to Kelly. 'You work here? So do I!'

'What? You live in Nafplio?' she asked, trying to conceal her bemusement.

'No, of course not. You know me, I love Athens too much! But I have a new job now. I am a sales manager for a shoe company and I travel around Greece. Me and one of my salesmen are spending a few days helping in a big shoe store that's opening here in Nafplio this weekend. Our company has provided them with a large shipment of our summer collection, and we'll be having all sorts of displays to make the merchandise stand out as much as possible.'

He seemed excited about it all, but it didn't rub off on her in the least. Once again, she noticed he hadn't taken any interest in her, didn't ask why she'd chosen to live in Nafplio or what her job was. *Typical Makis.* She eyed him as he went on about shoes and his new job, and she grew all the more bored and annoyed with him by the second.

When Alex hefted the heavy guitar package with a grunt, repositioning it more evenly under his arm, her eyes widened, 'Oh, I am so sorry, Alex. You've been carrying that for a while, haven't you? Well, Makis, we'd better go. It was nice to see you ag—'

Ignoring her, Makis took a step closer to Alex. 'Oh! You bought a guitar! You playing?' Makis air-strummed with his free hand and pretended to act like a rock legend while Kelly and Alex watched speechless. The two of them exchanged a look, Kelly trying to convey to him how sorry she felt.

Without giving Makis a reply, Kelly offered her hand. 'Well, it's been nice to see you, Makis. Good luck with it all.'

To her surprise, he took her hand and captured it in his own, moving closer. 'Wait! You can't just leave! Give me your number and I'll call you! I'll be here for a few more days. We should have lunch or something.' His eyes lit up and he let go of her hand to slap himself on the forehead. 'Idiot! What am I saying? Why wait? Have lunch with me today! Please? I can meet you, say, in about an hour?' He checked his watch. 'Let me just go to the shop and sort out some loose ends. I can meet you in that café where we used to go together back in the day. Remember? The one in Syntagma Square? You used to love their *loukoumades*.'

He winked, then waited, and she stood there, appalled. Not only because she'd taken his comment about the *loukoumades* as another nasty jab at her fattiness at the time, but because, once again, he was saying things that would make it clear to Alex that she and Makis had a thing together once. Not to mention the way he'd cradled her hand like that. Male friends just don't take that many liberties with women.

Her chest feeling tight, she turned to check on Alex and found him looking quite uncomfortable. Now, he kept hefting the package over and over again, beads of sweat on his brow, and he kept brushing it and his hair, feet restless, full of energy as if he was about to run a sprint and couldn't wait to start.

'I am so sorry, Alex. Let's go.' She touched his arm and beckoned him and, as she started to go with him, she said to Makis, 'Sorry. Got to run. Maybe I'll see you around.'

To her absolute horror, he made it awkward by hurrying behind them and shouting. 'Wait! You still have the same mobile number?'

Her own voice sounded regretful to her ears when she responded as if on auto-pilot, 'Yes, I do.'

'Well, I'll call you in an hour. See how you feel about lunch then!' He winked, relentless in his advances, just as she remembered him. A relentless go-getter. That's what he had been from day one. He'd flirted with her and kept calling her until she said yes to going out. And later, until she agreed to move in with him. Funnily enough, in the beginning, she used to be charmed by him being so confident, so insistent. Now, she wasn't exactly charmed, but perhaps it felt a little good too. Satisfying. To be honest, it stroked her ego deliciously.

Perhaps it will be good for me to dangle the gorgeous, fit, thin, sexy new me in front of his smug face. Yes. It will teach him a lesson to dump me the way he did. And if he has any ideas about trying his luck with me again, it'll be a laugh. Go on, Kelly. The poor devil is practically begging to get turned down!

She smiled confidently then, hoping her mischief wasn't showing. Still walking away, and as Alex was hurrying a little forward now, evidently eager to put down the heavy package in his office a moment sooner, she looked over her shoulder and told Makis with a little wave, 'Okay. Call me. But not for lunch. I am having lunch with Alex today.' She offered a triumphant little smile. 'But I can meet you for coffee in that place you mentioned. Tomorrow morning, maybe. Call me later... This afternoon.' Then, without waiting for a reaction, she turned to look in front of her. Rushing to catch up with Alex, she squeezed his arm gently and said sorry that she'd kept him waiting.

Chapter 35

Alex banged his fist on his desk. 'This is the worst timing ever! Just as I was about to talk to her, this cretin comes into the picture!'

Across from him in his office, his friend Dimos eyed him with sympathy, his lips pressed together. 'I'm sorry, Alex. And I hate to say I told you so, but I did tell you, didn't I? Kelly is a serious catch and she'd just landed on your lap. You shouldn't have waited for so long. I mean, she's already there in your house, running it, having great relations with your kids. And you clearly have feelings for her. So what's been holding you back? I never understood.'

'I told you what held me back; what still does, actually.'

Dimos tutted, rolling his eyes for emphasis. 'Oh, give it a rest already, Alex! It's just a dream, for god's sake.'

'It's not just a dream, Dimos. It's a recurrent one. It's persistent. It's got to mean something.'

'What? Those chains your late wife is tied up with on your bed? What *can* it mean?'

'They're not chains any more,' he said, distracted, his eyes staring into the distance at the quaint lane beyond the window pane.

'What?'

He turned to face his friend with a soft sigh. 'I said they're not chains now. It's been a week now that, in the dream, they've turned into strings of pearls.'

Dimos dropped his jaw, then shook his head in disbelief. 'The plot thickens. Are you serious?'

Alex put out his hands and gesticulated frantically as he said, 'What do you want me to say? It's a dream. I can't control it.'

'So what does it even mean? Do pearls have a special meaning for you?'

'No... I mean, Lauren used to wear a beautiful pearl necklace. But that's it. I cannot think of anything else that might be a possible association in my mind...'

'Look, it doesn't matter. Forget it, okay?'

'But that's just it, Dimos. I can't just forget it! The fact that I keep seeing Lauren in my sleep has to mean I am not ready yet to move on, right?'

'Nonsense. This is probably a catch twenty-two. As long as you see the dream, you think you're not ready, but it seems to me that as long as you think that, you'll only keep seeing the dream.' He raised a hand and twirled it in mid-air, his head tilted. 'You know what I mean?'

Alex closed his hand on top of his head, capturing thick clumps of hair as if he were drowning and attempting to grab and pull himself out of the water. All of a sudden, he let go and huffed, leaning back in his chair with such force that the poor thing squeaked in protest. 'Aaaargh! This is driving me insane!'

Dimos put up a hand. 'Perhaps if you see a specialist?'

Alex leaned forward abruptly, causing the back of the chair to squeak again. 'You mean a shrink?'

'Well, yes. If it's going to help... I have a friend, who—'

Alex put up his hand. 'Look! Dimos, I appreciate it, but I won't go to a shrink. I am just fine in my head. And if you must know, I feel there's more than meets the eye here.'

'Like what?'

'You know what... I've told you... I think that Lauren—'

'Oh no! Not that again! Surely you still don't think that Lauren's haunting your house!'

Alex put up both hands this time, his features pinched. 'You know what? Just forget it. I can't discuss this now. All I need you to do is help me out with Kelly. What do I do?'

Dimos leaned back in his chair with a heavy sigh. 'So, you're sure she's meeting that moron for coffee?'

'Yes... and I can't even bear to think that they could get back together. After we met him this morning, we came back here and I asked her surreptitiously about him. She told me they had a relationship for three years and even lived together. But he was constantly putting her down. She said she was overweight at the time and not feeling good about herself. Said that it was actually the way he mistreated her that urged her to change her lifestyle and start running... She said she owes him that.'

Dimos scrunched up his face, flinching. 'Ouch. I don't like that last bit.'

'Then again, she said he cheated on her, and she called him a couple of interesting names.'

'That's comforting.'

'So? Do you think they'll get back together now?'

'If he cheated on her, she's not likely to go back to him with open arms, now, is she?'

He shrugged a shoulder. 'I don't know... So many people forgive and forget.'

'Oh, for goodness sake, Alex! Don't be so damn insecure. You're also in her life, remember? She may not be so quick to consider patching up her relationship with him. After all, it's not like she actively sought to contact him. It was a chance meeting, right? And you did say she seems to like you?'

'Yes, definitely.' He smiled broadly, feeling himself relax, his heart swelling at the very thought that she could be his girl one day. Kelly was just perfect. Since the day they visited Bourtzi, where he had first felt sparks sizzling between them as he held her hand, just after her scarf had almost blown away, he'd been thinking about her night and day.

By now, it was getting increasingly difficult to act nonchalant around her and to keep his hands off her too. He had particular trouble with that, seeing that he was her boss. Lauren had always teased him that he was forever exploring everything with his hands. Her, especially. And now, all he wanted to do was touch Kelly when he talked to her, squeezing her shoulder or forearm gently as he shared a joke or praised her for her work while aching inside for a chance to squeeze her whole in his embrace.

'Hey! Buddy!'

Alex came to with a start, realizing he had fallen into a trance as he watched people come and go outside his office window. He shook his head and eyed his friend sheepishly. 'Sorry. It's been a weird day...'

'Mm-hm...' He seemed amused, about to burst into laughter.

'Dimos. Don't. It's not funny.'

He tilted his head and gave an impish smile. 'It is a little.'

Alex flung out his arms. 'So what do I do?'

'Nothing. Let Kelly meet the guy for coffee, then act as a friend and ask her how it went. You should be able to gauge from her reaction what this blockhead's prospects are with her.'

Alex shook his head fiercely. 'That's not good enough.'

Dimos shrugged. 'What else can you do?'

'I want to be there when they meet. See for myself.'

'Are you nuts?'

'I wouldn't go and get a table, Dimos. But I can always find an excuse and pass by, you know?'

'Pass by?'

'Yes, like on my way to a café or to shop something. You know?'

'So you'll just act like you happened to pass by and noticed them and go over there to say hi?'

'Exactly.'

'What would that do for you?'

'I'd get the vibes, you know? I'm pretty good at reading people, and I'm a master at reading body language.'

'Well, that should be easy for anyone to read. If they're not holding hands, or if he doesn't have his tongue stuck down her throat, you'll be okay.'

'Stop teasing, Dimos! I'm in torment here!'

'Okay, okay...'

Alex huffed, then looked away, his face melted, the very thought of losing Kelly causing his insides to tumble like clothes in the washing machine.

'That bad, huh?'

In lieu of an answer, he nodded firmly once.

'Okay. So you say she asked him to phone her in the afternoon so they can arrange to meet tomorrow morning?'

Alex signed. 'That's right...'

'Do you even know where they'll be going?'

'I don't know exactly. He mentioned he'd take her to one of the cafés on Syntagma Square, but without naming it, unfortunately.'

'That doesn't help much then...'

'I know that. But he said she always ordered *loukoumades* whenever they visited it in the past. Does that help?'

Dimos's eyes lit up as he bent forward to slap his knee. 'Of course, it does. You lucky rat! I know exactly which café has that on the menu. My nieces from Athens insist my sister take them there for *loukoumades* whenever they visit town.' He brought his chair closer to the desk and leaned forward. 'Now listen!'

Alex rubbed his hands profusely and listened to his friend as he spoke bright-faced, his heart accelerating with excitement.

*****

Kelly hung up her phone after talking to Makis. As she had asked him, he had called her in the afternoon. It turned out he had to go back to Athens urgently and stay for a day or two, so they arranged to meet on Sunday at eleven a.m. at that old café in Syntagma Square. Makis planned to arrive at Nafplio early Sunday morning, go to the shop first thing, and then meet her for coffee, possibly brunch too.

Kelly was determined to only have a coffee and eat nothing in his presence. Bile rose in her throat at the very thought of what it was like in the past to eat in his company, the way he always put her down. But, somehow, she managed to feel excited about their upcoming encounter. She couldn't wait to find closure with that idiot and felt fortunate he had proposed to go to one of the places where he used to upset her all the time in the past with his nasty comments.

Back then, she didn't have much self-esteem and kept chastising herself for her weakness, her pathetic lack of basic discipline. Food ruled her life and was forever on her mind back then. Whenever they visited that particular café during their many weekend breaks in Nafplio, she could never resist the *loukoumades.* A mouthwatering picture of the dish was printed on the menu... She could still see it clearly in her mind. Golden fried balls of dough slathered in lashings of honey and runny hazelnut paste. The sight of the photograph on the menu used to make her heart stop with longing.

And every time the *loukoumades* arrived and she attacked them with gusto, Makis would tut loudly, then launch into one of his long lectures as she ate them, making them taste like balls of hay infused with vinegar. She never did enjoy a single serving of *loukoumades* in that place. It was impossible to do with his fierce criticism in her ears about her sugar cravings and about how he preferred her to be thin and fit. At the same time, he'd point to all the pretty girls that sat at the nearby tables or passed by, to show her the perfect examples of what he thought was 'beautiful' and 'normal'.

Kelly gritted her teeth at the distant memories. Time hadn't done enough, it seemed, to lessen the pain they elicited. Putting her phone down on the kitchen island, she thanked herself for her drive to change her life so dramatically since then, and to become the fit, happy, assertive woman she was now. It had all started from her conscious decision to change her life, starting from her body. Now she knew that to change anything, to *be* anything, all it takes is a conscious decision. Life simply arranges its cosmic forces perfectly to make the change happen, the power of the shift proportionate to the firmness of the decision in a person's mind.

Likewise, now, she made a firm decision to find closure in that café, should Makis dare even hint on rekindling their old romance or pointing at another girl to make a nasty comment. *What a joke he is!*

Chuckling to herself, she went to the fridge to take out a carton of orange juice and four of her homemade energy bars. She poured juice in four glasses and put them on a tray with the energy bars to take them outside.

She and the boys had just returned from walking Charlie around the green, then up and down the hill. Their daily exercise had turned into their favourite routine, something that had strengthened her bond with the boys and the dog in record time while benefiting them all equally.

More than anyone, it had benefited Nikos, of course. Since he had finished the run and received his medal, the two bullies had changed their attitude towards him and seemingly had communicated it clearly enough to the other kids in school. No one gave him any trouble any more.

Tommy was playing less with his mother's jewellery these days. Instead, she'd find him at his desk in the evenings writing letters to his grandad, as he told her. Kelly imagined this continued to help him process his grief over his mother's passing.

As for Stratos, his face glowed every time he and his father reminisced about the earlier years when Lauren was around. The only thing that worried her about him was his being so shy with girls. He had admitted, after all, that he liked that beautiful girl that had passed them by at the stadium, but he had seemed crippled with fear just thinking about talking to her. From what he said, she understood it was because of his acne problem.

Yet, these days, his complexion glowed with freshness and there were no rough, red patches any more, thanks to the fabulous herb-based cosmetics she'd found online. It seemed there were no products she could buy to boost his teenage confidence, though. She'd have to try harder to fix that herself.

As for Alex, she wasn't sure how things were with him, and if he seemed happier at all. All she knew was that she craved his every look, his every word and touch, with every fiber of her being. Images of him filled her head once more, causing her to sigh deeply, but then she remembered she had no time for daydreaming.

Shaking her head, she willed herself to stop lingering by the kitchen island. The boys were sitting outside on the porch, surely desperate for a cool drink. As she made her way there hastily, she wondered how she could help Stratos. His birthday was coming up, after all. What better time for him to receive the gift of friendship—if not the love—of the girl that monopolized his dreams?

Chapter 36

Kelly and the boys were drinking their cool refreshments on the porch, shooting the breeze, when suddenly Stratos nearly spurted his drink, then clamped his mouth shut with an urgent hand. Eyes popping with alarm, he swallowed his last sip with a loud gulp.

Panicking, Kelly turned to him, thinking he was choking, but found him staring goggle-eyed at two girls who were strolling past the house along the pavement.

Kelly recognized one of them; it was Eleni – the girl they had seen outside the stadium last Sunday.

'That was Eleni, wasn't it?' she said to Stratos, once the girls were out of sight, nudging him on the arm as she sat beside him. His brothers erupted in smooching noises, teasing him, in between giggling and chortling.

Stratos admonished them, which worked to suppress their laughter a little. He gave Kelly a furtive glance and then let out a deep sigh as his eyes rested on the empty street. 'Yes...'

'That bad, huh?'

''Fraid so.'

'So, does she live close by?'

'Six doors that way.' He pointed to the right, then heaved another sigh, which caused more chortling and teasing from his brothers.

'Nikos! Tommy! Stop already. It's not funny!' he complained, pointing at them in succession with a sharp finger, his cheeks flushing red.

Kelly served the younger boys a look of disapproval, which caused them both to shrink visibly on their chairs and bow their heads. Taking advantage of the silence, she turned to Stratos again. 'Come on, Stratos. Let me throw a birthday party for you. Then you can invite Eleni. You never know. She may like you, too.'

'Impossible.'

'How do you know?'

'I just know, okay?' He shot his hands up toward his cheeks. 'With this skin?'

'Oh, come on! That's an excuse! Your complexion looks so much better these days and you know it!'

'Yeah? And what about my being so skinny? Look at me!' He began to gesticulate, pointing at himself here and there, the look in his eyes desperate. 'Besides. My nose is too big... And I hate these ghastly, knobbly knees of mine!'

Taken aback by this sudden outburst, all Kelly could do was stare as he kept on slapping various parts of his body that he wasn't happy about. 'Now, you're being silly, Stratos. There's nothing wrong with you. You look exactly how a tall and thin young man should look. To me, you look perfect—'

Stratos shook his head profusely, then pointed sharply towards the street. 'Kelly, did you not you see her just now? *She* looks perfect! And she walks smoothly like a catwalk model, like her feet hover above the ground!'

'So? What if she does?' She put up her hands. 'Look, Stratos. All I am saying is, your obvious wrong idea about your looks is not realistic. Ask her to come to your birthday party. What do you have to lose?'

'She'd laugh in my face, Kelly. No way!'

A tense silence ensued for a while, then Kelly said, 'Okay. Forget asking Eleni. But I'd still like to organize a party for you for Saturday night. Would that be okay?'

He shrugged, visibly upset.

She was about to thank him for what she thought had been a silent "yes", when he piped up in a whiny voice, 'But what's the point without Eleni?'

She turned to find him hunched over, shoulders slumped, his eyes glued to his sneakers. Reaching out with a tender hand, she tousled his hair. That caused him to look up and offer a wry smile.

'You silly thing. What's the point of a birthday party, I hear you say? Well, presents of course! Snacks, sandwich bombs and...' she scratched her head as she thought on her feet about what other food she could prepare, '...cheese pies, spinach pies...' Giving a wicked smile, she added, '...and my mean tiramisu, of course! Judging from the fact you had the most pieces last time I made it, I presume that would be okay?'

To her satisfaction, his eyes sparkled with a hint of enthusiasm. She gave a lopsided grin. 'Unless you'd prefer a bought cake?'

'No, your tiramisu would be great, thank you. Will you buy that same thick cream to make it again? It blows up the size of the thing!'

He was back to his normal self now, smiling brightly, and she pinched his cheek with affection. 'Of course. Whatever the birthday boy wants.'

Tommy, who had left the table for a while, returned with two of their many board games and set them down on the table. They were Ludo and Monopoly. Nikos pointed at Ludo and Tommy looked at Kelly and Stratos, waiting. When they said they were happy to play too, he set it all out and grabbed the dice, like he always did, wanting to go first.

Of course, no one minded as usual, and soon they had all made their first move. Before Kelly got to play her second one, she heard someone calling her name in a hushed voice and turned to find Alan standing behind the fence. He had a fisherman's hat on today that looked very fitting on him. One of his hands was up in a greeting gesture, the other before his mouth, where he'd put up a finger.

Intrigued by his secretive manner, Kelly acknowledged him with a slight tilt of her chin and a faint smile, and he beckoned her closer.

As soon as she stood to approach him, Charlie, who had been lying on the grass absorbing the sunshine with half-closed eyes, jerked upright. His tail wagging frantically, he followed her to the fence and, when she stopped there, he lay by her feet.

Kelly petted him on the head, then straightened and gave a smile to Alan, who stood before her now, his features a little tense, like he was worried.

'Hi, Alan. What is it? Everything okay, I hope?' She had whispered her words too, guessing he didn't want to be heard talking to her, for whatever reason. Her eyes flew to the open kitchen window of his house. His wife, whom she still hadn't met, was obviously cooking in there. Tantalizing smells of meat casserole enriched with cinnamon, bay leaf and cloves wafted in the air. She wondered if he was being secretive because of his wife being around. But why should he be?

Alan whispered her name then, causing her to turn her attention to him anew. Her brows shot up when she saw him place his finger over his lips in a shushing gesture before saying, 'I hope you don't mind... But I overheard your conversation with Stratos earlier. And I have an idea.'

'An idea? For what?'

Eyes lighting up, he raised both hands and whispered, 'Please keep it down, Kelly. I don't want him to know I am trying to help.' He looked over her shoulder where the boys were playing. They were crouched over the board, engrossed. From what she gathered, Tommy had just tried to cheat by making an extra move on the board and the others were admonishing him.

'Classic Tommy!' she said rolling her eyes, but kept her voice down to a barely audible whisper to satisfy Alan's request, even if she didn't understand.

'So, listen, Kelly. About Eleni. I know how she can come to the party without Stratos having to invite her.'

She leaned closer, opening her eyes wide. 'You do?'

'Yes. Easy. Eleni's little brother is the same age as Tommy. Tell Tommy and Nikos they can invite a couple of their school friends each, as they're bound to feel isolated with only Stratos's classmates around. Tommy is bound to invite Panayiotis, Eleni's little brother. He is his best friend and they're inseparable in school.'

'That's great info, Alan. But how would that make Eleni come too?'

'Eleni is overprotective of her little brother so she'll want to tag along. Their parents are the same towards the boy... You see, Panayiotis was born seriously ill and had to undergo a series of complicated operations as a toddler.'

'Oh, wow... But, how do you know about that?'

'Well, of course, I know. I was one of the neighbours who kept visiting the hospital back then to give blood for the boy's surgeries.'

'Oh... really? That was so nice of you, Alan.'

'Well, anyway. That's old history now. Focus here, Kelly!' He balled both fists before his chest, still whispering his words. He threw another concerned glance towards the boys, and she did too.

All three were still engrossed in the board game. Charlie at her feet began to whine, and she looked down. 'What is it, buddy?'

'He's always following you around these days, isn't he?' said Alan, his face relaxed as he smiled widely.

Kelly nodded with an easy smile, then bent over to caress Charlie's head, paying special attention to his ears. The pug raised itself, placing his feet on her shins so she could reach him more easily.

'Look how accommodating that little rascal can be when it comes to getting petted!' he said, and they both laughed.

It seemed to be something he hadn't intended to do, because as soon as he exploded with laughter, he stiffened up, a hand flying upwards to clamp his mouth shut.

She furrowed her brow and said, 'I must say, Alan. You're acting very weird today. What's wrong?'

'I told you, Kelly. I overheard you earlier. I want to help with Eleni, but I don't want Stratos to know I interfered.'

Before she could say anything, Stratos's voice echoed from behind her. 'Come, Kelly! You've missed your place twice as it is!'

Kelly turned to find all the boys gazing at her, looking expectant. She waved dismissively and said, 'You guys go ahead and play without me. I'm just happy standing here and—' She turned before her to find Alan had turned into a pillar of stone. Still dumbfounded, but eager to help him relax again, she turned her attention back to the boys. 'Anyway. You guys play, okay? I'm happy over here.'

When the boys did as she asked, she faced Alan, who had only relaxed slightly in the interim. 'Alan, what's wrong? You have to tell me.'

Alan sighed deeply. 'If you must know...' He took a crumpled piece of paper from his pocket and opened it up. 'This is the last letter I received from my grandson.'

She looked at it, wondering why it was crumpled, and noticed it was covered with mud stains, just like the last one she'd seen him hold. But most of all, she wondered what that letter said because Alan seemed quite upset. 'Did you receive bad news? Is that it?'

'No, I didn't.'

She looked at him, waiting, hoping to decipher from his expression what the problem was. Nothing made sense. Then he said, 'I crumpled the letter myself, you see...'

'Why did you do that?'

'Because I'm upset, Kelly. I miss him... I so wish I could hold him, tell him how much I love him, face to face.'

'I am sure he knows how much you love him, Alan.'

'Yes, I know... I guess... I love all my grandchildren, Kelly, don't get me wrong, but I have a soft spot for my youngest. I always have, and I am ashamed to admit I miss him the most.' His head was bowed now and under the brim of his fisherman's hat, she couldn't see his eyes.

'I am sure your grandson loves and misses you very much too, Alan. Writing to you is sound proof that he does.'

Alan looked up, his eyes misty. 'Yes, I know that. Thanks, Kelly.'

Kelly gave a soft sigh. 'The boys' grandparents live in Salonica, as you probably know, and Tommy misses his grandfather a lot, too... Hope your grandchildren don't live as far as that.'

Alan shook his head wistfully. 'I wish. Mine are a lot farther from me. They might as well be on the moon.'

'I'm sorry.'

'Well, it can't be helped, I guess. That's life. But, regardless of the distance, it's important to tell our loved ones how much we love them. Every day.'

'Yes, I'll agree with that. And I know what you mean. I miss my grandmother a lot... When she was still around, I showed her my love every day, but I don't think I told her the words 'I love you' enough times, you know? And I think of the times I disappointed her too, the times I was quick with her, or unfair... the times I could have sat with her, but preferred to do other things, mundane things, than spend quality time with her.'

Kelly's voice trailed off when she realized she'd said too much. The pain she kept in check inside had escaped again, rising from the pit of her stomach, causing her chest to tighten.

To her surprise, Alan reached out then and squeezed her shoulder gently. She looked up from the dog, who still lay on the grass by her feet, and found his blue eyes were gazing benevolently into hers. They were so peaceful, making her feel the same, and it made her thankful.

'Kelly, we're all human. Don't beat yourself up for the mistakes you've made. Love makes everything all right in the end. I am sure your grandmother knows that you love her.'

'Thank you, Alan. You're so right...' she said, feeling magnetized by his gaze.

He squeezed her shoulder again, and she felt warmth radiating from there into her heart, causing it to bloom like a spring rose.

'Listen, Kelly. Love is timeless. It never dies. It transcends everything. Even death. It survived the loss of your grandmother, just as it survived the loss of Lauren. Those kids know it...' He pointed at them with his head and added, 'Just as it will survive my own passing...' His features darkened then, and he removed his hand, taking a step back and straightening.

She stared, perplexed, as he looked away to gaze absently at his stunning flower patches, his lips pressed together.

What did he just say? Is he sick and dying? Is this why he's upset? She ached to know but didn't dare ask any more questions.

Before either of them could say anything else, Stratos's voice reached her ears, causing her to turn around.

'Come, Kelly! Look! We got the Monopoly out, and you know what these two are like! I need back up. Please can you be the banker and make sure these cheaters behave?' he said, laughing.

She gave a nod, then turned to Alan to find he had backed away further into his garden. With a wistful smile, he waved across the distance and said, 'Go to the boys, Kelly. And remember what I said about Eleni and her brother. I'll keep my fingers crossed for Stratos!' His face brightened then, just as he looked away, before going up the steps of his house to enter through the front door.

Chapter 37

Everyone Stratos had invited came to the party, the house soon filling with the joyful voices of teenagers and younger children. A few of Nikos's classmates turned up and a couple of Tommy's friends too, including Panayiotis, who arrived with his older sister, Eleni, in tow.

When Kelly opened the door to find Eleni and her brother on the doorstep, she tried her best to conceal her delight as she beckoned them in frantically. Stratos's face was a picture when he spotted them across the busy living room and rushed over to say hi, wide-eyed.

Stratos took Eleni to sit with him by the stereo with a few of their school friends. There, they chatted happily and watched their other classmates, who danced in the centre of the living room.

Nikos and Tommy took a selection of treats in four bowls and urged their classmates to follow them upstairs. They told Kelly and Alex they were all going to sit in Nikos's room, taking turns in playing on his games console.

Watching the teenagers dance and enjoy themselves from a deserted kitchen, Kelly and Alex rubbed their hands together and grinned at each other, eager for the time when Stratos would open his presents. His friends' offerings were all placed on the kitchen island, a colourful display of wrapped up gifts in all sizes. Alex hadn't shown his oversized present to his son yet, and Kelly's was rather delicate so she kept it hidden safely in a cupboard. Both couldn't wait to see him open them.

*****

Stratos cleared his throat and tried to sound nonchalant as he raised his voice over the blaring dance music. 'So glad you could come, Eleni.'

'Oh, I wouldn't miss it for the world!' she said, her eyes bright. She was sitting beside him, their arms almost touching. Stratos noticed she kept twirling one of her long strands at the end between two fingers. He thought it was the most enthralling sight he'd ever seen. And every time she looked up at him, she licked her lips before speaking, looking down momentarily at the same time. It made his knees weak, and he didn't know why.

Enchanted, Stratos swallowed hard just as she did it again. *Oh, Eleni... Have mercy on me!* Once again, he craned his neck and looked away, pretending to watch the others dance, and moving his head along with the beat. But his mind was still captured by the image of Eleni, her eyes gazing into his, and he couldn't keep away. He turned to her anew and chuckled. Appearing nonchalant seemed to him to be the best way to try to keep his sanity. Sitting so close to her made his chest feel tight, so tight he could hardly breathe.

Taking a shallow breath, he managed a weak smile and said, 'I am surprised you came tonight, Eleni. I didn't think this would be your thing.'

She tilted her head, her perfectly sculpted brows hugging each other. 'Why would you say that?'

'Oh... ah...' He looked away. *Idiot! Well done! You've just spoiled everything!* He shrugged. 'Nothing... I meant nothing by it. I'm an idiot. Don't mind me.' He looked up and found her eyes again, those clear pools of blue, and held on to them for dear life. Once again, they seemed to call to him, inviting him to dive into them and never get out, even if it meant drowning. *What a bliss would that be, to be forever trapped in her gaze, to always be near her, never to leave her side...*

'Stratos?' He heard her say and realized, in his panic, that he'd been staring at her for a while, his stupid mind wandering again.

He cleared his throat for the umpteenth time, looking away with a frantic shake of his head. 'I told you I'm an idiot.'

To his absolute, paralyzing panic, he felt a delicious, velvety warmth in his hand, then a gentle squeeze. As if in a dream, he looked down, to find she'd taken his hand in hers to rest it on her lap over her tight jeans. In the blink of an eye, the room that was filled with his friends swaying to the music disappeared into nothing. He might as well have been in a barren field with her then, in the middle of nowhere, with only the soft whisper of the wind in his ears.

'You're not an idiot. Don't say that again, Stratos. I think… I think you're *everything*, actually.'

'Everything?' It was by sheer miracle, it seemed to him, that he'd found his voice and managed to utter the word. Now, it felt like he was dreaming. The look in her eyes had taken on a different quality. It had softened, having taken on the pull of the strongest magnet. *What is she saying to me?*

Without meaning to, he squeezed her hand tightly and leaned closer. 'What do you mean I am everything?'

He saw it then. She had just swallowed hard. He knew all about that. And now it was clear. The air caught in his lungs, and he smiled faintly, unbelieving. Now, her eyes mirrored his own apprehension. But he didn't have time to say something and break the awkward silence, because she opened her mouth right then, that sweet, phenomenally shaped mouth of hers, and said, 'To me, Stratos. I meant that you're everything *to me.*'

'I am?' He squeezed her hand again, and she gave a chuckle, leaning closer.

'Why do you think I came over here tonight uninvited? I'm glad Tommy invited Panayiotis over as… that gave me an excuse to come here, too. Because I *had* to come… even though you didn't invite me.' She took a steadying breath, then tilted her head to ask, 'By the way, why didn't you invite me, Stratos?'

His heart racing, Stratos didn't know what to say. But the look in her eyes was warm and encouraging, and the tender sensation of her hand in his gave him courage. The words escaped his lips before he could stop himself. 'Because I was terrified that if I did you'd say no, Eleni...'

'What? I'd never say no to coming to your birthday party!' She served him a look of mild exasperation, the one he used to scold his younger brothers for doing or saying something silly. It made him laugh, encouraging him further.

'I'm sorry, Eleni. It's just that you're too wonderful, too perfect... I thought you wouldn't want to be anywhere near me.'

It was her turn, it seemed, to laugh. It was a nervous giggle, even he could tell. *Oh, my God! She likes me! She actually likes me!* His heart beat so hard against his chest he could hardly bear it now. That's when she leaned closer and left a lingering kiss on his cheek. He turned to look at her afterwards, and she smiled, daringly this time. 'That's not true, Stratos. I'd go anywhere with you.'

'Really?'

She nodded fervently, her eyes pinned on his.

'But why with me? You're the most beautiful girl in the whole school. You could pick anyone you wanted.'

'Oh come on now, Stratos. You want me to say it?'

'Say what?'

'That I love... I love... your voice, okay?'

Stratos stared mutely at her for a few moments, unbelieving, and then she pointed at one of their classmates, who was dancing a little further away. It was his friend whose father had been teaching him how to play the guitar.

'See Stathis over there?' she said with an open smile. 'He was the one who introduced me to your singing. I saw him watch one of your recordings on his phone one day. His dad was playing the guitar, and you were sitting beside him strumming on another one while you sang...' She made a pause to smile wickedly, her hand raised in a dismissive wave that exuded humour. 'Agreed, the guitar's not your strong point yet; you need more practice there!'

Stratos offered a cocky smile. 'Hey, girl! I know which recording you're referring to. That was months ago. I'm a lot better now! And if I had a guitar here I'd show you tonight!' He chortled, his free hand gesticulating frantically as he added, 'And how can you say I'm not good? I'm *almost* as good as Robert Pattinson!'

They both laughed, then she added, deadpan, 'I'd love for you to play the guitar for me. But let me just say... Your strong point is definitely singing... When you sing, you sound like an angel, Stratos. So, if you must know, it's your voice that made me...' she cleared her throat, '...made me become your fan... Not that you're bad-looking either.' She pressed her lips together, nodding humorously as she looked him up and down, pretending to appraise him.

'Is that right?' he said laughing, joining her own, fresh peals of laughter. Their hands were still entwined, and it was already something, he knew, he'd never tire of.

❊❊❊❊❊

'Come on, kids! Let's all find a seat around the table! It's cake time!' Alex's voice echoed from the living room as Kelly opened the fridge to get the tiramisu cake out. It looked just perfect, decorated with cocoa powder and confetti sprinkles. Feeling pleased with her effort, she placed thirteen festive candles on it, then nodded to Alex across the open space and he switched off the lights.

Everyone exclaimed with wonder as she paced to the living room where the coffee table had been cleared. A sea of youngsters was sitting on the sofa, the armchairs, the dining room chairs, and many sat on the thick carpet, the floor filling with the casual sight of legs dressed in jeans and sneakers. It reminded Kelly of the time when she was a teenager too, when every single thing was a matter of life or death, every feeling an extreme, every bad day, the end of life as she knew it.

Earlier, surreptitiously, she'd been stealing glances at Stratos and Eleni as they sat together by the stereo, seemingly oblivious to the rest of the world. It hadn't taken much effort to realize that what she'd been hoping for had actually happened. Now, Eleni was sitting next to Stratos on the sofa, and he had one arm around her shoulders. He seemed larger than life and she had trouble keeping herself from whooping with delight.

Smiling widely, she placed the tiramisu cake on the coffee table and turned around, looking for a place to sit just as Alex switched the lights back on. Everyone cheered and Stratos's face grew animated with exuberance as he gazed at his lit-up cake. He looked up at Kelly, eyes dancing, and her heart melted.

'Thank you, Kelly, this is wonderful!' he said, and she felt a tug on her arm. She turned to find Alex had brought a chair from the kitchen for her to sit on. 'Sit, Kelly. Right here.'

'Where will you sit? Let me get you a chair.' She moved to go, but he held her arm gently and chuckled. 'To sit where? Look!' he said with a little laugh. It was true. The floor was covered with teens sitting with their legs crossed, and those who sat at the feet of their friends' chairs, leaned against them, their legs spread out. 'There's no room, Kelly. I'll just stand.'

'Oh no, don't stand. You sit, I will stand. Honestly. I don't mind.'

'No way, Kelly. I could never sit and leave you standing.'

'Neither could I,' she said, chuckling. She tried hard to find a solution, aware all eyes were trained on them. She felt bad stalling the festive procedure for everyone but couldn't leave Alex standing like an outsider in the party of his own son.

Stratos then made a suggestion that made perfect sense, not to mention caused her heart to skip a beat. 'Oh, hurry up already!' He raised a shoulder. 'You guys can share the chair, surely.'

Kelly turned to meet Alex's eyes, to find him smiling, a wicked gleam in his eye. He sat on the chair and beckoned to her to sit on his lap. 'I surely don't mind, if you don't...'

Of course, she didn't mind, so she obliged him without a moment's hesitation. Sitting on Alex's lap felt amazing. The only problem was she found it extremely embarrassing, and difficult to look nonchalant before a crowd of young people while her heart raced. Its rhythm accelerated even further when Alex put his arms around her, lacing them over her tummy loosely. It felt like sitting in the seat of a fun fair ride the moment the bar drops down before you to keep you safe in place. She chuckled at the thought. *A roller coaster. Yep, that's what this is. Probably the craziest one I've ever been on, Disneyland's Thunder Mountain included!*

Everyone began to sing "happy birthday", pulling her gently out of her reverie. At the end, Stratos blew out his candles and everyone clapped their hands. Some of Stratos's friends nudged him on the arm and teased him, saying they had guessed what his secret wish was, causing him and Eleni to chuckle nervously.

Kelly watched all that, feeling elated, but at the same time was unable to relax. It was impossible not to feel on edge while sitting on Alex's lap. His heady scent caused her to reel. As if that weren't enough, his hands soon closed around her to hold her again after the applause they'd all broken into moments earlier. The warm feeling of his hands over her stomach caused her heart to melt. It took all her self-restraint not to raise her hands up from her lap to cup his own tenderly.

Moments later, when all the youngsters, Stratos and Eleni included, trained their eyes on her, she realized in panic that it was time for her to cut the cake. Of course, it was down to her. Who else would do it? Realization must have hit Alex at the same time. Both of them jumped up from that chair simultaneously as if it had given them a zap of electricity.

Running a sweaty hand through her hair, Kelly hurried to the kitchen to get a knife and a cake server, and Alex rushed behind her, offering to get plates and dessert spoons.

Soon, everyone had been served, the earlier awkwardness forgotten, and Kelly was relaxing on a chair chatting with Alex, who sat beside her on another chair. The music had resumed and a lot of the youngsters were dancing.

Stratos and Eleni were nowhere in sight. It had grown warm in the room and, as this was a mild night, Alex had opened the tall windows to the porch.

Many youngsters were sitting outside on the chairs enjoying the quiet night, and others sat on the lawn, chatting and laughing. Kelly looked outside and imagined Stratos and Eleni were sitting somewhere out there too, under the stars, perhaps in the most isolated corner of the garden they could find. *Yep. A classic move. Well done, Stratos.*

She felt proud of him again as if he were her own son, and the feeling, once more, felt familiar. Instinctively, she fiddled with Lauren's scarf in her hair, wondering if having committed to wearing it daily had resulted in her being just as haunted by her as poor old Charlie was. The thought didn't panic her, though. If anything, it warmed her heart. She loved feeling like part of this family. If it were up to her, she'd never choose to leave it behind.

She turned her head the other way, to find Alex laughing. Tommy was sitting on his knee talking to him, but she couldn't hear what they were saying over the loud music.

Then, Nikos, who stood with two of his friends on the other side of the room, beckoned to Tommy to approach. Nikos and the other boys were all holding bowls full of treats. Sandwich triangles, bite-sized cheese pies, *dolmadakia*, and cheese puffs. As soon as Tommy joined them, they all made a beeline for the stairs.

Kelly had been up there once to check on the younger children. Since the beginning of the party, they'd all been happy to stay up there playing games in Nikos's room. They'd only come down for a little while, just enough to sing happy birthday to Stratos and have a slice of tiramisu. Now, it seemed, they were itching to return to their own party upstairs.

Chuckling, she made a mental note to go check on them again a little later, just to make sure they were kept well fed and hydrated.

Chapter 38

Half an hour later or so, Alex went upstairs, then outside into the garden, to get everyone to gather in the living room anew so Stratos could open his presents. The birthday boy returned from outside holding hands with Eleni, their faces flushed, eyes sparkling.

Stratos opened all his presents from his friends, receiving a multitude of music CDs, and some of his favourite movies too that clearly his friends knew he liked. Others had bought him a selection of cool accessories and gadgets for his computer and phone, causing him to hyperventilate with excitement. Every time he turned to Eleni to show her the odd present that made him ignite with delight, she'd smile and look at him with evident adoration.

When Kelly and Alex brought their presents to the room, there was a hush, because of the oversized article Alex was carrying.

Wide-eyed and full of intrigue, Stratos kissed his father on both cheeks and took the package from his hands.

But, rather than ripping it open, to Kelly's surprise, he set it down gently before his feet, then turned to her, expectant. Kelly was holding a much smaller package for him, but it seemed to intrigue him even more. 'Kelly, thank you so much. You didn't have to get me anything.'

'What? Rubbish! Of course, I did. Besides, it's only a little something for your room. I hope you like it,' she said, handing the present to him.

Stratos sat back down and placed it on his lap, then began to open it. His eyes grew huge and he let out an exclamation of pure joy to find that it was a picture of him, his mother and father when he was only small. Kelly had had it blown up, having taken permission from Alex to take it from his old photo collection so the local shop could do it. She had bought a beautiful copper frame decorated with autumn leaves to place it in, and he seemed to love it. It was the size of a small poster and could be hung up on the wall.

Stratos fell into Kelly's arms, clutching her tightly against him with a fervour that surprised her. When he moved back, his eyes were misted over, his voice frail when he said, 'This is the perfect gift. Thank you so much, Kelly.'

She gave a mischievous grin. 'Oh, trust me. You haven't seen the perfect gift yet. Open your father's.'

In the meantime, Alex had placed another smaller packet that contained an amplifier beside the large one. He'd only got that from the same shop the previous day.

'What? I have two gifts from you, Dad?' Stratos asked, but Alex didn't offer a response. Kelly took one look at him and could tell he was bursting at the seams to see Stratos's reaction.

With intrigue alight in his eyes, Stratos sat back down.

'Start with the big one, Son!' said Alex with a bright smile.

Stratos's face grew serious, yet his eyes danced with enthusiasm when he turned the hefty package to stand it on its side before his feet. He began to rip the wrapping paper with urgent hands, and once he saw the picture of the guitar on the cardboard box underneath, he let out a squeal that filled the room and caused everyone to applaud and cheer.

Ecstatic, Stratos leaped up and fell into his father's arms.

Afterwards, the boy returned to his seat and unwrapped the guitar fully. Before he'd even attempted to open the box, his father reminded him about the other package, chuckling. Stratos opened that too, and the sight of the amplifier caused him to burst into squeals of exuberance again. Soon, he was clapping his hands together and laughing, telling Eleni how glad he was that he could play the guitar for her that night, after all.

A few minutes later, the guitar was all set up and he began to strum it awkwardly at first, then with more confidence, seeing that this was the very first time that he'd put his hands on an electric guitar. He said it felt strange to strum it and have "that magical electric sound" come out of it, and everyone laughed. Then, Stathis, who had played an electric guitar before, since his father, a professional musician, owned two, showed Alex the ropes.

And now, Stratos was sitting beside Eleni, gazing into her face, a face that seemed to melt with sheer adoration for him. She looked as if she was about to burst into tears as he began to sing to her before everyone.

A hush spread all over the room when the first chords of Wonderful Tonight by Eric Clapton began to play. When Stratos's velvet voice reverberated around the walls, even the kids came down from upstairs and huddled together in a corner to listen.

Kelly watched, spellbound, as Stratos sang, his eyes shifting from Eleni's face to his sparkling new guitar, then back up to her again. His voice was angelic, his high notes causing a shiver to course through Kelly's spine, his smooth legato sensational.

At the end of the song, everyone applauded, and Eleni left a kiss on his cheek, whispering in his ear. His eyes ignited, then he turned to his father with a thumbs up, mouthing a thank you, before he turned his attention to Eleni again. Stathis then played music on the stereo, and the crowd of youngsters animated anew into a sea of bodies swaying to the lively beat.

Alex wiped a tear from his eyes, then approached Kelly, who had been standing a little further away all this time, her back against the wall.

When he came to stand before her, he said, 'Thank you, Kelly. What happened tonight, my boy's happiness... I owe it all to you...' His voice trailed off, and then, lips pressed together, he took her into his arms and embraced her tightly.

Her mind lost in a whirl, and having temporarily lost her voice, she squeezed him against her with the same intensity of sentiment. When they parted, she put a hand on his cheek to caress it gently. 'I know no other man who deserves happiness more than you do, Alex. Same goes for your beautiful children. And I'll be here to make sure you all stay happy, for as long as you want me to. That's a promise.'

'Oh Kelly, that makes me so happy to hear, because… because I…'

*****

Alex scolded himself for being so tongue-tied. She was standing right there, the overhead light sending beams to dance as they reflected on her eyes, causing them to look spectacular, a breathtaking sight. Maybe that's why he felt so weak all of a sudden, like his lungs had lost the capacity to expand, making it hard to breathe. The timing was terrible, since his heart had just begun to gallop beneath his chest.

Nikos hurried past him in a blur, coming from the stairs, an empty bowl in his hand. 'Come, Tommy,' he shouted without looking back. 'Hurry! Let's get a few sodas up this time too!'

It was the word 'hurry' that caused alarm bells to ring in Alex's mind, calling him to action, and his eyes to turn away from Kelly and follow Nikos who sped past him. The boy had overdone it tonight, going up and down the stairs with his younger brother and their friends all night. It was so dangerous. And unlike any other day, they were unsupervised tonight. He hated to do it, to leave Kelly at this crucial moment, when in this noisy room all he wanted to do was to lean closer and whisper in her ear all he wanted to say, then take her outside to sit on the lawn, like the youngsters did tonight. His deep feelings for her made him feel like a youngster too. But this was serious. And damn dangerous. He had to tell Nikos to be more careful. He wasn't allowed to hurry on the stairs, let alone prompt Tommy to do so.

He excused himself, without looking at Kelly, and followed Nikos speedily into the living room. Since the music was blaring, calling out to him would have been futile, so he took hold of his arm to stop him.

Nikos spun around and Alex opened his mouth to tell him off, but then a horrible sound echoed from the stairs. It was so alarming, so awful to register that, at first, Alex refused to accept it, telling himself that it was something else, not what he feared.

The thud was followed by a crashing sound. He knew then Tommy had fallen on the stairs, running behind his brother, carrying something fragile that had crashed to the floor.

Dreading what he would find, he spun around, all the same, his heart stopping when he saw Tommy sprawled out on his back at the bottom of the steps, a smashed bowl scattered in big chunks and tiny shards beside him. Crying out, he rushed to him but, just as he passed by Kelly on his way, the unthinkable happened. Her eyes, looking hypnotic, suddenly closed shut and she collapsed to the floor right by his feet, unconscious.

What followed was mayhem. Stratos materialized beside him instantly and, with resolve that surprised him, he told him to go check on Tommy while he helped Kelly come around.

Alex, as if hypnotized, listened to his son and rushed to squat beside Tommy, careful not to tread on any of the large pieces of glass. He tapped Tommy's cheeks with a light hand and called his name, his voice frail and panicky in his own ears as he realized the boy was unconscious. He was lying on his back, which didn't make sense. Surely, had he fallen down the stairs, he'd have landed on his front?

His train of thought ended abruptly when Nikos attempted to approach. Alex flailed out one arm to stop him from coming any closer and stepping on the shattered glass.

The agonizing moments finally ended when Tommy's eyelids fluttered open. Alex's lungs inflated back into life, allowing him to breathe again. He caressed the boy's head as he began to come to, then his eyes flitted towards the living room, where Stratos and Eleni were kneeling before Kelly, trying to bring her around.

He saw her begin to move, then open her eyes, and he let out a long sigh of relief. He couldn't understand what had happened to her, and the fact she had collapsed at the exact moment that Tommy crashed onto the floor felt impossible, or rather, the probability had to be astronomically low. But then, strange things never ceased to happen since she came into their lives.

All he could do now was return his full attention to Tommy, who looked more alive with every passing moment, and hope that Kelly was all right, too. It was crowded in the living room and it had felt stuffy at times. Perhaps she needed some fresh air. Yes, that had to be it. She was a marathon runner, for goodness sakes. Fit as a fiddle. What else could it be?

Shaking his head, he turned his attention back to Tommy and smiled with amazement. The boy was smiling back at him, still sprawled out on the floor. 'Hi, Dad. What am I doing here?'

Alex caressed his hair and grinned. 'You fell, you silly boy. What did I tell you about running on the stairs?'

'Sorry, Dad.'

'Do you feel okay? Are you dizzy?'

'I'm okay. Mummy took me in her arms… but I don't know how I got here on the floor because I fell asleep…'

Alex felt a shiver course down his spine, the tiny hairs on the nape of his neck standing to attention. 'What? What do you mean Mummy took you in her arms?'

Tommy pressed his lips together and moved to sit up. Alex supported his back, pushing him gently forward until the boy was sitting up on the floor, Alex's protective arm around his shoulders.

Trying to contain his mystification, he asked as nonchalantly as he could muster: 'Tommy, what did you mean about Mummy?'

The little boy let out a soft sigh, then pinned his eyes on his father to say, 'She was here, Dad. Just now... She took me in her arms and stopped me from falling. I heard her whisper my name. It was her. I just know, okay?'

'What are you talking about, Tommy? Mummy's in heaven, you know that...'

'I know you don't believe me, Dad... But it's true. I wasn't on the last step when I tripped. I was halfway down the stairs. Mummy took me in her arms and lifted me in the air. That's when she whispered to me. Then, I fell asleep.'

Alex, stunned to silence, gazed into his eyes for a few more moments. When Tommy moved to stand, Alex stood first, helping the boy to his feet. Then, he swept him up in his arms to make sure he didn't step on the glass.

Stratos then approached with a handheld broom and a dustpan to remove the debris from the floor.

Alex whipped his head around to find Kelly was sitting on a chair receiving the attention of Eleni and another girl. She was sipping from a glass of water, her hand on her head. The music had stopped playing and everyone was standing around her, concern ablaze on their faces.

With Tommy still in his arms, he was about to walk over there to check on her when a young voice echoed from behind him, causing him to turn around.

Nikos was standing near the bottom of the steps with Filippos, his best friend, the latter shaking his head fiercely. 'Mr Alex!' he burst out. 'Tommy is telling the truth. Oh, my God! I can't believe what I just saw!' He brought both his hands on his head, chest heaving.

'What are you talking about, Filippos?' said Alex.

Nikos spoke this time. 'I didn't see it, Dad, but Filippos was following Tommy down the stairs and saw the whole thing. Tommy was halfway down the stairs when he tripped.

But then, he sort of hovered over the rest of the steps, somehow turned on his back, and landed softly on the floor, in slow motion... All the while, the bowl he'd been holding, floated in the air over the steps and crashed to the floor beside Tommy. It was almost like, it, too, was held by an invisible hand.'

'An invisible hand?' said Alex, his brow heavily furrowed, and when he met Tommy's eyes, he received a tight-lipped response and nothing else, but his boy's eyes were bright with evident satisfaction.

Alex huffed with exasperation. 'Oh, come on, Nikos! What are you saying? This is crazy!'

'How else would you explain that he landed on his back and not on his front, Dad?' Even if he had tripped on the bottom step, he couldn't have landed the way he did!'

Alex exchanged mute glances with Nikos and Filippos for a few moments, stunned to silence. Then, he nodded to them and turned away. Somehow, he had started to believe.

Still holding Tommy in his arms, he turned to check on Kelly again, across the short distance between them, and found her sitting in that same chair, listening intently as Stratos spoke close to her ear.

Yet, her eyes were locked on Alex, her face alight with awe and he knew instantly that she agreed.

Indeed. A little miracle had happened here tonight.

*****

Kelly saw Alex approach with Tommy in his arms. The last few moments had been a shock. She'd had this strange, sudden loss of consciousness, and had come to on the floor a little later under the gaze of a multitude of concerned youngsters. Finally, her heart had begun to beat easily again. Relief washed over her like a soothing warm shower to see

Tommy was safe, unscathed from the accident that Stratos had just informed her he had on the stairs.

Charlie, who had been upstairs with the younger children all this time, scurried down the steps and walked straight up to her, his eyes bright as Lauren's voice echoed inside her mind: 'I apologize, Kelly. I had to save my boy! And I needed a surge of energy from you to do it... I'm sorry I rendered you unconscious in the process. You do understand, don't you?'

Still surrounded by a small crowd of teenagers, Kelly nodded surreptitiously, and in her mind, she told Lauren that she'd have done the exact same thing had she been in her place. Then, managing a smile as nonchalant as she could muster, she stood to smile at Alex, who'd just arrived before her, to caress Tommy's head and make sure he was all right.

Alex asked her how she was feeling, and she assured him she was fine. Then, she prompted Stratos to turn the music back on again on the stereo. Moments later, the sea of youngsters was flowing before her eyes as they danced again like nothing strange had just happened.

But she knew... She knew something big had happened tonight. Lauren had just proved she had become strong enough to be able to save her child from a nasty fall, thanks to her. This gave her a tremendous sense of purpose.

Tommy asked to be excused and soon made his way upstairs with Nikos and the other boys, their hands laden with snacks and cans of soda, but this time they all made a point of advancing up the stairs with extra caution.

Chortling, Alex turned his attention to Kelly and rolled his eyes. 'What an evening, huh?'

In his gaze, she saw a spark of adoration then, and it melted her inside like an ice lolly left out on a scorching summer's day.

All she could do was nod mutely and gaze into his eyes that sparkled under the strong overhead light. One of her favourite songs, "Happy" by Farrell Williams, echoed loudly from the speakers, causing her, despite herself, to begin to bop in place to the cheerful beat.

As if on cue, Alex gave an open, irresistible smile, took her hand and said, 'Fancy a dance? Come on! Let's show those kids we're not as old as they think!' He pretended to wipe sweat off his brow and tremble, then pointed a little further, where there was a square inch of clear dance floor space, it seemed.

He must have registered her reluctance because he tugged her gently by the hand and added, 'Come on! Let's not think about it too much, let's just do it! YOLO, right? Isn't that what the kids say these days?'

She giggled. 'To be honest, I have no idea what that means.'

'Apparently, it means, "You Only Live Once".'

Grinning, she let him lead her closer to the youngsters, then they both started to bop and sway, their faces bright.

'Actually,' she piped up after a while, shouting to be heard, 'Since none of the kids care to watch us dance, I think the right term here is 'Klein Mein'.'

He raised his brows, his body jerking backwards as he began to dance frantically, arms and legs akimbo in a hysterical way that made her giggle. She guessed he didn't normally dance that way, and he seemed satisfied by the way he entertained her. A heartbeat later, he leaned closer and said, 'Okay. Please take me out of my misery and tell me what that means. I'll never guess.'

She scrunched up her face with humour, then said, 'Loosely translated, 'Klein Mein' means, excuse my French, 'Who gives a shit'?'

His face brightened with mirth even further to hear that. 'Oh! I shall enjoy using that one at work!' With a whooping sound, he took her hands and they began to sway together, their laughter drowned out in the hurricane of sound that enveloped them as it blasted from the stereo speakers.

Running Haunted

Chapter 39

Kelly left the house early for her appointment the next morning to meet Makis in town. She paced to the car deep in thought.

Despite her energetic evening at the party and having gone to bed well after two a.m., she'd awakened full of beans, feeling cheerful. But then, at breakfast, which she had with Alex and the boys, things changed. Alex said something vague about taking Nikos and Tommy for a walk, then wished her a nice morning looking rather aloof. He left the house with the boys before she'd even dressed to go.

All that had unsettled her, because he knew she was going to town to meet Makis... On the same day when she and Alex met him in town, Alex had told her that it would be no problem if she and "her friend" wanted to go out in the evening on a weekday and "catch up". She thought that was sweet, but was also disappointed that he seemed so accommodating about her meeting another guy.

She'd replied to him that wouldn't be necessary because she and Makis had arranged to meet on Sunday morning at that old café in Syntagma square. To her disappointment, he'd smiled then and changed the subject, clearly disinterested to know more.

That, combined with his equal indifference this morning, had caused her to feel quite deflated, but as she got into the driver's seat she told herself Alex was just being helpful and tactful as usual. It didn't necessarily mean he wasn't interested in her or feeling threatened by the idea of Makis claiming her.

Driving to town, she gradually put aside her unsettling thoughts about Alex and began to focus on Makis. She was determined to give him a piece of her mind that morning given half the chance. It made her feel in control, the knowledge that, since she no longer had feelings for him and knew him so well, he was going to be like putty in her hands that morning, unlike the way he always used to manipulate her in the past.

Walking up to the café, she found Makis sitting, like he always used to, under the awning near the front, facing the square "to watch the world go by", as he used to say. Still, she always knew that all he wanted to do was check out the pretty girls.

She felt herself tense up just thinking about it but, as she neared him, she arranged her features into the most relaxed and agreeable expression she could muster. Before she'd reached the table, Makis sprung upright, reaching out to hold her hand and kiss her on the cheeks. He had never been so gallant before; then again, neither had she been the hottie that she knew she was now.

'Kelly! Oh, my goodness, you look amazing!' he said, looking her up and down, his gaze lingering on her perfectly sculpted legs and medium-heeled shoes. She'd made an effort to wear a short, flowing skirt, something she hardly ever did, and definitely not in the daytime. But it had worked and he was drooling all over her, his eyes now darting back and forth between her face and bosom, even though the latter was perfectly hidden under her casual shirt.

'Thanks, Makis. You don't look bad yourself...' she said with a forced smile, hoping it did well to conceal her disdain.

Seemingly none the wiser, he smiled and offered her a seat, typically the one that faced the café so he could sit across from her with a view to the square.

Oh, no you don't... Not today, Mister. Kelly pointed to the seat he'd been occupying before and stepped past him to flop herself on it, a wicked smile on her lips. 'I prefer this one, actually.'

He stood still for a few moments, looking clearly lost for words, something that brought her contentment to new heights. She brought a hand over her mouth, pretending to cough lightly. His expression was priceless.

Finally, he said, 'That's strange! You always sat facing the café, remember?'

She shrugged. 'Well, I'm not the same person any more, I guess!' She chortled. *This is so much fun already!*

He rolled his eyes. 'That's for sure!' With a wicked smile, he dragged the chair, placing it beside her so he could also have a view to the square but kept a respectful distance from her. As soon as he sat down, he rubbed his hands. 'Doesn't matter. Means I'll get to sit closer to you so I can have a bit of the view as well. Remember the old days, Kelly? They were wonderful. And it's just as wonderful that we met here again, after so long. Maybe it's a sign...' He brought down his voice a notch to say the last sentence, leaning towards her, his pupils dilating.

Kelly leaned back in her seat and scrunched up her brows. 'A sign for what?'

As if scolded, he straightened, his hand flying up to push his short curly hair back from his forehead before saying, 'I don't know, I guess it means we were meant to meet again.' He met her eyes and chuckled. 'And this gives me a chance to apologize properly. We didn't part on the best of terms, did we, Kelly? I acted like an asshole. I know it now. And—'

Kelly raised her hand. 'Let me just stop you there, Makis. I've come here to have a coffee with an old friend. That's all. I'm not interested in apologies, or bringing up details of a past I've taken pains to put behind me.'

For a few seconds, he seemed shocked and rather disappointed that she'd stopped him from saying what he clearly had rehearsed to say. Then, he raised his shoulders and, taking the menu from the table, he said, 'Sure. Whatever you say, Kelly. Let me just say, though, that it's quite evident you've really moved on since I last saw you. Well done, you.'

'Thanks,' she mumbled, just as a waiter approached to welcome them and offer her a second menu to look at. Just like the one Makis was holding, it was a plastic-coated single sheet with pictures on both sides. When the waiter left with the promise to return soon, the awkward silence that ensued felt so heavy she knew he felt it too. But if he was feeling bad in any way, she was uninterested. But glad, too. *Oh, so glad.*

Putting down the menu, she gave a luxurious sigh, then said, 'I think I'll have a cappuccino.'

He looked up, an impish grin on his face. 'I guess some things never change.'

'Yes, it's always been my favourite coffee, I do admit.'

'Oh, don't I know it.'

'Don't tell me... Double espresso for you? Whipped cream on top?'

He flailed out his arms comically and chuckled. 'Busted.'

She chortled, realizing this was the most relaxed exchange between them so far.

'I told you some things never change, didn't I?' He winked at her and pointed to the menu with his head. 'And you're having *loukoumades*, I am guessing?'

She shook her head, then gave a lopsided grin, as she pointed to her torso with two sharp fingers. 'No way. Do I look like I eat *loukoumades* these days?'

He seemed almost upset for a few moments, staring at her flat tummy forlornly, then looked up and said with a soft sigh, 'I guess some things *do* change...' He tilted his head, leaning forward a little. 'Do you ever think of the old days, Kelly? Of us, I mean?'

'Think of us? No, I don't, Makis. And to tell you the truth, I can't believe you're asking me that... Why would I think back on a time when I was so miserable?'

'I don't mean when it ended, I mean when we used to be together... *happy* together.'

Kelly sighed deeply in lieu of an answer and looked away, wondering if it had been a mistake to say yes to meeting him. Clearly, he wanted to talk about their common past for some reason, and she found it impossible to do. She'd have to make it perfectly clear she wasn't having it. And if he couldn't respect that, if he couldn't move on to other,

Running Haunted

painless subjects, then she'd just have to leave. But, before she could say anything, the waiter materialized before them again.

They both gave their orders for coffee and when he was gone, she gave a sigh and uttered, 'Look, Makis...'

He raised both hands and shook them mid-air, cutting her short. 'It's okay, Kelly. I get it. You don't want to talk about the past. I won't mention it again.'

She nodded with an easy smile. 'Thanks.'

Another awkward silence filled the air between them and, during this time, they both watched the world go by, and also glanced at the other patrons, who enjoyed coffee and desserts with friends and family, chatting idly.

The children at the tables all around seemed restless in their seats unless there was a dessert spoon in their hands. More children played on the square, kicking a ball or chasing each other. Their cheerful voices reached Kelly's ears, causing her to remember the past again. *I cannot believe I wanted to marry this bozohead and have his children! Just look at him!*

She could watch him without worrying he'd see her now, seeing that he had his eyes pinned on two young girls that were passing by. They looked barely out of puberty, both lanky, with long, flowing blonde hair. One of them wore a simple white shirt and a tight pair of jeans, while the other was dressed in a super-mini skirt that barely covered her underwear, her cropped top leaving her stomach fully exposed.

No wonder Makis was following them both with his eyes, the latter especially. *Yes, you piece of shit. You bet, some things never change...* He always had wandering eyes that loved to rest on young, feminine, exposed flesh.

Once the girls were out of sight, he turned to face her, his expression dreamy. 'Oh... It's such an amazing sunny day... and how fabulous to be back here... with you again.'

Kelly had trouble swallowing down the bile that had risen from her stomach while he ogled the girls earlier. Giving him a furtive glance, she looked over her shoulder with a huff. 'Where's that waiter? I need coffee. Slept very little last night.'

He leaned forward, the sparkle in his eyes that once used to charm her so much returning to haunt her. 'Oh? Do tell!'

For a few moments, she felt captured by his deep blue eyes that, once, she never missed a chance to lose herself in. They sparkled like the surface of an azure sea, still and perfect on a warm summer's day. Willing herself to remember they belonged to a man that had treated her like dirt once, she forced herself to look away. She tossed a long strand of her hair behind her shoulder, smiled faintly and said, 'I was at a birthday party.'

'Oh? A friend of yours?'

'Actually, it was my boss's son's birthday. He turned thirteen. We had the party at his house. I got to bed after two a.m. and that's too late for me. Plus, there was dancing...' She tried to laugh, to sound nonchalant, hoping to fool him. And every time she looked away, she felt compelled to meet his eyes again, those eyes so full of humour that had captured her once more, much to her dismay. She was shocked to realize that, and mad at herself too. *Oh, you stupid girl! Don't you forget what he did! He cheated with your colleague. You caught him in your apartment, on your bed, for goodness' sake!*

Luckily, the waiter brought the coffees then, and she picked up her cup at once, drinking thirstily from it. He drank a few sips from his espresso too, while watching her with great interest, the amusement in his eyes never subsiding. Finally, he put his cup down on the table, tilted his head, and said with a chuckle, 'You surely have changed, Kelly.'

Holding her coffee cup near her lips, she eyed him with what she hoped passed for contained amusement and said nothing. She took a long sip, desperate for the delicious, frothy drink to distract her senses. Out of the blue, that all-too-familiar feeling of fondness for Makis had begun to rise up from the pit of her stomach like a coiled snake.

She thought she'd killed that vile serpent ages ago; the one that had been coaxing her to keep loving that creep, despite the way he constantly put her down in the past, trashing her already tiny sense of self-worth.

'Wow! Nafplio has a lot of tourists! And it's only early spring!' he exclaimed all of a sudden, forcing her to return to the present. 'And there are some pretty girls around. Ooh! Look at her! Her legs go all the way up to her armpits! Phoar! She looks like an F1 Grid girl in that skimpy red outfit!'

Shocked, Kelly looked to where he kept pointing with his head, her mouth gaping open. Not because she marveled at the admittedly perfect model looks of the girl in question, but because he'd done again what she'd always hated the most – pointing out to her all the pretty girls in sight.

She opened and closed her mouth a couple of times, feeling like a fish that'd been left out of the water too long. Her lungs had lost the capacity to expand with air; either that or she had stopped breathing for a while. She couldn't tell, so she willed herself to take a deep breath.

Makis was oblivious to her discomfort, fully engaged in his beloved game of spot-the-pretty-girl, and she considered standing and walking away without saying a word. But then, as if in a dream, she saw Alex, Nikos and Tommy coming into view on the square.

Before she could react, Alex spotted her too and raised his hand. 'Oh! Kelly! Hi!'

This caused the boys to turn their heads and greet her just as excitedly.

Before she knew it, she was gesturing them frantically to come over, even though Alex had already started to approach, a wide grin across his face.

Chapter 40

'Kelly! Oh, hi! Nice to see you again. Makis, is it?' Alex said, offering him his hand.

Makis shook his hand and greeted him, a relaxed expression on his face.

When Alex introduced the children, Makis's eyes lingered a little more on Nikos. Kelly knew exactly why. Makis's parents were overweight and the sight of them had always disgusted him while growing up. He had an aversion to people who had piled on the kilos, which had made it an absolute mystery to her how they'd wound up together in the first place. That was a mystery she knew she'd never solve, though she'd been thinner when she met him and gained a lot of weight in the course of their relationship.

After the introductions were finished, Alex, looking a little awkward all of a sudden, put his hands on his waist and exhaled, then looked at Kelly with a grin.

Kelly's heart skipped a beat when he fixed his bright eyes on her. Was it her or did he seem lost for words? 'So? Have you guys been for a walk?' she asked to break the uncomfortable lull in the conversation.

Before he could answer, Tommy, the typical chatterbox, beat him to it. 'Yeah! We went to the seafront! Dad bought us ice cream and we had them at the lighthouse! We saw a fisherman and he gave me this!' He opened his hand, showing her a dried-up seahorse.

'Oh, that's so pretty!'

'I am giving it to you, Kelly. Take it!'

'What? Are you sure? You don't want it?'

Alex chuckled. 'Trust me, he's sure. He told me he was going to give it to you as soon as we turned away from the man's boat.'

'Aww! That's so sweet! Thank you, Tommy!' She took the seahorse from his hand and left a kiss on his cheek, then placed it on the table beside her empty cup.

'Kelly?' piped up Nikos. 'Did you know you can now hire four-wheel bikes with two seats on the seafront? Dad said we can hire one next time we go there. You should come! We'll get two!'

Kelly giggled and nodded excitedly. 'I'd love to do that with you guys.' Then, she turned to Alex. 'Have you spoken to Stratos on the phone? Did Eleni visit him as they planned?'

'Yes, he said she arrived shortly after you left.' He flicked his wrist and grinned. 'Oh! I could hear Eleni giggling in the background when I spoke to him. I asked if they wanted to catch a bus and meet us here, but they were happy to stay alone at home.' He rolled his eyes and let out that adorable laugh of his that made his face glow. 'Duh! Young love... Of course, they prefer to be at home alone.' He pulled a face and twirled his hand in the air. 'What was I thinking?'

Everyone erupted in amused noises, Nikos's snorting laugh rising above them all, causing Kelly to giggle, just to hear it. Nikos had the wickedest laugh. She looked at him and Tommy standing on either side of their father and felt a pull of affinity towards them all. It made the sight of Makis foreign by comparison.

What the heck's wrong with me? To think I even entertained the thought for a moment that Makis and I could... that we could ever... Oh, look at me. I can't even say it, and there I was earlier, feeling magnetized by his eyes! Stupid, stupid girl!

Makis's voice broke her reverie. 'So, is that your son who had his birthday yesterday?' he asked Alex.

'Yes... Stratos. He turned thirteen. Perfect time for him to get a girlfriend, I guess,' he said chortling again, his eyes on Kelly. He seemed so proud of his oldest, but not only because he'd got his first girlfriend. Kelly knew that.

'Well, happy birthday to him!' said Makis. *'Chronia polla!* And I hope that'll be the first girlfriend of many to come.' Makis raised his half-empty cup of coffee with a devilish smile.

Alex gave a dismissive wave. 'Oh, trust me. Stratos is going to be even more monogamous than I ever was. He's head over heels in love with this girl. He'll probably wind up marrying her.' He chortled, happy sounds emitting from his perfectly sculpted lips, rendering Kelly magnetized. She was aware her eyes were caressing him with absolute adoration and didn't care if Makis caught her doing it.

Makis gave a little laugh, then winked. 'Well, if they're so in love, maybe you shouldn't have left them on their own if you don't mind me saying so.'

'Makis!' burst out Kelly, appalled, but Alex shook his head to signal that he didn't mind. He offered a little laugh, but a shadow had descended over his eyes following Makis's inappropriate comment.

'Trust me...' said Alex finally, 'All Stratos wants to do is sit with Eleni and play music on his computer for them, if not play his guitar and sing for her again. He did that last night...' He turned to Kelly. 'He sang so wonderfully, didn't he, Kelly?'

She smiled sweetly at him. 'He surely did.'

Alex put his hands in his pockets, looked behind him at the square, shifted his weight from foot to foot for a bit, then said, 'Well, we'd better go, guys!' He tousled Tommy's hair and both boys looked up at him smiling. Pointing to the kids, he looked at Kelly and Makis and said, 'See these smiles? They know what's coming!'

'What's coming?' asked Makis and, knowing him as well as she did, Kelly knew he was just humouring Alex; he wasn't really interested. Judging from the way he had been tapping his lighter on top of his pack of cigarettes for the last minute, she knew he was restless and guessed he wasn't happy they had come over.

Alex seemed oblivious to Makis's vexation. 'I promised them *souvlaki*, that's why. We're going to have a walk up to the clock tower, then come back down here to buy the *souvlakis* from our favourite shop. You know which one, Kelly, don't you? The one we all went to last weekend for dinner? To celebrate Nikos's triumph at the stadium?'

He winked at Kelly, threw a furtive glance to Makis, who seemed bemused, then looked at Kelly again, eyes crinkling at the edges, to add, 'And after that, we'll head home. We're buying enough *souvlakis* for Eleni too, of course. I'm guessing she'll be staying all day.'

He rolled his eyes again, clearly in high spirits over his son's happiness. 'And we're getting two for you, Kelly.' A shadow crossed his face, his smile fading, as he tilted his head and added, 'That is, if you *are* coming home for lunch?' He gave a thin smile, threw Makis another fleeting glance and turned to Kelly again to say, 'No problem if you're eating out, though. You can have your *souvlakis* tonight.'

The words that were coming out of his mouth were one thing, but what his eyes were saying was another. His vibes reached her across the ether warm and sticky like honey, causing her heart to melt. *Oh, Alex! This idiot means nothing to me!*

She gave him the warmest smile she probably ever gave anyone, and watched as his features relaxed, a broad smile blossoming on his handsome face. 'I'll be home for lunch, Alex!' She put up a playful finger to shake it mid-air. 'And you guys make sure to wait for me! You know what to get me, don't you?'

Alex chortled. 'I can assure you, I am buying two chicken *gyro pitta souvlakis* with your name on it!'

She giggled at that, satisfied, almost oblivious to Makis's presence by then.

Grinning, Alex waved to both Kelly and Makis, and so did the kids as they all turned to go. As soon as he'd taken a couple of steps with the boys, he turned again to say, 'Oh! I am so looking forward to the party this Saturday night, Kelly!'

Once again, she melted as their eyes met. 'So am I, Alex.'

With one last dashing smile, he was off with the boys, all open smiles and waving hands, and that made her feel all fuzzy inside. That same incredible pull she'd felt earlier returned inside her, making it feel unbearable to sit there once they were gone.

Makis's voice, stern and agitated, broke her reverie. 'What was that about another party? Are you guys an item, if I may ask?'

'What? No! Of course not. He's my boss,' she said, features scrunched up as if he'd said something ridiculous, even though she wished it more than anything else.

He scoffed. 'Well, it's none of my business, but you guys sound like a couple. So, what is that upcoming party he mentioned then?'

She waved dismissively. 'Oh. That. Just a work do...' She avoided his eyes.

Makis kept silent for a few moments, then muttered, 'What an idiot... Fancy him trusting two young teens in love to be alone at home and be all prim and proper!'

She darted her eyes at him, her brow wrinkled. 'Huh?'

'I'm talking about his teenage son and his girlfriend. What is he thinking allowing them to be on their own in the house?'

She leaned closer, her brow etched. 'Just what do you imagine they're up to? You don't even know Stratos. He's not that kind of boy!'

He gave a dismissive wave. 'Oh come on! He's a boy, isn't he? Since he's alone with that girl, he's doing to her what nature intended right now.'

'What? No way! Stratos is not like that!' she said, her eyes widening, causing him to laugh like a hyena.

'I can't believe—' She stopped short. His ridiculous notion had caused her to hyperventilate.

Makis didn't seem to notice. He was still laughing like an idiot and waving dismissively. She had indeed forgotten just how vile he could be. Other than his usual bad traits that used to hurt her, he also tended to take liberties and talk out of his ass about people he didn't know at all; just like he'd done with Alex earlier, just like he thought he knew Stratos better than anyone else, even though he'd never even laid eyes on him.

She was still shocked into silence when he let out a guffaw, then piped up, 'And did you see that chubby kid? Your boss is a moron! Fancy feeding him ice cream, then *souvlaki* for lunch! What's the menu for tonight, I wonder? Double-cheese pizza and doughnuts?' He screwed up his face and did a cartwheel in the air beside his ear, then added, 'The man is crazy. I mean, what is he hoping for?'

Kelly blinked a few times, unable to believe this was happening. 'Nikos is on a diet, one I've put him on actually, and I'll have you know that this is his cheat day! That's why he's eating ice cream and that's why, today, he can have any other sugary or fatty treat he damn well pleases!' By the time she'd finished her sentence, her voice was booming.

And now, she realized she had sprung upright and was standing stooped over him. In the process, she must have pushed the small table forward because the full glass of water that stood before her had spilled. Thankfully, the little seahorse beside it remained unaffected.

'Shhhh! People are looking! Don't shout!' Makis urged her in a hushed tone, embarrassment ablaze on his face.

'I don't care!' After following his eyes only briefly to confirm that people were indeed looking, she turned her furious gaze towards him again, to find he was cringing in his chair like a scolded child before a stern teacher. Patting the air down with both hands, he was now coaxing her to sit, all the while looking around him apprehensively.

A furtive look over her shoulder confirmed that several of the patrons continued to stare, some of them laughing now in the same deriding manner he had laughed moments ago about Alex and his family. *Serves you right, you bastard. Karma's come right back atcha!*

Inside, she was laughing at him too, behind her stern, furious exterior. Makis hated drawing attention to himself in public – another remnant of his painful upbringing. As a child and youngster, he avoided being seen with his overweight parents. Whenever people jeered at them, which happened a lot, he could never handle the embarrassment he felt. Being here now, under the scrutiny of total strangers, with her scolding him like that, was his worst nightmare. Still, she couldn't find a shred of sympathy in her for him. Not that she even tried.

She threw her hands in the air and exhaled loudly. 'You know what, Makis? Let's just forget it! You clearly haven't changed at all since I last saw you!'

He gave her a sheepish look before looking down at his lap to say in a frail voice, 'What does that even mean, for goodness sake? And do sit back down... please!'

'No, I won't sit back down. I'm done *enjoying* your fine company,' she said, her voice dripping with sarcasm. 'I'll just say my piece and then I'll be out of your hair. And what I mean, since you asked, is that you've just demonstrated to me, in all their glory, the all too familiar, *worst* parts of you! Ever since I arrived here, you haven't stopped looking at all the pretty girls, like you always used to! You even pointed out that leggy brunette in the red dress to me! So let me ask you, Makis... Do I look like one of your bloody mates? Don't you realize it's offensive to say these things to a woman? That it's sexist? And as for Alex, you don't know him, and you cannot judge him! And speaking out of your ass about his older son being alone with a girl and predicting how he'll act with her makes you look stupid. Don't judge what you don't know!'

Her words seemed to jerk Makis back into life. His face bright, he pinned his eyes on her and began to gesticulate wildly. 'Whoah! Relax, already! What's this? All I wanted to do was sit with you quietly and have coffee. To reminisce about the good old days—'

'That's just it, Makis! There *are no* good old days! There was just you being a *malaka* and me being the idiot who forever put up with it all because I had no self-esteem to speak of! So don't you talk to me about the *old days*!' She did air-quotes, huffing loudly, and he bent his head again.

Pointing at him with a sharp finger she shouted: 'Look at me when I'm talking to you! Look at me and listen!' That caused him to look up and gaze at her again, with a pathetic look in his eyes now, clearly having abandoned the hope he'd be avoiding a public ridicule today.

She took a steadying breath and carried on, 'Makis, all I feel about the *old days* is disbelief. For all the things I put up with that I never should have...' She took a moment to steady herself, then added, 'Do you know what I'd do if I could go back in time to catch you in our bed with my colleague again?'

A collective exclamation was raised by the onlookers all around them, which she ignored, along with the visible cringe on his face. She paused for a few moments, just to enjoy the sight of him shaking his head ruefully as he stared at his lap, and continued, 'Remember that day, Makis? I'm so thankful I changed my mind and caught an earlier bus from Efi's that day. Thought I was going to find you in bed still, the way I'd left you in the morning. You'd said you were coming down with a cold and needed to rest that Sunday, just to sleep or watch TV, remember? I brought us pizza and I was whistling happily on my way in, but then I caught you red-handed, didn't I? Trust me, I wouldn't react the same way if I could turn back time now!'

'Oh, for Pete's sake, Kelly... Why bring all that up again now?'

'Because it's the most despicable act among all the ones you've ever done, and, somehow, it's the only one I'd left completely unanswered, tiptoeing around it for the super-short time we spent together in the house after that as if what you did was *my* fault and not yours!'

She gave a deep sigh, then added, 'You wanted to talk about the old days so here it is! And I'm telling you this, Makis: I feel sorry. Because when I caught you and that cheap tart butt-naked in our bed I did the wrong thing. I should have got the biggest and the fattest wooden ladle from the cutlery draw and whopped her ass and yours until they were as blue as a *melitzana*!

'But what did I do? I stormed back out without uttering a peep, even though you saw me standing there, then I ran down the street, where I found a quiet corner to cry my eyes out. And all the while, Makis... All the while, I kept telling myself *I* must have done something wrong to deserve it, that *I* must have gained too much weight for you to want me! Did you hear that? Can you even comprehend, somewhere inside that useless, thick skull of yours, the kind of hell you'd put me through by that point?'

Before she knew it, she was pounding her open palm on the table, continuing to air her exasperation while he pleaded with her to stop. All the while, both of them raised even more eyebrows from the onlookers, but she didn't care, unlike him, who had by now shrunk in his chair looking half his normal size.

Finally, she squared her shoulders, exhaled luxuriously, then said in a calm manner, 'Makis, coming here today to meet you was a mistake. A *big* mistake. But I hope, for your sake, that you've learned something here. As you've obviously realized by now, I am not the same woman you once knew. And yet, you are the *exact* same man, if not worse, I fear. As for Alex, he's the kind of man you'll never be, no matter how hard you try. But, for your sake, I'll give you some advice. Do visit a therapist, for crying out loud! You're nearing thirty-five... You have to rid yourself of the traumas of your childhood. Not that it was your parents that inflicted them on you. No, you did that to yourself, Makis. You have only yourself to blame...

'You see, there's nothing wrong with being overweight per se, if one's happy to be that way, and provided, of course, that the excess weight does not present a major health risk. Your parents loved to eat all the wrong things, to make all the wrong lifestyle choices, but they loved you, Makis. And you know what? At the end of the day, them being that way benefited you greatly. Think about it... They gave you the drive to remain fit and lean all your life. That's something you can thank them for, surely. Hold on to that silver lining and take it from there... Heal yourself already. You're not a child anymore. You're an adult now. It's embarrassing.'

With that, she picked up from the table the seahorse Tommy had given her and said bitterly, 'Even the little boy who gave me this, is a better man than you'll ever be.'

He said nothing when their eyes met for a moment but the shame in his eyes was palpable, and she acknowledged his inner pain with a silent nod, hoping her words would sink deep into his heart and mind, enough for him to change, for his own good. For the sake of the happy times they shared once, she wished it for him deep in her heart.

With a huge sigh, she placed the seahorse carefully in an inside pocket of her bag and took out her wallet.

Under his mute gaze, she placed a banknote on the table that covered the price of both the coffees and a generous tip. She didn't want anything left to remind her of him any more, not even a sense of obligation to him if he were to buy her the coffee.

She saw confusion, then a mixture of embarrassment and sorrow deepen in his eyes when she said, 'Good bye, Makis. With all my heart, I wish you happiness.' Then, she walked away without looking back, leaving behind her a heavy, dead silence across the entire seating area.

Chapter 41

As soon as Alex got home with Nikos and Tommy, he sent them upstairs to change into sweats and wash their hands. As soon as they were gone, he sped to the front door and slipped out onto the porch to make a quick call in private.

'Dimos! I'm back!' he said as soon as his friend picked up.

'Oh! You sound excited!'

'It all went according to plan! Thank you so much!'

'Did you take the kids along as I advised you?'

'Yes! And get this! A fisherman gave Tommy a dried-out seahorse, and he only went and gave it to Kelly before that moron. It was wonderful! You should have seen his face! We were interacting like a big happy family. He must have felt like an outright outsider!'

'Yes! That's exactly what we wanted! So you think it worked? He realized he's up against something too big to compete with?'

Alex shrugged. 'Well, I hope so... I also did the *souvlaki* thing we'd discussed, mentioning I knew what Kelly's favourite was and how we'd gone to the shop together last weekend after Nikos's run at the stadium. I did all you told me to, to make the guy realize we're all domesticated and close... like a family.'

'Brilliant! So, how did you leave it? What did the guy say?'

'Not much... Actually, towards the end, he kept looking at me like he wanted to wring my neck!'

In lieu of an answer, Dimos exploded in loud guffaws.

Alex laughed along, then said, 'I owe you, Dimos...' His voice rang solemn in his own ears now, the ache in his heart for Kelly mushrooming, reaching down to burn his insides. He was so close now to confessing his love to her he could taste it.

'My pleasure, old pal. Did you remember to squeeze in a mention of my upcoming party at the very end?'

'Of course! Oh! I can't wait... The days can't pass quickly enough, to be honest.'

'Good! And I'll make sure it all goes smoothly for you at the party, my old friend.'

'You think Kelly likes me too then? That she'll say yes to being my girl?'

'She'd be mad to say no, Alex... And I bet she knows what a catch you are... Don't worry about it.'

'I'm broken goods, Dimos... That's what I am...'

'Don't be stupid, Alex. Who isn't?'

Alex shook his head. 'But—'

'No buts. Listen, mate... I'll tell you one thing I've learned from personal experience, and I urge you to take it to heart because it's absolutely true: The best relationships aren't made between two perfect people... They're made between two people who are broken, much like jigsaw puzzle pieces. And what happens is... These two broken bits find a perfect match in each other, resulting in creating a masterpiece through their union. Together, they're no longer broken. Do you understand?'

'Yes, mate... I think I do... Thanks.'

'Good. To me, it sounds like Kelly needs to mend her broken pieces in connection to yours as well. Chin up, my friend. From what you've told me, it seems to me she needs you as much as you do her...'

Alex took a deep breath, wishing all his friend had said was true. He opened his mouth to speak, to thank him again for being there, but then saw Kelly park the car outside and his heart leaped. 'Oh! Kelly's here. Talk later, pal!'

He ended the call and rushed back inside before she could spot him. Gliding to the kitchen, he half-placed and half-threw his phone on the island, then rushed to the fridge to get vegetables out for the salad.

By the time Kelly had walked in, he was standing before the kitchen sink, washing cherry tomatoes, peppers and cucumbers.

Kelly walked in with a bright smile and announced she'd stopped by one of the boutiques on her way home to buy a new dress for the party. She looked elated, saying how glad she was to live in a touristy town where the shops were open even on Sundays.

Curious, he moved closer to take a look inside her carrier bag, but she slapped his wrist playfully and said he had to wait until Saturday to see it.

Chuckling, he watched as she rushed to the stairs, then up to her room, having promised to be back down shortly to help with setting the table.

*****

Kelly stepped onto the landing to find Charlie sitting on the carpet outside her room. She greeted him with a pat on his head, then whispered to him softly.

Charlie whimpered, the way he did when he wasn't himself. The glassy look in his eyes confirmed he was under Lauren's spell.

'What is it, Charlie? What is she up to now?' she asked with humour, even though she knew she wouldn't get an answer.

As soon as she opened the door to her bedroom, the pug rushed inside and stood by her bedside table yelping in the familiar way he did every time he wanted something. But this time, it wasn't his favourite treat or a walk he was after. Instead, he kept looking at the scarf she had left on the bedside table, and she knew instantly what he wanted her to do.

Kelly gave a frown. 'You want me to wear it? She wants to talk to me, doesn't she?' She rolled her eyes and chuckled. 'I swear! Sometimes, you might as well be a ringing telephone, Charlie! Except, instead of ringing, you bark every time Lauren has something to say, or you give me that adorable glassy look!' She caressed his head, which seemed to quieten him, then she picked up the scarf. This time, she didn't need to wear it to make a connection.

As soon as her fingertips touched the fabric, Lauren's voice sounded pitch-perfect in her mind. 'Kelly! Talk to me! I can sense this guy is of no interest to you any more!'

'What? How can you possibly know that?'

'I can read your vibes, Kelly! And I can hear your thoughts... I am as surprised as you are!'

'Really?'

'Look... Can you walk to the mirror? I'd like to talk face-to-face if you don't mind?'

'Sure...' Of course, Kelly didn't mind. By now, Lauren felt more like a girlfriend and less than a ghost. She was surprised to realize that fact as she walked to the dresser, knowing already that when Lauren was gone she was going to miss her.

As soon as she looked in the mirror, Lauren's face appeared surrounded by a cotton-white mist. Rays of light pierced through it here and there, giving it the sparkle of diamonds. 'Oh! That's beautiful...' Kelly uttered, her mouth gaping open as she admired the effect that caused Lauren's face to glow.

Lauren looked left and right, then her eyes rolled upwards comically as she glanced over her head. 'Oh! I hadn't realized that until now. It must be my excitement! Soon, I'll be ready to leave.'

She must have noticed Kelly's sad expression to hear the last words, because she lifted her chin and added, 'Hey, Kelly... Don't do that... Don't be sad for me. I am no longer of this world and need to go where I was intended to go to in the first place after my passing. You realize that, don't you?'

Kelly nodded firmly. A knot had lodged in her throat stopping her from voicing her assent.

'Besides, there's no need to be sad for me. If you must know, I am getting excited. I can't wait to see heaven, to be with my parents there...'

'Yes, yes of course...' said Kelly, trying not to cry.

Lauren smiled widely, obviously eager to change the subject and lift the mood. 'Anyway! I won't keep you long! Alex never liked a cold *souvlaki*!' She giggled, then added, 'So, tell me, Kelly... How did it go with the guy? What did he do, for you to feel so indignant towards him?'

Kelly gave an exasperated sigh. 'Oh, Lauren... Makis is just a waste of space... I certainly don't know what came over me, saying yes to seeing him again. I can't wait to tell Alex that meeting him was a disaster. I'd hate for him to think I still have eyes for him!'

Lauren's face got animated with alarm. 'No! Please! Don't tell him, Kelly!'

'Not tell him? But why?'

'Because he's jealous and that's good...'

'He is?'

'Of course, he is! He adores you, darling! Last night in his room he was tormented knowing you'd meet Makis today. He kept tossing and turning. He couldn't sleep and called Dimos to talk to in the wee hours of the morning.' She gave a little laugh and added, 'I won't tell you what they said, but I'll just say Dimos knows and he's helping him win your heart.' She paused for a moment, then exploded in a hearty laugh before saying, 'As if that was necessary!'

Kelly was thrilled to hear all that, and she turned her head sideways, pretending to eye Lauren with disdain. 'Great to see you having a laugh with the romantic aspirations of the living!'

Lauren giggled. 'Never thought it would be so much fun watching humanity. I am almost tempted to stay.'

Kelly's brows shot up. 'Are you?'

'No! I'm joking, of course! I want this house to become for you and Alex the same love nest that it used to be for me.

And I want you to have it with all my heart, with all that is left of me anyway... My soul yearns for your happiness and Alex's, Kelly. That's all I want. To make sure you guys are happy together. And then I'll be ready to go. I know my children are happy. They adore you and see a mother in you already.'

Kelly broke into sobs to hear all that, her shoulders shaking as she cried.

Soothingly, Lauren said, 'Don't cry, Kelly. Not for me, anyway. That's the way life is. We're all passers by here on this good Earth. That's why only love matters. Because in the end, this is all that is left behind. Everything else evaporates in the face of death. Stop crying now. We can't have you shedding tears over the *souvlakis* and spoil everyone's meal. You hear? Chin up!'

Kelly reached for a paper hankie from the box on the top of the dresser and wiped her nose, then Lauren said, 'Now listen up because we don't have much time. Alex, Eleni and the boys are downstairs setting the table right now, and they'll be calling you soon. First of all: Wear the scarf now and keep it on throughout this coming week, day and night, until Saturday when the party takes place. Secondly: Before you leave the house that evening, I want you to put the scarf around Charlie's neck. This is important! Don't forget!'

'Of course. I won't...' said Kelly, listening intently, and agreeing to everything, even though she couldn't understand the reasons.

'Good! Now, listen for the last part: I want you to wear at the party the pearl necklace I gave you... I knew you guys would find a special occasion sooner or later to go out dancing, and the party is the perfect one for you to wear it. You will, Kelly, won't you? It's very important that you do.'

'Yes, Lauren. I'll do everything you ask me.'

Lauren's face bloomed with excitement, then she said, 'I know Alex will ask you to be his girl at the party... When he tries to kiss you, kiss him back, Kelly! And then, after you do, here's what I want you to tell him...'

Chapter 42

Kelly descended the stairs, careful in her step because of her new, high-heel shoes she had bought for the party. She wasn't used to wearing heels but was determined to look her best for Alex – not to mention intent on matching his height as they danced tonight.

'We don't want him crooking his neck when he leans in to kiss you, do we?' Kelly heard Lauren joke inside her head like an excited fairy-godmother. She could hear her because Charlie was slowly descending the stairs behind her, like a maid-in-waiting, looking cute with Lauren's scarf around his neck, just as Lauren had requested.

When Kelly entered the kitchen, her humorous thoughts ended abruptly. There, by the kitchen island, stood Alex in a tux, more gorgeous than ever before, but the sight was anything but pleasant. Stella, who had arrived to mind the kids, stood before him.

She had her back to Kelly, but Alex, who faced her, noticed her coming in. She saw the admiration in his eyes and it pleased her, guessing he loved the look of her new wine-pink taffeta dress.

Stella, obviously following Alex's gaze, spun around and raised her chin at Kelly. 'Hi. You okay?' It sufficed her to say, clearly still determined to act coldly towards her. Kelly caught her scanning her up and down, eyes narrowed.

Just then, Kelly heard Lauren whisper inside her head with glee, 'Yes. That's right. She's going to the dance with the prince. You. Stay here. Like an ugly step-sister!' Kelly brought a hand before her lips, pretending to cough while trying to suppress her need to laugh out loud.

'Hi, Stella. Thank you for coming tonight,' said Kelly, trying to contain both her amusement and her annoyance.

Stella's features were hardened, her envy palpable as her eyes, intense, flitted from Alex to Kelly and back, her lips so tight they looked like an etched line on her face. 'Don't mention it. Happy to help,' she finally said, looking down at the oversized handbag she was holding.

Kelly wondered why Stella had brought such a large bag to baby-sit next door for a few hours, but she quickly dismissed the thought. It was difficult to dwell on anything else with Alex, who looked so heartstoppingly dashing, standing close to her, his eyes never leaving her. She smiled at him, enchanted, and he smiled back.

'I love your new dress, Kelly. It's fabulous. No. Resplendent. That's the right word, I believe.'

'Thank you,' she replied, her heart blooming with the compliment. 'And I love your tux.'

He looked down at his front and chuckled. 'Thanks. Thought I'd take it out of the wardrobe where it'd been collecting dust. I've only worn it once before in my life.'

'Well, it's just perfect,' she said, unable to take her eyes off it, off him, off the idyllic picture of the perfect man for her. Inside, she felt excited. Lauren had said he was going to kiss her tonight. But as much as the thought made her heart leap, she was mystified. *How does Lauren know? Maybe it's just her wishful thinking. I'd hate to be disappointed. I'll take it with a pinch of salt. But... gosh... wouldn't it be nice?*

The pug emitted a single bark then, causing her and Alex to break the gaze they'd been locked in. They both turned to Stella, to find her looking down at the dog, her brow furrowed. 'What's with the scarf?' she finally asked, pointing to Charlie with a single rigid finger.

'Oh. Tommy put that on him,' lied Kelly. 'You know, for fun.'

'Ah,' said Stella, tilting her head back as if to show understanding, but her expression revealed quite the opposite. She seemed annoyed with them, if anything.

If she's so against us all, and if it bothers her so much to be here, then why did she come? Why didn't she say no? In the short, awkward silence that ensued, Kelly decided Stella was simply besotted with Alex. She'd do anything for him. He'd asked her for help so she obliged. But, clearly, she hadn't accepted whole-heartedly. *As long as she's nice to the kids. Otherwise, I'll give her a piece of my mind!*

'Kelly? Ready to go?' she heard, and turned to find Alex, his head tilted, a sweet smile on his lips.

'Yes.' She mirrored his expression, then threw Stella a curt glance to say goodbye as she headed for the door, her clutch bag in hand. As she paced to the front door, she heard Alex say goodbye to Stella and remind her she could sit and watch TV until supper. The food was ready in the oven and the kids were keeping themselves entertained in their rooms.

Kelly chuckled to hear that last bit. She knew for a fact the boys didn't intend to spend an extra moment with Stella if they could help it. They'd all told her and Alex they didn't want her in the house, Tommy especially. But since Alex had already asked Stella, he couldn't go back on it. So the boys had settled for only spending time with her during their meal, and even then they didn't intend to engage her in conversation. They'd all made it clear they were going to spend the rest of the time together upstairs. She could stay in the living room on her own watching TV all night if she wanted.

Alex had been taken aback by these adamant statements and had shared his mystification with Kelly. As for her, she didn't think it was too strange. Stella wasn't exactly likeable, plus she had been awkward with Kelly, and it made sense that the kids would side with the latter, feeling hostile to the woman who didn't treat her with courtesy. Or perhaps they shared their mother's feelings for her without knowing it…

Kelly thought of all that as she waited for Alex to join her at the front door. Her mind wandered further. She wasn't exactly sure why Lauren disliked Stella… Perhaps it was because the latter wanted Alex for herself and Lauren didn't deem her fit to be a step-mother to her children. Or, maybe, the three of them had bad history. In any case, it made perfect sense to Kelly why anyone would dislike Stella.

Her deep thoughts ended as soon as Alex appeared at the hallway, his hand put out to open, then hold the door for her to enter. 'Thank you, Alex,' she said to him, as they went out into the fragrant spring night.

An electric lantern cast a generous yellow light over the threshold, allowing them to see where they were going. The garden roses smelled sweet in the semi-darkness, the scent of the freshly cut lawn heady and intoxicating in Kelly's nostrils. She took in a luxurious breath and tilted her head back to find the clear night sky was strewn with stars.

'Heaven...' she said, feeling like a true Cinderella off to the ball with her handsome prince. She'd never before owned a dress half as beautiful, nor had she ever worn anything like this as a slim woman, the one she truly accepted and felt proud of. Not that her previous, over-sized self didn't deserve to be accepted or to be proud of. But that was another woman; one that Makis had been constantly putting down depriving her of any sense of self-worth.

Since then, her major lifestyle change had granted her a whirlwind of enthralling new experiences, ultimately bringing her here, in Nafplio to live this dream, with this man who had given her a glimpse of a perfect family life. And she wanted it. Oh, how she wanted it. Ghost and all...

Lauren had been part of the package from day one, it seemed. But Lauren wasn't going to stay with them forever. And tonight, if Lauren's obscure plan unfolded perfectly, she and Alex could finally get closer...

'Kelly?' Alex whispered, breaking her reverie, and she turned around in the semi-darkness, to find him standing before her, the expression on his handsome face revealing amusement. 'The dance? Don't you want to go?' He chuckled. 'Happy to stay out here with you all night, if you prefer...'

She gave an amused smile, about to say that of course they were going to the dance, but found it difficult to speak.

If anything, she felt her lungs void of air. He'd captured her gaze, rendering her bewitched, helpless. She saw him take a deep breath, and then, he reached out and clasped her hand.

It felt warm, his fingertips caressing the palm of her hand. 'I'll go anywhere with you, Kelly. Just say the word. This night is yours and mine to do as we please...'

Stunned, she watched as he leaned in slowly, his eyes soft, his expression serious. *Oh, God. Is this it? Is he going to kiss me right here? Outside the house? With Stella probably looking from the window?*

Instinctively, she broke his magnetizing gaze, somehow, and turned to look over her shoulder, just in time to catch Stella peeking through the living room window, having stuck her head out from the side of the tall frame. Kelly saw her brows shoot up with surprise for a split second before she disappeared from view.

I knew she was watching! 'Mad cow...' Kelly whispered, then beckoned Alex to the door. 'Come on, Alex. Let's not stand here any longer.'

'What is it?' He looked at the window, obviously failing to understand what had just happened, then back at her. 'Where are we going?' he asked, perplexed.

She threw out her hands and gave a little laugh. 'To the dance, of course! I didn't dress up like a meringue for nothing!' She tilted her head and gave a crooked grin. 'Hope you have your best dancing shoes on, matey!'

'Of course!' Alex's eyes exploded with mirth as he followed her along the concrete path to the front gate, their hands tightly entwined.

Chapter 43

The dance was held at a function hall in the outskirts of town. It was a rural setting that consisted of a converted old estate house, an enchanting olive grove in front of it, and vineries all around, as far as the eye could see.

Kelly and Alex parked in a beautiful court before the imposing façade of the estate house. It was early still but they were surprised to see many cars were parked there already. Hardly anyone was about, and they guessed the party had to be well underway inside.

Getting out of the car, Kelly marveled at the serene sight, her eyes caressing a line of leafy trees at the opposite end of the court. Their leaves trembled in the soft breeze, branches swaying gently as if in greeting.

Once they entered the building, then the reception hall itself, they found themselves swept away by a large wave of humanity that pulsated with exuberance before their eyes. Pop music blasted from the speakers, and many people danced to the frantic beat. Others sat at their tables enjoying finger food from large platters and chilled white wine from fluted glasses.

Dimos's face lit up as soon as he saw Kelly and Alex. He was standing near the entrance with another man looking excited as he greeted two guests who had just come in.

'Hey! Welcome, you two!' Dimos said as soon as the guests had moved towards the tables.

Kelly and Alex shook his eager hand, and Dimos introduced them to the other man, who turned out to be his purchasing manager. Then, he beckoned them to follow, taking them to a remote table, away from the dance floor.

'I picked this table, especially for you, guys. It's small and sits only two so you can... chat comfortably,' he said with a cryptic smile. Kelly chuckled, intrigued, and Alex nodded appreciatively. As soon as they sat, Dimos bent over Alex and added with a devilish smile, 'I picked it especially for you, my friend. You need quiet to hear properly. Old age and all that!'

Alex gave him a mock-punch on the jaw, then the two old friends pretended to mock-punch each other on the chest for a few moments, causing Kelly to titter. Before she could say anything, Dimos was gone with a friendly pat on her back and a wicked smile. His purchasing manager was beckoning urgently from the entrance for him to meet an elderly couple that had just arrived.

Alex turned to Kelly with a chuckle. 'You have to forgive Dimos. And me. He's such a big kid that never changed since high school. And when he's around, I can't help acting the same.'

She chuckled. 'Nothing wrong with friendly banter between two old friends. You should see me hanging out with Efi. We turn practically into twelve-year-olds in no time.'

Alex chortled and reached for the wine bottle that sat in an ice bucket on the table. He filled two glasses and offered her one. 'Let's drink to that, Kelly. To old friends. Old friends... and new ones, too.'

*****

Dinner was exquisite and, at some point, Dimos gave a speech while people sampled the fine courses and the many side dishes on offer. The speech was peppered with hilarious jokes that had people weeping with laughter. Dimos was relaying the hardships and the multiple streaks of bad luck encountered by him and his team in the beginning of his business's operation, but he relayed it all in a humorous light. There was no negativity involved, only laughter, and it was all about the lessons learned, the wisdom attained. As Kelly listened, she laughed like a drain, while realizing that this had to be the best way to remember every bad situation in life – by seeing the funny side, or at least by acknowledging the merits gained from every negative experience.

Thinking of her own past troubles, she couldn't help but chuckle to herself as she recalled Makis's face when she told him off at the café. Then, she turned to her side to steal a glance at Alex, her heart skipping a beat. *Oh, Alex... How much I want you...*

He was laughing at his friend's jokes, eyes twinkling with gaiety, and she told herself how lucky she was that Makis had come into her life. If it hadn't been for him to put her down constantly, she'd never have found it in herself to make this huge lifestyle change. She never would have come to Nafplio to run a marathon and meet Alex... Alex, who, in such a short time, had become all she wanted, all she yearned for.

A thundering round of applause filled the room, snapping her out of her deep thoughts, and she raised both hands to applaud too, as Dimos, at the end of his speech, bowed, and patted his heart to thank everyone.

As soon as he stepped down from the podium, he rushed to them. 'All okay, guys? Can I get you anything else?'

They both assured him they were fine and congratulated him on his great speech. By then, they'd finished their hearty meal and drunk the full bottle on their table. When Dimos noticed the empty bottle he snapped his fingers at a passing waiter and asked him to bring another to the table. Alex and Kelly protested, saying they weren't going to drink any more, but he waved at them dismissively.

When the bottle arrived he filled their glasses and got one for himself too. He raised his glass to them and said, 'To old friends and new!' causing Alex and Kelly to turn to each other blank-faced.

'What? What did I say?' said Dimos, shrugging with mystification.

Alex chuckled. 'Nothing, mate. It's just that Kelly and I toasted the exact same thing earlier.'

Dimos gave a guffaw and patted them both on their backs frantically. 'See? Goes to show we are all on the same wavelength here.'

They drank, then Alex excused himself to go to the Gents.

As soon as he was gone, Dimos sat in his chair and leaned towards her. 'Can I ask you something, Kelly? Between you and me? You won't tell Alex I asked you?'

She leaned forward too. 'Yes, of course, Dimos.'

'Forgive me, Kelly... I know it's not my place. But you seem like such a good girl... And it's just that... Alex mentioned your ex-boyfriend was in town, a guy who, from what he said, had made you unhappy in the past. Again, forgive me, but can I just say... There are good men in the world, Kelly. It's worth looking a little further. And, sometimes, the best man is right before your eyes, you know?' His eyes, glazed over, captured hers for a moment as he paused, then he went on, 'That guy, Makis, sounds like bad news to me. You deserve so much better.' He twisted his lips, then put up both hands as he leaned back in his chair. 'Please forgive me, okay?' He patted his heart and added, 'I've drunk quite a bit already, I know. Tell me to shut up if I am taking liberties. But, as I said, you seem like such a good girl. And I had to say.'

Kelly straightened in her chair and shook her hands frantically. 'Oh, it's okay. I don't mind, Dimos. It's sweet, actually. Thank you for caring enough to tell me this.'

'So? This guy, Makis... You're not getting back together with him, are you?'

She shook her head fiercely, then scoffed. 'No! That's not happening. Ever. Trust me.'

Dimos practically jumped in his seat to hear that, and then patted her shoulder to say, 'Oh! So happy to hear that, Kelly. So happy to hear that!'

A little later, he excused himself and went. Kelly watched him make a beeline for the Gents and smiled to herself. She hoped he was going straight to Alex to tell him that Makis was not a threat. Because if that was the case it meant that Alex cared for her, enough to tell his best friend.

The previous night, Lauren had told her that, if the opportunity arose at the party, she could tell Alex that she wasn't interested in Makis any more. And she had just done that, in a way, through Dimos.

Feeling hopeful, Kelly took a deep breath and drank from her glass, one hand caressing Lauren's pearl necklace around her neck. *Oh, Lauren... How I want your plan to unfold tonight, whatever it is!*

*****

Alex returned from the Gents gliding across the floor. It was evident from his glowing face that Dimos had delivered the good news to him. Shortly after returning to his seat, he raised his glass and, with a simple toast of 'cheers' this time, downed half the glass in one go, then loosened the tie in his collar.

Leaning towards Kelly, he engaged her in small talk, his eyes never leaving hers.

Kelly's heart skipped a beat, then began to soar when he put his hand over hers on the table. Looking pensive, his eyes on their hands, he sought her fingertips, to caress them with his own.

They had already got up and danced twice earlier, but only to dance music. And now, the first slow song of the night began to play. He looked up, mesmerizing her with his laughing eyes, then tilted his head and asked her to dance. She stood, a hand over her chest as she willed her heart's crazy rhythm to subside. Still holding her hand, he led her to the dance floor.

They embraced lovingly in the company of a few other dancing couples, but to her, it seemed as if they were alone now... The lights had dimmed down and tiny coloured lights had come on to swirl slowly upon them, rendering the atmosphere magical.

'Kelly?' he asked after a few moments, and she moved back to seek his eyes. 'Yes, Alex?'

'In case you're wondering... Nothing ever happened between Stella and me. Though... to be honest, something did happen, just this once, but I wasn't responsible for it.'

She knitted her brows. 'I don't understand.'

He took what looked like a steadying breath before saying, 'Well... You know she used to come and babysit sometimes, on the few occasions that I was out for the evening?'

'Mm-hm...'

'Well... On one of those nights, when I returned home late after a function at the hotel, I do admit... I made the mistake of offering her a drink before she left.' He scrunched up his face. 'I didn't know her then, how weird she could be. I was just trying to be friendly. And, to be frank, I was lonely...' He continued, looking away. 'I needed people to talk to after losing Lauren. Especially late at night when loneliness hit me the hardest during that first year... I still remember how impossible I found it back then to sleep alone in the bed...' His eyes lit up with alarm, darting back to her when he added, 'Not that I ever intended to get Stella in my bed!'

Kelly chuckled. 'Relax, I know, that... Just tell me what happened.'

'Well, after I had my nightcap, I sort of dozed off on the living room sofa. Then, somehow, I came around with her lips on mine.'

Kelly widened her eyes. 'You kissed her?'

'No! How could I have done that, Kelly? This is Stella we're talking about, for goodness sakes! *She* kissed *me*! While I was dozing! That's what I meant!'

'Oh!'

He gave a labored sigh. 'So, it got awkward after that, because she sort of came on to me and I had to tell her I don't see her that way. She left the house at once, acting all upset, but since then, she's been baking us all muffins, offering to babysit 'whenever needed' and trying to make herself useful in general. I think she's a little besotted with me.'

She chuckled. 'You think?'

He rolled his eyes. 'Well, I can assure you, though, I never encouraged her in the slightest.' He tutted and darted his eyes skywards before saying, 'That is, if you exclude my offer to her of a drink, or asking her to babysit a couple of times... I know it sounds like I've done my bit to give her the wrong idea, but I honestly never intended to do that...'

'Alex? Why are you telling me all this?'

'Because I want you to know I am not interested in her romantically in the slightest. In case you've been wondering.'

'But you feel bad for encouraging her inadvertently, is that it?'

'I guess so...'

She pressed her lips together but said nothing.

'What? Tell me what you're thinking, Kelly.'

'Well, I was never going to tell you what I think... It's not my business...'

He gave an encouraging nod. 'But...'

'But... to be fair, by inviting her to babysit tonight, you're sort of encouraging her again. Sorry, Alex, but that was totally the wrong move on your part.'

He shook his head ruefully. 'I am an idiot. You're so right. Talk about giving a dog a biscuit and expecting it to go away.'

'Exactly.'

'My kids were right... And so are you. What's wrong with me? Even Charlie has more brains than I do these days.'

'Hey... Don't beat yourself up about it any more. So, what if Stella thinks she's got a foot in the door just because you invited her to mind the kids for a few hours? Start from tomorrow. Encourage her no more. But stick to it this time. Come hell or high water!'

'Hell or high water. Right!' he said, nodding profusely.

They smiled to each other, then fell quiet as they continued to dance, but the corners of his lips remained curled up in a Cheshire-cat smile.

A little later, he gave a faint gasp and she pulled back, about to ask what was the matter, when he said, 'Kelly? Can I ask you something?'

'Yes?'

'I don't mean to sound awkward but... I just noticed your pearls... and I recognize the clasp. It has a butterfly on it. Lauren had a pearl necklace just like that...'

'Oh...' She brushed the exquisite pearls with tender fingertips at the front. 'Yes, they are, in fact, Lauren's pearls. Remember I told you Charlie gave me her scarf?'

Alex nodded firmly, so she carried on, 'Well, he brought me her pearl necklace too on a separate occasion. As weird as that may sound...'

His brows shot up. 'Really?'

'Yes... I know it's hard to believe, Alex, but it's true. I assure you, I'd never lay a finger on Lauren's things. And if I was the type to do such a thing, I hope you'll agree I'm not dumb enough to wear in your presence something I'd stolen from you.'

He removed one hand from her waist to shake it desperately before her. 'Kelly, you don't need to explain yourself like that. Of course, you couldn't have taken it. It never even crossed my mind.'

'So you believe me?'

'That the dog brought it to you?'

'Yes.'

'I guess I do, yeah... And to tell you the truth, I think the dog must be picking up some strange vibes...'

'What vibes?' she asked, pretending she didn't know and hoping to find out what he believed.

'Well, I mean all the strange things that have been happening to us... Like that Sunday when we visited the fort of Bourtzi and we kept coming across things that were relevant to Lauren, or the night of Stratos's birthday party. Remember the strange accident that Tommy had on the stairs? It makes one think, doesn't it?'

'Yes, of course, it does...'

'So you agree... that Lauren... may be...'

She waited, nodding encouragingly. She knew he was aware that Lauren's spirit was watching them all. He'd told her as much in the house before, after all. But she could tell he had trouble believing it fully.

'Well... Would you think I'm mad if I told you that... that I believe Lauren's spirit is not just "with us" in the typical sense... but that she's kind of... haunting the house?'

'Alex... All I'll say is... hold that thought. I promise that before the night is over, I'll tell you more.'

'Are you saying that you know something I don't?'

'Yes. Yes, I do. Later tonight, when the time is right, I'll tell you all about it. And then you can decide if you believe me or not.'

Alex pleaded with his eyes but she shook her head. Lauren had told her he had to kiss her first before she were to say what she had to say.

'Nuh-uh... I said, not now, Alex... Please wait. Now, dance, you!' she said, tapping him on the nose playfully, and he gave a sweet smile, lifting the mood for them both.

They swayed silently to the end of the song, and then, a heart-rending piano melody followed. When Adele began to sing, it touched Kelly so much that the hairs on the back of her neck stood on end.

Alex tightened his grip around her waist, pulling her closer, and she responded in kind, holding on to his broad shoulders as if life depended on it, breathing the heady fragrance of his cologne until she felt intoxicated, until it felt as necessary as oxygen for her survival.

By then, her head was spinning with desire, and she found herself begging silently for him to reach down with his lips and seal hers at last. As if on cue, he bent his head and left a tender kiss on her neck. The touch of his lips on her skin felt amazing, and the warmth of his breath caused her knees to buckle.

'Oh Kelly...' she heard him say feebly.

As if in a daze, she moved back, just enough so she could see his face clearly. She was too stunned to speak, too settled in her newly found brand of heaven to find her voice.

'Kelly... Dimos told me about Makis... Is it true? Can we... Is there a chance that I... that you and I—'

His eyes were burning like embers, and his lips were half-open as he waited for her answer, his breath, urgent now, tickling her face. She heard herself say 'Yes,' and then he took her lips at last, for a kiss so passionate, so lingering, so urgent, that it knocked the air out of her lungs.

And then, something peculiar happened. At the time, Alex had both his hands around her waist, and she had hers looped around his neck. So neither of them could have caught her necklace that, out of the blue, broke into bits, the precious pearls falling to the marble floor to scatter away with a soft rattling noise. Kelly felt them break away around her neck so she gave a start, snapping her eyes open, and he did the same.

By the time she'd realized what had happened, Alex was already crouched at her feet, picking the pearls in handfuls first, then one by one, to place them in his trousers pocket with urgency. It wasn't only that they were precious, real pearls that had belonged to his late wife, but also, he wanted to avoid other people from slipping if they happened to step on them. As he picked the precious tiny spheres, he kept alerting people to move back to be safe.

Shortly, with Kelly picking the odd pearl that he'd missed, they seemed to have retrieved them all. Alex seemed as giddy as she felt now. He took her hand and they rushed back to the table to put the pearls somewhere safe. Kelly opened her clutch bag and Alex emptied his pocket to place the pearls inside a zipped up compartment.

With that done, they sat closely together at the table, their hands entwined, and he said with a chuckle, 'Talk about bad timing... I am sorry the necklace broke just as we gave our first kiss, Kelly...'

She gave a knowing smile and shook her head. 'I'm not, Alex. Because I know something you don't know, remember?'

His face ignited with excitement. 'Go on! Tell me, Kelly. If it's about Lauren, I have to know. I need to do something, anything, to help, if I can. I get the feeling she's in the house, but not happy to be there...'

'That's exactly what has been going on, Alex. And you've just set her free.'

His eyes grew wide as he leaned closer. 'I have? But how?'

'By kissing me, silly... Lauren told me so herself. And she has a message for you... She hopes that it will prove to you that I am telling the truth about her. I can communicate with her, Alex... We have proper conversations. We have for a while.'

Alex had grown frozen, like a slab of ice. He straightened and let go of her hand, brushing his hair with his own urgently. His eyes looked glazed, focusing far, mouth gaping open as he tried to process what he had just heard.

Chapter 44

It was midnight and all Alex's kids were fast asleep, a blissful dead quiet long having spread around the house. Stella hadn't seen much of the boys all evening, but they'd been making noise, be it talking loudly, or playing music upstairs. Tommy had been playing with that darn dog that barked loudly, and it'd been hard to concentrate on her movie. And that god-awful screeching from Stratos's guitar had simply driven her nuts.

Other than that, the spoiled brats had only shown their faces for a while, just enough so they could eat their *pastichio* in the kitchen. They'd then returned upstairs to stir up even more of a racket than before till they grew tired enough to go to bed.

It had been an easy night, other than that. She'd found the table made when she arrived, and the salad was in a bowl in the fridge already cut up. All she had to do was dress the salad and set the plates on the table, then left the kids to eat on their own. She had already had a light lunch next door so she returned to the TV movie, enjoying her solitude while they ate, thankfully, in dead silence. All she heard was soft whispers coming from the kitchen, and from time to time, she'd turn to find them stealing glances her way, only to look away again when she caught them looking.

It had been quite a drag to her, having to interact with the kids, who obviously didn't like her any more than that snooty cow, Kelly, did. Not that she liked any of them either. But she loved Alex, and she'd never give up hoping that one day she could get him to see her in a different light. So far, she hadn't had much luck, but who succeeded in anything without perseverance, right?

Now that the kids had long gone to bed and her movie had finished, she poured herself a glass of brandy from the drinks cabinet to relax on the sofa, her mind returning again to that fateful night when Alex had offered her a drink. And later, she'd lost her mind when she saw him leaning back on the sofa, eyes closed. He was just too handsome to resist.

Before she knew it, she had kissed him and he'd woken up, looking so appalled it had really stung. But then, the next time he asked her to babysit, she'd found consolation by doing something behind his back. It had felt only fair after the upset he had caused her. In a way, you could say, he had it coming…

Stella had long made up her mind to do the same thing again tonight. After all, she deserved some kind of remuneration for her trouble. Alex was ungrateful, and he had hurt her. Now that those awful kids of his had fallen asleep was the perfect time to set her plan to motion.

Laughing wickedly, she finished the last dregs of her drink and went straight to the kitchen sink. She was going to wash the glass, dry it and put it back in the cupboard so no one would know she'd poured a drink for herself, any more than they were going to know what she was about to do upstairs…

*****

Lauren watched as Stella went up the stairs stealthily, her oversized bag slung over her shoulder, looking like a well-prepared little mouse that had just come out of its hole to get some cheese. 'You haven't gotten over your thieving thirst yet, have you, you nasty lunatic? You've done this twice already! But this time, I'm strong! And this time, I'm not going to just watch. I'm going to *get you!*' Lauren shouted, but because Charlie wasn't around to meld her energy with his, no one heard her.

Now, she was strong enough, thanks to the scarf that was super-charged with Kelly's energy after all these days of her wearing it non-stop. It meant that now, if Lauren spoke, *anyone* would hear her. As long as Charlie was present, of course.

Like a flash, Lauren glided through Tommy's door that was left ajar and whispered to the dog's ear. 'Come on! I need you! She's going to my bedroom! The time has come!'

Charlie jumped to his feet, his paws never making a sound as he scampered to the door and pushed it open with his nose. With a grunt, he sped to the master bedroom, Lauren gliding behind him.

✶✶✶✶✶

Stella stood before the wardrobe, malice colouring her features dark, causing her mouth to shrink to the size of a button. She stared into the open compartment on the very right, grunting, her eyes slit. 'Aaaargh! No-no-no! Where are the Armani dresses, the Stella McCartney shirt? The Zara trouser suit? Where did everything go?' She opened the next compartment with haste. 'The bags are gone too! And all the scarves! What the heck?'

Despite her rising vexation, she'd managed to speak at a low volume. She'd also had the good sense to shut the bedroom door on her way in, so the kids sleeping in their rooms wouldn't hear anything. But now, she felt her ire rising. Desperate to contain it, she put up an urgent hand to clamp her mouth shut. Her eyes protruded from their sockets as she stood still, muffling herself, poised like a mad dog that stood in a corner pondering who to bite next.

Finally, she put her hand back down and gazed at the two near-empty wardrobe compartments forlornly. 'At least the jewellery is here still. I'll help myself to that... It's okay...' she whispered to herself and managed a faint smile.

Eyes glinting, she reached for the jewellery case and opened the lid. Sure enough, it was just as full to the brim as the last time she'd seen it. She had her eye on specific matching sets and was pleased to find they were all still there. Picking two necklaces with matching bracelets she threw them into her bag that she still carried on her shoulder. Her face grew wild with frenzy. She'd only just begun...

Chuckling to herself with glee, she removed the upper tray of the jewellery case to get to the many golden rings she knew were underneath. She picked the one that had the biggest stone on it—a huge, sparkling ruby—and was about to try it on when, suddenly, the door swung wide open.

Somehow, it didn't make a sound, nor did the dog that stormed inside to run straight at her feet. And then, the weirdest thing happened. The dog began to bark, but even though his mouth kept moving, no sound came out. And then, of all things, a voice filled the room, a female one that chilled her blood.

'Stella! Put my ring back in the case now! My other jewellery too! I saw you!' she heard, clear as day, as the dog's mouth and tongue kept moving, producing that eerie human voice, somehow.

Stella gawped, the shock so great that she dropped the ring. It landed on the carpet with a soft thud. As soon as it did, it bounced off it, impossibly, and now kept rising, right before her eyes, until it landed softly back into the jewellery case as if by an invisible hand.

'Eeeek!' shrieked Stella, thankfully, not too loudly. As numbed by shock as she was, it occurred to her that things would get even worse if the children awoke. With a trembling hand, she clamped her mouth shut again, the agonizing scream brewing inside her contained in time, reduced to a muffled whimper.

Now, she was sure she'd turned ashen, judging from the look of her other hand that she'd put out before her. It was as white as fresh snow and trembling. Her mind drawing a blank, she used it to pinch herself hard on her other arm, just to make sure she was dreaming. She hoped she was...

because if she wasn't, then what was happening before her eyes? It couldn't possibly be real, could it?

'Wake up, Stella! Wake up, already!' she commanded in a hushed tone, her voice wavering, as she pinched herself hard again and again. 'Ouch! Ooh! Argh!' she kept uttering each time the pain hit her, causing the female voice to erupt into a wicked laugh so eerie, so chilling, that she knew if she didn't bolt anytime soon, she'd surely faint from terror.

The dog was immobile before her, staring at her with glassy eyes, its lips curled back as it showed its teeth. But instead of a snarl, that awful laugh kept reaching her ears.

'How can this be real?' she whispered to herself, spent, her heartbeat so frenetic it reverberated in her ears, echoing like a hammer hitting the anvil.

Panicking further, she put up both hands up to her ears and whimpered, 'Please! Please! What do you want from me? Who are you? *Where* are you?' She looked around desperately but found no origin for the voice. Still, in her mind, she had a well-formed idea about who that could be. She had known Lauren in life, after all. She had recognized the voice. But the notion was unthinkable.

'That's right... You know who I am!' echoed the voice, now, impossibly, inside her head this time, causing Stella's heartbeat to reach a frenetic rhythm. It made her head reel, but she still refused to believe this was happening. 'It can't be... You can't be Lauren. Lauren is dead...' she mumbled, her voice frail like a sobbing child's.

'Dead as a doornail, as they say. You're right about that. But that doesn't mean I'm going to go away and leave my husband at the hands of a conniving, thieving woman such as yourself!'

Stella began to tremble from head to toe but, stubborn as she was, she refused to believe it. Instead of running, like any other person would have done, she began to slap herself hard on the face this time, determined to get to the bottom of the mystery. 'Wake up, Stella! Come on! This is crazy!'

'Crazy? I'll show you *crazy*!' The moment the voice said that, something resembling a fog materialized before the mirror on the other side of the room. Stella paced hesitantly towards it and as soon as she got there, the fog dispersed, but then a face formed, clear as day, in the mirror.

'Lauren?' she whispered, trembling like a leaf.

'Finally, you recognize me. Yes, I am Lauren. The one you've been stealing from!' Lauren's face contorted with anger, tongues of fire shooting out from her head in the mirror in all directions. Now, she looked menacing like Medusa, except, her headdress consisted of fire bolts instead of live snakes.

'Aaaargh!' cried Stella, this time not caring if anyone heard her. With her bag still over her shoulder, she turned around, ran past the dog and bolted out of the room like it was on fire.

As she ran down the stairs, and all the way to the front door, Lauren's wicked laughter echoed behind her, chilling her blood, sounding like a screeching bat, straight out of hell, its claws clamped to the hem of her skirt. The dog ran behind her all the way too. She could feel its breath at her heels and dreaded it would sink its teeth in her flesh at any moment. Luckily, she rushed out of the door and swung it shut before the dog could reach her.

Alone in the night, the silence blissful, her wobbly legs gave out and she collapsed to the floor tiles. Whimpering, she caught her breath for only a moment, then jolted upright and ran to the safety of her home.

✽✽✽✽✽

'Good riddance to you, missy!' shouted Lauren, then gave a luxurious sigh. 'Aaah... splendid! One more thing crossed off my list. She gave a little laugh and eyed the dog with tenderness. He was sitting behind the closed door, panting from the exertion.

'Thank you for your help. We showed her, didn't we?'

The dog eyed her with adoration and gave a single bark.

'Now, go and get some rest,' she told him. 'We have one last job to do tomorrow morning, then we're finally done. I promise. And I need to rest too... It has taken all my energy to chase that awful woman away. I'm feeling all the more faint with every passing moment... Oh... I hope Kelly returns here shortly. She's the only one who can help me get the energy I need to stay here a little longer... for that precious, final goodbye to my family.'

Chapter 45

'I'm sorry, Kelly. I'm having a lot of trouble believing all this...' Alex heaved a long sigh and turned the last corner, the car now cruising down the street to the house.

Kelly looked at him silently for a few moments as he drove, his eyes on the road, but they seemed to be focusing way further, into the mists of the mystery she'd been relaying to him for the past hour or so. Back at the party, less than an hour ago, she had finally delivered Lauren's message, telling Alex that the chains he'd been using to keep her here all this time had broken when he finally kissed Kelly. With that kiss, he had proved to Lauren that it was all right for her to finally depart for good.

Alex had astounded Kelly afterwards when he told her he'd been having a recurrent dream in which he kept seeing Lauren chained on the bed with him. What's more, the last time he saw the dream, the chains had taken on the shape of pearls... In a way, Lauren had been trying to talk to him too all this time, urging him to let her go.

When they exchanged this information at the party, Alex had no choice but to take Lauren's message to heart. It was just too amazing to ignore, the connection of the pearl necklace with his dream, and the fact that it had broken just when he kissed Kelly.

Still, when she began to tell him how Lauren had been talking to her inside her head or appearing in the mirror, always in Charlie's presence, Alex had grown doubtful. As much as he wanted to believe Kelly, he just couldn't bring himself to do it. He had asked for more proof. Thankfully, Kelly had plenty to give. She just needed to get Charlie and show him.

As soon as he parked the car, they got out and hurried to the house. Once inside, the serenity of it in the wee hours of the morning enveloped them like a caress.

Running Haunted

Only a small lamp illuminated the interior. It stood on a side table in the living room, and they headed straight there to find that Stella was nowhere in sight.

'What the heck? Where is Stella?' asked Alex, his brow furrowed.

Kelly shook her head. 'You don't suppose she kept one of the boys company and fell asleep in their room? Tommy's, maybe?'

Alex scrunched up his face. 'No way. Tommy wouldn't want her in his room...'

'Then where is she?' Kelly whispered and went to the corridor to check if the light in the small bathroom was on. That wasn't the case but, to make sure, she opened the door slowly, only to confirm Stella wasn't in there.

After they gazed at each other mutely for a few moments, Alex shrugged and said, 'Oh well. Why are we surprised? The woman's tapped. I'm guessing she got tired of waiting for us and just left. Let's go check on the boys.'

A little later, having checked the rooms, they ascertained the kids were all sleeping soundly and that Stella was definitely gone. Kelly had caressed the dog's head when they entered Tommy's room, and he had sprung on his feet to follow them downstairs as if he knew she needed him to.

When she and Alex came to stand by the kitchen table, she turned to him and pointed to the dog. 'You see this scarf? I've been wearing it for days on end on purpose. Day and night. Lauren asked me to. She said it would help.'

'Help? Like, how?'

'So my life energy would amplify her own, what little she has left, allowing her to communicate with us. She has been complaining from time to time about her energy waning. I don't know why she asked me to put the scarf on the dog tonight... But, in any case, with the scarf and the dog here, I am sure I can get her to talk to me...'

Alex widened his eyes. 'Really? Will I be able to hear her too?'

'I don't know... Let's see.' She closed her eyes. 'Lauren? Can you hear me? Can you talk?'

After a few seconds, hearing nothing, she opened one eye and darted it to Alex, lips twisting. 'I am sorry. She's not answering.' She shrugged one shoulder and opened the other eye too. 'Problem is, I can never summon her. She's the one who talks to me whenever she wants to.'

'Well, that won't help us much tonight, will it?' said Alex with a quiet laugh.

Giving a playful smile, she put her hands on her waist to say, 'Hey! I am ridiculing myself here, and you're having a laugh? That's not right.'

'Well... I am sure if she wants to talk to you, she will do it in her own time. Lauren's always had her own mind. You could never tell her what to do. Believe me, I tried.' He gave a chuckle, then put his arms around her. 'Don't worry. I know Lauren's here. I can feel it. And I want to do all I can to help her find peace.'

'But you don't believe that she talks to me.'

'Let's just say I need to see that to believe it. Or, at least, to hear it.'

Kelly fell silent for a moment or two, then snapped her fingers. 'I remembered! Lauren said if I give you her message and you don't believe me, to tell you that you're a baboon! She said you'll know.'

Alex's eyes lit up, then he shook his head with amazement. 'How... How do you know that she used to call me that?'

'Huh! See? I *am* telling the truth!' Kelly had another idea that would serve as solid proof. Setting her jaw, she pulled back from their embrace, causing him to remove his hands, and she stooped down to pat the dog's head. 'If you can hear me, please, do this with me, Lauren. On the kitchen chair. Let me show him that, at least.'

The dog's eyes lit up to hear these words as if he understood, causing Kelly to take heart.

Alex seemed puzzled, about to speak, and she put up a hand to give a little wave. 'Just let me show you...'

With Alex and the dog following her with her eyes, Kelly spun around, went to the side of the table and dragged the chair where no one ever sat.

Alex's hand shot up, fingers splayed out. 'Hey, Kelly. Please don't sit in that chair. Charlie will protest, and his barks will wake up the kids!'

Kelly shook her head with a knowing smile. 'Don't worry. He won't do it this time. Trust me.'

Mystified, Alex stepped closer as Kelly slowly sat on the chair. The dog had come to stand near her feet but never barked or even whimpered. If anything, he seemed frozen, exactly how he looked whenever she trained him, waiting for the next command so he could get his chocolate treat.

Alex's jaw gaped open. 'How... is this even possible?'

Instead of answering him, Kelly patted her lap and Charlie jumped onto it, settling on there and looking up at her face adoringly.

Alex dragged another chair nearby and plonked himself on it like a lump of lead. 'Oh my God! What just happened?'

Kelly eyed him lovingly, a satisfied smile on her face. 'See? I knew he wasn't going to mind. Because Lauren communicates with the dog too, and she wants me to show you...'

'Show me, what?' he whispered, eyes burning with intrigue.

She put out a hand to pat his, and he gripped it like his life depended on it. She sighed, then said, 'It's all right, Alex. I know how hard this is for you and the children. But believe me when I tell you, I know because Lauren has told me. In every painful detail. And I know things about her that you don't know...'

'Like... what?' he mumbled.

'Well, for one, I know she still sits on this chair when you all eat. Every time. That's why Charlie never let anybody sit here after she passed away. That's why he never let me sit here either until today.'

'Oh my God...'

Kelly eyed him with deep sympathy for a moment or two, then carried on, 'I also know that when she was still alive, Lauren used to sit here with Charlie on her lap, telling you she could sit on this chair forever, watching you all... her family, her "most precious jewels". That's what she used to call you and the kids, didn't she?'

In lieu of an answer, Alex nodded once, then wiped a tear that flowed down his cheek.

She squeezed his hand with feeling. 'It's okay. I understand. Lauren was a warm, wonderful person, and I am sure you miss her a lot. You loved her so much, after all. And love remains in our hearts always. Death doesn't have the power to extinguish the force of love. Nothing does. And even though you set Lauren free tonight, she'll always stay with us. Her love will, for sure.'

'And you don't mind that?' he asked, lips twitching.

'Mind? Of course not. Lauren has become a precious friend of mine... And I know she wants us to be together. We have her blessing, Alex. All's good.'

Alex put his arm around her and they both leaned in closer for a kiss. It lasted very little, but it was just as tender as before, and it helped Kelly feel confident that Alex had finally believed.

After a short silence, he spoke first, his voice feeble. 'So... Is Lauren still here, you think?'

'*I know* she is, Alex.'

'I hope you're right... and that she'll say goodbye, at least to you, before she goes. Sadly, the kids and I never got the chance to say goodbye to her...'

'I... I meant to ask... How did she die, Alex? Was it an accident?'

Alex shook his head, then heaved a long sigh. 'No... Believe it or not, it was a stroke, despite her young years. It happened out of the blue. We had just come back from the supermarket. We were putting away the groceries, rowing about something stupid, something trivial... and, suddenly, she just collapsed. Moments later, she died in my arms right here in the kitchen. But she died peacefully. She just took one good look at me, her eyes intense as if she wanted to take the image of me along with her, then she closed her eyes, and that was it.' He took a steadying breath and added, 'Seeing her die without pain or anguish, without upset, has been my only saving grace...'

'Oh my God, Alex... it must have been terrible for you. To lose her like that, all of a sudden. I shudder to think what you've been through, especially in the beginning.'

Alex set his jaw. 'It was hard. I won't lie. But I had to keep functioning, you know? For the kids. I had to keep working at the hotel and to mind them at home the rest of the time, and to take care of them in every way I could.' He gave a wry smile. 'To be honest, I still don't know how I pulled through.'

She caressed his hand in hers. 'Alex, sometimes, we don't know our strengths until the need arises to be super-tough. Only then do we realize who we really are; what kind of metal we're really made of. No doubt, you've made a journey of self-discovery through this, so I don't believe for a moment you don't know how you pulled through. I am sure you do.'

'I guess you're right... And, to be frank, the whole experience has taught me a lot about myself. While Lauren was my wife, I thought I was just the bread winner, and maybe the dad for the weekends, you know? I wasn't really that close to the kids from day to day, because of my demanding job.'

'Yes, I can imagine... And now that I think of it, it makes sense why Lauren felt the need to linger. Not just so she could watch you as you took over in all things as a parent, but also because she never got to say goodbye properly to you guys.'

'You're right, Kelly. And, hopefully, today, the kids and I will have the chance to say goodbye to her at last.'

'I hope so, too. But she's going to need a ton of energy to do it. She barely manages a minute or so at a time to talk to me... And I don't understand why she's not speaking to me tonight. Normally, she'd readily do it with the scarf right here.' She pointed to the scarf around Charlie's neck and sighed. 'I wonder if she's weaker than normal right now, for whatever reason...' She shook her head and mumbled, 'If only we had something else to amplify her energy a little so I could talk to her...'

All at once, a bright idea formed in her mind. She placed Charlie carefully back on the floor and stood like a spring. 'Stay here! Back in a sec!' she said breathlessly as she dashed towards the stairs.

✳✳✳✳✳

Kelly returned a little later, one hand closed into a fist stretched out before her as she approached the table. Alex leaned forward in his chair when she plopped on the same one as before, and Charlie stepped closer to sit on the floor, his eyes trained on her.

Kelly opened her hand on the table to show him the remnants of the broken pearl necklace in her palm. The precious orbs glinted under the overhead light in a mesmerizing way.

'I don't understand. Why did you bring them here?' asked Alex, but Kelly put up a hand when she heard a murmur brew inside her mind. 'Please, Alex. Let me listen. I think the pearls I've been wearing all night are helping. I can hear something...'

Alex fell silent and seemed to have stopped breathing as he gazed into her face intently.

Slowly, Kelly began to make out through the murmur a scattered vowel or two, then a sigh. Finally, she heard Lauren in a faint whisper. 'Sorry about earlier, Kelly. I could hear you both talking but I couldn't respond. Too weak... I...'

'Please, Lauren! Don't go just yet...' said Kelly, under Alex's agonizing gaze.

'I want... I want to say goodbye to you all... Tomorrow morning... Can you help me please, Kelly?'

'Of course! Tell me what to do!'

'The scarf...' Lauren's wavering voice went on inside Kelly's mind, and Alex continued to watch mutely, obviously hearing only her part of the conversation. Kelly saw the hope and the heartache in his eyes and it broke her own heart, too.

'Wear the scarf overnight, Kelly. And put the pearls under your pillow. Let's hope that, tomorrow... I'll be able to talk to you all before I go,' Lauren added with huge effort.

Kelly was grateful to have received clear instructions. She gave a bright smile, causing Alex to mirror it, his face alight with relief first, then excitement.

'Tell her I will always love her. And that I'm thankful, so thankful that she brought you to my life.'

'You can tell her that yourself, my love. Tomorrow morning. When she intends to talk to you all.'

Alex's face went ablaze with awe. He swallowed hard and gazed back at Kelly for a few moments, eyes glazed over, his Adam's apple bobbing like a buoy in a tumultuous sea.

✶✶✶✶✶

A little later, they were saying goodbye with another kiss, a more fervent one this time, at the top of the stairs. Mid-kiss, Alex gave a soft grunt and pulled her to him, tugging gently towards his wide open bedroom door.

With a cunning smile, Kelly pulled back and shook a finger at him. 'No, you don't, Mister Impatient... We're not alone, remember?'

Alex raised his eyes comically to the ceiling, then turned his neck left, then right, before pinning them back on her to say under his breath, 'You think she's watching us, huh?'

'My guess? Always.' She saw him flinch and chuckled softly, then whispered, 'But don't worry. She *wants* us to be together. So, technically, she'd be happy to see us spend the night in your bed. It's just that I feel awkward about it, you know? I can't do this while she's here...' She shrugged, chewing her lower lip.

His eyes brightened as he got hold of her shoulders to rub them gently. 'Of course. I understand. I wasn't thinking. I am sorry, Kelly.'

'It's okay.' She gave a wicked smile. 'Believe me. It was hard to say no just then. I want this as much as you do. I want you, Alex...'

'So do I, Kelly. Oh... so much...' he whispered, his voice trailing off as he took her lips again.

Afterwards, he let her go and watched as she paced to her room, looking at him over her shoulder, her high heels making no sound on the carpet. Giggling softly like two lovesick teenagers, they waved at each other from their bedroom doors before closing them with a blown out kiss.

Kelly placed the pearls under her pillow and wore the scarf loosely around her neck as per Lauren's request. As she lay down to cover herself with the duvet, she gave a yawn.

Closing her eyes, she whispered in the darkness, 'Thank you so much, Lauren. For tonight... for Alex... and I hope you will get yourself suitably energized overnight. Your family is waiting eagerly to meet you tomorrow morning.'

Chapter 46

Kelly awoke with her alarm clock at eight a.m., feeling rested, despite having slept for only five hours. She dressed and went downstairs to find Alex getting mugs out of the cupboard.

The coffee maker was bubbling away, and two plates of buttered bread were sitting beside it on the counter.

'Wow!' she said, as she neared him. 'What time did you get up?'

He looped an arm around her waist, pulling her to him for a tender kiss. 'Good morning, my love. About ten minutes ago.'

She saw the warmth in his eyes as he held her, her heart soaring like a young swallow in the spring. 'How did you sleep?'

He gave a yawn. 'Like a log.'

'Me too,' she said with a chuckle, then tilted her head to ask, 'So why do you think Stella left like that last night? Are you going to ask her?'

He shook his head. 'I don't know and I don't care. The least words I exchange with her from now on the better. So, no, I'm not going to ask her why she left. But I can say a simple thank you to her for minding the kids... That's enough, isn't it?' He cocked his eye at her and gave a lopsided smile. 'Unless you think we should put her on our list for a Christmas hamper?'

She slapped his wrist with a chortle. 'Hey! There's no such thing as a Christmas hamper in Greece. So I know you're not serious!' She winked and added, 'But you could buy her a kilo of *kourabiedes*.'

He gave a guffaw, then his face became serious when he said, 'Oh... I am so happy you came into my life, Kelly. You changed me, you changed the kids, you *transformed* our lives completely. All, in a matter of weeks... Hey! Are you sure you're a marathon runner and not a sprinter? You, my girl... You're super-fast!'

He squeezed her in his arms and they giggled as they swayed together playfully from side to side.

When they finally sobered up, she met his tender gaze and said, 'I'm just as happy to have found you all, Alex.... But you know it wasn't just me. Without Lauren, I couldn't have done much...'

'Yes, I realize that. And I could sense all along that she's here. Thank goodness for your special gift that allowed you to connect with her. Hopefully, we all will this morning.' He gave a bright smile. 'I can't wait... and I hope it won't freak the kids out.'

She gave a dismissive wave. 'Freak out? It's their mother, Alex. Of course they won't freak out. Besides, they all realize Lauren's been around, watching us, protecting us, trying to make contact. They'll be beside themselves with joy if she manages to make a proper appearance today.'

'Oh, Kelly, I hope you're right...' He squeezed her in his arms before burying his face in her neck. 'Oh my... You smell so good... I could eat you up...' he said after a short pause.

She pulled back and caressed his cheek, a playful smile on her lips. 'You can have the toast for now...' She mirrored his grin to add, 'And afterwards, we'll go wake up the kids. We'll explain about their mother, then I'll do my best to help her say a proper goodbye to you all.'

✵✵✵✵✵

By nine o' clock, Kelly and Alex had gathered the kids around the kitchen table. Over breakfast, they confirmed to them what they all already knew in a way – that their mother's spirit had been lingering in the house. The children grew excited, especially when Kelly relayed how she had been able to speak to their mother all this time and even see her in the mirror.

Instead of freaking out as Alex feared, they became ecstatic, begging Kelly to summon their mother so they could see her too. When she responded that this was exactly what she planned to do they erupted in whooping sounds and squeals of delight.

Alex then took over to warn them that perhaps this wasn't going to be possible, seeing that their mother's spirit had been very weak the previous night when Kelly tried to make contact.

Kelly showed them the scarf that she wore in her hair, and the pearls, which she'd brought downstairs. She had placed them in a little glass bowl that sat on the table before them all.

For a while, a short silence spread around the room as everyone stared at the remnants of their mother's old pearl necklace. Stratos said he remembered her wearing it and couldn't help but shed a tear.

Kelly, who sat beside him, squeezed his shoulder, as Alex, across the table, patted his hand.

Then, Kelly had an idea. She turned to Tommy and asked him to bring the tin box of old photos that they now kept in the living room under the coffee table. The little boy was forever sitting with it on the sofa to browse through them.

When Tommy handed the box to Kelly, she removed the lid and placed it on the table. Then, she looked at the children in succession to say, 'I am guessing your mother's greatest tonic is your love for her, hence placing the photos here that have been recently charged with that love since you've been holding them in your hands daily.'

She lowered her gaze to look at Charlie, who had been sitting expectantly by her feet all this time. She'd already explained to the boys that Charlie was haunted in some odd way, communicating with their mother, probably all the time.

Kelly gave a soft sigh, eyeing the dog with hope, and said, 'Come on, buddy. Do your thing. Can you call her over?'

Charlie gave a single bark, his eyes bright like live coal, and jumped readily onto the vacant chair at the head of the table. As soon as his paws landed on there with a soft rustle from his nails, a grey haze began to rise, seemingly from the chair, eliciting a collective gasp from the others, who watched, mouths agape.

Kelly took a moment to inspect everyone's expressions. They all seemed equally enthralled and, thankfully, there was no trace of trepidation or fear in the children's eyes, far from what Alex had worried about.

As if he could read her thoughts, he turned to look at her then, and they exchanged an encouraging smile, before returning their attention back to the dog.

The haze had turned pure white and was now starting to take on the shape of a faint apparition. It was the outline of a womanly figure and it was transparent, allowing them to see the kitchen island behind it.

In an instant, the outline disappeared, giving its place to Lauren's ghostly form. It was crystal clear, leaving no doubt in anyone's mind that she was right there, sitting with them, the same doggie on her lap, like in the old days when she was living.

A deathly silence spread around the table as everyone seemed to be either fighting back tears, or trying to find the right words. Alex seemed to be doing both.

Lauren broke the eerie silence first. 'Hello, everyone! Yes, it's me... But don't look so shocked, my darlings! I may look a little different, but I'm still me...' She turned to Alex, her eyes full of tenderness, to say, 'My love, I wish you happiness, you know that. That's why I stayed...'

He seemed tongue-tied, tears now flowing freely from his eyes.

Smiling at him, Lauren whispered, 'I know... I know... I love you too. I always will. We never got the chance to say goodbye properly, but now we finally have that chance. Thanks to Kelly, who has given us all this gift of communication.'

Alex took a steadying breath and said, 'I am also very thankful, Lauren. Both to you and Kelly. Thank you for staying behind to take care of us all. Until you knew we were okay. You should be an angel, Lauren. You deserve this, delaying the gratification of the perfect paradise that's surely in store for you to linger here with us.'

Lauren erupted in a guffaw, to everyone's surprise, then said, 'Oh, I am no angel! But for you all, I'll always be one. Your *own* angel. Forever. That's a promise.'

Everyone's faces frowned with feeling, the sentiments clearly overflowing in their hearts. Lauren, seemingly attuned, realized and put up a hand. 'Ah, no! Please! I am already dead and buried, and I am not here to witness another funeral. I want to see happy faces on my way out. Okay?'

To please her, everyone began to perk up, then offer faint smiles that grew brighter under her encouraging gaze.

'That's better...' she said, then turned to Alex. 'And as for you, you have a big reason to be smiling. As of today, your new life begins with Kelly.' She looked at them both tenderly and added, 'You have my full blessing. I couldn't have found you a better woman...'

Kelly exchanged a curious look with Alex, and when they both turned back to Lauren, the latter nodded with satisfaction.

Next, Lauren's gaze rested upon her children, who looked back at her with evident awe. Her eyes were soft as they moved from face to face, a hand on her heart. 'My darlings, I love you all so much... I won't get the chance to watch you grow into the wonderful men you're bound to become, but I'll always love you... In your loving hearts, I'll always be right here... with you. I promise.'

Stratos cleared his throat, then said, 'Mum? Is this really you?'

'Yes, Stratos. I am as real as can be, beyond my grave.'

'Cool!'

She laughed in response, causing everyone to do the same. A short lull ensued, then she said, 'Stratos, I am so happy you are singing and playing the guitar... You sing like an angel, you always have. I know it's something you love, so I hope you'll keep on doing it...'

'Yes, Mum. Always. You've always encouraged me and I thank you for that.'

'Stratos, pursuing the things we love the most is a surefire way to find the kind of happiness that lasts. Never give up on the things you love. No matter who tries to stop you. Make no mistake: Life will keep throwing you into one tempest after another, like it's meant to do, but your love will remain the compass. Always. It will see you through in life, no matter the hardship. And I say this to all you boys...'

She looked at all her children in succession, then Alex and Kelly. 'All of you... Hold on to what you have, to what you love. Happiness in life is everyone's God-given right. Anyone who tells you otherwise is a fool who will know it when it's far too late.'

Everyone nodded, seemingly lost in thought.

'Nikos?' Lauren asked, causing him to straighten in his chair, his eyes sparkling.

'Yes, Mum?' he said in a frail voice.

'I am so proud of you. For not giving in to bullying, for always believing in yourself. For staying upbeat, self-loving and kind to others, despite all that nasty stuff. And, ultimately, for seeking a better you. Look what you've managed in such a short time! You're amazing!' She clapped her hands with glee, but no sound came out.

As if wanting to compensate for that, everyone put their hands together and began to clap, the sound reverberating around the walls. In response, Lauren's apparition turned brighter, more solid, somehow, causing everyone to gawp.

Lauren gave a little laugh. 'Why do you look so astonished? Everything in this world you live in is about energy, about vibration. Happiness and joy raise them both. Gratitude too. And love is the greatest force of nature. You have filled the room with all the above. It's no surprise I feel stronger by the second...' She winked and added, 'Carry on, and I'll come back to life within the hour.'

Tommy jumped visibly in his chair, then leaned towards her like a cut flower in a vase leaning towards the sunshine. 'Really?'

Her gaiety disappeared from her face, eyes softening to say, 'No, Tommy. That was a joke. Life and death are up to God and no one can tamper with that. But thank you for your excitement.'

Tommy pressed his lips together and lowered his head. 'Oh.'

'Don't be sad, Tommy. You have your whole life ahead of you. And I'll be with you, walking with you, every step of the way. As long as you keep me in your heart.'

'Yes, Mummy. I will. I always will.' As he gazed into her face, he wiped a tear from his cheek, then said, 'Mummy? Can I ask you something before you go?'

'Of course, my love.'

'Why did Charlie bring me your necklaces to play with?'

'Because I could sense you missed me... and my necklaces are charged with my energy from when I wore them in life, my darling. I knew they would bring you comfort.' She tilted her head. 'They did, didn't they?'

'Yes, Mummy, lots...'

'I am glad to hear it. Now, can you do something for me too, Tommy?'

'Yes. Anything...'

'I want you to stop writing to Grandad. He needs to rest now.'

Kelly was taken aback. *What did that mean? What does writing to his grandfather in Salonica have to do with him resting? Resting… like, how?*

Before she could voice her curiosity, Alex spoke first. 'What do you mean, Lauren? Then, turning to Tommy, he added, 'Have you been writing to your grandad?'

'Yes, Dad,' he said, head bent.

Lauren shook her head. 'Don't admonish him, Alex. He didn't do anything wrong. He was trying to manage his grief and to express his thoughts, that's all. He's been writing about you, too, worrying about you as you battled with your own grief. Only good things came out of Tommy writing to his grandfather, believe me.'

'Of course, I have no problem with him writing the letters. I just don't understand. Where did he get the stamps? How did he post the letters?'

Tommy, head still bent, cut in to say, 'I didn't use stamps, Daddy…'

Alex's brows shot up. 'What do you mean? You just threw them in a post box? Oh, Tommy… They don't get delivered without stamps. You know that…'

Tommy remained silent, shoulders slumped, as he continued to stare at his lap.

Alex waited for a few moments, then opened his mouth to speak to Tommy again, but Lauren cut in.

'Alex, listen to me… He hasn't been writing to his grandad in Salonica… He's been writing to his grandad Alan. Next door.'

Chapter 47

Lauren had disappeared, this time forever for certain, shortly after dropping the bomb that Alan, who lived next door, was her father.

For reasons Kelly didn't understand, everyone had stared goggle-eyed to hear Tommy had been writing to Alan, but nothing else was said about it because Lauren then announced her energy was waning. With one last affirmation of her love to them all and a blown out kiss, she was gone, leaving the dog sitting on the chair looking rather drowsy.

Shortly, under everyone's mute gaze, the dog's eyelids drooped, then closed firmly shut and he dozed off, beginning to snore.

Now, everyone seemed just as numb as Kelly, slumped in their seats, each lost in their own thoughts. Luckily, there were no tears, not even from the children, and Kelly felt thankful for that. She felt thankful for everything today. For Lauren especially, who had left only after everything in the house had become perfect. She'd made sure that even Kelly, a total stranger, was happy before she sought her well-deserved eternal peace.

Finally, when she felt she had allowed enough respectful silence after Lauren's final departure, she gave a frown and said, 'So, Tommy, I didn't know Alan was your grandad...' She turned to Alex and the other children too, to add, 'How come all this time your grandparents never visited us here? And you never visit next door either. If you don't mind me asking, why is that?'

'Visit?' said Nikos, raising his brows.

'Yes...' she answered, dumbfounded, then noticed everyone looked at her in a strange manner. 'What? What did I say?'

'Why should we visit next door?' asked Alex.

'Uh... So the kids can see their grandparents?'

'See them?' asked Alex. 'How could they? They've both passed away, Kelly.'

A few moments of dead silence ensued and when the penny finally dropped, Kelly brought both hands to her head. 'Oh. My. God.'

Alex's face fell, then ignited with astonishment. 'You didn't! You saw Lauren's parents too? How? When?'

The children seemed frozen and too dumbfounded to speak, but Alex had become fully animated. He turned towards her in his chair and put an urgent hand on her arm. 'Kelly? Tell me! When did you see them?'

She shook her head. 'I only saw Alan. On several occasions. We talked. He gave me advice...' She scratched her head, trying to remember. Her eyes lit up, then she said to Tommy, 'Wait a minute! I saw him reading one of your letters! How do you give them to him? How is it possible?'

'He got my letter? You saw him read it?' asked Tommy, his eyes wide like cartwheels.

'Yes, I did. Actually, it was heavily stained with mud.'

'Mud?' asked Alex with a deep frown.

'Yes. I presumed it was because he is such an avid gardener. I thought maybe he had touched it with soiled hands after working in his flower patches.'

'What flower patches?' said Alex. 'There are none next door, Kelly! The property is derelict. It's been for years...'

'What? Of course, there are flowers next door! And a beautiful, recently painted house!' She rubbed her forehead hard, squeezing her eyes shut, trying to focus her thoughts. Moments later, she snapped her eyes open and turned to Alex, who still watched her intently, jaw slack.

'It all looks so lived in next door!' she protested. 'The kitchen window is always open... I've been smelling your mother-in-law's cooking every day, for goodness sake!'

Alex took her hand gently. 'Come, Kelly... Let's all go in the garden and you can tell us all what you see next door.'

*****

Outside on the lawn, Kelly looked up to the sky and closed her eyes for a few moments, willing herself to clear her head as the strong sunshine caressed her face.

When she opened her eyes again, she found the others looking at her expectantly, so she beckoned and they all neared the fence. She walked to it on unsteady legs, her eyes focusing at the property next door, her astonishment growing with every step. *What's this? Where are the flowers? The fresh coat of paint on the walls? The pristine tiles on the roof?*

What she saw before her now seemed impossible. All she could do was stand before the fence and hold it with both hands as if she feared she'd collapse if she were to let go. All the while, the others' eyes flitted from Alan's property to her, then back again. 'It's dilapidated... you're right...' she said feebly.

Alex put an arm around her waist as if he knew she felt unstable on her feet, and she gave him a mute gaze, unable to express her thoughts.

It was one thing to know all along she'd been communicating with Lauren's ghost, and another to think she'd been talking to a living neighbour to realize, only now, that it had all been a vision – another haunting she didn't have the faintest idea about. Until now. Thoughts returned to her mind with torrential speed, and she whirled around to point vaguely towards their front door.

'He told me about the spare key in the flower pot over there the day I locked myself out... I didn't tell you...' she said to Alex, '... but that's what he did. To help me. And he told me how to get Eleni to come to your party, Stratos... He's been taking care of all of you, of all of us...'

'So you didn't see Granny?' interrupted Nikos.

'No... But she must have been around.' She pointed to the window that stood closest to the fence on the decrepit old house. The paint on the closed shutters was heavily chipped, the woodwork long turned black, weatherbeaten.

'This window was open every day... I've been tortured by so many tantalizing food aromas for weeks...'

Alex chuckled. 'Not surprised. My mother-in-law was an excellent cook.'

'I miss her curries, I know that!' said Stratos, and Nikos agreed with a nod.

Kelly sensed the latter was about to cry so she pulled him in for a hug.

After a few moments of silence, Alex turned to Tommy. 'So, how did you give your grandfather the letters?'

Tommy pointed downwards. There was a hole in one of the wood planks at the bottom of the fence.

'I meant to repair that... Never got around to doing it,' said Alex, his voice heavy with regret.

'You've been leaving them in your grandfather's garden through the opening?' asked Kelly, and Tommy nodded, then crouched down, put his hand through the opening and retracted it moments later. In his hand, he was now holding a bunch of weathered, folded pieces of paper. All of them were muddy and crumpled with the indication that they'd been sodden by rain.

'Oh Tommy...' said Kelly, and knelt before him to give him a hug as soon as he put the letters back on his grandfather's side of the fence. His property was overgrown with weeds and thistles, and there was no sign left of the flower patches that she'd been admiring all this time.

Tommy pulled back from Kelly's embrace and looked up to his father. 'So, where is Grandad now? Isn't he going to talk to us too?'

Alex seemed tongue-tied so Kelly caressed the boy's head, causing him to look at her as they both stood back on their feet. 'No, Tommy. Your grandparents are no longer here... I am guessing they left together with your mother today.'

Tommy set his chin. 'How do you know that?'

'Because, today, for the first time, I can see a derelict house, like you all do. If Grandad was still here, I'd be able to see him. I am sorry... But don't be sad, Tommy. I am sure your grandparents love you and will remain in your hearts always, just like your mummy will.'

Tommy gave a faint smile, and Alex pulled her and all the children together into a group hug. Afterwards, he said, 'I love you, guys. But as of today, no more sadness, okay? Mummy and your grandparents have left us with their blessing. Let's make the best of it. What do you say?'

The children began to cheer, then walked up ahead, as they all made their way back to the front door.

Ambling hand-in-hand, Kelly asked Alex, 'When did they die, your in-laws?'

'Oh... Same year as Lauren did. Three years ago. They died together, in a road accident. We never got the chance to say goodbye to them either... And, actually, Lauren passed away just six months *after* they did. The doctors said her stroke may have been caused by her grief... She just couldn't shake the pain of their loss. They had always been incredibly close.'

Kelly paused to look over her shoulder at the derelict house once more, her heart heavy with sadness.

He did the same and said, 'Now that I am finally moving on, maybe I should deal with it properly... fix it up and put it up for rent. Alan transferred the ownership to the kids in his will. I guess I had been too stuck in my own sense of loss to deal with it until now.'

Kelly gave him an encouraging smile. 'I'll help you, my love. You and me. We'll fix everything. We'll make our life perfect. You will see.'

She smiled, and he did too, their gazes locked together as they pulled each other closer for a kiss, but before their lips could meet they heard the children explode with squeals of excitement. They were calling them over from the front path near the garden gate.

Getting closer, they saw that Stratos was holding a large carrier bag and removing some odd items from it to hand them to his brothers. They were scarves in beautiful designs, four shoulder bags, and a medium-sized paper box with a lid.

Nikos, who was holding the box, gave it to Kelly when she asked.

Intrigued, she opened it to find inside a messy tangle of golden chains, necklaces, rings and bracelets. Some of them were adorned with semi-precious gems or pearls. 'Oh, my!'

Alex leaned closer to take a look. 'Wait a minute! These are Lauren's! How did they get here?'

He dashed to the gate to open it and look up and down the street, then hurried back in. 'There's no one in sight. Did you see anyone leave the bag here, boys?'

'No! Tommy said the bag was already here when we came outside,' replied Nikos. 'When we turned away from looking at Grandad's house he ran straight to it, and we all gathered to see what's inside.'

Alex's brows knit as he turned to Stratos. 'Is there anything else in the bag?'

Instead of answering, Stratos gave a cheeky grin and put on a pair of dark designer sunglasses. They looked feminine.

'Where did you get these?'

'They were in the bag too, Dad!' said Stratos with a chortle. 'Do you think they're parting gifts from Mum?' he asked Kelly.

'Of course not...' she said, her mind whirling, as she pointed to the glasses. 'Can I see them, Stratos?'

When he handed them to her she turned them in her hands this way and that until it finally hit her. 'Dolce e Gabbana!' she said triumphantly. 'Of course! Stella! She had a pair like that... Remember Alex? She got funny when I mentioned the brand that day when she was wearing them. By her fence over there?'

She pointed to it, and he looked that way, then struck the side of his head with a rigid hand. 'Of course! But... what the heck? How does she have Lauren's things? I'll go ask her!'

In the meantime, Stratos had taken another, more careful look at the bag to find a single piece of paper inside. He handed it to Kelly and she shouted out to Alex, who was walking away. 'Wait! Alex! There's a note!'

He returned, his face animated with intrigue, and they all huddled together as Kelly began to read.

Dear Alex,
I apologise. Please tell Lauren I am very sorry. I only took these things to remember her by. I didn't know she'd be angry.
I'll tell you what. From now on, I'll keep to my side of the fence and you keep to yours. I don't want any more trouble. And, again, I am sorry. This is all I took, cross my heart. It's all a terrible misunderstanding. And I hope you and Lauren will forgive me in time.
Stella

Their collective laughter erupted in the yard, reaching high into the fresh morning air. And, just like that, their annoyance over Stella, along with any remnants of their past heartaches, dispersed in the sunshine, carried away by the force of Lauren's love.

Epilogue

It was a sunny Sunday in late May with soaring temperatures when the family got in the car and drove to Tolo. It wasn't just an outing for their first swim that year, but a day out to celebrate a special occasion.

On the previous night, having taken Kelly out for dinner at a fancy hotel in Akronafplia while Stratos and Eleni minded the younger boys back home, Alex had popped the big question. Kelly had had to choke back the tears to say yes.

She had been expecting it, of course, seeing that from the day Lauren departed from the house, their love had been going from strength to strength. Already, they shared the same bed, and the kids saw a loving mother in her.

The ring with the dazzling single diamond on Kelly's finger only served to confirm what she and Alex already knew: that they'd found the perfect match in each other.

Now, stretched out on the sand, their towels side-by-side under a large beach umbrella, Kelly and Alex sat together, looking out to sea. Charlie lay between them, snoring away.

In the shallows, Nikos and Tommy splashed about, tossing a ball at each other. Behind the umbrella, Stratos and Eleni sat inside a small beach tent, just big enough for two. She was gazing into his face with adoration, twirling a strand of her hair coyly as he played his guitar and sang to her. Few people were about at the time. They didn't seem to mind, and some even moved their heads along with the melody.

Alex chuckled, having just stolen another look their way. 'Darn. I didn't think to sell tickets. We're losing money here.'

'Don't laugh, you never know. Stratos could very well be the next Chris Martin. You know, the singer of Coldplay?'

Alex scrunched up his face, a finger on his nose as he pretended to look pensive. 'Ooh. I don't know about that... Is this his style?'

'Definitely. He even looks like him a bit. And he certainly has the same British accent.'

He pulled a face of mock disappointment. 'Shoot. I was hoping for Bruce Springsteen.'

'Hm. The talent may be there, but the accent's all wrong.'

They erupted in peals of laughter, just as Nikos and Tommy began to call from the shallows for them all to go in.

Stratos and Eleni agreed to toss the ball around with them, and Charlie awoke, eager to follow them into the water. Kelly took him off the lead and he went splashing madly into the shallows to receive pats on his head from the children.

Alex then asked Kelly to go with him to the café nearby for a *frappé*. She was happy to, so they stood to go. The children complained when they heard, coaxing them to join them in the water instead, but Alex promised to bring them all ice cream. That seemed to end all protestations.

The seating area of the café was on higher ground, partly over the water. Kelly and Alex sat at a vacant table by the stone ledge that was adorned with ceramic pots of geraniums in various colours. The sea view was spectacular from up there, allowing them to admire the whole bay and the tiny islands of Romvi and Koronissi. A rainbow of small boats and pedaloes floated peacefully on the sparkling water as far as the eye could see.

As their backs rested on the large, cushioned chairs on offer, Alex gave a luxurious sigh. 'Now, that's what I'm talking about. I'd begun to worry my body would bend permanently in the same of an L from sitting under the umbrella like that.'

Kelly laughed and he joined her as he put an arm around her shoulders. She leaned in and kissed him tenderly on the lips, then said, 'Tell me you're not one of those men who intend to grow old before their time. And don't you dare stop going to the gym! If I see any flab, I'm out!'

He tickled her, and she erupted in giggles. Neither of them bothered to look around, in case anyone watched. They simply didn't care.

Alex removed his fingertips from her stomach, allowing her to breathe easily again, and said, 'Same here, missy.'

She tilted her head. 'I know you don't mean that.'

He tapped her nose and replied, 'Neither do you.'

'Of course, I don't,' she whispered, 'I'll still love you when you've grown all wrinkly and toothless.'

'What if I lose all my hair?' he teased.

She eyed him with adoration. 'I'll love you just the same.'

'And... what if my bum stops being... you know... chewable?'

She pulled back from their embrace, studying his face intently, and he began to laugh out loud.

She slapped his chest playfully. 'No! I don't believe you! You read my message on your phone that day in your office!'

'Of course, I did!'

'So, you knew I fancied you when you found me in there, and all this time I thought I had deleted it before you saw it?' She buried her face in her hands. 'Oh no...'

He chortled. 'Well, I did see it... And it both enthralled and amused me no end. Of course, I guessed you'd sent it to me by mistake and knew that when you realized, you'd be tortured by worry and shame.'

'Oh... You have no idea...' she said, shuddering at the distant memory as she looked away.

He squeezed her to him and laughed out loud. 'Come here you! Never in my life would I have imagined you'd have the cheek to come over to my office to delete the message! When I checked my phone after my meeting and saw it wasn't there any more, well...' he burst into a snorting laugh, then added, '...and since I'd found you in my office when I got in, it was easy to put two and two together.'

'Oh, God... How embarrassing!' she said, cringing in his embrace.

Squeezing her tightly, he caressed her cheek and gazed into her eyes. 'No, that wasn't embarrassing. It was a godsend! I was so unsure about confessing my feelings to you that if it hadn't been for that mishap of yours, I probably would never have plucked up the courage to do it.'

That caused a torrent of thoughts to enter Kelly's mind. She remembered the pug had been acting strangely that morning back home, causing her mind to run astray, enough for her to confuse the two threads, thinking she was writing to Efi instead of Alex.

'It was Charlie, you know...' she told him with a big smile. 'He kept barking, bothering me at home that morning, causing me to look up from my phone screen. He even bit me, for goodness sake! I am sure Lauren was behind all this.'

Alex gave a knowing smile and nodded, then sat back in his chair, pulling her gently to him. They looked out to sea in silence for a few moments, clinging to each other. The vast blue mass of water was calm. Gentle waves lapped on the shore, foaming gently on the golden sand.

Finally, he said, 'Thinking back now, I am sure Lauren orchestrated the whole thing. I wouldn't be surprised if she did something to cause us to meet that first day on the seafront in Nafplio.'

'You know? I wouldn't put it past her. But I don't need to know... I am just happy to be here, happy at last, with you.'

Seemingly too moved for words, Alex leaned in and kissed her, conveying with the fervour of his lips and his embrace all that his words might have failed to express.

After they enjoyed their coffees, they bought ice creams for everyone and returned to the kids, who came out of the water at once to get their treats.

Afterwards, Alex rented out a pedalo at the pier nearby, and they all jumped on it to go for a ride.

In the deep water, the salty breeze filled with their happy sounds as they squealed and called to each other excitedly, diving off into the crystal clear water.

*****

High up in the sky, so high that, from up there, the pedalo looked like a speck of dust, Lauren and her parents looked down and revelled at the sight. Somehow, they could still see everyone's smiling faces and the sunlight dancing in their eyes.

'I have to hand it to you, Lauren,' said Alan. 'You picked the perfect girl to take care of your family!'

'Thanks, Dad. And you've been an amazing helper in my plan.'

'Oh, I did nothing compared to your mother. She did all the hard work.'

'Yes, of course! Poor Mum! She got the short end of the stick!'

Alan winked at her. 'You mean she *fetched* it?'

'Ha ha, yes! And now she's *dog tired*, bless her.'

Alan's face brightened further. 'Hey! Maybe we should take her to see a *dog-tor! Dog-tor?* Get it?'

Quick as a flash, Lauren replied, 'Yeah! A shrink! And he'll probably tell her she's *barking* mad!'

'After a *paws*, no doubt!'

The two dissolved in hysterics, and Lauren's mother, who walked just two steps ahead, looked behind her shoulder, and said, 'I can hear you okay? Honestly! Talk about rubbing it in! You two have conspired against me to give me the worst role in your little scheme.' She gave a deep frown, but the others could tell she didn't really mean it.

Alan chuckled. 'Oh, come on. How hard can it be to inhabit a little doggie for a while?'

'Hard? The word doesn't half-describe it... All Charlie did all day was slobber, and eat and lick things he wasn't supposed to. And don't get me started on him passing wind!

Ah! The fumes! Enough to stop a nuclear reactor in its tracks!'

Lauren and Alan took her by the hands, chortling, and the three began to stroll upon the clouds towards a brilliant beam of light. It awaited to take them even higher, to the green pastures of Heaven that were long overdue.

One of their angel guides had said they were allowed to stay in this semi-earthly, semi-ethereal plane for just a few more days to keep an eye on their family, and today was their last day. But that was okay. They were all ready to go, their hearts full of love, all three of them certain of the happiness of their loved ones left behind. They didn't even feel the need to look down to check on them one last time.

As soon as they entered the beam, it began to raise them higher, the sound of their laughter amplifying, booming, as it reverberated around the ether.

THE END

Thank you for reading Running Haunted. Keep turning the pages for recommended reads, a note from the author and more!

Did you know? Every time one of my readers forgets to write a review, a Greek gets so upset they forget to pick the olives from their trees. It just breaks my heart! Tell me what you thought of my book and help the Greeks continue to pour olive oil in their salads!

Please leave a short review on Amazon. It will be greatly appreciated!
US: https://www.amazon.com/dp/B0853CMP1V
UK: https://www.amazon.co.uk/dp/B0853CMP1V

More from this author

Lizzie arrives on the idyllic Greek island of Corfu but far from feeling excited, her heart is heavy. She is here to claim back her twin brother who was kidnapped twenty years earlier on her previous visit. In a cave. By an evil witch.

When Lizzie sees her brother again, she receives the shock of her life. The witch has tricked her… As if this weren't enough, Stamatis, a handsome local, steals her heart to complicate her life even further…

"It's a step up from Mills and Boon - much more Mary Stewart than Barbara Cartland, with a bit of Gothic horror and Harry Potter-esque magic in the mix. And it's certainly a page-turner." ~Hilary Whitton Paipeti, author of In the Footsteps of Lawrence Durrell and Gerald Durrell in Corfu

Available in paperback, kindle boxset or kindle episodes!
Amazon US: http://www.amazon.com/dp/B07J4V96RP
Amazon UK: https://www.amazon.co.uk/dp/B07J4V96RP

FREE eBOOK!

Treat yourself today to this wonderful collection of short stories that highlight various kinds of love. Not just the romantic kind, but also love for family, pets, and country. Facets of Love will introduce you to stunning locations around Greece. The fantasy elements contained in some of the stories are bound to enchant you!

"I loved the variety of voices, characters and motifs I encountered. From blooming love, second chance love, to the innocence of children, grandma's wise words, to Greek pride."
~Alina's Bookish Hideout Blog

Visit: http://effrosyniwrites.com/yours-for-free/

When Sofia falls in love, a mourning spirit begins to haunt her...

Sofia Aspioti, a young student, arrives on the idyllic island of Corfu for her annual summer break. Because of her strict upbringing, Sofia is discontented with her life. Her parents expect her to be the model daughter, so she keeps her heart locked away, avoiding boys, to keep herself out of trouble.

When she falls in love with Danny, a charming British tourist, he shows her a fun side of life she becomes addicted to. Now, for the first time, Sofia dares to go against her family's strict rules, and to follow her heart. Just as life becomes the sweetest it's ever been, strange dreams about a woman dressed in black begin to haunt her...

"I could feel the warm sun and sandy beaches even on a cold dreary day." ~Helen Johnson Brumbaugh, Amazon reviewer

Amazon US: http://www.amazon.com/dp/B00LGNYEPC
Amazon UK: https://www.amazon.co.uk/dp/B00LGNYEPC

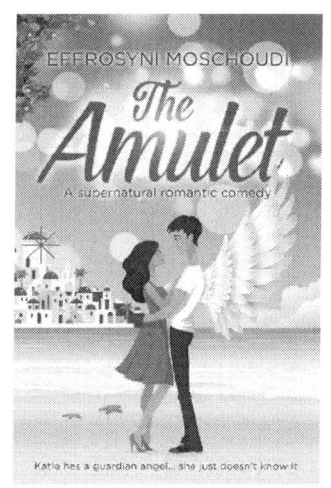

Katie has a guardian angel . . . she just doesn't know it. Plus, she's falling for him.

When Katie loses her office job, a gypsy woman hands her an amulet for good luck. Next, she gets hired as hotel receptionist on the Greek island of Sifnos. One of the guests, heart-stoppingly handsome Aggelos, saves the day whenever she needs help.

Katie is intrigued by him and his quirky friends, unaware that he is a guardian angel that came with the amulet. As she falls in love, the unanswered questions pile up, driving her crazy... Will Katie get her happily-ever-after? It may take a miracle; but on an island as magical as Sifnos, anything is possible!

"What a stunning read! You can feel the summer heat and taste the sumptuous Greek dishes as the words just leap from the page." ~Readers' Favorite

"What a wonderful imagination the author has, I felt as if I was living in the book and found it hard to put it down." ~Jean Symonds, Amazon.co.uk reviewer

Amazon US: http://www.amazon.com/dp/B01MCZ2UOU
Amazon UK: https://www.amazon.co.uk/dp/B01MCZ2UOU

A note from the author

I started writing Running Haunted in early 2019, at a time when my mother was undergoing chemo. The writing progress was slow, my worry over her wellbeing steadily growing. As a result, this story that began as a light-hearted romantic comedy wound up dramatic in places, enriched with the theme of the undying love of a mother, who, even beyond the grave was reluctant to leave her loved ones behind just yet.

I knew from back then I was going to dedicate the book to my mother, yet I couldn't imagine I was going to lose her, nor that her cancer was going to spread even further and so fast, making our family life a nightmare, and her the absolute martyr.

My mother, Ioanna, passed away on February 12, 2020, and even though she is gone, I am comforted to think she is now at peace, suffering no longer, just like the character that inspired her.

Dear reader, if you've lost a dear family member, I hope this story stirs in you the right feeling that can comfort you, the way it happens to me as I now read what The Muse has offered.

For my travel guide to Nafplio and a bunch of stunning photos, visit my blog: http://bit.ly/2rhA1ev

I hope you've enjoyed the many references to Greek food in this book. For my delicious Greek recipes, go here: http://bit.ly/1L9GuKu

Acknowledgements

I offer sincere and plentiful thanks to my beta readers, the wonderful bookworms and supportive friends I am blessed with. Once again, they have all set aside time in their busy lives to give my newest baby their tender loving care, and for that, I am grateful beyond words. In no particular order, they are: Hilary Whitton Paipeti, Louise Mullarkey, Jean Symonds, MM Jaye, Wendy Gilops, Anne Bateman, Vicki Harrison, Colleen Chesebro, and Cheryl Worrall.

As always, I owe tons of gratitude to my husband Andy for his support as I pursue my dreams.

To all my readers, a big thank you! Because of you, I continue to give vent to the benevolent, whimsical voices in my head. Being able to share them with you is a true blessing for me. Every morsel of your feedback spurs me on to keep creating stories you will love.

If you've just discovered me, please know that I am thankful and deeply honoured that you've chosen one of my stories among the millions on Amazon!

About the author

Effrosyni Moschoudi was born and raised in Athens, Greece. As a child, she loved to sit alone in her garden scribbling rhymes about flowers, butterflies, and ants. Today, she writes books for the romantic at heart. She lives in a quaint seaside town near Athens with her husband Andy. Her mind forever drifts to her beloved island of Corfu.

Her debut novel, The Necklace of Goddess Athena, won a silver medal in the 2017 book awards of Readers' Favorite. The Ebb, her romance set in Moraitika, Corfu that's inspired from her summers there in the 1980s, is an ABNA Q-Finalist.

Effrosyni's novels are Amazon bestsellers, having hit #1 several times, and are available in kindle and paperback format.

Go here to grab FREE PDF books by this author: http://effrosyniwrites.com/free-stuff/

Visit Effrosyni's website to check out her travel guide to south Corfu, a plethora of blog posts about her life in Greece, book reviews and lots more: http://effrosyniwrites.com

Make sure to join her newsletter to receive her news and special offers: http://effrosyniwrites.com/yours-for-free/

**Email her at contact@effrosyniwrites.com

**Friend her on Facebook:
https://www.facebook.com/efrosini.moschoudi

**Like her Facebook page:
https://www.facebook.com/authoreffrosyni

**Follow her on Twitter: https://twitter.com/frostiemoss

**Find her on Goodreads:
https://www.goodreads.com/author/show/7362780.Effrosyni_Moschoudi

**Follow her blogs. The first one below is perfect for bookworms (many author interviews and book reviews). On the second blog, you'll find her yummy Greek recipes!
http://www.effrosyniwrites.com
http://www.effrosinimoss.wordpress.com

Printed in Great Britain
by Amazon